LAWRENCE SANDERS

"A master storyteller."   —*King Features*

"A writer who has matured into one of our great ones."
—*Pittsburgh Press*

"One of the most consistently satisfying 'entertainment' novelists in America today."   —*Washington Post*

"The amazing thing about Sanders is that he never disappoints his reader."   —*USA Today*

"It's a sin not to enjoy Sanders!"
Columbia State (SC)

Praise for THE TIMOTHY FILES

"A book worth buying . . . Sanders shines!" —*Houston Post*

"Entertaining . . . well-plotted . . . a new hard-boiled hero!"   —*Cincinnati Post*

"Originality and energy . . . It's fun to watch a private investigator in action!"   —*Associated Press*

"Chilling . . . superbly capturing the flavor of New York . . . Good reading!"   —*Virginia Pilot & Ledger Star*

Lawrence SANDERS

Timothy's GAME

B

BERKLEY BOOKS, NEW YORK

This Berkley book contains the complete
text of the original hardcover edition.
It has been completely reset in a typeface
designed for easy reading and was printed
from new film.

TIMOTHY'S GAME

A Berkley Book / published by arrangement with
the author

PRINTING HISTORY
G. P. Putnam's Sons edition / July 1988
Berkley edition / July 1989

ISBN: 0-425-11641-7

A BERKLEY BOOK ® TM 757,375
Berkley Books are published by The Berkley Publishing Group,
200 Madison Avenue, New York, New York 10016.
The name "BERKLEY" and the "B" logo
are trademarks belonging to Berkley Publishing Corporation.

PRINTED IN THE UNITED STATES OF AMERICA

10 9 8 7 6 5 4 3 2 1

"Sex is dead. Money is the sex of our time."
　　　　　—Sally Steiner

BOOK I

Run, Sally, Run!

<u>One</u>

Jake Steiner, a crude and growly man, slams down his fork. "What *is* this shit?" he demands.

"It's fettucini primavera, pa," Sally says. "Martha made the pasta herself, and all the spring vegetables are fresh. Try it; you'll like it."

"I won't try it, and I won't like it. Whatever happened to a nice brisket and a boiled potato?"

"You know what the doctor told you about that," his daughter says, then jerks a thumb at his tumbler of whiskey and water. "And about *that.*"

"Screw the doctor," Jake says wrathfully. "There are more old drunks than old doctors."

He gets up from the table, stalks over to the marble-topped sideboard, takes a cigar from a humidor. He bites off the cigar tip and spits it into a crystal ashtray.

"I'll pick up something to eat later," he says. "I gotta go out."

"Yeah," Sally says. "To Ozone Park. It's payoff night. Those fucking bandits."

"Watch your mouth," he says sharply. "Act like a lady; talk nice."

She finishes her fettucini, watching as he scrapes a kitchen match across the marble slab and lights his cigar.

"I gotta import these matches from Florida," he tells her. "You can't buy scratch-anywhere matches around here. Would you believe it?" He puffs importantly, twirling the cigar in his heavy lips. "What are you doing tonight?"

"I'm going up and sit with ma awhile. Give Martha a chance to have some dinner and clean up."

"And then?"

"I thought I'd drive into New York and take in a movie. There's a new Woody Allen."

"Bullshit," her father says. "You're going to see that fairy brother of yours. Well, don't give him my love."

"Believe me," Sally says, "he can live without it."

They glare at each other, then Jake pushes back the sliding glass door and stamps out onto the tiled terrace to smoke his cigar, taking his whiskey glass with him.

Sally goes up to her mother's bedroom on the second floor. Martha is feeding the invalid. Rebecca Steiner's hands and lower legs are so crippled with rheumatoid arthritis that she cannot walk, cannot hold a spoon.

"How was dinner, ma?" Sally asks.

"Delicious," Becky says, smiling brightly. "And I'll bet your father wouldn't take even a little taste."

"You'd win your bet. Martha, why don't you go down and have your dinner. I'll sit with ma for a while."

The old black woman nods. "There's a nice piece of strawberry cheesecake, Miz Steiner," she says to the woman in the wheelchair. "Just the way you like it."

Sally leans over her mother. "How about the cheesecake?" she asks.

"Well, maybe just a bite. I hate to disappoint Martha; she works so hard."

"Ho-ho," Sally says. "If I know you, you'll finish the whole slice. Come on now, open wide."

She feeds the cheesecake to Rebecca, then holds the mug of coffee close so her mother can sip through a straw.

"You're going out tonight?" Becky asks. "It's Saturday. You got maybe a date?"

"Nah, ma. I'm driving over to New York to see Eddie."

"That's nice. You'll give him my love?"

"Of course. Don't I always?"

"Listen, Sally, in New York you'll be careful?"

"I'm always careful. I can take care of myself, ma; you know that."

They watch the evening news on television, and then sit gossiping about an aunt who is on her third husband and has recently taken up with a beach boy in Hawaii.

Rebecca Steiner is shocked, but Sally says, "Let her have her fun; she can afford it."

Martha comes back up, carrying her knitting, and she and Mrs. Steiner settle down for a night of television. Then, at eleven o'clock, Rebecca will be put to bed, and Martha will retire to her own bedroom to read the Bible.

"Dad still downstairs?" Sally asks her.

"Oh, yeah," Martha says. "Stomping up and down and cursing."

"Sure. What else."

She goes downstairs to find her father pulling on his leather trench coat. He has a fresh, unlighted cigar clamped between his teeth.

"How is she?" he asks.

"Why don't you go up occasionally and take a look?" Sally says angrily.

"I can't take it," her father says, groaning. "I see her like that, and I remember . . ."

"Yeah, well, she's the same; no change."

He nods and tugs down a floppy tweed cap. "It's chilling off out there, Sal. Wear a coat."

"I will, pa."

"You want a lift?"

"No, I'll take my car."

"You got your pistol?"

"In the glove compartment."

"You get in trouble, don't be afraid to use it."

"I'll use it. Pa, watch your back with those ginzos."

"Listen, when I can't handle momsers like that, I'll be ready for Mount Zion."

Suddenly, unexpectedly, he comes close to touch her cheek with his fingertips.

"It's a great life if you don't weaken," he says, looking into her eyes.

"I'm surviving," Sally Steiner says.

"Yeah," he says. "See you tomorrow, kiddo. Don't take any wooden nickels."

She watches from the window until he drives away in his black Cadillac Eldorado. Then she struggles into a long sweater coat that cost a week's salary at one of those Italian boutiques on Madison Avenue. She backs her silver Mazda RX-7 out of the three-car garage. She checks the glove compartment to make certain the loaded pistol is there, then heads for Manhattan.

* * *

Jake Steiner drives from Smithtown into Ozone Park. He parks in front of a narrow brick building, windows painted black. There is a small sign over the doorway: THE MIAMI FISHING AND SOCIAL CLUB.

Jake gets out of his Cadillac, knowing the hubcaps are safe. There is no thievery on this street. And no muggings, no littering, no graffiti. Maybe the cops drive through once a week, but the locals take care of everything.

There are a few geezers in the front room, playing cards and drinking red wine. They don't look up when the door opens. But the mastodon behind the bar eyeballs Steiner and pours a waterglass of whiskey, splash of water, no ice. Jake pulls out a fat roll of bills, peels off a twenty, hands it over.

"For your favorite charity," he says.

"Yeah," the bartender says, and moves his head toward the back room.

Steiner carries his whiskey through a doorway curtained with strings of glass beads, most of them chipped or broken. There is one round wooden table back there, surrounded with six chairs that look ready to collapse at the first shout. The tabletop has a big brownish stain in the center. It could be a wine spill or it could be a blood spill; Jake doesn't know and doesn't wonder.

Two men are sitting there: Vic Angelo and his underboss and driver, Mario Corsini. They've got a bottle of Chivas Regal between them, and their four-ounce shotglasses are full. Only Vic gets to his feet when Steiner enters. He spreads his arms wide.

"Jew bastard," he says, grinning.

"Wop sonofabitch," Jake says.

They embrace, turning their heads carefully aside so they won't mash their cigars. They look alike: short, porky through chest and shoulders, with big bellies, fleshy faces, manicures, and pinkie rings.

"Hiya, Mario," Jake says.

Corsini nods.

"How's the family?" Angelo asks, pulling out a chair for Jake.

"Couldn't be better. Yours?"

"Likewise, thank God. So here we are again. A month gone by. Can you believe it?"

"Yeah," Steiner says, taking a gulp of his drink, "I can believe it."

He tugs a white envelope from the inside pocket of his jacket and slides it across the table to Angelo.

"My tax return," he says.

Vic smiles and pushes the envelope to Corsini. "I don't even have to count it," he says. "I trust you. How long we been good friends, Jake?"

"Too long," Steiner says, and Mario Corsini stirs restlessly.

"Yeah, well, we got a little business to discuss here," Angelo says, sipping his scotch delicately. "Like they say, good news and bad news. I'll give you the bad first. We're upping your dues two biggies a month."

Steiner slams a meaty fist down on the table. It rocks; their drinks slop over.

"Two more a month?" he says. "What kind of shit is this?"

"Take it easy," Vic Angelo says soothingly. "Everyone in Manhattan and Brooklyn is getting hit for another grand."

"But I get hit for two? That's because I'm such a good friend of yours—right?"

"Don't be such a fucking firecracker," Vic says. He turns to his underboss. "He's a firecracker, ain't he, Mario?"

"Yeah," Corsini says. He's a saber of a man, with a complexion more yellowish than olive.

"You didn't give me a chance to tell you the good news," Angelo says to Steiner. "We're giving you a new territory. South of where your dump is now. Along Eleventh Avenue to Twenty-third Street."

"Yeah?" Jake says suspiciously. "What happened to Pitzak?"

"He retired," Vic says.

"Where to? Forest Lawn?"

"I don't like jokes like that," Corsini says. "It's not respectful."

"What the fuck do I care what you like or don't like," Steiner says. He swallows whiskey. "So the bottom line is that my tariff goes up two Gs, and I get Eleventh Avenue down to Twenty-third Street. Right?"

"And all the garbage you can eat," Corsini says.

"Listen, sonny boy," Jake says. "One man's trash is another man's treasure. You're drinking Chivas Regal. That's where it comes from—my garbage.''

"Hey hey," Angelo says. "Let's talk like gentlemen. So you start on Monday, Jake. You can handle the business?"

"Maybe I'll need a new truck or two. Let me see how much there is."

"You need more trucks," Vic says, "don't buy new ones. We can give you a good deal on Pitzak's fleet."

"Oh-ho," Steiner says. "It's like that, is it?"

"That's the way it is," Corsini says. "You take over Pitzak's district, you take over his trucks. From us."

"I love you wise guys," Jake says. "You got more angles than worms."

"If you're shorting," Angelo says gently, "we can always make you a loan to buy the trucks. Low vigorish."

"Thanks for nothing," Steiner says bitterly. "I wouldn't touch your loans with my schlong. I'll manage."

"One more thing," Vic says. "We want you to take on a new man. He's been over from the old country six months now. Strictly legit. He's got his papers and all that shit. A good loader for you. A nice young boy. He'll work hard, and he's strong."

"Yeah?" Jake says. "He speaka da English?"

"As good as you and me," Angelo assures him.

"What about the union?"

"It's fixed," Vic says. "No problem."

"If I'm taking over Pitzak's organization," Steiner says, "what do I need a new man for?"

"Because he's my cousin," Mario Corsini says.

They drain their drinks, and Jake rises.

"It's been a lovely evening," he says. "I've enjoyed every minute of it."

He nods at them and marches out, leaving his empty whiskey glass and chewed cigar butt on the table.

"I don't trust that scuzz," Mario says, filling their shotglasses with scotch. "He's got no respect."

"He's got his problems," Vic says. "A crippled wife. A fag son. And his daughter—who the hell knows what she is. What a house he's going home to."

"Only he ain't going home," Corsini says. "He's going to Brooklyn. He keeps a bimbo on Park Slope. He bought a co-op for her."

Angelo stares at him. "No shit?" he says. "How did you find that out?"

"I like to know who we're dealing with. You never know when it might come in handy."

"A young twist?"

"Oh, sure. And a looker. He makes it with her three or four times a week. Sometimes in the afternoon, sometimes at night."

"The old fart," Vic Angelo says admiringly. "I never would have guessed. I wonder if his wife knows."

"I'll bet that smartass daughter of his knows," Corsini says. "I can't figure her. You never know what she's thinking."

Manhattan comes across the bridge, the harsh and cluttered city where civility is a foreign language and the brittle natives speak in screams. Sally Steiner loves it; it is her turf. All the rough and raucous people she buffets—hostility is a way of life. Speak softly and you are dead.

She dropped out of Barnard after two years. Those women—she had nothing in common with them; they had never been wounded. They were all Bendel and Bermuda. What did they know about their grimy, ruttish city and the desperate, charged life about them? They floated as Sally strode—and counted herself fortunate.

Her brother lives in Hell's Kitchen on a mean and ramshackle street awaiting the wrecker's ball. Eddie works on the top floor of a five-story walk-up. The original red brick façade is now festooned with whiskers of peeling gray paint, and the stone stoop is cracked and sprouting.

His apartment is spacious enough, but ill proportioned, and furnished with cast-offs and gutter salvage. But the ceilings are high; there is a skylight. Room enough for easel, taboret, paints, palettes, brushes. And white walls for his unsold paintings: a crash of color.

He has his mother's beauty and his father's body: a swan's head atop a pit bull. When he embraces Sally, she smells turps and a whiff of garlic on his scraggly blond mustache.

"Spaghetti again?" she asks. "A'la olio?"

"Again," he says with his quirky smile.

"I can't complain; we had fettucini. Ma sends her love. Pa doesn't send his."

Eddie nods. "How is the old man?"

"Terrible. Smoking and drinking up a storm. I don't know why he's paying that fancy Park Avenue doc. He never does what he's told."

"He's still got the girl in Brooklyn?"

"Oh, sure. I can't blame him for that. Can you?"

"Yes," Eddie Steiner says, "I can blame him."

They sit side by side on a dilapidated couch, one broken leg propped on a telephone directory. Eddie pours them glasses of a harsh chianti.

"How you doing, kiddo?" Sally asks him.

"I'm doing okay," he says. "A gallery down in the East Village wants to give me a show."

"Hey! That's great!"

He shakes his head. "Not yet. I'm not ready. I'm still working."

Sally looks around at the paintings on the walls, the half-blank canvas on the easel.

"Your stuff is getting brighter, isn't it?"

"Oh, you noticed that, did you? Yeah," he says, laughing, "I'm coming out of my blue mood. And I'm getting away from the abstract bullshit. More representational. How do you like that head over there? The little one on top."

"Jesus," Sally says, "who the hell is *she?*"

"A bag lady. I dragged her up here to pose. I did some fast pencil sketches, gave her a couple of bucks, and then did the oil. I like it."

"I do, too, Eddie."

"Then take it; it's yours."

"Nah, I couldn't do that. Sell it. Prove to pa you're a genius."

"Who the hell cares what he thinks. I talked to ma a couple of days ago. She sounded as cheerful as ever."

"Yeah, she never complains. Where's Paul?"

"Bartending at a joint on Eighth Avenue. It's just a part-time thing, but it brings in some loot. Including that wine you're drinking."

"Paul's a sweetheart," Sally says.

Her brother smiles. "I think so, too," he says. "Hey, listen, there's something I've been wanting to ask you."

"Ask away."

"I want to do a painting of you. A nude. Will you pose for me?"

"A nude? What the hell for? You've seen me in a bathing suit. You know the kind of body I've got. My God, Eddie, I'm a dumpster."

"You've got a very strong body," he tells her. "Good musculature. Great legs."

"And no tits."

"I'm not doing a centerfold. I see you sitting on a heavy stool, bending forward. Very determined, very aggressive. Against a thick red swirly background laid on with a palette knife. And you looming out. What do you say?"

"Let me think about it—okay? You've never seen me naked before."

"Sure I have," he says cheerfully. "You were five and I was seven. You were taking a shower, and I peeked through the keyhole."

"You louse!" she cries, punching his arm. "Well, I've added a few pounds since then."

"And a few brains," he says, leaning forward to kiss her cheek. "So *good* to see you, sweetie. But you seem down. Problems?"

"Well, you know, with ma and pa. And you."

"Me?" he says, amused. "I'm no problem."

"And me," she goes on. "I'm a problem. I'm not doing what I want to be doing."

"Which is? Making money?"

"Sure," she says, challenging him. "That's what it's all about, isn't it?"

"I guess," he says, sighing. "The bottom line."

"You better believe it, buster. I see these guys raking in the bucks. . . . Like those banditos pa went to pay off tonight. I've got more brains than they've got, but they're living off our sweat. What kind of crap is that?"

"Life is unfair," he says, smiling and pouring them more wine.

"If you let it be unfair. Not me. I'm going to be out there grabbing like all the rest—if I ever get the chance."

He looks at his paintings hanging on the walls. "There's more than just greed, Sally."

"Says who? What? Tell me what."

"Satisfaction with your work. Love. Joy. Sex."

"Sex?" she says. "Sex is dead. Money is the sex of our time."

He doesn't reply. They sit silently, comfortable with each other.

"You're a meatball," she says finally.

"I know," he says. "But a contented meatball. Are you contented, Sal?"

"Contented?" she says. "When you're contented, you're dead. Once you stop climbing, you slide right back down into the grave."

"Oh, wow," he says. "That's heavy."

She drains her wine, rises, digs into her shoulder bag. She comes up with bills, smacks them into his palm.

"Here's a couple of hundred," she says. "Go buy yourself some paint and spaghetti. And a haircut."

"Sally, I can't—"

"Screw it," she says roughly. "It's not my dough. I'll take it out of petty cash at the office. Pa will never know the difference."

"You're sure?"

"I'm sure."

Before she leaves, he embraces her again.

"You'll think about posing for me?"

"I will. I really will."

"I love you, Sal."

"And I love you. Stay well and say hello to Paul for me. I'll be in touch."

She gets back to Smithtown a little before midnight. Goes up to her mother's bedroom and opens the door cautiously. The night-light is on, and Becky is snoring grandly. Sally goes back downstairs to the office-den. The books for the accountant and tax attorney and IRS are kept in the office safe of Steiner Waste Control on Eleventh Avenue in Manhattan. The *real* books are kept here, in a small safe disguised as a cocktail table.

She spends a half-hour crunching numbers, using a pocket calculator that has no memory. Profits are up over the corresponding week of the previous year. But not enough. The tax paid to the bentnoses for the right to collect garbage is a constant drain. Go sue city hall.

Next she flips through the current issue of *Barron's* to see how their equities are doing. A small uptick. Jake lets his daughter do all the investing. "I can't be bothered with that shit." He doesn't know an option from a future, but he can read the bottom line. Every month. Then it's a grudging "Not bad" or a furious "You trying to bankrupt me?"

Sally pushes the papers away on the big, leather-topped desk scarred with burns from her father's cigars. She sits brooding, biting at the hard skin around her thumbnail.

They're doing okay—but nothing sensational. Most people would consider the Steiners rich, but they're not *rich* rich—which is all that counts. It's not for lack of trying; the want is there. But what Sally calls the Big Chance just hasn't come along. She can buy a thousand shares of this and a thousand shares of that, and maybe make a few bucks. Terrific.

But she's also bought some dogs and, on paper, the Steiner portfolio is earning about ten percent annually. Hurrah. She'd be doing better if she socked all their cash away in tax exempts. But where's the fun there? She doesn't go to the racetracks or to Vegas; stocks are her wheel of fortune. She knows that playing the market is a crapshoot, but once tried, never denied.

Later, naked in bed, hands locked behind her head, she tries to concentrate on the Big Chance and how it might be finagled. But all she can think about is Eddie asking her to pose in the nude.

That's the nicest thing that's happened to her in years.

Judy Bering, the receptionist-secretary, opens the door of Sally's office and sticks her head in.

"There's a guy out here," she says. "Claims he was hired and told to report for work this morning."

"Yeah," Sally says, "pa told me he'd show up. What's his name?"

"Anthony Ricci."

"Sure," Sally says. "What else? What's he like?"

Judy rolls her eyes heavenward. "A Popsicle," she says.

Ricci comes in, an Adonis, carrying his cap and wearing a smile that lights up the dingy office.

"Good morning, miss," he says. "I am Anthony Ricci, and I am to work here as a loader."

"Yeah," Sally says, "so I heard. My name is Sally

Steiner. I'm the boss's daughter. Sit down. Have a cigarette if you like. You got all your papers?''

"Oh, sure. Right here."

He digs into his jacket pocket, slides the documents across Sally's desk. She flips through them quickly.

"Everything looks okay," she says. "You been over here six months?"

"Maybe seven," he says. "I never want to go back."

"You speak good English."

"I thank you. I study hard."

"Good for you," Sally says. "You know what a loader does? He lifts heavy cans of garbage and dumps them into the back of a truck. You can handle that?"

Again that high-intensity smile. Ricci lifts his arms, flexes his biceps. "I can handle," he says.

"Uh-huh," Sally says. "We've had three hernias in the past year. They call you Tony, I suppose."

"That's right. Tony."

"Well, Tony, the boss isn't in right now. He's out inspecting a new territory we just took over. He should be back soon, but meanwhile I'll show you around. Come along with me."

As they're going out the door, he flashes those brilliant choppers again and asks, "You married?"

"What's it to you?" Sally says sharply.

She shows him around the dump: sheds, unloading docks, compactors, maintenance garage, shower and locker room. She leaves him with old gimpy Ed Fogleman who got a leg caught in a mulcher but won't quit. Jake Steiner keeps him on as a kind of plant caretaker, and is happy to have him.

Sally goes back to her office, draws her third cup of black coffee of the day from the big perk in Judy Bering's cubbyhole, and gets back to her paperwork.

She is vice president and truck dispatcher at Steiner Waste Control. She directs, controls, hires, fires, praises, berates, curses, and occasionally comforts a crew of tough men, drivers and loaders, who make a living from their strength and their sweat. They work hard (Sally sees to that), and they live hard.

But Sally does more than schedule garbage trucks. She's the office manager. She leans over the shoulder of the bookkeeper. She solicits and reviews bids on new equipment. She negotiates contracts with old and new customers. She deals with the union and approves all the city, state, and federal bumf required, including environmental reports.

Big job. Stress. Tension. Dealing with a lot of hardnoses. But she thrives on it. Because she's a woman making her way in this coarse men's world of the bribed and the bribers, the petty crooks, the thugs on the take, and the smiling lads with their knives hidden up their sleeves. Sally Steiner loves it because it's alive, with a gross vitality that keeps her alert and steaming.

At about 12:30, she runs across Eleventh Avenue and has a pastrami and Swiss on a seeded roll, with iced tea, at the Stardust Diner. She and Mabel, the waitress, exchange ribald comments about the crazy Greek chef who recently flipped a hamburger so high that it stuck to the tin ceiling.

She returns to the Steiner dump. A loaded truck is coming in, driven by Terry Mulloy, a redheaded, red-faced harp. Sitting beside him is his loader, a black named Leroy Hamilton who's big enough to play noseguard for the Rams. Both these guys are beer hounds, and on a hot day you want to stand well upwind from them.

"Hey, Sally baby," Terry calls, waving. "How'ya doing?"

"Surviving," she says, walking up to the truck. "How you two putzes doing?"

"Great," Leroy says. "We're getting a better class of crap today. You know that restaurant on Thirty-eighth? I picked out enough steak scraps to feed my Doberman for a week."

"Bull*shit!*" Sally says. "You two morons are going to have a barbecue tonight."

They laugh. "Hey, baby," Terry says, "when are you and me going to make it? A night on the town. Maybe a show. A great dinner. All you can eat."

"No, thanks," Sally says. "I got no use for shorthorns."

She flips a hand and starts away. "Don't knock it until you've tried it," Terry Mulloy yells after her.

She goes back to her office, smiling. That guy will never give up. But it's okay; she can handle him. And she enjoys the rude challenge.

She works on the next week's schedule, assigning drivers and loaders to the Steiner fleet of trucks. For a couple of years now she's been trying to convince her father to computerize the whole operation. But Jake continues to resist. It's not that they can't afford it; he just doesn't want to turn control over to machines; he's got to see those scraps of paper with numbers scrawled on them.

Late in the afternoon he comes lumping into Sally's office, collapses in the armchair alongside her desk.

"Jesus, Jake," she says, "you smell like a distillery. You been hitting the sauce hard today."

"A lot of people I had to see." He takes off his hat. His balding head is covered with sweat. It's been a warm April day; he looks wiped out.

"You want something?" she asks anxiously. "Coffee? A cold Coke?"

"Nah," he says, "I'm okay. Just let me rest a minute."

"You look like the wrath of God."

"Yeah, well, I've been on the go since this morning. What's been going on around here?"

"Nothing much. The new guy showed up. His name's Tony Ricci."

"That figures," Jake says. "He's Mario Corsini's cousin. Did I tell you that?"

"Yeah, pa, you told me."

"What kind of a guy?"

"A good-looking boy. Fresh—but that's okay."

"Wait'll he puts in a week lifting hundred-pound cans of dreck, he won't be so fresh. You can handle him?"

"Oh, sure, pa. No problem. So tell me, how does the new territory look?"

"Not so bad," Jake says. He takes out his handkerchief, wipes his face. He straightens up in the chair. "Pitzak had some good wheels. Three Loadmaster compactor trucks only a few years old. The rest of the stuff is shit, but still rolling. Their dispatcher is a lush; he doesn't know his ass from his elbow; you'll have to take over."

"Okay, pa, I can do that. What about the customers?"

"Mostly industrial, thank God. Some restaurants, some diners, two apartment houses. But most of the stuff is clean. Like scrap wood, steel shavings, and so forth. There's one paint factory and one chemical outfit that might give us some trouble. We'll have to dump in Jersey. And three or four printers. But that's only paper, so that's no problem there. We can bale and sell."

"What kind of printers?"

"One does magazines, a couple do catalogs and brochures, and one does printing for Wall Street outfits. Annual reports, documents, prospectuses, stuff like that."

"Yeah?" Sally Steiner says. "That's interesting."

Two

LATE IN MAY, Timothy Cone comes off a case that's a real doozy. Cone's an investigator for Haldering & Co., an outfit on John Street that provides "financial intelligence" for corporate and individual clients.

Early in May, a venture capital partnership hired Haldering to look into something called Ozam Biotechnology, Inc. Ozam had been advertising in the business media with big headlines: NEW ISSUE! Shares of Ozam available at ten bucks.

The legal and accounting departments of Haldering & Co. couldn't find any record of Ozam anywhere. It apparently had no bank accounts, wasn't chartered by the State of New York, nor was it registered with the Securities and Exchange Commission.

So Timothy Cone went to work. He soon found there were two other eyes doing the same thing: a guy from the SEC and a woman from the Manhattan District Attorney's office.

The three finally discover that Ozam just doesn't exist. It is an out-and-out stock swindle dreamed up by a con man named Porfirio Le Blanc. How much loot he took in on those fraudulent ads they never do determine, but it must have been hefty because when Porfirio flies the coop, he flies first-class to Bolivia.

No one is interested in trying to extradite the rascal; just getting him out of the country is enough. So the Immigration and Naturalization Service is told to put Señor Le Blanc on the "watch list," and Timothy Cone returns to his cubbyhole office to write out his report.

When he tosses it onto the desk of Samantha Whatley, who bosses the five Haldering & Co. investigators, he slumps in the doorway while she reads it.

"You're a lousy speller," she tells him. Then she shakes

her head in disbelief. "Can you believe this? A guy takes out
ads in newspapers, and people send him money. *Fan*-tastic."

"It's happened before," Cone says, shrugging. "Years
ago there was an ex-carny pitchman working the Midwest. He
bought ads in small-town newspapers. All the ad said was:
'Last chance to send in your dollar,' with a P.O. Box number
in Chicago. He was doing okay until the postal guys caught
up with him."

"Barnum was right," Sam says. "Well, here's a new one
for you."

She holds out a file folder, and Cone shuffles forward to
take it.

"What is it?" he asks. "Some guy selling the Brooklyn
Bridge?"

"No," Sam says, "this is heavy stuff. The client is Pistol
and Burns. You know them?"

"The investment bankers? Sure, I know them. Very old.
Very conservative. What's their problem?"

"They think they may have a leak in their Mergers and
Acquisitions Department."

"Oh-ho. Another inside trading scam?"

"Could be," Samantha says. "Tim, this is a new client
with mucho dinero. Will you, for God's sake, try to dress
neatly and talk like a gentleman."

"Don't I always?"

She stares at him. "Out!" she says.

Back in his office, he opens a fresh pack of Camels (second
of the day) and lights up. He parks his scuffed yellow work
shoes atop the scarred desk, and starts flipping through the
Pistol & Burns file.

It's a sad story of unbridled greed—and a not uncommon
one. About a year ago, P&B is engineering a buyout between
a big food-products conglomerate and a smaller outfit that's
making a nice buck with a nationwide chain of stores that sell
cookies, all kinds, made on the premises, guaranteed fresh
every morning. The takeover is a marriage made in heaven.
Or, as they say on Wall Street, the synergism is there.

As usual, the ladies and gents in the Mergers and Acquisitions Department of Pistol & Burns work in conditions of
secrecy that would do credit to the CIA—so word of the impending deal won't leak out prematurely. But it does. The

computers of the Securities and Exchange Commission pick up evidence of heavy trading in the cookie company in the weeks prior to the signing of the buyout documents and the public announcement. The cookie stock goes up almost ten points.

So the SEC launches an investigation to try to discover the insider leak. It turns out that a yuppie-type in the Mortgage Insurance Department of Pistol & Burns, who has nothing to do with mergers and acquisitions and is supposed to know zilch about them, is a drinking buddy of another yuppie in the M&A section. Not only that, but they're both doing coke and shagging the same twitch who supplies the nose candy and also dances naked at a joint on East 38th Street called Aristotle's Dream.

The whole thing is a mess. The two Pistol & Burns' yuppies confess their sins and admit they made almost a quarter-mil dealing in shares and options of the cookie corporation in the month prior to the takeover. What's worse, they were paid for their insider information by arbitrageurs and attorneys who work for other investment bankers.

This clique of insiders, all with MBAs or law degrees, make a nice buck until the SEC lowers the boom, and everyone has to cough up their profits, pay fines, and is banned from the securities business for three years. The two original Pistol & Burns insiders also get a year in the slammer, which means they'll be out in four or five months. There is no record of what happens to the skin dancer at Aristotle's Dream.

The entire scandal is a painful embarrassment for Pistol & Burns. It is one of the few remaining investment-banker partnerships on the Street. The original partners, Leonard K. Pistol and G. Watson Burns, have long since gone to the great trading pit in the sky, but the present partners try to preserve the stern probity and high principles and ideals of the two founders. Their oil portraits glower down on the executive dining room, spoiling a lot of appetites.

But Pistol & Burns muddles through, cooperating fully with investigators and prosecutors from the SEC and district attorney's office. P&B also appoints one of the senior partners, Mr. G. Fergus Twiggs, to be Chief of Internal Security. He institutes a series of reforms to make certain such an insider coup will never again tarnish the reputation of such a venerable and respected institution.

(Which somewhat amuses students of the history of our nation's financial community. They happen to know that Leonard K. Pistol kept a teenage mistress, and G. Watson Burns drank a quart of brandy every day, without fail, and once had to be dissuaded from making a cash offer to buy the U.S. Government.)

Timothy Cone, reading all this with enjoyment, pauses long enough to light another cigarette and call down to the local deli for a cheeseburger, an order of French fries, a kosher dill, and two cold Heinekens. He munches on his lunch as he continues reading the preliminary report provided by the client.

After enduring the shame of what comes to be known on Wall Street as The Great Cookie Caper, and after tightening up their internal security precautions, Pistol & Burns now finds itself facing another disgrace involving insider trading.

They're in the last stages of finagling a leveraged buyout of a corporation that makes clothes for kiddies, including diapers with the label of a hotshot lingerie designer and little striped overalls just like gandy dancers once wore. The buyers are a group of the company's top executives, and the transaction includes an issue of junk bonds.

Everything is kept strictly hush-hush, and the number of people with a need to know is kept to a minimum. But during the last two weeks, the volume of trading in Wee Tot Fashions, Inc., usually minuscule, has quadrupled, with the stock up five bucks. An investigator from the SEC is already haunting the paneled corridors of Pistol & Burns, trying to discover who is leaking word of the upcoming deal.

"This state of affairs cannot be allowed to continue," Mr. G. Fergus Twiggs concludes firmly.

So Timothy Cone calls the phone number on the letterhead of the client's report.

"Pistol and Burns." A woman's voice: brisk and efficient.

"Could I speak to Mr. Twiggs?"

"May I ask who is calling?"

"Sure," Cone says cheerfully.

Long pause.

"Who is calling, please," she says faintly.

"Timothy Cone. I'm an investigator with Haldering and Company."

After a wait of almost a minute, he's put through. Twiggs

has a deep, rumbling voice. Cone thinks it sounds rum-soaked, aged in oak casks, but maybe that's the way all old investment bankers talk. Cone wouldn't know; he doesn't play croquet.

Their conversation is brief. G. Fergus Twiggs agrees to meet at 10:00 A.M. the following morning to discuss "this disastrous and lamentable situation."

"Uh-huh," Cone says. "Okay, I'll be at your office at ten tomorrow morning. Who's the SEC investigator?"

"His name is Jeremy Bigelow. Do you know him?"

"Yeah," Cone says, "I know Jerry. I worked a case with him earlier this month. Good man."

"Seems rather young to me," Twiggs says, and then sighs. "But at my age, everyone seems rather young to me."

Cone smiles. The guy sounds almost human.

It's a close and grainy evening; when he walks home from John Street to his loft on lower Broadway, he can taste the air on his tongue. It isn't nice. He stops at local stores to buy a large jar of spaghetti with meat sauce, a jug of Gallo Hearty Burgundy, and a link of kielbasa for Cleo, his neutered tom-cat, who eats everything, including cockroaches, fish heads, chicken bones—and thrives.

Cone notes mournfully that the outer door of his cast-iron commercial building has once again been jimmied—an al-most weekly occurrence. Since it is now later than 6:00 P.M., the ancient birdcage elevator is shut down for the night, so he climbs the six flights of iron staircase to his apartment.

Cleo is waiting for him, and gives him the ankle-rub treat-ment, crying piteously, until he hands over the sausage. Then the cat takes its treasure under the old claw-footed bathtub and gnaws contentedly while the Wall Street dick mixes him-self a vodka and water. He works on that as he heats up the spaghetti in a battered saucepan and sets his desk that doubles as a dining table. The china and cutlery are bits and pieces of this and that. The wineglasses are empty jars of Smucker's orange marmalade.

Samantha Whatley shows up a little after seven o'clock. She's picked up a container of mixed greens at a salad bar, and also has two strawberry tarts for dessert and a small chunk of halvah for Cleo.

An hour later, they've got their feet up on the littered table and are drinking noggins of cheap Italian brandy with black coffee. They decide to save the tarts, but Cleo gets the halvah, mewling with delight.

"Good dinner," Cone says.

"Not very," Sam says. "Do you have to buy canned spaghetti?"

"It wasn't canned," he tells her. "It came in a jar."

"Whatever. Is it so difficult to buy a package of pasta, boil it up, and add your own sauce?"

"Oh-ho," he says, beginning to steam, "now I'm supposed to be a gourmet cook, am I? Bull*shit!* Either eat what the kitchen provides or bring your own. And now that we got that settled, you staying the night?"

"Half the night," she says. "Maybe till midnight or so."

"Okay," he says equably. "I'll put you in a cab."

"My hero," she says. "You talk to Pistol and Burns?"

"Yep. I'm seeing G. Fergus Twiggs tomorrow morning at ten. I'll be in late."

"So what else is new?" She looks at the mattress on the linoleum floor of the loft. It's been spread with clean sheets. "I feel horny," she says.

"So what else is new?" he says.

Timothy Cone is a scrawny, hawkish man who's never learned to shave close enough. Samantha Whatley is a tall drink of water with the lean body of a fashion model and the muscles of a woman at home on a balance beam. He is taller, but stooped, with a shambling gait. She is sharp-featured: coffin jaw and blue-green eyes. His spiky hair is gingery; her long auburn hair is usually worn up, tightly coiled. His nose is a hatchet, and his big ears flop. Her back is hard and elegant. His skin is pale, freckled. She is dark, with a ropy body that holds secret curves and warm shadows. He is all splinters, with the look of a worn farmer: pulled tendons, used muscles.

They have nothing in common except . . .

Naked on the floor mattress they have another skirmish. Not combat so much as guerrilla warfare with no winners and no losers. They will not surrender, either of them, but assault each other with whimpers and yelps, awaiting the end of the world. They think capitulation shameful, and their passion is fed by their pride.

They recognize something of this. Their relationship is sexual chess that must inevitably end in a draw. Still, the sweat and grunts are pleasure enough for two closed-in people who would rather slit their wrists than admit their vulnerability.

Shortly after midnight, he conducts her downstairs and stops an empty cab.

"Take care," she says lightly.

"Yeah," Cone says. "You, too."

Then he goes back up to his desolate loft, eats both strawberry tarts, drinks a jar of vodka, and wonders what the hell it's all about.

The offices of Pistol & Burns, Investment Bankers, on Wall Street, look like a genteel but slightly frowsty gentlemen's club. The paneled walls display antique hunting prints in brass frames. The carpeting seems ankle-deep. Employees tiptoe rather than walk, and speak in hushed whispers. Even the ring of telephones is muted to a polite buzz. The atmosphere bespeaks old wealth, and Timothy Cone is impressed—not for the first time—by the comfortable serenity that avarice can create.

He is kept waiting only ten minutes, which he endures stoically, and then is ushered into the private office of G. Fergus Twiggs, P&B's Chief of Internal Security. This chamber, as large as Cone's loft, is more of the same. But on the floor is an enormous, worn Persian prayer rug, and on the beige walls are oak-framed watercolors of sailing yachts, most with spinnakers set.

G. Fergus Twiggs is a veritable toby jug of a man: short, squat, plump, with a smile and manner so beneficent that the Wall Street dick can see him with a pewter tankard of ale in one fist and a clay pipe in the other.

He is clad in a three-piece, dove gray flannel suit of such surpassing softness that it could have been woven from the webs of white, Anglo-Saxon, Protestant spiders. But the pale blue eyes are not soft, nor do they twinkle. They are the unblinking, basilisk eyes of an investment banker.

"Thank you for coming by," Twiggs says genially, shaking hands. He gets Cone seated in a leather chair alongside his mastodonic desk. "I needn't tell you how upsetting this entire matter has become; the whole house is disturbed."

"Look, Mr. Twiggs," Cone says, "there's not much I can

do about the Wee Tot Fashions deal. The cat is out of the bag on that one. You'll just have to take your lumps.''

"I realize that. The problem is how to prevent it from happening again.''

"You can't,'' Timothy says. "Unless you figure a way to repeal human greed—and I doubt if you can do that. Listen, how do you define insider trading?''

"Define it?'' Twiggs says, looking at him curiously. "Why, it's the illegal use of confidential information about planned or impending financial activities for the purpose of making a personal profit.''

"Yeah, well, that sounds very neat, but it's not that simple. Insider trading has never been exactly defined, even by the Supreme Court. Let me give you a for-instance. Suppose one of your guys is working every night on a megabuck deal. His wife is furious because he's continually late for dinner. So, to explain his long hours, he tells her he's slaving on this big buyout of the ABC Corporation by the XYZ Corporation. His wife mentions it to her hairdresser. He mentions it to another customer. She tells her husband. The husband mentions it to his car dealer, and the dealer runs out and buys ABC Corporation stock and winds up making a bundle. Now who's guilty there? The original investment banker didn't profit from his inside knowledge; he just had a big mouth. And the guy who did profit, the car dealer, was just betting on a stock tip. He didn't have any inside knowledge. How do you stop that kind of thing?''

"Yes,'' Twiggs says slowly, "I see what you mean.''

"Also,'' Cone goes on, "the leak on the Wee Tot Fashions deal may not have been in your house at all. The arbitrageurs have a zillion ways of sniffing out a deal in the making while it's still in the talking stage. They pick up one little hint, hear one little rumor, that XYZ is going to make an offer for ABC, and they go to work. They try to track the whereabouts of the chairman, president, and CEO of both corporations. They'll even check the takeoffs, flight plans, and landings of corporate jets. They'll bribe secretaries, porters, pilots, chauffeurs, office cleaning ladies, security guards—anyone who can possibly add to their poop on who is meeting whom and what's going on. There's a lot of money to be made on advance knowledge of deals in the works, and the arbs want some of it. But I wouldn't call that insider trading—would you? It's just shrewd investigative work by guys who want a piece of the action.''

"I suppose you're right," the little man says, rubbing his forehead wearily. "Very depressing. That men would go to such lengths to make a profit. It wasn't like that in the old days.''

"Maybe, maybe not," Cone says. "In the old days there was only a handful of people who knew about a deal in the making—just the principals and a few lawyers—so it was relatively easy to spot the gonnif if someone leaked or made an illegal profit on his own. But now, in any big-money deal, there are hundreds of people with inside knowledge: corporate officers and their staffs, the investment bankers and their staffs, attorneys and their staffs, accountants and their staffs. Then you've got secretaries, telephone operators, and messengers. Any one of them could spill or make a dirty buck.''

"Ah, me," Twiggs says, sighing. "So you believe it's impossible to stop insider trading?''

"Sure it is," Cone says cheerily. "As long as people's itch for a dollar overrides their ethics or morals or whatever the hell you want to call them.''

"I should think that heavier penalties might be effective.''

"Yeah?" Cone says. "Ever hear of the 'hangup gimmick'?''

"The hangup gimmick? What on earth is that?''

"An arbitrageur hears a rumor that ABC Corporation may be bought out by the XYZ Corporation. The arb has a drinking buddy with the legal firm that handles ABC. He calls his lawyer buddy and says, 'I hear XYZ has made an offer for ABC. If the rumor is true, don't say a word. I'll stay on the phone. But if you're silent and then hang up after ten seconds, I'll know which way to jump, and you'll get your share.' So the ten seconds pass in silence, the lawyer hangs up, and the arb rushes to buy ABC stock. Who do you prosecute? The attorney, the insider, hasn't leaked a word, and can swear to it in a court of law. How do you prosecute him? There are a hundred scams like that. So when you talk about heavier punishment for insider trading, you've got to realize how tough it is to get a conviction.''

G. Fergus Twiggs gives him a quirky smile. "Are you trying to talk yourself out of a job, Mr. Cone?''

"Nah. I just want you to understand the problems involved. And I'd like to know what you expect Haldering and Company to do about them."

The investment banker takes a handsome pipe from his top desk drawer. He looks down at it, fondles it, then strokes the bowl slowly between his fleshy nose and cheek, inspecting it as skin oil brings out the grain of the brier.

"Being Chief of Internal Security at Pistol and Burns," he says ruefully, "is not a task I sought or relish. I have had no experience in this rather distasteful field. I suppose I was selected for the job because, though it may be difficult for you to believe, I am the youngest of the senior partners. In any event, what'd I'd like you to do is spend as much time in our offices as you feel is necessary and review all the security precautions I have instituted. Be as critical as you like. Make any suggestions you wish that will make insider trading at Pistol and Burns, if not impossible, then at least more difficult."

"Yeah," Cone says, "I can do that. As long as you understand I can't make the place airtight. No one can. I'll tackle your setup like I was an employee, out to make a dishonest buck from trading on inside secrets. That should be easy; I've got a criminal mind."

Mr. Twiggs smiles again and rises. "I think you're exactly the man for the job," he says. "When do you plan to start?"

"How about tomorrow? Could you spread the word to guards and secretaries and such that I'll be wandering around the place and have no intention of boosting women's purses or swiping a typewriter?"

"Certainly. Is there anything else you need?"

"I don't think so, thanks. I'd start today, but first I want to compare notes with Jeremy Bigelow, the SEC investigator. Maybe he's got some ideas on how the Wee Tot Fashions deal was leaked."

He walks back to John Street. It's a warm, springy day, but the wind is boisterous, and Cone isn't sweating in his ratty olive drab parka and black leather cap. He shambles up Broadway, thinking of the interview and wondering if Twiggs himself might not be making a quick, illicit buck on Pistol & Burns' deals. The guy looks like Santa Claus, but maybe his bag is stuffed with illegal greenbacks.

The Wall Street dick ponders how much gelt it would take

for him, Cone, to turn sour. Half a mil? A mil? Five mil? But that kind of thinking is strictly wet dreams; no one is going to offer him that much loot to go rancid. Besides, what's the point of being rich? Right now he's got a job, a place to sleep, a rotten cat, and enough pocket money to buy beer and ham hocks. He even has Samantha—sort of. What more could a growing boy want?

Back in his cubbyhole office, he takes off cap and anorak and lets them drop to the floor because some office thief has snaffled his coat tree. He lights his fourth or fifth cigarette of the day and sits down behind his scarred desk. He calls Jeremy Bigelow at the Securities and Exchange Commission.

"Jerry?"

"Speaking. Who's this?"

"Timothy Cone at Haldering and Company."

"Hey, old buddy! I was thinking of giving you a call. I hear you guys got the Pistol and Burns account."

"Bad news travels fast. Listen, Jerry, you looked into a possible leak on the Wee Tot Fashions deal, didn't you?"

"That's right." Bigelow's voice turns cautious. "I've been working it. You got something for me?"

"Not a jot or tittle, or tot or jittle, whichever the hell it is. Anyway, it adds up to zilch. But I'd like to buy you lunch and pick your brains."

"Lunch? Today?"

"Sure."

"Why not," the SEC investigator says. "Where?"

"I feel like eating street food. Okay by you?"

Bigelow sighs. "The last of the big-time spenders," he says. "All right, I'll eat street. I'll even come over to your place. Meet you outside at, say, twelve-thirty. How does that sound?"

"Just right. There's a new stand near Trinity that's selling hot roti goat. How does that grab you?"

"Instant ulcers—but I'll give it a go. See you."

They meet outside the Haldering & Co. office and start ambling down Broadway. The day has thickened, with clotted clouds blocking out the sun. There's a smell of rain in the air, but it hasn't stopped the lunch-hour throngs from flocking to the street for their falafel fix.

Manhattan is the biggest outdoor buffet in the world. Especially in the financial district, the umbrella carts, vans, trucks, and knockdown booths are all over the place. Foul weather or fair, the street vendors are out hustling and probably dreaming of the day they can build their taco stand into The Four Seasons or maybe sell franchises.

What do you feel like eating? Not falafel? Not hot roti goat? Not tacos? Then how about fried chicken with jalapeño sauce, seeded rolls with cold cuts, sausage heroes, gyros, foot-long franks, turkey hamburgers, pizza, soups hot and cold, Acapulco salads, shish kebab, Philadelphia steak sandwiches, burritos, shrimp parmesan, tortillas, Ben & Jerry's ice cream, chocolate-covered Oreos, coffee, tea, milk, colas, cakes, pies, pastries, nuts, fresh fruit? Sound okay? And you never have to leave a tip!

Cone and Jeremy Bigelow begin their peripatetic luncheon. The first stop is for barley and mushroom soup. They throw away the plastic spoons and drink the rich sludge directly from the foam containers. They try the hot roti goat. Not bad. Then they stop at a Chinese booth for slivers of bamboo stuck through chunks of barbecued pork and kiwi slices. Then cans of cola and ice cream bars covered with a quarter-inch of dark Belgian chocolate.

They eat as they stroll, as everyone else is doing. Meanwhile, between sips and bites, they talk shop.

"What's your take on that Twiggs?" Cone asks.

"I think he's straight," Bigelow says. "A gentleman of the old school. But not too swift when it comes to street smarts. He wanted to hook up everyone at Pistol and Burns to a lie detector. I had to explain to him how easy it is to beat the machine."

"Yeah," Cone says. "Like urinalysis for drugs. There's a couple of ways you can beat that even with an observer there watching you pee in a plastic cup."

"Please," the SEC man says, "not while I'm eating."

"So how do you figure the Wee Tot Fashions leak? The arbitrageurs?"

"I think so, and that's what I'm going to put in my report. I don't believe anyone at Pistol and Burns was on the take. It was just rumor and good detective work by the arbs. Those guys can put two and two together and come up with twenty-two. We checked all the trading in Wee Tot in the last few weeks. Not the odd lots, of course. Just the big trades, like ten thousand shares and up. Most were handled by brokerage houses the arbs use. I looked for personal connections with Pistol and Burns staff, and came up with zip. There was one big trade, ten thousand shares, by an amateur. A woman named Sally Steiner. But she works for a garbage collection outfit on Eleventh Avenue. She couldn't have any access to inside information. She plays the market for fun and games, and just made a lucky pick. Other than that, there's nothing to justify our pushing this thing any farther. What's your interest in this, Tim? What does Twiggs expect Haldering and Company to do?''

"He just wants me to double-check his security precautions.''

"That sounds easy enough,'' Jeremy Bigelow says. "Most of these investment banking houses are as holey as Swiss cheese. You could stroll in and walk out with their checkbooks, and no one would notice, especially if you were dressed like a Harvard MBA.''

The SEC investigator is a self-assured guy with such strength of character that he can eat one salted peanut. When Cone first met him, Bigelow came on strong, like working for the Securities and Exchange Commission was akin to holding high office in the Papacy. The Wall Street dick had to swat him down a few times, but then Jerry relaxed, and they were able to work together without too much hassle.

He's a beanpole of a gink who equates height with superiority—but that's okay; superior shrimps cause more trouble. Cone admires him because he can drink gin martinis. Cone loves gin martinis but can't handle them, and leaves them strictly alone—especially since an incident several years ago when he ended up in Hoboken, N.J., in bed with a lady midget.

"I got to get back to the treadmill,'' Bigelow says. "Thanks for the lunch. I'll probably be popping Tums all afternoon, but it tasted good. Let's eat street again—my treat next time.''

"Sure,'' Cone says. "Listen, that woman you mentioned who made the big trade in Wee Tot Fashions. . . . What was her name?''

"Sally Steiner. Why the interest?''

"Did you talk to her?''

"Of course,'' Bigelow says, offended. "That's what

they're paying me coolie wages for. She's a tough bimbo who practically runs that waste disposal business I told you about. Her father owns it. She claims she bought Wee Tot stock because she wants to get out of garbage and open a store that sells kids' clothes. She figured the annual reports of Wee Tot would help her learn the business. It makes sense."

"Sure it does," Timothy Cone says. "Nice seeing you again, Jerry. Give my best to the wife."

Bigelow looks at him. "How do you know I'm married?" he asks. "I never told you that."

"Beats me," Cone says, shrugging. "I just assumed. You've got that married look. Also, you've got a pinched band of skin around your third finger, left hand, where I figure you wear a ring but maybe take it off during the day in case you meet something interesting."

Bigelow laughs. "You goddamn sherlock," he says. "You've got me dead to rights. I better watch myself with you; you're dangerous."

"Nah," Cone says, "not me. I'm just a snoop. Thanks, Jerry."

"For what?"

"All the info you gave me—like Sally Steiner and so forth. I owe you one."

"Look," the SEC man says, "if you find out anything more about the Wee Tot Fashions leak, you'll let me know?"

"Absolutely," the Wall Street dick vows. "I'm no glory hound."

They shake hands, and Cone watches the other man move away, towering over everyone else on the street. Then he trudges back to Haldering & Co. He stops on the way to buy a knish. He's still hungry.

Three

MAY IS A rackety month for Sally Steiner. She is living in a jungle and giving as good or better than the blows and bites she endures.

"Listen, Jake," she says to her father, "I'm going to take a few hours off this afternoon to go see some customers."

"Yeah?" he says, looking up from his tipsheet. "Who?"

"The new people we got from Pitzak."

"I already seen them."

She sighs. "You *saw* them, pa. But so what? I'm the one they call with their kvetches. I want to know who I'm dealing with."

"So do what you want to do," he says. He puts aside his chewed cigar and picks up his whiskey and water. "You're going to do it anyway, no matter what I say. So why ask?"

"I didn't ask," she says, as prickly as he. "I'm telling you."

But there is only one customer she wants to visit: Bechtold Printing, downtown on Tenth Avenue. She's planned this interview and dressed for it. Black gabardine suit. High-necked blouse. No jewelry. Opaque pantyhose. Clunky shoes. With a leather portfolio under her arm. The earnest executive.

"Mr. Frederick Bechtold, please," she says to the lumpy blond receptionist, handing over her business card. "From Steiner Waste Control."

The klutz takes a look at the card. "He's in the pressroom," she says. "I'll see."

It's almost five minutes before the owner comes out, a chunky slob of a man. He's wearing a cap of folded newsprint and an ink-smeared apron that doesn't hide a belly so round that it looks like he's swallowed a spittoon.

"Zo," he says, peering at her card. "Sally Steiner. You are related to Steiner Waste Control?"

"Daughter," she says brightly. "I just stopped by to see if you're satisfied with our service, Mr. Bechtold. Any complaints? Any way we can improve?"

He looks at her in amazement. "Eight years with Pitzak," he says, "and he never came around. No, lady, no complaints. You pick up twice a week, right on schedule. My contract with Pitzak is still good?"

"Absolutely," Sally says. "We'll honor the prices. Nice place you got here, Mr. Bechtold. I've heard about your reputation for top-quality financial printing."

"Zo?" he says, with a smile that isn't much. "I do the best. The *best!* You'd like to see my pressroom?"

"Very much."

It's a cavern, with noise and clatter bouncing off cinderblock walls. There's one enormous rotary, quiet now, and four smaller presses clanking along and piling up printed sheets. Sally is surprised at the small work-force—no more than a half-dozen men, all wearing ink-smeared aprons and newsprint caps. Two guys are typing away at word processors. One man is operating a cutter, another a binder. A young black is stacking and packing completed work in cardboard cartons.

"This is my pride," Frederick Bechtold says, placing his hand gently on the big rotary. "West German. High-speed. The very *best*. Six colors in one run. And I use high-gloss inks from Sweden. Expensive, but the people I deal with want only the best."

"You have some big Wall Street accounts, Mr. Bechtold?"

"Absolutely," he affirms. "For them, everything must be just zo."

"Annual reports?" Sally suggests.

"For the color, yes. And in black-and-white, we do brochures, documents, instruction booklets, proxy statements—everything. They know they can depend on Bechtold Printing. They give me a deadline, and I meet it. I have never been late. Never!"

Sally shakes her head in wonderment. "A marvelous operation," she says. "Nice to have met you, Mr. Bechtold. You ever have any complaints about our service, you just give me a call and I'll take care of it."

She goes back to the office and gets to work. First, she finds gimpy Ed Fogleman, who runs the dump.

"Ed," Sally says, "we got a new customer: Bechtold Printing, on Tenth Avenue. It's a clean job; practically all their shit is paper. We'll pick up twice a week. Is there any place we can store the barrels for a day or so before we bale?"

He peers at her, puzzled. "Why do you want to do that, Sal?"

She's prepared for questions. "Because I got a look at their operation, and they use everything from coated stock to blotting paper. Up to now we've been baling everything from good rag to newsprint in the same bundle. I figure maybe we could make an extra buck if we separate the good from the lousy and sell different qualities of scrap paper at different prices."

"Yeah," the old man says slowly, "that makes sense. But who's going to spend the time separating all the stuff? Sounds to me like a full-time job—and there goes your profit."

"That's why I want to hold out the Bechtold barrels," Sally says patiently. "To see if it would be worth our while. Where can I put them temporarily?"

Fogleman chews his scraggly mustache. "Maybe in the storeroom," he says finally. "I can make space. It's against fire regulations 'cause we got inflammables in there, but if it's only for a day or so, who's to know?"

"Thanks, Ed," Sally says gratefully. "I'll get the barrels out as soon as I can."

She goes back to her office and looks out the window every time a truck rolls into the dump. She goes running when she spots Terry Mulloy and Leroy Hamilton in their big Loadmaster compactor.

"Hey, you paskudniks," she yells, and they stop. Terry leans out the window.

"Sally baby," he says, grinning. "You've finally decided you can't resist my green Irish joint."

"Up yours, moron," she says. "Listen, I'm revising schedules and pulling you two bums off that chemical plant on Twenty-fourth Street and giving you Bechtold Printing on Tenth Avenue."

"God bless the woman who birthed you," Leroy Hamilton

says. "That chemical place smells something fierce. Gets in your hair, your clothes; you can almost taste that stink."

"Yeah," Sally says, "well, now you've got Bechtold. A nice clean job. Practically all paper. Pickups on Tuesday and Thursday. When you get the stuff, keep it in separate barrels and leave them in the storeroom. Ed Fogleman will show you where."

"What the hell for?" Mulloy asks.

"You know what curiosity did to the cat, don't you?"

"I don't know from cats," he says. "All I know is pussy."

She gives him the finger and stalks away, followed by their whistles.

On Thursday night, she complains to her father and Judy Bering about having to work late on a couple of workmen's compensation cases. It's almost seven o'clock before they leave, and she sees Ed Fogleman drag himself home. Then the dump is almost deserted; only the night watchman is in his hut at the locked gate, flipping through his dog-eared copies of *Penthouse*.

She goes out to the storeroom, puts on the light, starts digging through the barrels of scrap paper from Bechtold. It's almost all six-color coated stock. Someone is running a slick annual report, and the discarded sheets are preliminary press proofs with colors out of register and black type too heavy or too faint.

That's not what she's looking for. She spends more time with black-on-white proof sheets: documents, proxy statements, prospectuses. Nothing of any interest. She gives up and drives home. The next morning she tells Fogleman to empty the barrels and bale everything.

She goes through the same routine on the following Tuesday evening with similar results. She's beginning to think her wild idea, her Big Chance, is a dud. But on the next Thursday night she finds some interesting proof sheets on Pistol & Burns letterheads. She scans them hastily. They look like a plan for a leveraged buyout of Wee Tot Fashions, Inc. She gathers up all the pages she can find that mention Wee Tot, crams them in her leather portfolio, and drives home to Smithtown, singing along with Linda Ronstadt on her stereo deck.

She stops up to visit with her mother for a while. Then when Becky and Martha settle down for an evening of TV, Sally rushes downstairs to the den. She's too excited to eat, but pours herself a Perrier before she goes over the Pistol & Burns documents scavenged from Bechtold's scrap. She reads them three times because some of the type is blurred, and she has to use a magnifying glass to make out certain words and phrases.

Then she does swift computations on her pocket calculator. The next morning she calls her stockbroker and sells some of the dogs in the Steiner portfolio, taking a tax loss. But she accumulates enough funds to buy 10,000 shares of Wee Tot Fashions at a total cost of about $48,000, including commission. Have a hunch, bet a bunch.

A week later, after following the market anxiously, she sells out her Wee Tot stake for about $112,000, and is so elated and unbelieving that she doesn't know whether to weep or laugh.

And a week after that, she's having a coffee with Judy Bering in the outer office when a tall, thin guy, nicely dressed, walks in and smiles at the two women.

"I'm looking for Sally Steiner," he says.

"That's me," Sally says. "Who are you?"

He hands her a card. "Jeremy Bigelow," he says. "Securities and Exchange Commission."

She's sitting naked on a three-legged kitchen stool, hunching forward.

"I think I'm getting splinters in my ass," she says.

"Shut up," Eddie says, "and try to hold that pose. Don't relax. Make yourself tight and hard."

She *is* tight and hard. Her body has a rude grace, heavy through shoulders and hips. Not much waist. The thighs are pillars tapering to unexpectedly slender ankles. A muscled woman. Her skin is satin.

"When's Paul coming back?" she asks.

Her brother sighs. "I told you. He'll ring before he comes up. Don't get so antsy."

He continues sketching, using a soft carpenter's pencil on a pad of grainy paper. He works swiftly, limning her body with quick slashes, flipping pages, trying to catch her solidity, the aggressiveness of her flesh. He was right: She does loom.

After a while she forgets that she's exhibiting herself in front of her brother and thinks about why she's there. Because she wants something from him—or rather from his consenting adult, Paul Ramsey.

That visit from the SEC investigator spooked her. The guy wanted to know how come she had sprung for 10,000 shares of Wee Tot Fashions, Inc. Had she heard something? Did someone tell her something? Did she know anyone at Wee Tot? At Pistol & Burns? Why, suddenly, did she buy such a big block of that particular equity?

Without pause, she scammed the guy silly. She was proud of that. She wanted to get out of garbage hauling, she told him, and open a store that sold kids' clothes. She bought Wee Tot to get their annual reports so she could learn more about the business. Besides, she owned a dozen other stocks. She was in the market for kicks.

He departed, apparently satisfied, and Sally went back to her own office. She was sweating. What if Jeremy Bigelow subpoenas Steiner's customer list and discovers they're collecting trash from Bechtold, who does confidential printing for Pistol & Burns? What if he comes poking around, asking questions of Ed Fogleman, Terry Mulloy, Leroy Hamilton, and learns she's been putting aside barrels of Bechtold waste? Curtains!

She decides she handled her Big Chance stupidly. Too many people involved, too many potential witnesses. And she purchased the stock in her own name. Idiotic! And she bought 10K shares. That would be a trip wire to alert anyone investigating the possibility of insider trading.

Eddie's phone rings. Three times. Then stops.

"That's Paul," he says. "He'll be up in about ten minutes. You can get dressed now. I got some good stuff. But I'll need a couple more sessions."

"Sure," she says. "Anytime."

To her surprise, she finds she's no longer self-conscious, and when Eddie helps her hook up her bra in back, she thinks it's a nice, brotherly thing for him to do. By the time Paul Ramsey shows up, Sally is dressed and sipping a glass of their lousy chianti.

Paul is a tall blond with a sweet smile and more teeth than he really needs. He's got a laid-back manner, and Eddie says that when the world blows up, Paul is going to be the one who murmurs, "Oh, yeah? Cool."

Sally has already decided what she wants to do. She's going to continue picking through Bechtold Printing trash. But if she finds another lead on a takeover, merger, or buyout, she can't invest in her own name, or in the name of anyone else connected with Steiner Waste Control. Too risky. And the stock purchase has got to be less than 10,000 shares.

"Paul," she says, "I got a proposition for you."

"Sorry," he says with his seraphic grin, "my evenings are occupied."

She tells him what she wants. She'll give him the name of a stockbroker. He's to open an account by purchasing shares of AT&T. She'll give him the money. After that, he'll buy and sell on her instructions.

"I'll pay all the losses," she says. "You get five percent of the profits. How about it?"

The two men look at each other.

"Go for it, Paul," Eddie Steiner advises. "My little sister is a financial genius."

"Okay," Paul Ramsey says, shrugging. "Why not?"

Sally has come prepared. She hands over a manila envelope with $2,500 in cash and the name and phone number of her stockbroker.

"Stick with me, kid," she tells Paul, kissing his cheek, "and you'll be wearing diamonds."

"I prefer emeralds," he says.

She goes back to the office, pondering her next move. She's walking from her parking slot when she meets Anthony Ricci. The kid is wearing tight jeans and a Stanley Kowalski T-shirt, and he looks beautiful.

"Hey, Tony," Sally says. "How's it going? You like the job?"

"No," he says with his 100-watt smile, "but the money is good."

"All money is good," she tells him. "The loading—you can handle it?"

"Sure," he says. "I've done worse. Maybe someday I'll be a driver—no?"

"Why not? We have a lot of turnover. Hang in there, kiddo."

She goes into her office, parks her feet on her desk, and

tries to figure how to paw through the Bechtold garbage without endangering Steiner Waste Control. She decides she can't do it by herself. She's got to use fronts, some bubbleheads who won't have a glimmer of what she's doing. She looks out the window and sees Terry Mulloy and Leroy Hamilton wheeling onto the tarmac to dump their load.

"Oh, yeah," Sally breathes.

The next morning, at breakfast, Jake Steiner says to his daughter, "You better take your car. I'll be gone all afternoon. I got things to do."

"Sure, pa," she says. "I'll drive in."

They don't look at each other. She knows about his "things to do." He's going to shtup his twist in Brooklyn.

He drives to the dump in his Cadillac and she follows in her Mazda. By the time she arrives at the office, Jake is on his second cigar and third black coffee. He's also nibbling on a tot of schnapps from a bottle he keeps in his desk.

"You're killing yourself, pa," Sally says.

"Tell me about it," he says, not looking up from his *Times*.

She keeps glancing out her window, watching for the big Loadmaster crewed by Mulloy and Hamilton. Finally, a little after noon, she sees it coming in. She knows the guys are going to take their lunch break. She grabs her shoulder bag and goes running out. She has to wait until they wash up in the locker room.

"Hey, you bums," she says. "Want a free lunch?"

"Whee!" Leroy says. "Christmas in May. What's the occasion, Sally baby?"

"She wants to make nice-nice," Terry says. "I told you she'd come around eventually."

"This is strictly business, you schmuck," Sally says. "Come on, let's go over to the Stardust."

She picks out a table in a back corner of the diner. They give Mabel their order: three cheeseburgers, home fries, cole slaw, and beer.

"Can either of you guys get hold of a pickup or a van?" she asks them.

They look at each other.

"What for?" Mulloy says.

"It's a special job. I need a pickup every Tuesday and

Thursday. I want you to load it with the barrels of Bechtold Printing scrap, drive out to my house in Smithtown, and leave the barrels in the garage. The next Tuesday or Thursday when you bring the new barrels out, you pick up the old ones and bring them back here to the dump for baling. Got that?''

"What's this all about?" Terry asks.

"It's about an extra hundred a week for each of you. In cash. Off the books."

They think about that awhile, chomping their cheeseburgers.

"I got a cousin with an old, beat-up Chevy van," Hamilton says slowly. "I could maybe borrow it on Tuesdays and Thursdays. Probably get it for five bucks a shot and gas."

"I'll pay," Sally says promptly. "However you want to work it. Just get those Bechtold barrels out to Smithtown twice a week. I'll rig your Tuesday and Thursday schedules so you'll have plenty of time to make the round trip. Maybe one of you better stick in town on the big truck, and the other guy makes the drive out to the Island in the van."

"But we get a hundred each?" Mulloy says.

"That's right. Per week. Cash. Off the books."

"No trouble with the buttons?" Hamilton says.

"What trouble?" Sally says. "Anyone asks questions, you know from nothing; you're just following the orders of the boss."

"Sounds good to me," Mulloy says, glancing at Hamilton.

"I'll play along," Hamilton says.

She goes back to the office, sets to work rearranging pickup schedules. She lightens up on Mulloy and Hamilton's Tuesday and Thursday assignments so one or both of them will be able to work in the round trip to Smithtown. It's about three o'clock, and Jake is long gone in his Cadillac, when Judy Bering comes into her office.

"There's a woman on the phone," she says. "She's crying. Sounds hysterical. Something about your father."

"Jesus," Sally says, knowing this can't be good. "All right, put her on my line."

She listens awhile to the wails, the sobs, the incoherent babbling. Finally she figures out what has happened.

"What's your name?" she says sharply, interrupting the woman's desperate howls.

"What? What?"

"Your name. What's your name?"

"Dotty. My name is Dotty."

"Dotty what?"

"Uh, Dotty Rosher."

"All right now, Dotty, listen to me. Lock your door and get dressed. Go into the living room and just sit there. Don't do a goddamn thing. Don't call anyone or talk to anyone. I'm coming to help you. To *help* you, Dotty. I'll be there as soon as I can. Now give me your address and phone number."

She makes quick notes, hangs up, then has the presence of mind to go to the office safe. They keep the petty cash in there, but it's hardly "petty"—almost five thousand in small bills in case the local cops come around, or the fire inspectors, plumbing inspectors, electrical inspectors, sanitation inspectors. The petty cash is not for bribes, exactly. Just goodwill.

Sally grabs up a handful of twenties and fifties, stuffs them in her shoulder bag. She stalks out, grim-faced.

"I listened in, Sal," Judy Bering says, beginning to weep. "I'm sorry."

"Yeah," Sally Steiner says.

She drives her Mazda like a maniac, but crosstown traffic is murder, and it's almost an hour and a half before she gets over to Park Slope.

Dotty Rosher turns out to be a little thing, a piece of fluff. A strong west wind would blow her away. She's got wide blue eyes, a mop of frizzy blond curls, Cupid's-bow lips, and a pair of lungs that make Sally look like a boy. She's fully dressed—for all the good that does.

"Where is he?" Sally demands.

"I got your phone number from his business card. It was in his wallet, but I swear I didn't—"

"Where is he?" Sally screams at her.

"In the bedroom. He just, you know, just went out. I thought he had fainted or something, but then I couldn't—"

"Shut your yap," Sally says savagely.

She goes into the bedroom. The body of her father, naked, is lying on rumpled pink sheets. His mouth is open, eyes staring. He is dead, dead, dead. She looks down at the pale, flaccid flesh and varicose veins with distaste. His shrunken penis is lost in a nest of wiry gray hair.

"You son of a bitch," Sally says bitterly, then bends to kiss his clammy cheek.

She goes back into the living room and tells Dotty Rosher what must be done.

"I can't. I just can't."

"You do it," Sally says stonily, "or I walk out of here right now and leave you with a naked corpse. You can explain it to the cops. Is that what you want?"

So, together, they dress the remains of Jake Steiner, wrestling with his heavy body while they struggle to get him into undershirt and shorts, knitted sport shirt, trousers, jacket, socks and shoes. They remember to lace up the shoes, close his fly. Then they drag him off the bed into the living room, tugging him by the armpits, his heels scuffing the shag rug. They get the body seated in an armchair, head flopped forward, arms dangling.

Dotty Rosher looks ready to pass out. Her mouth is working, and she's beginning to claw at her throat.

"You better get a drink of something," Sally advises.

"I think I'll have a Grasshopper," Dotty says faintly. "They're really delicious. Would you like one?"

"No, thanks. Go have your Grasshopper."

Sally fetches her father's half-full tumbler of cognac from the bedroom and sets it on the end table alongside his armchair. Then she tips it over so the brandy spills on the table and drips down onto the rug. She inspects the scene, then knocks the tipped glass to the floor. Now it looks authentic: man with history of heart trouble stricken with an attack while drinking.

Dotty comes back with her Grasshopper, looking a little perkier. Sally outlines the scenario for her, speaking slowly and distinctly.

"My father owned this apartment, but you rented it from him. Got that? He and I came up to collect next month's rent. *He and I* came here together. That's very important. Can you remember that? We were sitting in the living room talking, and you offered us drinks. I didn't want anything, but Jake had a glass of brandy. He took a couple of swallows and suddenly collapsed. We tried to revive him but nothing helped. Got all that?"

Dotty nods.

"Just keep your mouth shut," Sally says, "and let me do

the talking. Okay? You behave and there'll be a nice piece of change in it for you. Capeesh?''

''What?''

''Do you understand what I'm telling you?''

''Oh, sure.''

So Sally calls 911 and explains that her father has died unexpectedly, and since he had a history of heart trouble, she thinks it was a sudden attack.

While they're waiting for the paramedics and cops, she makes three more calls. The first is to Judy Bering.

''He's gone,'' Sally says. ''I may not be in for a couple of days. I'm depending on you to keep the wheels turning.''

''Sally, I'm sorry, so sorry.''

''I know, kiddo, and thanks. Listen, if anyone comes around asking questions, just tell them you know from nothing and refer them to me. Okay?''

''Of course, Sal. I can keep my mouth shut.''

''That's the way to do it. I'll let you know when the service is scheduled in case you and any of the guys want to come.''

''I'll take up a collection. For flowers.''

''Yeah, that would be nice.''

Her second call is to Jake's personal physician. She explains that her father dropped dead after drinking half a glass of brandy.

''I'm not surprised,'' the doctor says. ''I warned him, but he wouldn't listen. I'm sorry, Sally.''

''Yeah, thanks. I guess they'll take the body to the Medical Examiner, won't they?''

''That's the customary procedure if no physician was present at the time of death.''

''Do you know anyone there? I mean, I'd like to get the body released as soon as possible.''

''I understand. I'll do everything I can.''

''Thanks, doc. I knew I could count on you.''

Finally she calls Eddie, tells him the true story of their father's death, and what she's doing to cover it up. Her brother starts weeping, a soft, keening sound.

''I loved him,'' he says. ''I really did.''

''I know, baby.''

''Jesus,'' Eddie says, ''this will be the end of ma.''

''Nah,'' Sally says. ''Becky is stronger than you think. Eddie, can you come out to Smithtown? I want you there when I tell her. Take a cab if you have to. You've got enough money?''

"I can manage. I'll be there as soon as possible."

"Bring Paul if you like. You can stay there for a few days. Until the funeral. Plenty of room for both of you."

"Yeah, maybe we'll do that. Sal, are you all right?"

"I'm surviving."

"My God," he says, "I couldn't have done what you did. I wouldn't have the balls for it."

"Sure you would," she says.

The paramedics and cops show up. Jake Steiner is pronounced definitely dead. Statements are taken from both Sally Steiner and Dotty Rosher. While a uniformed cop is scribbling in his notebook, the plainclothesman in charge, a big, beefy guy, wanders about the apartment, hands in his pockets. He seems to be whistling noiselessly.

The body is finally removed on a gurney, covered with a rubber sheet. The plainclothesman crooks a finger at Sally, and the two go into the kitchen. The cop fishes in his pocket and comes up with a little plastic bag. Inside is a chewed cigar butt.

"You forgot this," he says, staring at Sally. "It was in the ashtray on the table next to the bed."

She dips into her shoulder bag, picks out two fifty-dollar bills.

"For your favorite charity," she says.

"Thank you," he says, taking the money and handing her the plastic bag. "My sincere condolences on your loss."

She's in the funeral home, holding herself together while a parade of old guys come up and tell her what a mensch her father was. They were Jake's gin rummy and pinochle pals, and all Sally can say is, "Thank you very much."

Then the uniformed doorman tells her there's a man downstairs who'd like to talk to her. His name is Mario Corsini.

"Jesus X," Sally says. "All right, I'll be down in a minute."

She looks around. Everything seems under control. Eddie is holding up well, and they hired a special van with a lift so Becky in her wheelchair could be transported to the funeral home and eventually to the cemetery. Paul is there. Martha is there. And a crowd of relatives, friends, and neighbors. More people than Sally expected. Dotty Rosher isn't there. *Got tsu danken!*

The hearse is parked at the curb, followed by a long line of black limousines. The chauffeurs have congregated, and are smoking up a storm and laughing. The single Cadillac limousine parked across the street is a stretch job, silver gray.

"Mr. Angelo would like to talk to you," Corsini says.

"Now?" Sally says indignantly. "Can't it wait?"

"Just a couple of minutes," he says. "We didn't want to come inside."

"I'd have kicked your ass out," she says, and means it.

She crosses the street and climbs into the back, alongside Vic Angelo. Corsini sits up front behind the wheel, but turns sideways so he can keep an eye on Sally and listen to what's going on.

"My sincere condolences on your loss," Angelo says.

"Thanks."

"Your father was an old friend."

"Uh-huh."

"But now we got a business problem. The garbage dump. Who inherits?"

"My mother, my brother, me."

"And who's going to run it?"

"Who do you think?" Sally says angrily. "Me. I've practically been running the joint for the past ten years."

"It's no business for a woman," Angelo says, shaking his head regretfully. "Too rough. We'll make you a nice offer."

"Screw your offer," Sally says wrathfully. "I'm hanging on to the dump. You'll still get your tax. Jake is dead, but the business belongs to my family and that's where it's going to stay."

Mario Corsini grins. Or at least he shows a mouthful of big, yellowed teeth. "I don't think so," he says.

Sally stares at the two bandidos. If she had her pistol she would have popped both of them, right there. She knows exactly what they can do to Steiner Waste Control: trouble with the union, trouble with city inspectors, maybe firebombs in the trucks if they want to play hard. There's no way she can fight that. She could run to the DA and scream about the monthly payoffs—but where's the proof?

"All right," she says, "you want to take over, you can do it. But you'll be throwing away a fortune."

"What's that supposed to mean?" Angelo says.

"You guys ever play the stock market?" Sally asks.

Four

"I'M GOING TO gird a loin," Timothy Cone says.

"You're going to *what?*" Samantha Whatley demands.

"Haven't you ever girded your loins? It's something like hoisting yourself with your own petard."

"Oh, shut up," she says crossly, "and get to work."

"That's what I'm trying to tell you," he explains patiently. "I'll be out of the office the rest of the week. I'm supposed to investigate internal security at Pistol and Burns, and make suggestions for improvements."

"Then *do* it!"

He slouches out of her office and ambles down Broadway to Wall Street. It's a sultry day, and he's happy he left his raincoat at home. He's wearing his black leather cap and his old corduroy suit.

G. Fergus Twiggs must have spread the word because, after identifying himself, the Wall Street dick has no problems getting into Pistol & Burns. He's allowed to roam the hushed corridors, examine offices, poke into closets, and check the fire escape doors to see if they can be opened from the outside.

Cone doesn't leave the offices during the lunch hour because he wants to see if any high-powered executives come reeling back, their eyes glazed with a three-martini lunch. He strikes out on that; all the P&B employees seem sober, industrious, and dull.

"Look," he says to Mr. Twiggs at the end of the first day, "I'll put everything in a final report, but there are things you should do immediately, so I think I better pass them along to you personally every day."

"It's that bad, is it?" the cherubic senior partner says.

"It's not a disaster," Cone says, "but you've got to learn to operate defensively. I don't mean you've got to make this place into a fortress, but you should take some more precautions. Or one of these days some outlaws are going to stroll in here and waltz out with the family jewels.''

''What kind of precautions?''

''Well, for starters, you've got one security guard on the front door. I'm sure he's a fine old gentleman, but he is old and he is fat. It would take him a while to suck in his gut before he could get that big revolver out of his dogleg holster. Get a younger guy on the door. Get another two or three to wander around. They can be nicely dressed, but armed and maybe wearing badges.''

''What else?'' Twiggs says, making notes.

''All your typewriters and business machines should be bolted to the desks. You can even get attachments with burglar alarms, if you want to go that far. But you've got a zillion dollars' worth of portable machinery in here that could be carted off with no trouble at all. Bolt it down.''

''Good idea,'' the senior partner says. ''Anything else?''

''Yeah, those paper shredders you're using to destroy confidential documents. . . . They're antiques. Shredded documents can be pasted together again. The Iranians taught us that when they re-created CIA secret memos from strips of paper lifted from the shredders in our embassy. You need new models that turn paper into confetti.''

''Excellent suggestion. More?''

''Not today,'' Cone says. ''I'll be back tomorrow and take a closer look. I'll stop by at the end of the day and give you my report.''

''I think you're doing a fine job.''

''It's all practical stuff. It's not going to stop insider leaks, but it may help. Like keeping a cleaning woman who's on the take from delivering the contents of your wastebaskets to some wise guys.''

At the end of the second day, he says to Twiggs, ''This one is going to cost you bucks. You've got your Mergers and Acquisitions people scattered all over the place. An office here, an office there. That's an invitation to leaks. You've got to consolidate that whole department. They can still have their individual offices, but all of them have to be in the same area. And that area has to be behind a locked door that can only be opened by authorized personnel with a computer-coded card.''

"It's beginning to sound more and more like a fortress," Twiggs says with a wan smile.

Cone shrugs. "You want to cut down on the possibility of leaks? This is one way to do it."

On his final day at Pistol & Burns, he says to the senior partner, "This one is going to cost you *big* bucks. Your M and A people are writing too many office memos, too many suggestions, projections, analyses of upcoming deals—and all on paper."

"We've got to communicate," Twiggs protests.

"Not on paper you don't. Computerize the whole operation. If anyone has something to say on a possible takeover, buyout, or merger, he puts it on the computer. Anyone else who's involved can call it up on his monitor—but only if he knows the code word. You understand? Nothing typed on paper. And everything in the computer coded so that it can only be retrieved by personnel who have a need to know, and have the key word or number allowing them access. Also, the computer can keep a list of who requests access to the record."

G. Fergus Twiggs shakes his head dolefully. "What's the world coming to?" he asks.

"Beats the hell out of me," Timothy Cone says.

He plods back to Haldering & Co. to pick up his salary check. He figures he's done a decent job for Pistol & Burns. If they want to follow his suggestions, fine. If not, it's no skin off his ass.

But something is gnawing at him. Something he heard or saw that flicks on a red light. Maybe it was something Bigelow said, or Twiggs. Maybe it was something he observed at Pistol & Burns. He shakes his head violently, but can't dislodge whatever it is. It nags him, a fragment of peanut caught in his teeth.

When he gets back to his office, there's a message on his desk: Call Jeremy Bigelow. So, without taking off his cap, Cone phones the SEC investigator.

"Hiya, old buddy," Jerry says breezily. "How did you make out at Pistol and Burns?"

"Like you said, it's as holey as Swiss cheese. I gave them some ways to close the holes."

"But no evidence of an insider leak?"

"I didn't find any."

"That's a relief. I wrote in my report it was the arbs who caused the run-up of the stock. I guess I was right."

"Uh-huh," Cone says.

"So much for the good news. Now comes the bad. We got another squeal on insider trading."

"Oh, Jesus," the Wall Street dick says. "Don't tell me it's a Pistol and Burns' deal."

"No, this one is at Snellig Firsten Holbrook. You know the outfit?"

"The junk bond specialists?"

"That's right. They're supposed to have the best security on the Street, but they're handling a leveraged buyout and someone is onto it. The stock of the takee is going up, up, up. Listen, could you and I meet on Monday? Maybe we can figure out what's going on."

"Maybe," Cone says, striving mightily to recall what he cannot remember.

He wakes the next morning, hoping the night's sleep has brought to mind what he's been trying to recollect; sleep does that sometimes. But all he can remember is the entire pepperoni pizza he ate the night before.

He goes over to Samantha's place on Saturday night. She won't be seen with him in public, fearing someone from Haldering will spot them and office gossip will start. That's okay with Cone; he's willing to play by her rules.

She serves a dinner of baked chicken, Spanish rice, and a salad. They also have a bottle of chilled Orvieto which puts them in a mellow mood. They have a nice, pleasant evening of fun and games, and Cone is home by 1:00 A.M. He gives Cleo fresh water and some of the chicken skin and bones he doggie-bagged from Sam's dinner.

Sunday is just as relaxed. He futzes around the loft, smokes two packs of Camels, drinks about a pint of vodka, with water, and digs his way through *Barron's* and the Business Section of the *New York Times*. In the evening he has a one-pound can of beef stew with a heel of French bread he finds in the refrigerator, so hard that he has to soak it in the stew to render it edible. Cleo gets the remainder of the chicken scraps.

On Monday he's late for work, as usual. Jeremy Bigelow shows up at ten o'clock, carrying a fat briefcase. Cone calls down to the local deli for two black coffees and two toasted bagels with a schmear. They wait for their breakfast to arrive before they get down to business.

"Look," Cone says, "it would help if you could tell me how the SEC works on insider trading scams. Then maybe I'll know what you're talking about."

"It's a two-level operation," Jerry says, gnawing on his bagel. "We get a lead and start gathering facts. That's where I come in. If we can't find any evidence of hanky-panky, the investigation is usually dropped. If things look sour, the staff goes to the Commission and gets an order for a formal inquiry. That's when we get power of subpoena."

"Yeah, but what gets you moving? Where do the leads come from?"

"Computers mostly. We couldn't live without them. You know how many companies are listed on all the stock exchanges in the country?"

"No idea."

"Neither do I—exactly. But I'd guess about twelve thousand. How could you check all those every day by hand? Imfuckingpossible. So the computers are programmed to pick up unusual activity. Say a stock has been trading an average of fifty thousand shares a day for months and months. Suddenly the trading volume goes up to maybe a million shares a day. The computer flashes a red light, bells go off, and an American flag pops from the top of the machine and starts waving madly back and forth."

"And that's when you move in?"

"Sure," Bigelow says. "We want to know who's trading. Most of the time it's entirely innocent. A rumor got floated on Wall Street, and a lot of amateur arbitrageurs are hopping on what they hope will be a bandwagon—and probably won't."

"So your computers do it all?"

"Hell, no. Just the first line of defense. We also get tips from brokerage houses. *Their* computers pick up unusual trading activity. They report to us because they don't want to get their balls caught in the wringer. Also, we get anonymous tips from divorced wives and husbands who want the boom lowered on their former mates. And sometimes we get squeals from honest executives who know or suspect the guy in the next office is buying or selling illegally on the basis of the next quarterly earnings report."

"You check out the executives first?"

"Of course. If they're officers of the company, they've got to declare buys and sells. If they don't, they're in the soup."

"Look," the Wall Street dick says, "I know you haven't got the time or staff to check out every piddling little trade. I mean you're not going to investigate Joe E. Clunk of Hanging Dog, North Carolina, who bought ten shares of this or that. So what do you look for?"

"Generally I look for trades of ten thousand shares or more. But if a corporation officer is involved, he's as guilty if he trades a hundred shares as he would be if he traded a hundred thousand on the basis of inside knowledge."

"But he could get his relatives and friends to trade for him."

"Of course," Jerry says, grinning. "Happens all the time. That's when we've got to play detective, track down relationships, and tell them all they've committed a no-no."

"And what do they get for that?"

"Usually they have to surrender their profits, pay a fine, and are put on probation. A few go to the clink."

"For how long?"

"I think the longest sentence for insider trading has been four years."

"Which means the guy is out in eighteen months."

"Probably," Bigelow says, shrugging. "But that's not my problem. I'm supposed to make the case. What the judge decides is something else again."

Cone lights up a cigarette, after offering the pack to the other man. But Jerry declines.

"I stopped smoking four years ago," he says virtuously. "You know what those things are doing to your lungs and heart?"

"Please," Cone says, holding up a hand. "I've heard all the lectures and none of them take. Let me enjoy my vices. Now what's this Snellig Firsten Holbrook deal you mentioned on the phone?"

"Like I said, it's a leveraged buyout. An old outfit named Trimbley and Diggs, up in Massachusetts. They make brooms, brushes, wooden clothespins, and stuff like that. But they also own some choice shorefront real estate. They went public about twenty years ago and have been paying a small dividend—but never missing a quarter. It's a small outfit,

Tim; General Motors it ain't. If their daily trading volume hits, say, ten thousand shares, it's a big day. Now the top executive officers want to buy them out, take the company private again, and develop their beachfront properties. Snellig Firsten Holbrook is handling the deal. But suddenly the daily volume is way up—almost a hundred thousand shares last Friday. Nobody can figure how the buyout leaked. Someone is gobbling up shares, and we want to know who.''

"The arbs?'' Cone asks.

Bigelow shakes his head. "I doubt it. Not enough loot in it for them.''

"Yeah,'' Cone says, "I can understand that. But what's all this got to do with me? I work for Haldering, and we don't have Snellig Firsten Holbrook as a client, or Trimbley and Diggs either. So why am I supposed to get involved?''

"One,'' Jeremy says, holding up a thumb, "as a personal favor to me. Two,'' he says, pointing a forefinger, "because it's a puzzle, and I've got you made as a guy who likes puzzles. And three,'' he adds, extending his middle finger, "who the hell do you think recommended you to Pistol and Burns?''

"Jesus,'' Cone says, "you're really calling in your chits, aren't you?''

"Just take a look at it, will you? I brought you computer printouts of trading and a record of the stock since the leveraged buyout got started.''

"What's it selling for now?''

"About eight dollars a share. A week ago it was four.''

"All right,'' the Wall Street dick says, sighing. "Leave your bumf and I'll take a look. No guarantees.''

"Thanks, Tim,'' Bigelow says gratefully. "In return, the SEC can be very cooperative with Haldering and Company if the occasion ever arises.''

"Who the hell cares?'' Cone says roughly. "When are you going to buy me a street lunch like you promised?''

"You give me a lead on this, I'll take you to The Four Seasons for dinner.''

"Yeah? They got ham hocks?''

He would never lie to Samantha Whatley on a personal matter. But he will lie to her *officially,* as his boss at Haldering & Co. That he can do with nary a qualm.

He lounges in the doorway of her office. "Listen," he says seriously, "I've got to go back to Pistol and Burns and finish up that job."

"Yeah?" she says. "I thought you were all done with them."

"I need a couple of more days. Clean up some odds and ends. Then I want to talk to Twiggs about the final report."

She looks at him suspiciously. "So what you're telling me is that you'll be out of the office again this week."

"Just until Wednesday or so. I'll have it wrapped up by then."

"You better," she says. "I've got three new files waiting for you."

"Gee, thanks, boss," he says. "That makes me feel warm all over."

Jeremy Bigelow has left his battered briefcase stuffed with all the skinny on the Trimbley & Diggs buyout.

"You can borrow the briefcase," he tells Cone. "But I want it back eventually."

"What for?" Cone asks. "Sentimental attachment? It's a piece of junk. You should pay me for taking it off your hands."

So he plods up Broadway in a warm drizzle, lugging the case and feeling no guilt at having conned Sam. The world isn't going to come to an end just because he finagled a couple of days off. Besides, it is a good cause: cooperation with an agency of the U.S. Government.

Back in his loft, he pops a tall can of Bud. Then he opens Bigelow's briefcase and dumps the contents onto his wooden table. He sets the empty case on the floor, and Cleo immediately jumps in and curls up contentedly.

"Leave your fleas in there," Cone tells the cat.

He reads all the papers and reads them again. Then he sits back and considers the case. It's pretty much as Bigelow described it. The first printed documents are dated about three weeks previously and deal with Snellig Firsten Holbrook's suggested plan for the proposed buyout of Trimbley & Diggs, Inc.

Subsequent printed documents amend and refine the plan. Then there's a letter assuring the principals involved that the required funds can be raised through the sale of high-risk bonds, and Snellig Firsten Holbrook has "every confidence" the bond issue will be oversubscribed.

All that is routine stuff, and Cone can't see anything freaky going on. What interests him more are the computer records of trading activity in Trimbley & Diggs. The volume began to climb about ten days ago, and the stock, listed on the Nasdaq National Market, rose in value steadily from about $4 a share to its current price of slightly over $8. Nice. The buyers are probably rubbing their sweaty palms with glee and wondering whether to hold on or sell and take the money and run.

Cone leans down to address Cleo, who is snoozing in the briefcase. "Sometimes the bulls make money," he says, "and sometimes the bears make money. It's the pigs who always get stuck."

But who are these lucky investors who doubled their stake in about ten days? Cone goes over the computerized trading records again, and what he finds amuses him. He can't spot any trades of 10,000 shares or more, but there are plenty for 9,000 shares. Timothy figures that's because a lot of wise guys have heard that the SEC is interested in trades of 10K-shares and over. If they buy or sell 9,000 shares, they think they're home free. Cone is surprised Jeremy Bigelow didn't spot that, and he wonders just how swift the guy is.

The big buyers of Trimbley & Diggs' stock are from all over the country, but seem to be concentrated in New York, Atlantic City, Miami, New Orleans, and Las Vegas. Also, most of the buyers' names end in vowels. That gets Cone's juices flowing because all those cities are big mob towns—which may mean something or absolutely nothing.

Since no one is going to finance his travels to investigate out-of-state buyers, he concentrates on the names of New York investors. One that catches his eye is a man named Paul Ramsey, who lives on 47th Street at an address that would place his residence west of Tenth Avenue.

That sets off alarm bells because, after Cone returned from Nam, he lived for two years in a five-story walk-up on 48th east of Tenth, and he knows what a slummy neighborhood that is. It's in the middle of Hell's Kitchen, with rundown tenements, sad mom-and-pop bodegas, dusty beer joints, and boarded-up buildings awaiting demolition.

Unless the whole area has been gentrified since Cone lived

there, it's hard to believe one of the residents is a stock market plunger. Not many ghetto dwellers deal in gold coins either.

He goes through the computer printouts for the fourth time, checking Paul Ramsey's trades. It looks to Cone like the guy now owns 27,000 shares of Trimbley & Diggs, Inc., bought at an average of six bucks a share. If he sells out today, he'll walk away with a profit of about $54,000. Not bad for someone who lives on streets where a mugger would be happy with a take of $10—enough for a vial of crack.

Cone pulls on his leather cap and takes his grungy raincoat in case the drizzle has thickened. Just before he leaves the loft, he checks the short-barreled S&W .357 in his ankle holster. Reassured, he ventures out to visit his old neighborhood.

"Guard!" he admonishes a startled Cleo before he leaves.

Down on the street, he finds the drizzle hasn't just thickened, it's as if someone has turned a tap on over Manhattan. And there's not a cab in sight. Cursing his luck, Cone bows his head against the rain and humps his way to the nearest subway station. He tries to figure the best way to get to 47th Street and Tenth Avenue, and finally realizes there is no "best" way. No matter what his route, he's going to get soaked.

But almost a half-hour later, when he exits at 50th Street and Eighth Avenue, the downpour has ended. The city remains a sauna, and Cone reflects morosely that all he needs is someone to beat him with birch branches. He carries his raincoat and splashes through puddles and running gutters down to 47th Street and westward to Tenth Avenue.

Ramsey's building looks the way Cone imagined it: peeling paint, torn shades, cracked windows. It is dreary and dying, and no way would you figure it as the residence of a Wall Street plunger.

There's a spindly-legged little girl on the sidewalk. She's about nine, and she's skipping rope to the repeated chant:

> *"Hubba, hubba, hubba,*
> *You better use a rubbeh,*
> *Or your ma will be a bubbeh."*

A freckled, red-haired boy is sitting on the sagging stoop, watching her. He looks to Cone to be about eleven, going on forty-six.

"You live here?" Cone asks him.

The kid stares at him coldly. "What's it to you?"

"I'm looking for Paul Ramsey. You know him?"

"I don't know nothing, I don't."

"He's supposed to live in this building."

"I'm not saying, I'm not."

"But you heard the name?"

"I told you I don't know, I told you."

Cone sighs. "Who are you—Joey Echo? All right, I'll see for myself."

He starts up the stoop. The kid stands up.

"Hey," he says, "you want to know about this guy, you want to know? Cost you a buck."

Cone digs out his wallet, fishes out a dollar, hands it over.

"I don't know nothing, I don't," the kid yells and darts away.

Outraged, Timothy watches the juvenile con man race down the street. Then he laughs at how easily he's been scammed. He figures that kid will end up President or doing ten-to-twenty in Attica.

He goes into the cramped vestibule that smells of urine and boiled cabbage. There's a bellplate but no names are listed in the slots. But there are names on the mailboxes. Two are listed for Apartment 5-A.

One is Paul Ramsey.

The other is Edward Steiner.

He gets a cab going downtown on Ninth Avenue. The hackie wants to talk baseball, but Cone isn't having any; he's got too much to brood about.

There's this woman, Sally Steiner, who goes for 10,000 shares in Wee Tot Fashions, Inc., in an insider trading scheme at Pistol & Burns. And there's this man, Paul Ramsey, who buys 27,000 shares of Trimbley & Diggs, Inc., in what is apparently another insider scam at Snellig Firsten Holbrook. And this Ramsey lives in an apartment with a guy named Edward Steiner.

Maybe the two Steiners aren't related, don't even know each other. Coincidences do happen—but don't bet on it. The Wall Street dick wonders how far he should push what he's already calling the "Steiner Connection."

He's back in the loft, pacing back and forth, when a light bulb flashes over his head, just like a character in a cartoon strip. And suddenly he remembers what he's been trying to recall these past few days, something he heard that struck a tinny note. It comes to him now.

Jeremy Bigelow said that when he interviewed Sally Steiner in the course of his investigation of the Wee Tot Fashions deal, she claimed she bought her 10,000 shares because she wanted to get Wee Tot's reports. She was planning to quit the garbage business. She hoped to learn more about the manufacture, distribution, and sale of children's clothing.

Now, as Cone well knows, people sometimes do buy stock to get a company's reports and possibly learn about the business. And sometimes they buy stock just so they can attend the annual meeting of stockholders and may get a free box lunch. But those objectives can be achieved by purchasing one share, ten, or maybe a hundred. But buying 10,000 shares just to get quarterly reports? Ridiculous!

Cone curses his own stupidity; he should have caught it from the start. It's obvious to him now that Sally Steiner bought her stake because she knew something or had heard something about the takeover of Wee Tot Fashions, and was out to make a quick buck.

He goes to the wall telephone in his greasy little kitchenette and calls Neal K. Davenport, a detective with the New York Police Department. He's worked with Davenport on a few things, and the city bull owes him.

"Hey, sherlock," the NYPD man says cheerily. "How'ya doing? I haven't heard from you in weeks. You've found another patsy in the Department?"

"Nah," Cone says, "nothing like that. I just haven't been working anything you'd be interested in."

"Glad to hear it. Every time you get me involved, I end up sweating my tush. So why are you calling now?"

"It's about the commercial garbage-collection business."

"Oh?" Davenport says. "Thinking of changing jobs, are you? I'd say you're eminently qualified. You want a letter of recommendation?"

"Cut the bullshit," Cone says, "and just tell me if I'm right. Private garbage collection, waste disposal, and cartage in Manhattan is pretty much controlled by the Families—correct?"

"So I've heard," the NYPD man says. "They're supposed to have the whole fucking city divided up into districts and neighborhoods. If you want to pick up shit, you've got to pay dues to the bentnoses. There was an investigation years ago, but nothing came of it. The DA's witness disappeared and hasn't been heard from since. So what else is new?''

"Thanks," Cone says. "Nice talking to you."

"Hey, wait a minute," Davenport says. "You got something on the mob's connection?"

"Not a thing," Cone assures him. "If I come across anything, you'll be the first to know."

"I won't hold my breath," the city cop says.

Cone hangs up and stares at Cleo thoughtfully.

"Something stinks," he tells the cat. "And it ain't garbage, kiddo."

Five

SALLY STALLS Vic Angelo and Mario Corsini for two weeks. It's a gamble; if she can't come up with a winner, then she loses Steiner Waste Control and access to inside secrets in trash collected from Bechtold Printing. And that'll be the end of her Big Chance.

She conned the two villains in Angelo's car outside the funeral home where Jake lay in his coffin.

"Look," she says to them, "I got a boyfriend on Wall Street. He's a lawyer in the Mergers and Acquisitions Department of a big investment banker. I won't tell you which one. Anyway, he gets in on the ground floor on mergers, takeovers, and buyouts. There's a lot of money to be made if you get advance notice of these deals. I've been making a mint. You guys let me keep Steiner Waste Control, and I'll feed you the same inside information I get from my boyfriend."

The two men stare at her, then turn to look at each other.

"I don't like it," Angelo says. "Insider trading is a federal rap. Who needs it?"

"Wait a minute, Vic," Corsini says. "The insider here is this girlie's boyfriend. If he wants to shoot off his mouth, it's his problem. The people he tells can claim they bought on a stock tip."

"Right!" Sally says enthusiastically. "I tell you it's foolproof. I've played four deals and haven't lost a cent."

Corsini gives her a two-bit smile. "And you invest for the boyfriend and then kick back to him. Have I got it straight, girlie?"

"Of course," she says. "Whaddya think? And don't call me girlie."

"I still don't like it," Angelo says, slowly peeling away the band from one of his fat Havanas. "Trouble with the Feds I don't want."

"Wouldn't hurt to take one little flier, Vic," Corsini says.

That's when the shtarkers agree to give her two weeks to come up with a winning tip. If she can do that, they'll talk a deal. If she fails, they'll buy Steiner Waste Control—on their terms. Sally goes along with that; she's got no choice.

By this time she's got Terry Mulloy and Leroy Hamilton organized. Trash from Bechtold Printing is being delivered to her Smithtown garage, and the stuff she's already pawed through is taken away and brought back to the Eleventh Avenue dump.

By the ninth day she's getting panicky. She's broken three fingernails grubbing through the Bechtold scrap, and all she's found is worthless first proofs of prospectuses and mass mailings to stockholders. But then, on a Thursday night, she hits paydirt.

There are crumpled pages with the letterhead of Snellig Firsten Holbrook. They outline a suggested plan for a leveraged buyout of an outfit called Trimbley & Diggs, Inc. Financing will include junk bonds and a hefty cash payment by company executives who are going to take T&D private as soon as they get control. The purpose, as far as Sally can make out, is to sell off or develop valuable shorefront real estate.

She looks up Trimbley & Diggs in that day's *Wall Street Journal* and finally finds the stock listed in Nasdaq. It's selling for four dollars a share. The next day she calls Paul Ramsey, tells him to buy 9,000 shares of T&D; she'll get the cash to him as soon as possible. Then she calls Mario Corsini at the number he gave her. He isn't in, but she leaves a message, and he calls back in fifteen minutes. Sally tells him she's ready for a meet.

He says they don't want to be seen with her in public, and that's okay with Sally. She suggests they come out late that night to her Smithtown home, say at midnight when her mother and housekeeper will be asleep, and they can talk without being interrupted or overheard.

Corsini doesn't like it. He implies her place may be bugged. He can't take the chance.

"Oh, for God's sake," Sally says disgustedly. "Why would I want to do a stupid thing like that? I'm in this thing deeper than you are. Look, if it'll make you feel any better, you drive out there, park in the driveway, and I'll come out and sit in the car. Your Cadillac's not bugged, is it?''

Corsini mutters darkly that he doesn't think so, but these days who the hell knows? Finally he agrees that they'll drive out that night and try to arrive at midnight. Sally gives him the address and directions on how to find her home.

She gets home early, fills a plate with the shrimp salad Martha has prepared, and takes it upstairs to have dinner with her mother. She and Becky watch the evening news on TV while they're eating, and then Sally goes downstairs while Martha gets her mother ready for bed. She works on her records and books in the den. Steiner Waste Control, with the addition of Pitzak's territory, is making a bundle. Jake would have been happy.

By eleven o'clock the house is silent. Sally sits quietly, plotting how she's going to get the cash to Paul Ramsey and how much, if anything, she should give to Dotty Rosher. That bubblehead has written a letter to Sally, claiming she's broke, and after all she did for Jake, she figures she should have something for her time and trouble. And silence.

Sally decides to turn Dotty's letter over to the Steiners' attorney, Ivan Belzig. He's a toughie and will know exactly how to handle an attempted shakedown like that.

At fifteen minutes before midnight, she's standing in the dimly lighted living room, peering out a window at the graveled driveway. It's almost ten minutes after twelve when the silver gray limousine comes purring up and coasts to a stop. The headlights are doused.

Sally snaps on the porch light and steps out the door. But before she can get down the steps, she sees Vic Angelo and Mario Corsini get out of the Cadillac and start toward the house, looking about them.

"You decided to come inside?" Sally asks as they approach.

"Yeah," Angelo says. "I figure you're straight. You'd be a fool not to be."

She leads the way into the den and offers them a drink, but they decline.

"We won't be here that long," Angelo says.

Both men light up cigars, Vic one of his thick Havanas and Mario a short, twisted stogie that looks like a hunk of black rope. The air grows fetid, and Sally switches the air conditioner to exhaust. She comes back to sit behind the desk. She looks at Vic Angelo, suddenly shocked at how much he reminds her of Jake.

"So?" she says briskly. "Have you decided? You want in? If you do, I've got a hot tip for you."

"Nah," Angelo says. "The stock market ain't for us. I talked to my lawyer about it. He says the risk of our being racked up on an insider trading charge is zip. But if we *do* get involved, then maybe the Feds start looking into our other activities—and that we can do without. So we're turning down your proposition."

She stares at the two men, feeling as if she's been kicked in the cruller. They return her stare with all the expression of Easter Island statues.

"So," Angelo goes on, "we take over Steiner Waste Control. My lawyer is drawing up the papers now. We'll pay you a nice price."

"A nice price!" Sally explodes. "My father started that business with one lousy, secondhand pickup truck. He worked his ass off to build it up, doing the driving and loading himself. And after I joined him, I worked just as hard. How can you put a 'fair price' on that? Goddamn it, that dump belongs to the Steiner family."

"Not anymore it doesn't," Angelo says coldly. "Look, private garbage collecting and cartage is a rough, dirty business. It's no place for a woman."

"Screw that!" Sally says wrathfully. "I can handle it."

"You don't need it, do you?" Mario Corsini says, speaking for the first time. "I mean, you got this boyfriend on Wall Street and you're cleaning up on inside tips. You've been making a mint. That's what you told us—right?"

"Well, yeah, sure," Sally says, beginning to feel desperate. "But the money to play the market comes from the business."

"That's your problem," Vic Angelo says, rising. "You're a smart lady; you'll find a way to work it. The papers for the sale of Steiner Waste Control will be ready in a couple of weeks. We've got to find someone to take over, but that's our problem. Thanks for inviting us to your home. Nice place."

Then they're gone. She watches the limousine pull slowly away. She digs her nails into her palms, determined not to cry. She turns off the porch light, locks and bolts the front door. Then she goes back into the den, slumps in her swivel chair, and in a low voice calls those two snakes every filthy name she can think of.

It's almost ten minutes before she begins to weep.

By Monday morning she's got her act together again. But her brain is churning like one of the compactors at the dump as she tries to find an out. All she knows is that no way, *no* way, are those skunks going to get control of her family's business.

She drives into the city, and before going to the office, stops at the bank that handles the company's accounts. She withdraws $36,000, telling the bank officer she's made a deal on a new truck, but the seller wants cash. She gets the money in hundred-dollar bills, neatly packed in a manila envelope. It's small enough to fit into her capacious shoulder bag, next to her loaded pistol.

When she gets to the dump, Judy Bering jerks a thumb at Sally's private office. "You got a visitor," she says in a low voice. "He wouldn't wait out here. Wouldn't give me his name. A mean bastard. He scares me. You want I should call the cops?"

"Not yet," Sally says. "If I need help, I'll yell."

She walks into her office with a hand in her shoulder bag, gripping the gun. Mario Corsini is seated in the armchair alongside her desk. Sally stops short, glares at him.

"Don't tell me," she says. "You came to count the paper clips. Afraid I'll steal something before you take over?"

"Nah," he says with a bleak smile. "Close the door and sit down. You and me gotta have a private talk."

"We did," Sally says. "On Friday night. Remember? So what more have we got to talk about?"

But she does as he says: closes the door and sits down behind her desk. She examines him in silence.

He really is a repellent man, with a pitted, ocherous complexion and eyes like wet coal. His shiny black hair is parted in the middle and plastered to his long skull like a gigolo or tango dancer of the 1920s. He's wearing morticians' clothes: black suit, white shirt, black tie, black socks, black shoes. No color. No jewelry. He looks like a deep shadow.

"I gotta tell you," he says. "I think Vic is making a big mistake."

"Don't tell me," Sally says bitterly, "tell him."

"I did," he says. "My point is this: We can take over this place anytime we want—but what's the hurry? Why not give you a chance to deliver the stock tips you promised? If you come through, maybe we could make more loot on the market than we can by taking over. If you can't deliver, then we grab the business. I told him all that but he wouldn't listen."

"And Vic's the boss," Sally says.

"That's right," Corsini says. "Vic's the boss. So I go along even when I don't agree. But there's more than one way to skin a cat. We got a lot of things going on, and there are ways I can stall our moving in on you."

"Yeah? What ways?"

"Just believe me when I tell you I can do it," Corsini says evasively. "But it means you'll have to play along with me. With *me*, not with Vic and me. You understand? He knows nothing about this. If he knew I was talking to you alone, he'd cut off my balls. I told him I was coming here to see how my cousin, Tony Ricci, was being treated."

"Well, he's doing okay. The kid's a hard worker—and ambitious."

"Yeah, I know. I had breakfast with him about an hour ago. He's all right; he does what I tell him. Anyway, what I want to toss at you is this: On Friday night you said you had a hot tip for us. Vic turned you down. I want you to give me the name of that stock. I'll invest my own money. Not Vic's money or our company's money, but *mine*, my personal funds. Now if your tip pans out, and I make a nice buck, then I go to Vic and say, 'Hey, that Sally Steiner wasn't shitting us; she really can deliver. Why don't we let her keep the dump as long as she keeps feeding us inside info on stocks.' What do you think of that?"

"I think it sucks," Sally says. "There are two things wrong. First of all, you could do exactly like you tell me, and Vic would still say screw it, we're taking over the business."

"Yeah," Corsini says, nodding, "that could happen. He's a stubborn guy who likes things his own way."

"Second of all," Sally says, "how do I know you're not scamming me? Maybe you just want to make a quick dollar on my tip and you couldn't care less if or when I lose the dump."

He looks at her admiringly. "You got more between your ears than pasta fagioli," he says. "And sure, you're exactly right; I could be conning you. But you're forgetting one thing: You got no choice. Without me, you're going to lose the business for sure. Play along with me and at least you got a chance.''

"I got other choices," she says hotly.

"Yeah?" he says with a death's-head grin. "Like what? Like running to the DA and ratting on us? You'd be cold in a week, and so would your mother and brother. Is that what you want?"

They sit a few moments in silence, eyes locked. They hear the sounds of the dump: trucks rumbling in and out, gears grinding, shouts and laughter. And beyond, the noises of the harsh, raucous city: sirens, whistles, the roar of traffic, and under all a thrumming as if the metropolis had a diapason of its own, coming up from underground vaults and vibrating the tallest towers.

Sally Steiner pulls a pad of scratch paper toward her and scribbles on the top sheet.

"The stock is Trimbley and Diggs," she says. "Nasdaq Market. Right now it's selling for about four bucks a share. And don't, for God's sake, buy more than nine thousand shares at a clip or the SEC might get interested."

Mario Corsini takes the slip of paper. "Nice doing business with you," he says politely.

He starts out the door. "Hey," she calls, and he turns back. "Thanks for not calling me girlie."

He inclines his head gravely as if her gratitude is merited.

She sits for about five minutes after he's gone, thinking about their conversation and wondering if she's doing the smart thing. But then she realizes the bastard was right: She really has no choice. As for his threat of what might happen to her, Becky, and Eddie if she goes to the cops, she has no doubt whatsoever that he and his thugs are capable of doing exactly what he said.

She pulls the phone toward her and calls Eddie.

"Hey, bro," she says. "How'ya doing?"

"Hanging in there," he says. "How are you, Sal?"

"Couldn't be better," she says brightly. "Paul around?"

"Won't be back till noon. He's auditioning for a commercial for a strawberry-flavored laxative."

"Beautiful," Sally says. "Could I pop over for a while?

I've got some cash to leave for him. Our first step on the way to fame and fortune.''

"Sure," he says. "Come ahead. Got time to pose?"

"Maybe an hour or so. Okay?"

She walks down to Eddie's apartment, stopping on the way to buy him a decent burgundy. It's a sprightly day, summer around the corner, and the blue sky, sharp sun, and kissing breeze make her feel like she owns the world. Life is a tease; that she knows. All souls dissolve; but meanwhile it can be a hoot if you keep running and never look back.

She poses nude for Eddie for almost an hour, sitting on that stupid stool and trying to make her body as tense, muscular, and aggressive as he commands. Finally he slaps his sketch pad shut.

"That's it," he says. "I've got all the studies I need. Now I'll start blocking out the canvas. This is going to be a good one, Sal; I just know it."

"Make me pretty," she says. "And about six inches taller and twenty pounds thinner."

"You're perfect the way you are."

"Marry me," she says. "And also pour me a wine while I get dressed."

They're sitting on the couch, drinking her burgundy, talking about their mother and whether or not they should try another doctor, when Paul Ramsey comes ambling in. He gives them a beamy smile.

"I didn't get the job," he reports. "They decided I wasn't the strawberry laxative type."

"Thank God," Eddie says. "I don't think I could stand seeing you in a commercial, coming out of a bathroom and grinning like a maniac."

"Paul," Sally says, taking the manila envelope out of her shoulder bag, "here's thirty-six thousand in hundred-dollar bills."

"Hey," he says, "that's cool."

"You opened a brokerage account?"

"Oh, sure. No sweat."

"Well, dump this lettuce in your personal checking account. Draw on it to buy nine thousand shares of Trimbley and Diggs. Your broker will find it on the Nasdaq exchange. I wrote it all out for you. Buy the stock today, as soon as possible. You've got five days to get a check to the broker.''

"Does this make me a tycoon?" Paul Ramsey asks.

"A junior tycoon," Sally tells him. "But we're just getting started.''

She sits in the one comfortable armchair in the apartment. Eddie and Paul sit close on the rickety couch. The three kid along for a while, chattering about this and that. But then Sally falls silent and listens while the two men, holding hands now, chivy one another as they plan what they're going to have for dinner and whose turn it is to do the cooking.

She can see the intimacy between them, a warm bond that may be fondness, may be affection, may be love. Whatever, each completes the other. They are easy together, and no strains show. There is a privacy there, and Sally finds it disturbing. For that kind of sharing is a foreign language to her and yet leaves her feeling cheated and bereft.

The stock of Trimbley & Diggs, Inc., is going up, up, up, and Sally is ecstatic. When it hits seven dollars, she has Paul Ramsey buy another 9,000 shares.

She also notes the trading volume of T&D is increasing as the value of the stock rises. She figures there's either an inside leak at Snellig Firsten Holbrook or the arbitrageurs have ferreted out the takeover and are looking to make a bundle. So is Sally. And so, apparently, is Mario Corsini. He calls her at home, late at night, a week after their talk in her office.

"Good tip," he says, his raspy voice revealing neither joy nor enthusiasm. "You buying more?"

"Thinking about it."

"How high do you think it'll go?"

"Who knows?" she says. "Ten. Twelve maybe."

"Twelve?" he says cautiously. "If it hits twelve, you think I should bail out?"

"Hey," she says, "I'm not your financial adviser. I gave you a good tip. What you do with it is your business. And what about *my* business? What's going to happen to Steiner Waste Control?"

"I'm working on it," he says. "Listen, one of the reasons I called: Tony Ricci will be late for work tomorrow. There's a family funeral, and I want him to be there. He'll show up around noon. Okay?"

"I guess it'll have to be," Sally says. "It'll screw up my truck schedules, but I'll work it out."

"You do that," Corsini says. "And if you get any more tips, let me know."

He hangs up abruptly, leaving Sally staring angrily at her dead phone. It infuriates her that she's enabling that gonnif to make even one lousy buck. It's she who's breaking her nails digging through garbage from Bechtold Printing. All Corsini has to do is call his broker.

She drives to work early the next morning, checks in at the office, then crosses Eleventh Avenue to the Stardust Diner. Terry Mulloy and Leroy Hamilton are seated at the back table. Both men are working on plates of three eggs over with a ham steak, a mountain of home fries, a stack of toast with butter and jelly, and coffee with cream and sugar. Sally joins them.

"You're both going to have coronaries," she says, and tells Mabel to bring her a plain bagel and a cup of black coffee.

It's payoff day, and she slips each man an envelope under the table.

"I thank you kindly," Hamilton says, pocketing his hundred. "And the best part is my wife don't know a thing about it."

"How long is this going to last?" Mulloy wants to know.

"Till I tell you to stop," Sally says. "What's the matter—getting all worn out, poor baby? I can always find two other imbeciles to handle Bechtold Printing."

"Nah," Leroy says, "no call to do that. We like the job, don't we, Terry?"

"Well, yeah," the redheaded harp says. "The money's good, but I'd like to know what's going down. I don't want to get my ass busted for a hundred a week."

"You worry too much," Sally says. "You know those three monkeys: See No Evil, Hear No Evil, Speak No Evil. That's the way you monkeys should be."

At about the same time, a silver gray Cadillac limousine pulls into a No Parking space in front of the marquee of the Hotel Bedlington on upper Madison Avenue.

"What're we stopping here for?" Angelo asks.

"Vic," Mario Corsini says, "we got plenty of time to get

downtown for the meet. I figured we'd grab some breakfast.
You like it here. The French toast—remember?''

"Oh, yeah," Angelo says. "Good idea."

They get out of the car. The uniformed doorman comes
forward, and Corsini slips him a sawbuck. "Take care of it,"
he says. "You have any trouble, we'll be in the dining
room."

"No trouble, sir," the doorman says. "No trouble at all."

The cavernous dining room is almost deserted; just one
wimp by himself and two old ladies together, sipping tea and
nibbling on dry rye toast. The two men take a corner table so
their backs are against the wall. Vic Angelo orders a large
glass of freshly squeezed orange juice, French toast with
plenty of butter and syrup, and decaf coffee. Mario Corsini
has warm blueberry muffins and regular coffee, black.

"Nice quiet place," Angelo says, looking around.

"Yeah," Corsini says. "You could plan a revolution in
here and no one would be the wiser. Also, it gives me a
chance to speak my piece."

"Oh, Jesus," Angelo says, groaning. "Not that Steiner
thing again. Lay off, Mario. We been over that twice, and
what I said still goes."

"I gotta tell you, Vic, I called and leaned on her. She gave
me that stock tip she told us about. I played it—on my own,
Vic, on my own—and it's almost doubled in a week."

Angelo stares at him, face rigid. "That wasn't very smart,
Mario. I told you I want no part of Wall Street. We're going
to take over the Steiner dump and that's it."

"Vic, will you listen just for a minute," Corsini says,
leaning over the table. "She wasn't conning us; she really
does have an inside pipeline. Maybe I'll triple my stake.
Jesus, we can make more with her than we can from garbage
and linen supply. And the—"

But then their breakfasts are served, and neither man
speaks until the waiter moves away.

"And the best part," Corsini continues earnestly, "is that
we don't have to kick anything upstairs. Let's face it, Vic,
we're hired hands. Messenger boys—right? Sure, we collect
plenty, but how much sticks to our fingers after we pay our
dues and grease the lousy politicians, the cops, the union
guys, and everyone else and their uncles? This thing with

Sally Steiner is a nice clean deal. What we make is what we keep. No dues, no payoffs.''

"You're talking shit," Angelo says, smothering his French toast with butter and syrup and beginning to wolf it down. He talks with his mouth full. "How long do you think it would take Fat Lonny to find out what's going on? He's no dope. Then he'll want to know why we didn't cut him in, and our ass is in a sling. Just forget about it, will ya, and let me finish my breakfast in peace. No more stock deals with Sally Steiner. As soon as the papers are ready, we're moving in on her. And that's final."

"If you say so, Vic. You're the boss."

They finish their food in silence, then light up cigars from Mario's gold Dunhill. When they get up to leave, Corsini stays behind a moment to inspect the check. He leaves enough cash on the table to cover it, with a generous tip.

They exit from the hotel together. Their Cadillac is still parked in front of the marquee.

Corsini slaps his jacket pocket. "Shit," he says, "I must have left my lighter on the table. I'll be right back."

He reenters the hotel. Vic Angelo gets into the front seat on the passenger side. He has closed the door when a young man comes out from between parked cars behind the limousine. He's wearing a black raincoat with the collar turned up and a black slouch hat with the brim pulled down.

He walks swiftly to the Cadillac. He pulls an automatic pistol from the pocket of his raincoat. He sticks his arm through the open window and fires four rapid shots into the startled face of Vic Angelo.

Then he walks quickly to a car double-parked north of the hotel. He gets in. The car pulls away.

The doorman, hearing the shots, comes running from the lobby. Mario Corsini comes running from the hotel. Pedestrians come running from all directions. They peer into the front seat of the limousine where Vic Angelo lies sprawled in a fountain of blood, still spouting. His face and half his head are blown away.

"Oh, my God," the doorman cries.

"I saw who done it," someone shouts. "It was a guy in a black raincoat."

"Call the police," someone yells.

"There's never a cop around when you need one," says Mario Corsini.

Sally Steiner wasn't born yesterday; after watching TV reports and reading newspaper accounts of the assassination at the Hotel Bedlington, she makes a shrewd guess at what actually went on and who's responsible. It's no skin off her teeth. Let the bastards kill each other; she couldn't care less.

The only thing that concerns her is how the death of Angelo is going to affect the future of Steiner Waste Control. She doesn't have to wait long to find out. Three days after the murder, she gets a call at the office from Mario Corsini.

"I'm driving out to your place tonight," he states. "About twelve. You'll be there?"

"Sure," she says. "Sorry about Angelo."

"Yeah," Corsini says. "He was an okay guy."

The prospect of being alone with that mobster at midnight is not a prospect that fills her with glee. She puts her loaded pistol in the top drawer of the desk. She doesn't think he'll try any rough stuff, but still. . . .

It's a balmy night, and she's strolling around the front lawn when the silver gray Cadillac pulls into the driveway a little after twelve. Sally goes back to the lighted porch and waits for Corsini to come up.

"Still got the same car," she observes.

"Yeah," he says. "I had to have the front seats re-covered."

In the den, she offers him a drink, and this time he accepts. She hasn't any Chivas Regal, but he takes a snifter of Rémy Martin. That was Jake's favorite, and no one has touched the bottle since he died.

"I'm taking over from Vic," Corsini announces. "It's been cleared. I don't want you coming to Ozone Park, so from now on you'll make your monthly payments to Tony Ricci, and he'll deliver. I'm bringing him along slowly. He'll be my driver one of these days."

"My monthly payments?" Sally says. "Does that mean I keep the dump?"

"For the time being," he says coldly. "Just keep running it the way you have, and we'll see. You got another stock for me?"

"No. Not yet."

He takes a sip of his cognac. "You better be extra nice to that boyfriend of yours," he advises. "Figure it this way: As long as you keep coming up with inside tips that pay off, that's how long you'll own Steiner Waste Control. You can understand that, can't you?"

"Yeah, sure; it isn't all that complicated."

"Well, now you know where you stand. I like everything open and aboveboard."

"Uh-huh," Sally says.

He sits back in the armchair, beginning to relax. He crosses his knees, inhales the aroma from his glass of brandy.

"Now about that Trimbley and Diggs stock," he says, watching to catch her reaction. "Right now I'm holding about a hundred thousand shares."

"What!"

"You heard me. A hundred thousand. But don't get your balls in an uproar. I only bought nine thousand in my own name. The other buys were made by friends of mine around the country. They'll get a cut of the profits. And none of them bought more than nine thousand shares each, so there's nothing to worry about."

"I hope you're right," Sally says nervously, biting at her thumbnail. "Jesus, you must have well over half a million tied up in that stock."

"About," he says carelessly. "I had to borrow to get up the kale. And the people I borrowed from wouldn't like it if I stiffed them. So I'm going to start taking some profits."

"Oh, my God!" Sally says despairingly. "Don't tell me you're going to dump a hundred thousand shares all at once? It'll kill the market."

"Whaddya think—I'm a klutz? Of course I'm not going to dump it all. I'm selling off little by little. It won't hurt the stock price. But I want to see some money. Enough to pay off the sharks. How much you in for?"

"As much as I can afford," Sally says. Then she figures she better prove her confidence in T&D. "I had eighteen thousand shares," she tells him, "and bought another nine this morning. Through a friend."

"That's smart," he says, nodding. "You really think it'll go to twelve bucks a share?"

"Now I think it may go to fifteen. It's a leveraged takeover, and from what my boyfriend tells me, it's going through.''

He finishes his drink, sets the crystal snifter carefully on the desk. He stands up to go.

''Just remember what I told you,'' he says. ''Your family keeps the business as long as you keep coming up with cash cows. That's fair enough, isn't it?''

''Oh, sure,'' Sally says, ''that's really fair.''

At the front door, he pauses and turns to her. He reaches out to stroke her cheek, but she jerks angrily away, and he gives her a mirthless smile.

''You're some woman,'' he says. ''You've got guts. I'd teach you how to be nice, but I don't want to ruin what you've got going with your Wall Street guy. That's where our loot's coming from, isn't it?''

She doesn't answer. Just glares at him. She watches until he gets in the Caddy and drives away. She goes back into the den and stares at his empty brandy glass. Enraged, she backhands it off the desk, hoping it will shatter into a hundred pieces. But it bounces harmlessly on the shag rug, and she leaves it there.

She sits stiffly in the swivel chair, thinking of what happened. After a while she cools, and the fact that he came on to her seems small potatoes compared to the fact that the stupid prick has sunk over a half-mil on a stock tip. Suddenly she strikes her forehead with a palm and groans.

Feverishly she digs out the most recent issue of Standard & Poor's Stock Guide. She looks up Trimbley & Diggs, Inc., and follows the numbers across to the column headed Capitalization. As she feared, T&D is very thinly capitalized. There is no preferred stock and only about 800,000 shares of common stock outstanding.

Then she begins laughing. It's possible that there's an insider leak at Snellig Firsten Holbrook, and it's possible that arbitrageurs have learned of the leveraged takeover and are buying T&D for a quick profit. But it now seems obvious that the run-up of the stock's price is mostly due to Sally buying 27,000 shares and Mario Corsini buying almost 100,000 shares.

Unknowingly, the two of them have been manipulating the goddamn stock! She can't stop laughing, but eventually sobers long enough to realize that their manipulation can work both ways. If Corsini is liquidating his holdings, she better do the same. Take the money and run—before the whole thing blows away like a house of cards in a sudden belch.

So she unloads her first purchase of 9,000 shares the next morning, making a profit of about $36,000. She gives Paul Ramsey his 5 percent, and he looks at the cash in bemusement.

"Cool," he says.

"I told you my sister is a financial genius," Eddie tells him. "She's a lousy cook, but she knows money."

So everything's coming up roses, and looking even better on Tuesday night when Sally, digging through the latest delivery of Bechtold Printing trash, finds smeared proofs on the letterhead of Pistol & Burns. There's a merger in the works between two food processing companies, one small, one big and cash-rich.

Sally smiles grimly. That should keep Corsini happy until she can figure a way to get that murdering punk out of her life—permanently.

<u>Six</u>

TIMOTHY CONE looks up the telephone number of Edward Steiner, West 47th Street, in the Manhattan directory and calls from the loft.

"Mr. Steiner?"

"Yes. Who's this?"

"Our name is Silas Farthingale. We are the director of client data for the Carlton Insurance Company. A Miss Sally Steiner has applied for a single-premium annuity policy with Carlton. It pays a death benefit, of course, and Miss Steiner has listed you as one of her beneficiaries, giving us your name and address. Unfortunately, she neglected to fill out the space in which the relationship should be stated. We have attempted to contact Miss Steiner, but she seems to be out. We wonder if you'd be willing to state your relationship to Miss Steiner so her application can be processed as expeditiously as possible."

"Sure," Eddie says, laughing. "I'm her brother."

"We thank you very much, Mr. Steiner."

So now Cone knows that much. The two, brother and sister, could be in it together, but he's inclined to think the woman is the mover and shaker in these stock deals. After all, she's the one who bought 10,000 shares of Wee Tot Fashions in her own name. Then Jeremy Bigelow shows up and asks questions. So now Sally is using a front: Paul Ramsey, her brother's roommate. And she's buying Trimbley & Diggs in 9,000-share lots, figuring that will keep the SEC off her tail.

And those other 9,000-share buys in cities all over the country? Maybe those buyers are friends of Sally Steiner, too. But that's so neat a solution that Cone is inclined to doubt it.

But none of his theorizing sheds any light on the Steiner

woman's pipeline into Wall Street. She must have an informant down there—unless . . .

She runs a garbage collection outfit, doesn't she? So maybe she's picking up trash from Pistol & Burns, Snellig Firsten Holbrook, and God knows how many other investment bankers and stockbrokers. And maybe she's flipping through that rubbish to glean her inside information. It's possible. Cone remembers warning G. Fergus Twiggs about safeguarding the contents of Pistol & Burns' wastebaskets by purchasing more efficient shredders.

He digs out the Manhattan Yellow Pages and, in the section headed Rubbish & Garbage Removal, finds the address and phone number he wants. He calls.

"Steiner Waste Control."

"My name is Herschel Dingby. I'm opening a restaurant in the Wall Street area in a month or so, and I'd like to talk to someone at your company to arrange for daily garbage collection."

"We don't service any customers below Fourteenth Street."

Bang! goes the phone. And *bang!* goes Timothy's theory of how Sally Steiner is getting her inside poop. He sighs and makes one more call.

"Pistol and Burns. May I help you?"

"Could I speak to Mr. G. Fergus Twiggs, please. Timothy Cone of Haldering and Company calling."

"Just a moment, please, sir."

It's more than a moment, but Cone waits patiently. Eventually the senior partner comes on the line, and they exchange brief pleasantries. Then the Wall Street dick gets down to business.

"Are you a betting man, Mr. Twiggs?"

Short pause, then: "I wouldn't be in this business if I wasn't. What do you want me to bet on?"

"Me," Cone says. "Look, I know that technically Haldering's job is finished at your shop. I submit a final report, you pay us off, and that's it. Only I don't want it to end right now. I'd like you to call Hiram Haldering and tell him you want to keep us on the payroll for another couple of weeks."

"And why should I do that, Mr. Cone?"

"Because I think I'm onto something that may—with

heavy emphasis on the *may*—uncover that Wee Tot Fashions leak from your office. And other insider leaks from other investment houses. No guarantees, but I think it's worth the bet that I'll come up with something. If not, then just write me off as another con artist.''

"No, Mr. Cone, I'd never do that.'' There is a long silence, then he says, "All right, I'll place a wager on you. I'll call Mr. Haldering immediately and tell him we require your services for another two weeks.''

"Thanks," Timothy says. "But I better warn you: I plan to rent a car. I'll need it to do the job. You'll get stuck for the expenses on that.''

G. Fergus Twiggs laughs. "Why not?'' he says. "In for a penny, in for a pound.''

That night Cone picks up a big box of baked lasagna, a container of cucumber salad, and a jug of burgundy. He cabs over to Samantha's apartment in the East Village. She pops the lasagna in the oven to warm it while he pours tumblers of wine. As usual, they plop down and eat on one of the oval rag rugs in her artsy-craftsy apartment.

"You'll never guess what happened,'' she says. "This afternoon that guy Twiggs called H.H. He wants you to keep on the Pistol and Burns case for another two weeks.''

"No kidding?'' Cone says, eating busily. "I wonder what he's got in mind.''

Sam looks at him suspiciously. "When you get that look on your puss,'' she says, "I begin to worry. You didn't have anything to do with Twiggs' call, did you?''

"Me? Come on! How could I convince a guy like that to spend more money on something I thought was signed, sealed, and delivered? I figured to complete the final report and that would be that.''

"Uh-huh,'' she says, still staring at him. "Well, now I'll have to parcel out those three new cases to the other guys, and they'll scream bloody murder. Tim, is there something you're not telling me?''

He holds up a palm. "I swear there's not. Have I ever lied to you?''

"Oh, Jesus,'' she says, sighing. "Now I *am* worried. You tight-mouthed bastard! I should have known better than to ask you.''

They finish their dinner and clean up the debris. Then they loll on the rug again, sipping fresh glasses of burgundy.

"Want to stay the night?" she asks him.

"Of course I want to stay. I'll split early in the morning before you're awake."

"What a life we lead," she says. "Fast action and quick goodbyes."

"Hey," he said, "don't get started on that. We agreed— remember? Either of us can blow the whistle any time, with no explanations, no excuses, no apologies."

She looks at him coldly. "I'd like to blow your whistle," she says, and they both crack up.

She wants to watch some stupid TV documentary about the Richest Man in the World. So Cone undresses and slips naked into bed, after removing her French dolls and chenille bedspread covered with little pink balls of fluff.

She keeps the volume down, and after a while he dozes, not really sleeping but floating drowsily between clean, crisp sheets, wondering if this really is, as he believes, the best time of his life.

He is dimly conscious of Sam clicking off the TV set and checking the chain and bolt on the outside door. He hears her moving about, going into the bathroom and coming out, undressing.

Then she slides into bed alongside him.

"Sleeping?" she whispers.

"Yes," he says.

"Liar. Want to wait till morning?"

"No."

She molds herself to his back, spoon-fashion, then reaches around to hold him. He can feel the fever of her body, and it's so nice having her close that he doesn't want to move.

"*Do* something," she urges.

"Whistle 'Dixie'?" he suggests. "Sing an aria? Crack my knuckles?"

She punches his ribs. "I'll crack more than that, buster."

Then he is no longer drowsy, and they attack each other with moaning kisses and caresses as hard as blows. Their bodies join in a curve as convoluted as a Möbius strip. Within moments they are engaged in hostile assaults, as if each is guilty of the other's need—for which there is no forgiveness.

They rampage across the bed, back and forth, and if there had been a chandelier overhead, they would have swung from that, two nutty acrobats socking together in midair. Curses are muffled, oaths gritted, and when they finally come to a sweated juncture, each believes it a selfish victory and is beamy and content.

Cone rents a Dodge Shadow because the name appeals to him. He intends using it to shadow and, if things get hairy, to dodge. It's a black two-door compact and has all the performance he'll need for city driving.

He gets the feel of it on a jaunt uptown. He drives by Steiner Waste Control on Eleventh Avenue and is surprised by the size of the dump—almost a city block wide. It's late afternoon, and the place seems relatively quiet with only a single truck unloading at a shed and another on the tarmac awaiting its turn.

He returns to the loft and phones Neal K. Davenport.

"Now what?" the NYPD detective demands. "I'm trying to eat a sausage hero, so make it fast."

"That's your lunch? At this time of day?"

"You think we get a regular lunch hour like you nine-to-five types? Fat chance! What's on your mind, sherlock?"

"You know anyone in the Organized Crime Bureau?"

"I might. Why are you asking? You got something for them?"

"Nah," Cone says. "Just a couple of questions."

"What the hell is this—a one-way street? When are you going to start coming up with some answers for us? What a hardnose you are! Okay, I'll play your little game. The guy I know in the Organized Crime outfit is Joe D'Amato. He looks and dresses like a college professor, but he's got more street smarts than you and I will ever have. I'll give him a call and tell him you're the worst brain-picker in the city. If he wants to talk to you, that's his problem."

"Thanks," Cone says. "That's one I owe you."

"*One!*" the city bull says, outraged. "What're you doing—counting on your thumbs? Use all your appendages and it comes to twenty-one. Do you read me, sonny boy?"

Cone hangs up softly. He finds the computer printouts Jeremy Bigelow gave him, and makes a list of all the out-of-town buyers who purchased 9,000 shares of Trimbley &

Diggs, Inc. There are ten of them, and Cone jots down their names and the cities where they bought the T&D stock.

Cleo has started to mewl sadly, so he changes the cat's litter, puts out fresh water, and then inspects the contents of his scarred, waist-high refrigerator to see what kind of a banquet man and beast can share. He finds three eggs, a hunk of salami, and a piece of greenish cheese sparked with jalapeño pepper flakes.

He cuts the salami into cubes, fries them up with the eggs, and sets out the cheese to provide his cholesterol overdose of the day. There's also a blackened banana for dessert. But everything tastes good to him, and Cleo has no objections except perhaps to the pepper cheese which makes the tom sneeze.

The phone doesn't ring until almost nine o'clock and, being a superstitious man, Cone goes to answer it with his fingers crossed.

"Yeah?" he says.

"Is this Timothy Cone?"

"That's right. Who's this?"

"Sergeant Joseph D'Amato. Neal Davenport said you wanted me to contact you."

"Yeah. Thanks."

"I should tell you this call is being taped. In the business I'm in, that's SOP. Okay with you?"

"Sure. All I got is a list of names and where they live. I was hoping you might be able to give me some skinny on them."

"Who are they?"

Cone sees no reason to hold back, especially if he wants a favor from this guy. "All of them bought big blocks of the same stock in the last two or three weeks. I think it may be an inside trading scam."

"Hey, wait a minute," D'Amato says. "That's a federal rap. No interest to us."

"It might," Cone says. "I think these guys are getting their tips from a woman who operates a private garbage removal service on the West Side of Manhattan. I got a feeling these guys are all wrongos, and they're in your files."

Silence a moment, then: "All right, let's have the names. Try to speak slowly and distinctly. My tape recorder is an antique. And spell out all the last names."

Cone does as he's told.

"That's it," he says when he's finished.

"A couple of the names ring a bell," the sergeant says. "And you're right: They are not nice people. I'll run them through the computer and see what turns up. I'll get back to you."

"Thanks."

"Neal tells me you're a secretive sonofabitch. If you're holding back, now's the time to tell me. I don't like doing a private eye's work unless there's something in it for me."

"I understand that, and I'm not holding back. I've given you all I've got."

"All right," D'Amato says. "But you cross me just once, and you've had it, pal. You capeesh?"

"I capeesh," Cone says.

That night, around eleven o'clock, he drives uptown again. He parks two blocks away from Steiner Waste Control and walks back. The dump is surrounded by a heavy chain-link fence, and the truck-filled tarmac is lighted by two floods. There's also a night watchman's shed inside the locked gate, and the guy himself is outside, looking up at the star-spangled sky. He's a chunky bruiser and he's not carrying a kielbasa in that belt holster.

Cone knows at once that there's no way he's going to break into the Steiner office and waltz out with their customer list. That leaves only one alternative, and he groans aloud when he thinks of the stultifying labor that will entail.

But he won't let go; he's done his share of donkeywork before and lived through it. So on Thursday morning, early, he's parked across Eleventh Avenue from Steiner Waste Control. He's come prepared with two deli sandwiches (bologna on rye with mustard, roast beef on white with mayo) and four cans of Miller beer in a plastic bag filled with ice cubes.

The garbage dump comes to life. Cone watches as the gate is unlocked and thrown open. Employees arrive, trucks are revved up, the gas pump is busy, and a short, stocky woman comes out of the office to yell something Cone can't hear at an old guy who comes limping from one of the corrugated steel sheds.

There are six huge Loadmaster compactor trucks, all painted yellow. Timothy thanks God and his good-luck angels when he sees that not only do the garbage trucks bear the legend Steiner Waste Control, but each has a big number painted on the side, 1 to 6. At least Cone won't be following the same truck for a week.

Because that's his plan; he can't think of a better way to find out who Sally Steiner is dealing with. He doesn't think she's got a Wall Street informant, so she must be getting her inside info from one of her customers. It's a long shot, but the only one Cone has.

Truck No. 4 pulls out first, and Cone starts up the Dodge Shadow and goes right after it. For the next seven hours he eats the truck's exhaust, going where it goes, stopping when it stops, returning to the dump when Truck No. 4 returns to drop a load.

Meanwhile he's making scrawled notes on the back of a brown envelope that originally contained a nasty letter from the IRS warning him that he owed Uncle Sam an additional $17.96. He logs the schedule of Truck No. 4: names and addresses of places it services: restaurants, apartment houses, diners, industrial buildings, taverns.

By the end of the day, sandwiches and beers consumed, Cone is bored and cranky, wondering if he's got the fire to keep this up for a week. What bugs him is the fear that each numbered truck may have a different schedule of rubbish pickups every day. If that's true, it'll take a month of Sundays to list all of Sally Steiner's customers.

But on Friday morning, he's there again, parked and waiting. Now there are big flatbeds pulling through the Steiner gate to load up with strapped bales of paper, and open-bed trucks being filled with cubes of compacted garbage to be taken, Cone presumes, to landfills on Long Island or New Jersey. And smaller trucks loading up with tons of swill for what eventual purpose Cone doesn't even want to imagine.

On Friday he follows Truck No. 2. On Monday he shadows Truck No. 5. And on Tuesday he takes off after Truck No. 3, beginning to think he's just spinning his wheels. But then, early Tuesday afternoon, something happens that makes it seem likely he hasn't been diddling himself.

Cone has already noted that the big Steiner trucks are operated by a crew of two, driver and loader. On Tuesday, Truck No. 3 is being driven by a redheaded guy with the map of Ireland spread all over his face. The loader is a broad-shouldered black who looks like he could nudge a locked door off its hinges with no trouble at all.

Everything in their Tuesday routine is normal and dull until about 1:00, when Truck No. 3 slows and turns into an alley-way alongside a one-story cinderblock building on lower Tenth Avenue. Cone parks across the street and opens his second pack of Camels of the day. From where he sits, he has a good view of the action.

The loader climbs down from the cab. But instead of hefting the cylindrical barrels of trash that have been put out for pickup, he exits the alley and starts walking up Tenth Avenue. Cone straightens up, interested enough to forget to light his cigarette.

In a couple of minutes, a battered Chevy van pulls into the alley and stops right behind the Steiner truck. The loader gets out of the Chevy, opens the back doors, and begins to lift the barrels into the van.

"What the hell?" Cone says aloud, and then realizes he's now got two cigarettes going at once. He licks thumb and forefinger and pinches one out, saving it carefully in the ash-tray. The van, loaded with four barrels, backs out of the alley and starts north on Tenth Avenue. Cone takes a quick look at the cinderblock building. It's got a brass plate next to the front door, but it's so small he can't read it from across the street. The yellow truck hasn't moved, so Cone gets rolling and follows the van.

What a journey that turns out to be! Up Tenth Avenue to 54th Street. East on 54th to Eighth Avenue. North on Eighth and onto Broadway. Up Broadway to 72nd Street. East on 72nd to Central Park West. North on CPW to 86th Street. A right turn and they're going through the Park at Traverse 3. Cone is happy he's got a full tank of gas.

He's keeping a tight tail on the van, but city traffic is heavy and it's doubtful if the loader will spot him, even if he's look-ing for a shadow. Cone doesn't think that likely; the guy is driving steadily at legal speeds and making no effort to jink.

On the East Side, they turn up First Avenue and continue north, almost to 125th Street. Now Cone guesses where they're heading: the Triborough Bridge. He wonders if this guy is making a hegira to Long Island to dump his four bar-rels in some deserted landfill. But that doesn't make sense; by rights, the contents of those barrels should have been taken back to the Steiner dump for disposal.

On they go, picking up speed now as traffic thins. They stop briefly to pay their tolls, then head across the span. Cone accelerates to pull the Dodge Shadow alongside the van. He glances sideways. The loader looks like he's enjoying life. He's smoking a plump cigar and slapping the steering wheel in time to radio music Cone can't hear.

They get onto the Long Island Expressway, moving at a lively clip. They turn off onto the Northern State Parkway, turn again onto the Sunken Meadow State Parkway. The van is slowing now, and Cone has time to look around. Pretty country. Plenty of trees. Some impressive homes with white picket fences.

Down Main Street in Smithtown and into an area where the homes are even bigger, set on wide lawns with white graveled driveways leading to the house and two- or three-car garages.

The Chevy van turns into one of those driveways. Cone continues down the road a piece, pulls onto the verge and parks. He hops out, lights a cigarette, and saunters back. He stands in the semi-concealment of a small copse of pines and watches the loader lug the four barrels, one at a time, into a neat white garage with a shingled roof.

The four cardboard barrels inside, the man starts bringing them out again and sliding them into the van—or so it seems; the barrels are identical in appearance. Timothy is flummoxed until he realizes what's going on. The guy has delivered four new barrels; he's picking up four old barrels that were already stored in the garage.

Cone sees the Steiner loader climb behind the wheel of the van. Away he goes. Cone will make book on exactly where he's heading: back to the city to make contact with Truck No. 3, dump the trash in the big yellow Loadmaster, and then return the empty barrels to the alleyway alongside that building on Tenth Avenue.

Cone stays where he is, eyeballing the garage and home. Nice place. The house is two stories high with a lot of windows. Weathered brick halfway up and white clapboard the rest of the way. A tiled terrace at one side with French doors from the house. All set on what looks to be a one-acre plot, at least, with a manicured lawn and a few pieces of Victorian cast-iron furniture scattered about.

He figures he'll meander up and see if there's a name on the mailbox. If someone braces him, he'll tell them he's the Avon Lady. But he doesn't have to use any subterfuge. He's no sooner started up the bricked walk to the front door when he spots a sign on a short post driven into the lawn. It reads: THE STEINERS.

"Ho-ho-ho," Cone says aloud. He goes back to his car, turns around, and heads for the city. He drives as fast as the cabs on the parkways and expressway, hoping to get back to Tenth Avenue before that business closes for the day. Traffic is heavy, but nothing like what's coming *from* the city; that's bumper-to-bumper.

He's back in Manhattan by four o'clock, but it takes him almost forty-five minutes to work his way over to the West Side. He finally parks on Ninth Avenue, with his watch nudging 5:00 P.M. He practically runs back to the one-story cinderblock building. The brass plate next to the front door reads: BECHTOLD PRINTING. Just that and nothing more.

The front door is still open, but when he pushes his way in, a blowsy blonde in the front office is putting on her hat. It looks like a velvet chamberpot.

"We're closed for the day," she tells Cone.

"Nah," he says, giving her what he fancies is a charming smile. "The front door is open. I just want to get some letterheads, bills, and business cards printed up."

"We don't do that kind of work," she says tartly.

"You don't?" he says. "Well, what kind of work do you do?"

"Financial printing," she says.

"Thank you very much," the Wall Street dick says, tipping his leather cap. "Sorry to bother you."

Back in the Dodge Shadow, he realizes he hasn't eaten all day. So he wolfs down his two deli sandwiches (salami and egg salad) and gulps two beers. All the ice cubes in his plastic sack have melted, and the beer is barely cool. But at least it's wet.

Then he drives back to his loft, whistling a merry tune.

He wakes Wednesday morning, mouth tasting like a wet wool sock and stomach ready to do a Krakatoa. He resolves never again to drink Italian brandy with kosher hot dogs, baked beans, and sauerkraut. Even Cleo, who shared the same meal, looks a mite peaked.

He trudges down to the office. It's an unexpectedly sharp day, with a keen, whistling wind. Breathing that etheric air is like having a decongestant inhaler plugged up each nostril. But by the time he hits John Street, he's feeling a lot better and figures he'll live to play the violin again.

"Thanks for stopping by," Samantha Whatley says bitterly. "So glad you could make it. And it isn't even payday."

"Hey," he says, "you know I've been busy with Pistol and Burns. Practically living with G. Fergus Twiggs."

"Practically living with him, huh? That's why you've got three messages on your desk to phone him as soon as possible."

"Oh," Cone says. "Well, something must have come up. I'll give him a call."

"That's more than you do for me," she says in a low voice. "You bastard!"

"I've really been busy," he says lamely, and flees to his own cubbyhole office before she starts bitching about his missing progress reports.

There are the three messages from Twiggs, and one from Joseph D'Amato. Cone calls the sergeant first.

"Christ, you're a hard man to get hold of," the NYPD detective says. "I called you at home a couple of times, then figured I'd try your office. Listen, you and I have got to have a talk."

"Sure. How about noon here in the office? We can have a sandwich and schmooze as long as you like."

"Suits me," D'Amato says. "I'll be there."

"You got something for me?" Cone asks hopefully.

"See you at noon," the sergeant says and hangs up.

Cone then calls G. Fergus Twiggs. Getting through to the senior partner of Pistol & Burns is akin to requesting an audience with the Q. of E., but the Wall Street dick waits patiently, and eventually Twiggs comes on the line. His normally cheery voice sounds dejected.

"I'm afraid we have another one," he reports.

"An insider leak?"

"Yes. On a deal that's barely gotten under way. I just don't understand it. Very depressing."

"I can be in your office in half an hour. I won't take much of your time, but I think it'll make you happier."

"Then by all means come ahead."

Timothy is in the office of P&B in twenty minutes, and moments later is closeted with the Chief of Internal Security. The plump little man is sagging. All he can manage is a tinselly smile.

"It's a merger," he tells Cone. "Two food processing companies. I prefer not to mention the names."

"Sure. That's okay."

"Anyway, it's still in the early stages. Surely no more than fifty people know about it. But there's already increased trading in the stock of the smaller company. The share price is up two dollars since Monday."

"Uh-huh," Cone says. "I suppose documents have been prepared."

"Of course. Preliminary proposals. Suggestions for stock swaps between the two companies. Analyses of the problems of merging the two management groups."

"And the documents have been printed up and distributed to those fifty people?"

"Naturally. They're all involved and have to be kept informed of what's going on."

"Who's your printer?"

"Bechtold Printing on Tenth Avenue. We've been using them for years. Absolutely trustworthy. Every Christmas Frederick Bechtold sends me a smoked ham."

"Do you know anyone at Snellig Firsten Holbrook?" Cone asks suddenly.

Twiggs looks at him, puzzled. "Yes, I know Greg Vandiver, a risk arbitrage attorney. He crews for me in the Saturday yacht races at our club."

"Will you call him right now, please, and ask him the name of the printer used by Snellig Firsten Holbrook. They got caught, too."

Twiggs makes the call and asks the question. Then he hangs up and stares grimly at Cone.

"Bechtold Printing on Tenth Avenue," he reports.

"Sure," Cone says. "And I'll bet a dozen other investment bankers and brokerage houses print at Bechtold."

"You mean Frederick Bechtold, that fine, upstanding man who sends me smoked hams, is leaking all his customers' secrets?"

"Nah, he's clean. But he's throwing out some valuable garbage."

Then Cone explains what's going on: How first press proofs are invariably discarded and more proofs are pulled until the density of the ink is correct, colors are in register, copy is properly centered on the page.

"All those fouled-up proofs are wadded up and thrown out. And along comes a private carter who picks up the barrels of trash and empties them into a truck. In this case, it's a garbage collector called Steiner Waste Control, on Eleventh Avenue. The boss is Sally Steiner, and she's a stock market maven. She knows what kind of work Bechtold is doing, and whenever a pickup is made at the printer, she has the barrels taken to her home in Smithtown. Then she paws through all those discarded press proofs looking for goodies. And finds them."

Twiggs' face reddens, he seems to swell, and for a moment Cone fears the senior partner is going to have cardiac arrest, or at least bust his braces. But suddenly Twiggs starts laughing, his face all squinched up, tears starting from his eyes. He pounds the desk with his fist.

"The garbage collector!" he says, sputtering. "Oh, God, that's good! That's beautiful! I'll dine off that story for years to come! And I believe every word of it."

"You can," Cone says, nodding. "A few years ago a financial printer was reading the stuff delivered to him by his Wall Street customers and buying and selling stocks on the basis of the documents he was given to print. He did great, and the SEC charged him with inside trading. I think it was the first insider case to end up in the Supreme Court. They found the guy Not Guilty, but they never did define exactly what constitutes inside trading. The garbage angle is just a new variation on an old scam."

"And what do we do now?"

"Nothing you can do about the merger that's in the works. The cat is out of the bag on that one. But for the future, you've got some choices. You can get yourself a new printer, with no guarantee that the same thing won't happen again. Or stick with Bechtold, but every time you give him something to print, send over a couple of guys who can make sure all preliminary proofs are destroyed. Or—and I like this one best—equip your Mergers and Acquisitions Department with the new desktop printers. You won't get six-color work or jazzy bindings, but you'll be able to reproduce most of the documents you need right here in your own shop, including graphs, charts, and tables. It's all done by computers, and the finished documents can be counted and coded so none of them go astray. The machines aren't cheap, but they'll save you a mint on commercial printing costs. And your security will be umpteen times better than if you send your secrets to an outside printer.''

"I'll look into it immediately," Twiggs says. "It makes sense. You're going to report this garbage collector to the SEC?"

"As soon as possible."

"And what's going to happen to—what's her name?"

"Sally Steiner. Well, I figure her for a smart, nervy lady. She probably thinks that if she's caught, she'll walk away from all this with a smile on her lips and a song in her heart. If she's the stand-up gonnif I think she is, she'll fight any attempt by the SEC to charge her or make her cough up her profits. What, actually, did she do? Dig through some barrels of rubbish, that's all. She's home free. That's what she thinks, and I hate to admit it, but she may be right.''

"I wonder," says G. Fergus Twiggs thoughtfully, "if she'd consider employment with an investment banker.''

Cone smiles and rises to leave. "You could do a lot worse," he says. "Nice meeting you, Mr. Twiggs. You put in that electronic printing system. It'll help.''

The senior partner shakes his hand fervently. "I appreciate everything you've done, Mr. Cone. It's a pleasure dealing with someone who enjoys his work.''

"Do I?" Timothy Cone says. "Yeah, I guess I do.''

Neal Davenport is right: Sergeant Joseph D'Amato looks and dresses like a college professor. He's a tall, gawky guy with a Mt. Rushmore face and big, spatulate hands. His tweed jacket has suede patches on the elbows, and his cordovan kilties are polished to a mirror gloss. He's smoking a long, thin cigarillo, so Cone thankfully lights up his ninth cigarette of the day.

He calls the local deli for cheeseburgers, fries, a couple of dills, and four cold cans of Bud. They talk and eat at the same time, occasionally waving a pickle slice or French fry in the air to make a point.

"Those names you gave me," D'Amato says. "All illegals. Members of the same Family."

"New York?" Cone asks.

"Yeah, but not the Big Five. These schmoes belong to a second-rate gang, bossed by a slimy toad whose monicker is Alonzo Departeur. He's not even an Italian, I'm happy to say, let alone Sicilian. He's known as Fat Lonny, and if you ever see him, you'll know why. The guy is obscenely obese."

"This Family of his—what're they into?"

D'Amato gestures with a pickle. "Think of them as hyenas, waiting around for scraps after the big Families make the kill. They couldn't operate without permission of the heavies. And, of course, they pay through the nose for the go-ahead."

"How do you know all this?" Cone asks curiously.

"Snitches," the sergeant says promptly. "We have informants in every New York Family. We catch a guy pulling something foul, and we give him a choice: Either he does ten years in the slammer or he turns and becomes our property. You'd be surprised at how many of those scuzzes are willing to work for us, singing their rotten little hearts out. We've even got some of them wired."

"Whatever happened to the code of silence?"

"Omertà? Forget it. Maybe ten years ago, but today it's every pirate for himself. Organized crime is becoming disorganized crime. Anyway, the names you gave me are all associated with the Departeur mob, headquartered in New York but with people all over the country. They do routine collections for the Big Five and are allowed to run some drug deals, loansharking, extortion, and a few other things like restaurants, nightclubs, and after-hour joints."

"Any connection with garbage collection?"

"Oh, yeah. And linen supply, liquor wholesaling, and some minor ripoffs of concrete companies, construction unions, plumbing contractors, and electrical equipment suppliers."

"Anything on Wall Street?"

"Not to my knowledge. The Big Five keep a lock on that. The reason I'm telling you all this is that one of the biggies in the Departeur Family was, until recently, a hood named Vic Angelo. You probably read of how he was scratched outside the Hotel Bedlington not too long ago. His job was taken over by his underboss, Mario Corsini. And Corsini was one of the names on your list—so that accounts for our interest."

"You think this Corsini arranged for Vic Angelo being chilled?"

"Definitely. It's common talk on the street, but we can't get enough real evidence to justify busting Corsini, let alone indicting him. But we keep hoping."

"Is this Corsini into extortion of private carters and garbage collectors?"

"Sure he is. Why do you ask?"

So, for the second time that morning, Cone describes the activities of Sally Steiner, and how she's been able to come up with those profitable stock tips.

"That's lovely," D'Amato says when Cone finishes. "I'd guess that she's passing her inside information along to Corsini. For what reason I don't know. Maybe she's got the hots for the guy. Some women think mobsters are king shits."

"Maybe," Cone says, "or maybe he's leaning on her, and those stock tips are what she has to pay to stay in business."

"Could be," the sergeant says. He blots his mouth delicately with a paper napkin, sits back, and lights another of his long cigarillos. "On the list you gave me, Mario Corsini's address was given as Atlantic City. Actually he lives in Queens but probably bought his stock through an Atlantic City broker. No law against that. Maybe the broker's a pal of his, or maybe one of the Departeur Family. Something bothering you?"

"I don't know," Cone says fretfully. "We've been blowing a lot of smoke, but there are damned few hard facts. It's all 'suppose' and 'maybe' and 'perhaps.' I don't think *every* private garbage and rubbish collector in New York is paying dues to the mob. I mean, we have no hard evidence that Mario Corsini or any other Mafia type is ripping off Steiner Waste Control. How can we prove a connection?"

Sergeant D'Amato gives Cone a soft smile. "About seven or eight months ago, Corsini brought a cousin over from the Old Country. It's legal; the kid has all his papers. His name is

Anthony Ricci. Anyway, in that list you gave me, there were two heavy stock buyers in Atlantic City. One was Mario Corsini. The other was Anthony Ricci.''

"So?" Cone says. "What does that prove?"

"Anthony Ricci works for Steiner Waste Control."

"Let me buy you another cheeseburger," Timothy Cone says.

Seven

"THERE YOU ARE," Eddie Steiner says, gesturing. "In all your primitive glory."

Sally stares at the completed oil painting propped on an easel. "Jesus!" she bursts out. "You made me look like a tough bimbo."

"You *are* a tough bimbo," her brother says. "But forget your vanity for a minute; what do you think of it as a painting?"

"It's good, Eddie," she says grudgingly.

"Good? The goddamned thing is magnificent. It's just one hell of a portrait. The best I've ever done. Ever will do. But then I'll never find a model like you again."

She moves closer to inspect the canvas.

"Careful," he warns. "Don't touch. It's still wet; I just finished it last night."

"I'm going to have to lose some weight," Sally says. "Look at those hips. And that ass. My God!"

"You're just a strong, solid woman, sis. Don't knock it."

"What are you going to do with it?"

"I told you about that gallery in the East Village that wants to give me a show. I finally agreed. I'll bet this thing will be the first to sell."

"I hope you're not going to call it *My Sister* or anything like that."

"Nah," he says, laughing. "I'm calling it *Manhattan*."

Good title, she thinks. In the nude body of a thrusting woman, he's caught the crude, exciting world she lives in. The colors are so raw they shriek, and sharp edges and jagged composition reflect the demonic rhythm of the city.

"Yeah," she says, "I think you got something there. If no one wants it, I'll buy it."

"And cut it up?" he teases.

"Never. When I'm old and gray, I'll look at it and remember," she says, smiling. "Well, look, here's a package for Paul. Cash and a note telling him what stocks to buy. Okay?"

"Sure. I'll give it to him. He likes the idea of being the Boy Wonder of Wall Street. Listen, Sal, you're not going to get into any trouble on this, are you?"

"Trouble? What trouble? I'm giving stock tips to a good friend, that's all. Nothing illegal about that."

"I hope not," Eddie says. "I'd hate to visit you up the river on the last Thursday of every month, bringing you some of Martha's strudel."

"Not a chance," she says confidently. "No one's going to lay a glove on me."

She walks back to the office, thinking of her portrait. It lights up that entire dingy apartment. The more she recalls it, the better she likes it. It's Manhattan, all right, but it's also Sally Steiner, shoving belligerently from the canvas.

"That's me," she says aloud. "A tough bimbo."

It's almost noon when she gets back to Steiner Waste Control. There are four big yellow trucks on the tarmac, waiting to unload. Most of the guys have gone across to the Stardust Diner for lunch, but Anthony Ricci is waiting in the outer office. She knows what he wants.

"Why don't you go to lunch," she says to Judy Bering. "I'll hold down the fort until you get back."

"I may be a little late, Sal. I want to get over to Bloomie's. They're having a sale on pantyhose."

"Take your time. Tony, come into my office."

The kid really is a beauty, no doubt about it, and she wonders what Eddie could do with him—and then decides she's never going to bring them together and find out. Paul Ramsey would kill her.

Ricci has a helmet of crisp, black curls, bedroom eyes, and a mouth artfully designed for kissing. That chiseled face might be vacuous except that, occasionally, the soft eyes smolder, the jaw sets, lips are pressed. And there, revealed, are temper, menace, an undisciplined wildness when the furious blood takes over.

He's got a muscled body and moves with the spring of a young animal. He's been working all morning, but he doesn't smell of garbage; he smells of male sweat with a musky undertone from the cologne he keeps in his locker and uses every time his truck returns to the dump.

"How's it going, Tony?" Sally asks him. "Like the job?"

"It's okay," the kid says. "For a while. I'm not about to spend the rest of my life lifting barrels of shit."

"You're not?" she says, putting him on. "And what have you got in mind—an executive job where you can wear monogrammed shirts and Armani suits?"

"Yeah," he says seriously, "I think I would like a desk job."

"With a secretary? A blue-eyed blonde with big knockers?"

He gives her the 100-watt grin. "Maybe. But not necessary."

"No, I don't imagine you have much trouble in that department. You got someone special, Tony?"

He shrugs. "I have many friends, but no one special, no. Mario, he'd like me to marry a woman he has picked out for me, but I don't think so. Her father is respected and wealthy, but she looks like a—like a—what is it that farmers put in their fields to frighten birds away?"

"A scarecrow?"

"Yeah," Ricci says, laughing, "she looks like a scarecrow. Not for me."

"What kind of a woman are you looking for?"

He leans toward her slightly, his dark, burning eyes locked with hers. "An older woman," he says in a low voice. "I am tired of young girls who talk only of clothes and rock stars and want to go to the most expensive restaurants and clubs. Yeah, I'm interested in older women."

"Because they're grateful?" Sally suggests.

He considers that. "It's true," he says finally, and she decides he may be an Adonis, but he's got no fucking brains. "Also," he continues, "older women are settled and know about life. They are smart about money, and they work hard."

"Uh-huh," Sally says. "Sounds to me like you've got it all figured out. An executive desk job—with or without a secretary—and an older woman you can tell your troubles to. And what would you give her? You'd be faithful, I suppose."

He doesn't realize she's kidding him, but sits back with a secret smile. "She would not care about that," he says.

"Where I come from, a man provides a home, food on the table, and takes care of his children. What he does outside the home is his business. The wife understands."

"Well, I wish you luck," Sally says. "I hope you find a rich older woman like that."

"I intend to," he says solemnly, staring at her with such intensity that she begins to get antsy.

"Well," she says, "let's get down to business." She slides a sealed white envelope from the top drawer of her desk and hands it to him. "You know what's in that, Tony?"

He nods soberly. "More than I make in a month for lifting garbage."

"You better believe it," Sally says. "So don't lose it or take off for Las Vegas. A receipt isn't necessary."

Her sarcasm floats right over those crisp, black curls. "A receipt?" he says, puzzled. "Mario didn't say anything about a receipt."

She wonders if this boy has all his marbles. "Forget it," she says. "Just a joke. Nice talking to you, Tony."

"Maybe some night we could have dinner," he says, more of a statement than a question. "I know a restaurant down on Mulberry Street. Not expensive, but the food is *delizioso*. Would you like to have dinner with me?"

She realizes that if Terry Mulloy had made the same proposal, she'd have told him to stuff it. "Sure," she says to Anthony Ricci. "Why not?"

After he's gone, she questions why she didn't cut him off at the knees. Not, she decides, because he's so beautiful and dumb. But he's Mario Corsini's cousin, and she has a presentiment that he might, someday, be of use to her. She has never forgotten that on the morning Vic Angelo was murdered, Ricci didn't get to work until noon.

She calls Mario, leaves a message, and he calls back in twenty minutes.

"I delivered the mail to Tony," she tells him.

"Okay," he says. "You got anything else for me?"

"Yeah," she says, and gives him the name of the smaller food processing company involved in the merger being engineered by Pistol & Burns.

"A good one?" Corsini asks.

"I'm in it," Sally says. "You suit yourself."

"It better be good," he says. "You know what's riding on it."

"You scare the pants off me," she says scornfully.

"I'd like to," he says, and she hangs up.

Timothy Cone and Jeremy Bigelow are "eating street" again. They're sauntering down through the financial district toward the Battery, stopping at carts and vans to pick up calzone, chicken wings in soy sauce, raw carrots, chocolate-chip cookies, gelato, and much, much more.

"I never want to work a case with you again," the SEC investigator says. "Every time we eat like this, I gain five pounds and my wife tells me she can't sleep because my stomach keeps rumbling all night."

"I got a cast-iron gut," Cone brags. "But nothing compared to my cat. That monster can chew nails and spit tacks."

"Lucky for him. How did you make out with those Trimbley and Diggs trading records I gave you?"

"I made out like a thief," Timothy says. "I found the leak."

Jeremy stops on the sidewalk, turns, stares at him. "You're kidding," he says.

"Scout's honor," Cone says, and for the third time he describes how Sally Steiner is digging through trash from Bechtold Printing and finding smeared proofs of confidential financial documents.

He tells Bigelow nothing about the Mario Corsini connection.

Twiggs had succumbed to hysterical guffaws after hearing the story, and Joe D'Amato had been amused, but the SEC man is infuriated.

"Son of a bitch," he says angrily. "I should have caught those nine-thousand-share trades. How did you break it?"

"A lot of luck."

"You told Pistol and Burns?"

"Oh, sure. Twiggs called me this morning. They've canned Bechtold and are switching to another commercial printer until they can put in a desktop printing system. Listen, Jerry, you better tell Snellig Firsten Holbrook."

"Yeah," the other man says worriedly. "I'll do that. You think the printer was in on it?"

"Nah," Cone says, "I think he's clean. He's just careless with his garbage, that's all."

"My God," Bigelow says, trying to wipe drips of gelato from his lapel, "do you realize what this means? We'll have to get hold of Bechtold's customer list—get a subpoena if we have to—and alert all his Wall Street customers about what's going on."

That's exactly what Cone wanted him to say. This guy is brainy, but not the hardest man in the world to manipulate.

"Yeah," he says sympathetically, "a lot of work. Maybe an easier way to handle it would be for you to pay a visit to Frederick Bechtold. Come on strong. Tell him what's been going down, and if he doesn't get rid of Steiner Waste Control and put in an incinerator or pulverizer, you're going to report him to every Wall Street customer he's got. He'll believe you because he'll already have the bad news from Pistol and Burns."

"It could be handled that way," Jeremy says thoughtfully. "A lot less work. No subpoenas, charges, and court trials."

"Sure," Cone agrees. "And why should an innocent printer suffer just because Sally Steiner has larceny in her heart."

They stop at an umbrella stand for a final giant chocolate chip cookie. They munch on those, holding paper napkins under their chins as they walk.

"Sally Steiner," Bigelow repeats. "What are we going to do about her?"

"What can you do?" Cone asks. "Let's face it: Your chances of making a legit charge against her for inside trading are zilch. She's a shrewd lady, and I'm betting she'll fight you every inch of the way. Maybe you can force her to cough up her profits—but I doubt it. Meanwhile the SEC will be getting a lot of lousy publicity. Everyone will be on Steiner's side and getting a big laugh out of how clever she was to beat the stock market."

"Yeah, you're right. If this was a megamillion deal, I'd push for a formal inquiry by the Commission. But how much could she have made? Half a million?"

"Probably less than that," Cone says, not mentioning how much Corsini and his pals might have cleared. "But the important thing is that you're closing her down. The moment you brace Bechtold, you know he's going to get rid of Steiner. She'll be losing a good customer and getting cut off from her source of inside scoop.''

"It makes sense," Jeremy says, nodding. "I'll just keep the whole thing on the investigative level and file a report saying the leak's been plugged."

"And take all the credit," Cone advises. "I don't want any glory. My job was with Pistol and Burns, and they're happy. The rest belongs to you."

"Thanks, Tim," Bigelow says gratefully. "Listen, you don't mind if I split, do you? I want to get uptown and start the ball rolling.''

"Go ahead," the Wall Street dick says. "Tell the printer it was all Sally Steiner's fault."

He watches the SEC man hurry away, tossing the remnants of his cookie into a litter basket. Cone finishes his, then turns and meanders uptown to Haldering & Co.

He's satisfied that he's put the first part of his plot into place. If he can stage-manage the second part, his scheme will have a chance. Except, he admits, everything depends on the reaction of Sally Steiner. All Cone can do is put the pressure on and hope she'll cave. She might not, but he's got to try it. It's his civic duty, he tells himself virtuously. And besides, the whole thing is a hoot.

Back in his office, he calls Joe D'Amato. Sorry, he's told, the sergeant is out and can't be reached. Cone leaves a message and begins to get skittery. A lot depends on timing, and if he can't get hold of D'Amato and persuade him to play along, the whole scam will collapse.

He chain-smokes two cigarettes and makes a half-assed attempt to compose his long-delayed progress reports. They should be submitted weekly to Samantha Whatley, but at the rate he's going, they've become monthly progress reports.

His phone doesn't ring until after four o'clock. By that time his throat is raw from smoking, and his "Yeah?" comes out like a croak.

"Joe D'Amato," the sergeant says. "Something wrong with your voice?"

"Too many coffin nails. Thanks for calling back. I need a favor."

"Yeah? And what might that be?"

"You got a phone number for Mario Corsini? I'd like to call him."

"What for? Wanna have lunch with him?"

"Nah, nothing like that." Then Cone explains what he has in mind. "It's risky," he acknowledges, "but I think it's got a chance, don't you?"

"Damned little," D'Amato says. "You're playing with fire, you know that?"

"Sure, but what have I got to lose? I figure if I go ahead with it, she'll think seriously about turning."

"Umm. Maybe."

"You want to make the call to Corsini yourself?"

"Hell, no. Self-preservation are the first, second, and third laws in this business, and I've got to cover my ass. I'm even going to erase the tape of this call."

"Does that mean you're going to give me Corsini's phone number?"

"I haven't got it. But I've got the number of a social club in Ozone Park where he hangs. Maybe they'll get a message to him to call you back. That's the best I can do."

"Good enough," Cone says. "Let's have it."

That evening, on the way home, he stops to buy some baked ham hocks, which he and Cleo dearly love, and a container of potato salad. But back in the loft, he postpones laying out the evening's feast until he calls that Ozone Park social club.

A man answers. "Yeah?" he says in a voice that sounds like someone has kicked his Adam's apple.

"I'd like to speak to Mr. Mario Corsini," Cone says politely.

"Who?"

"Mario Corsini."

"Never heard of him."

"Sure you have," Cone says.

"I'm telling you, mister, there's no one here by that name, and I never heard the name before."

"Well, look, if a man named Mario Corsini happens to stop by, will you ask him to call this number. It's really very important. Tell him it's about Sally Steiner. Got that? Sally Steiner."

He gives his phone number, repeating it twice, and hangs

up. Then he and Cleo go to work on the ham hocks and potato salad. Cleo takes a hunk of gristle under the bathtub for a late-night snack, and Cone mixes himself a vodka and water to cut the grease.

He doesn't read, listen to the radio, or watch TV. He just slouches at his desk, feet up, planning what he's going to say if Corsini calls.

The phone rings a little after eight o'clock, and he moves quickly to the kitchenette.

"Hello, asshole," Samantha Whatley says. "What're you doing?"

"Will you get off the line," he says. "I'm expecting an important call."

Silence. Then: "And what's this—chopped liver? Fuck you, buster!"

"Listen," he says desperately, "I'll call you when—"

But she hangs up, and he goes grumbling back to the vodka bottle. "Who needs her?" he shouts at a startled Cleo, then answers his own question. "I do," he says.

It's almost 9:30 when the phone rings again, and by that time Cone is feeling no pain and is ready to take on the entire Cosa Nostra and its Ladies' Auxiliary.

"Who's this?" a voice shouts.

"Am I speaking to Mr. Mario Corsini?"

"You tell me who you are or I hang up."

"Mr. Corsini, my name is Smedley Tonker, and I am an investigator with the Securities and Exchange Commission."

"So?"

"Forgive me for calling at this late hour," Cone goes on, wondering how many years he can get for impersonating a federal officer, "but we're working overtime investigating recent stock trading in Trimbley and Diggs, Incorporated. In the course of our investigation, careful examination of computer records shows that you and your associates took a very considerable long position in that stock."

"I don't know what the hell you're talking about."

"I'm sure you do, Mr. Corsini. Our records show a purchase of nine thousand shares by you personally through a broker in Atlantic City."

"I tell you it's all horseshit to me; I don't know nothing about it. And you said this call was about Sally Steiner. I never heard of the broad."

"You haven't? That's odd since your cousin, Anthony Ricci, works for Steiner Waste Control. Come on, Mr. Corsini, let's stop playing games. Our investigation shows you and your friends made your stock purchases on the basis of inside tips from Sally Steiner. Do you know how she got her information, Mr. Corsini?"

So, for the fourth time, Cone relates the tale of how trash from Bechtold Printing was delivered to Sally's Smithtown home, and how she rummaged through the garbage to find confidential financial documents.

"Are you claiming you knew nothing about Ms. Steiner's illegal activities, Mr. Corsini?"

"Talk to my lawyers, you putz!" the other man screams and hangs up.

Smiling happily, Cone goes back to his unfinished drink, polishes it off, and then returns to the phone to call Samantha Whatley.

It takes almost twenty minutes of sweet talk to soothe Sam into a growlingly genial mood. But finally they're calling each other "asshole" and "shithead" and planning a Saturday night dinner in the loft. Cone promises to supply pounds of barbecued ribs, a basket of extra-thick potato chips (garlic flavored), and some dill pickles as a green vegetable.

"I'll bring the dessert," Sam volunteers.

"Okay."

"What would you like?"

"You," he says.

Sally Steiner thinks of it later as Black Friday. It starts bad and gets progressively worse. On the drive into the city, some fucking cowboy cuts her off on the Long Island Expressway, and she almost rolls the Mazda onto the verge.

Then, when she gets to the office, she discovers the air conditioner has conked out, and it's a bloody hot day. There's a letter from the bank informing her that a check she deposited, from the guy who buys their baled paper, has been returned because of insufficient funds. There's also a crusty letter from the IRS telling her that Steiner Waste Control owes an additional $29,871.46 on the previous year's return, and they better come up with the funds—or else.

She's on the phone to the IRS for a long time, and when

she finally hangs up, sweating, Judy Bering comes in to tell her that Frederick Bechtold has called three times.

"He sounds like he's got steam coming out his ears," Judy reports. "He kept shouting in German. All I could catch was *verdammt, verdammt, verdammt*. It sounded like he wants to feed you into one of his high-speed presses."

"All right," Sally says, sighing, "I'll give him a call."

Bechtold immediately starts spluttering, roaring, and cursing her in German. She knows enough of the language to recognize some of the words he's using, and they're not nice.

"Now wait a minute," she says, getting pissed off.

"Zo!" he shouts. "I should wait a minute, should I? You, you *Dirne*, you will wait five years in jail. In prison you will wait."

"What the hell are you talking about?" she demands.

"Oh, yes, oh, yes," he says furiously. "My best customer you have cost me. And who knows how many more? Maybe all. Because you go through my trash, and you read my first proofs, and then you buy stocks, you *Schlampe!* You are fired, you understand that? And you will hear from my lawyers. For my loss of business, you will pay plenty, you bet."

Sally has been listening to this tirade while standing behind her desk. Now, knees suddenly trembling, she collapses into her swivel chair.

"Who told you all that?" she asks weakly.

"Who? I tell you who. A man from the United States Government, that's who. They know what you have been doing. Oh, yes, they know everything. And you will pay for what you have done. Thirty-six years I have been in this business, and my work is the best. The best! And you, you slut, you have destroyed—"

She hangs up softly and sits slumped forward, forehead resting on the heels of her hands. She tries to make sense of what's happened, but her brain's awhirl. Thoughts come, go, jostle, scream for attention, dissolve, return.

The government man he mentioned must have been that creep from the SEC. How did he find out? And if he knows about Sally's stock trading, then maybe Paul Ramsey is in danger. What can they do to him? What can they do to her? Goddamn it, she'll fight them! She had no inside knowledge of those deals—exactly. But will they charge her anyway?

Make her return the profits and fine her? A prison term? Ridiculous! It was no big deal. How the hell did they find out?

Suddenly frightened—not at possible punishment, but at possible loss of her investments—she phones Paul Ramsey. Thank God he's in, and she tells him to call his broker immediately and sell everything at the market price. Just unload totally.

"That's cool," he says.

"You'll do it, Paul? Right away?"

"Sure," he said, and his placidity helps calm her.

She closes the door to her office, and then calls Ivan Belzig, her attorney, and tells him everything. After he stops laughing, he gets indignant.

"And you couldn't pass the tips along to me?" he says. "What am I—an enemy?"

"Cut the shit, Ivan," Sally says. "Tell me, what can the SEC do to me?"

"I'll have to research it," he says cautiously, "but if you want a top-of-the-head opinion, they can't do a thing to you. You had no personal contact with any of the insiders who knew about those deals. All you did was use typical American chutzpah. They might want you to return your profits, but we'll fight that. Listen, they've closed down your operation, haven't they? That should be enough. If you hear from them, don't tell them a thing, not a thing—you understand? Just tell them to contact me; I'll handle it. And don't worry, honey; you'll come out of this smelling like roses."

"Thanks, Ivan," Sally says gratefully, feeling a lot better.

But when she hangs up the phone, she sees Mario Corsini standing in the doorway of her office.

"Thanks for knocking," she says angrily.

He comes close to the desk, leans forward on whitened knuckles. He stares at her with dead eyes from under the brim of a black fedora.

"Cunt!" he says venomously.

"I can explain," she starts. "I can—"

"You can explain shit!" he says, voice cold and hard. "A boyfriend on Wall Street, huh? And all the time you're digging through garbage. I should have known; that's your style, you no-good bitch. Now I got the SEC on my ass, and who knows what—"

"Listen," she interrupts desperately, "I just talked to my lawyer, and he says—"

"Fuck your lawyer," Corsini says, "and fuck you. The SEC works hand in glove with the Federal District Attorney, and he works with the FBI and God knows who else. So now I got the whole fucking government asking questions, like where did I get the money and do I know those guys who invested in other cities, and maybe the IRS is auditing my returns. All because of you, you lousy twat. Vic Angelo warned me this could happen. I should have listened to him. I swear to Christ I could off you right now for what you did to me."

"Hey," Sally says, "take it easy. You're imagining a lot of things that might not happen. Maybe you'll have to give back your profits and pay a fine. That's no big deal for a hotshot like you."

"No big deal, huh? And I should tell the sharks that? You got shit for brains? Oh, I'll work my way out of this, but I'm going to have to grease a lot of people. It's going to cost me, and guess who's going to pay?"

She doesn't answer.

Corsini looks around the office, goes to the window to peer out at the busy tarmac. "Nice place you got here," he says. "Good business, real estate, trucks. Plenty of assets. The papers are ready, and I've got a front lined up to make you a nice offer."

"I'll bet," Sally says stiffly. "But the business isn't for sale."

"Sure it is," Corsini says, taking out one of his twisted black cigars. He lights it and tosses the spent match onto Sally's desk. "This place is how I'm going to get my money back."

"But you haven't *lost* any money!" she yells at him. "You've *made* money on the tips I gave you. So why are you coming on so hard?"

He leans across the desk and blows cigar smoke in her face. "Because you tricked me," he says, his face twisted. "You played me for a sucker, you fucking whore. Now's my turn. You want to go on living, you sell the business; it's that simple."

She learned a long time ago that if you show weakness in the world she inhabits, you're finished. Jake taught her that.

"Give 'em an inch, and they'll take a mile," he told her. "You gotta stand up to the hardcases. They push, you push back. Otherwise you're flat on your tuchas, and they're walking all over you."

"Listen, you cocksucker," she says stonily, "you and your lousy front aren't coming anywhere near this place. The business belongs to my family, and that's where it's going to stay. I'm not signing any papers. Stick them up your ass and smoke them, you crap-faced motherfucker."

The hand holding the cigar starts to tremble, and he presses it against the side of the desk to steady it. She wonders how close he is to popping her then and there and doesn't care.

"Oh, you'll sell," he says in an unexpectedly soft voice. "Maybe you got the balls to fight me, but does your crippled mother or faggot brother? I'd start with them. I'd leave you for last, because before I was through, you'd be down on your knees, begging to sell."

"Screw you," Sally says with more bravado than she feels.

"There is one way you can keep the dump," Mario Corsini says thoughtfully, still staring at her. "You put out for me and maybe we can work a deal."

"Christ Almighty!" she cries. "Is that the only way you can get a woman?"

"I can get a lot of women," he says, snapping his fingers. "Like that. But I want you. I want to break you. Really put you over the hurdles." Then he starts describing exactly what he wants to do to her.

She jerks to her feet. "You prick!" she screams. "Get the hell out of my office."

"*Your* office?" he says, looking at her with a stretched grin. "Not for long."

Eight

It's STILL FRIDAY, and Sally Steiner wonders if this frigging day will ever end. If just one more schmuck starts swearing at her and calling her names, she's going to take out her pistol and *Bam!*—right in his family jewels.

Judy Bering goes out for lunch, and Sally calls over to the Stardust Diner for a tunafish on wheat and an iced tea. But when the sandwich arrives, it tastes like wallpaper paste, and after one bite she dumps the whole thing in her wastebasket. The tea is cold and wet, but that's about all.

Her stomach is still bubbling after that go-around with Mario Corsini. She rummages through her father's desk, still in the office, and finds his bottle of schnapps in the bottom drawer. It hasn't been touched since Jake died. She pours a dollop into her iced tea, but the mixture is so awful that she can't swallow more than a sip.

So she gets a plastic cup from the stack alongside the coffee percolator in the outer office and fills it with ice cubes fished out of her tea. Then she pours in the schnapps, a pear brandy strong enough to take the kink out of her hair. After the first swallow, which almost makes her gag, it begins to slide down a lot easier, killing off those butterflies in her gut.

She's pouring another when she looks up to see a tall, gangly man standing in the doorway. He's wearing a ratty corduroy suit and a black leather cap. He looks like a nut, and that's all Sally needs on this Black Friday: another brouhaha with an airhead.

"I'll take one of those," he says, jerking his chin at the schnapps bottle. His smile is quirky, but Sally decides he's not going to be a problem.

"Who the hell are you?" she demands, putting the bottle away.

"Sally Steiner?"

"That's right. And if you're selling, I'm not buying. So take a walk."

"I just wanted to talk to you for a few minutes."

"About what?"

"About Paul Ramsey."

"Oh, Jesus," she says, "are you from the SEC?"

"Nah," the gink says. "Do I dress like a guy from the SEC? My name is Timothy Cone, and I'm with Haldering and Company on John Street. We do financial investigations, mostly for corporate clients on Wall Street."

"Beat it, will you?" Sally says wearily. "I've already been investigated up and down, inside out, and both ways from the middle."

"I know," Cone says. "I'm the one who did it. Our client was Pistol and Burns. Wee Tot Fashions—remember that stock? And I was also in on the Trimbley and Diggs takeover leak."

She stares at him. "You're the bastard who blew the whistle on me?"

"I'm the bastard," he says cheerfully.

She sighs. "You make my day complete. All right," she says, taking out the bottle of pear brandy again, "get yourself a cup out there and we'll drink to my destruction."

"It's not that bad," he says. "Just listen to me for a minute."

He comes back with a plastic cup, sits in the armchair alongside her desk, and takes off his cap.

"How did you do it?" she asks, pouring him a stiff wallop of schnapps.

"Find out you were going through Bechtold's trash? I followed your trucks."

Her eyes widen. "You're kidding."

"No, that's how I did it. You were on the computer printouts of trading in Wee Tot Fashions. Then, on the records of Trimbley and Diggs, there was Paul Ramsey. I went up to see him, but came away when I found out he was living with your brother. So that led me back to you."

"How did you find out Eddie was my brother?"

"I called and told him he was a beneficiary on an insurance policy you had bought, and asked him what the relationship was. He told me you were his sister. Pardon me for saying it, but he's not too swift in the street-smarts department."

"Tell me something I don't know. For instance, tell me how many days you followed my trucks."

"Four."

"You were lucky."

"I know. I tailed the van with Bechtold's scrap out to your garage in Smithtown. After that it was a breeze."

Sally takes a deep swallow of her drink. Now it's going down as smooth as silk. "You're a real buttinsky, aren't you?" she says.

"That's right," he agrees, and his smile is unexpectedly charming. "That's what they pay me for. So I got Pistol and Burns to dump Bechtold, and I turned you in to the SEC. Sore?"

"Sore? Why should I be sore? You just ruined my life, that's all."

"Nah," Timothy says, leaning forward to pour himself another shot, "it's not that bad. Nothing is going to happen to Paul Ramsey. I just mentioned his name so you'd talk to me. And I doubt if the SEC will move in on you. They may want you to return your profits, but if you've got a good lawyer, you can fight that. Look, they've closed you down, haven't they? That's the important thing as far as they're concerned."

"So that's why you're here? To cheer me up?"

"Not exactly," Cone says, looking at her directly. "I wanted to talk to you about Corsini."

"Who?"

"Mario Corsini."

"Never heard of him," she says.

"Sure you have," Timothy says. "His cousin works for you. Anthony Ricci."

"My, you've been a busy little boy," she says, but her smile is glassy.

"It's all guesswork," he admits. "But I figure that Steiner Waste Control, like a lot of private carters in the city, pays off the mob to stay in business. I think Corsini is your collector. You gave him stock tips. What I don't know is whether you did that voluntarily or if he was leaning on you."

She stands suddenly, begins to pace back and forth behind her desk, arms crossed, holding her elbows. "You really are a meddler, aren't you?"

"That's right. So which was it? You gave him the tips out of the kindness of your heart or because he came on heavy?"

"None of your business," she says.

"It *is* my business," he insists. "I think Corsini is giving you a hard time, and you gave him the tips to keep him off your back."

She turns on him suddenly. "All right!" she cries. "I gave him the tips. What difference does it make why I did it? It's all over now, isn't it?"

"No, it's not all over," Cone continues doggedly. "By this time he and his pals have heard from the SEC, and Corsini knows where your tips were coming from. And he knows the SEC has closed you down. No more inside stock tips. So if he was squeezing you before, he'll squeeze you all the harder now. If he hasn't already."

She flops into her swivel chair, drains her drink, peers into the empty cup. "All right," she says, "but you didn't come here just to tell me the story of my life and brag how smart you are. You want something. What is it?"

He looks at her admiringly. "You've got the brains of the family," he says. "I want you to turn and blow the whistle on Corsini. Go to the cops and tell them about the shakedowns."

"And get my ass shot off," she says with a sour grin.

"No," Cone says, shaking his head. "The cops will give you and your family protection. Corsini and his bullyboys won't dare try anything. No way! They're shrewd enough to know that any rough stuff would raise a stink strong enough to convict them without a trial."

"You don't know them," Sally says. "They may be smart, but when someone crosses them or plays them for saps, they stop thinking. Then it's just their stupid pride, machismo, and hot blood. Then all they know is revenge."

"Bullshit!" Cone says. "Maybe ten years ago, but the new breed are weasels. They'll rat on their mothers to keep out of the clink. Listen, these guys aren't like they were in the *Untouchables*. It just takes one person like you to stand up to them. Then maybe a lot of other people in your business will say enough's enough, and help the cops put the shtarkers away."

"And if I don't?"

"You want to go on the way you've been going? Paying a lot to bentnoses just to make a living? What makes you think you'd still have a business?"

"What's that supposed to mean?"

"I told you that the SEC probably won't bring criminal charges. But what if the SEC and the Federal DA decide you're not being cooperative? You know what they can do if they want to? Just give the story to the newspapers and TV. It'll be the talk of Wall Street for at least eight hours. Long enough for a lot of people to decide to bring civil cases against you. Maybe even class-action suits. They'll say you manipulated the stocks—and there's something to that. Suppose a guy sold short in Trimbley and Diggs. He lost his stake because you drove the stock up on the basis of what he'll claim was inside information. The people trying to take over Trimbley and Diggs will probably have to pay a higher price because of what you did. Ditto the ones who bought Wee Tot Fashions. They can all sue if they want to. I'm not saying they'll collect, but your legal fees to fight those suits could bleed you dry."

"Oh-ho," Sally says. "First the carrot and now the stick."

"I'm just telling you what your situation is," Cone says. "You may be home free as far as the SEC is concerned, but you're not out of the woods yet. Those civil suits could demolish you. But if you become the Joan of Arc of the garbage business, I think the cops and the Manhattan DA will pass the word, and those civil cases will be quietly dropped. No one wants to sue the city's star witness who's performing a noble civic duty. Think it over. If you decide to play along, give me a call. Haldering and Company on John Street. I know a couple of New York's Finest. Like all cops they're hard-ons, but these guys you can trust. Say the word, and I'll set up a meet."

Sally makes no reply.

The Wall Street dick rises, pulls on his cap. "Thanks for the belts," he says. "Take my advice and go to the cops. Do yourself a favor."

After he's gone, she sits behind her desk a long time, swinging slowly back and forth in her swivel chair. What Cone said makes a lot of sense—to him. But, smart as he is, he doesn't know everything. He's got half the equation. Sally has the whole thing, all the pluses and minuses. And, at the moment, not a glimmer of how to solve it.

She rises, wanders over to the window. Truck No. 2 has just pulled up at the shed to unload. Anthony Ricci swings down from the cab. Sally stares at him a moment, then hurries out of the office.

"Tony!" she yells, and when he looks up, she beckons. He walks toward her smiling and wiping his face and neck with a red bandanna.

"It's a hot mother," he says as he comes up to her.

"Yeah," Sally says, "a killer. Listen, what about that dinner you were going to buy me."

He looks at her, startled. "You wanna go? Hey, that's great! How about tomorrow night?"

"Suits me."

"The joint is Brolio's on Mulberry just below Grand Street."

"I know a girl who got screwed on Delancey Street and thought it was Grand. All right, I'll meet you at Brolio's tomorrow night. What time?"

"About eight. Is that okay?"

"I'll be there," Sally says.

She sleeps late on Saturday morning. It's almost ten o'clock before she rises and pads naked to the window to peer out. Everything is swaddled in pearly fog, and Sally can't even see the garage. The house is silent, and the stillness is everywhere: no traffic noises, no bird calls, no distant thrum of airliners. She feels isolated, wrapped in cotton batting, and yearns for a shout or a whistle.

She pulls on jeans and a T-shirt and goes downstairs barefoot to the kitchen. She has a glass of V-8, an English muffin with orange marmalade, a cup of black coffee. She may be awake, but her brain isn't; she's moving senseless through a muffled world, unable to concentrate; the fog is in her.

She picks up the *Times* from the stoop, but can't read it. She pours herself another coffee, but can't taste it. She stubs her toe, but can't feel the pain.

"Zombie," she says aloud.

It angers her, this dazed feeling of being out of control, and it frightens her. She goes back upstairs to her bedroom and takes a shower as cold as she can endure. She stands under the water for almost twenty minutes, letting the needle spray bounce off her skull, face, shoulders, back, breasts, stomach, thatch, thighs—and start all her corpuscles dancing.

Gradually consciousness returns, confidence is reborn, resolve swells. She dresses again, goes down to the den, sits at her desk. She pulls a pen and scratch pad close and starts doodling, making scribbles: arrows, flowerpots, a radiant sun, stick figures running. She ponders what to do, how to do it, when.

Timothy Cone offered one option: go to the cops and spill the beans. That way she'd be able to hang on to Steiner Waste Control. Maybe she could get her mother and brother out of the city to reduce the danger to them. She has a queasy faith in her ability to protect herself.

A second option is to play along with Mario Corsini, put out for that devil until she can figure a way to fix his wagon for good. She actually considers letting that slob have his way, but then realizes it's impossible; the first time he tried, she'd vomit all over him; she knows it.

What it comes down to is that both options represent surrender, and that she cannot tolerate. She considers herself capable of coping with a raw, turbulent world. It's a matter of pride. If she gives up now, then her life is make-believe, and she is pretending to be someone she is not.

What would her father have done? Jake would never run to the cops for help; she is certain of that. Nor would he sacrifice his personal dignity to Mario Corsini or anyone like him. Making payoffs to the mob was distasteful to Jake, but just another business expense. If they had demanded something more, something that would diminish Jake as a mensch, Sally knows what her father's reaction would have been: He would have died fighting.

It's an ego thing, Sally decides, and there's no use denying it. She has bragged (to herself) that she is a woman with the brains and will to succeed in the violent, dog-eat-dog world of savage, scrambling men. If she is defeated now, her self-esteem shattered, she doesn't want to imagine what her future will be like. No future. None at all.

She draws the number 1 on her pad and strikes it out. Sketches the number 2 and crosses that out also. Then makes a big 3, and stares at it. A third option that did not suddenly occur to her, but has been growing in her mind like some kind of malignant tumor ever since she learned that her Big Chance was down the drain.

Option 3 is scary, no doubt about it, and she wonders if she has the balls for it. She thinks she might be able to bring it off, but the risks are horrendous. Failure would mean the loss of the business and, possibly, the loss of Sally Steiner.

It's a gamble, the biggest gamble she's ever made in her life. But she underlines the number 3 on her scratch pad with heavy strokes, and decides to go for broke. Jake would approve; she's certain of that. She starts plotting the details.

Later that day she calls Eddie. Paul Ramsey isn't there, but her brother assures her that Paul unloaded all the stocks and asked the broker to send him a check.

"Good enough," Sally says. "And you haven't had any unexpected visitors—like a guy from the SEC?"

"No one's showed up," Eddie says. "What's going on, Sal?"

"Nothing to worry about. When's your show at the gallery?"

"In about a month. Cocktail party at the opening. You'll come, won't you?"

"Wouldn't miss it for the world. I'll even tell everyone I posed for your masterpiece. Eddie . . ."

"Yeah, Sal?"

"I love you, baby."

He laughs. "What brought that on?"

"I just want to make sure you know."

"I know," her brother says, his voice soft. "And I love you, dear, and want the best for you."

She hangs up before she starts bawling. She goes upstairs to her mother's bedroom where Becky and Martha are playing backgammon, with the housekeeper shaking the dice cup for both of them. Sally sits with them awhile, watching the game and making them laugh with her ribald comments.

Martha goes downstairs to start dinner, and Sally pulls up a hassock alongside her mother's wheelchair.

"I won't be home for dinner, ma," she says. "I'm driving into the city. I got a date."

"A date?" Becky says, then smiles happily. "That's wonderful! But listen, you deserve, you work so hard. A nice boy?"

"Very nice. And very, very handsome." Then, knowing what her mother's reaction will be: "A regular John Garfield."

"Mazeltov!" Becky cries, and adds dreamily, "John Garfield. How I loved that man. So tell me, how did you meet?"

"Through business."

"He's got money?"

"Plenty."

"And what's his name?"

"Anthony. He's Italian."

"That's all right, too," her mother says. "I know some very nice Italian people. So where are you going?"

"To an Italian restaurant," Sally says, laughing. "Where else?"

"You'll be home early?"

"I don't think so. But I'll tell you about it in the morning."

"He lives in the city?"

"Yeah, ma."

"So you'll be driving home alone?"

Sally nods.

"Be careful. Drive with your windows up and the doors locked. You promise?"

"I promise."

Sally rises, then bends over her mother, embraces her, kisses her velvety cheeks. "I love you, ma."

Tears come to Becky's eyes. "I love you, too. I am so lucky, having a daughter like you. Every day I thank God."

"Yeah," Sally says huskily, "we're both lucky. Eat all your dinner and have a nice evening."

"You, too," her mother cries gaily. "Enjoy! Enjoy!"

Sally goes to her bedroom to get ready. Another shower, warm this time, with scented soap. She decides to wear her high-necked black sheath, figuring all the floozies Anthony Ricci has been dating probably dress like tarts with their tits spilling out. So she wears her conservative black with a pearl choker. And, examining herself in a full-length mirror, wonders sourly if she looks like the older wealthy woman that Ricci seeks.

It's a long drive into the city and down to Mulberry Street. But the trip goes swiftly as she runs scenarios through her mind, trying to decide the best way to spin this simpleton. It's been a long time since she's come on to a guy, and she hopes it's like riding a bicycle: You never forget how.

She gets down to Little Italy in plenty of time, but has to cruise around for a while, looking for a parking space. She finally finds an empty slot two blocks away. She slips the loaded pistol into her purse, locks the car, and walks back to Brolio's. It looks like a scuzzy joint to her, but you never know.

Tony is already there, thank God, waiting for her at a tiny, two-stool bar to the left of the entrance.

"Hey!" he says, coming forward to take both hands in his. "You made it! Have any trouble finding the place?"

"Not at all," Sally says, looking around. And then, with feigned surprise: "Tony, I like it. Very pretty."

"Nothing fancy," he says, shrugging. "But the food's great, and you can't beat the prices."

Sally sees a typical third-rate New York trattoria. Small, only nine tables, and all occupied except one. Crude murals of Vesuvius, the Colosseum, Venetian canals painted on wrinkled walls. Plastic plants in plastic pots. Checkered tablecloths. Dripping candles stuck in raffia-bound chianti bottles. Paper napkins. And hanging in the air, a miasma of garlic strong enough to scare off a hundred vampires.

Tony snaps his fingers, and a waiter swathed in a filthy apron comes hustling to usher them to the empty table and remove the Reserved card.

"A little wine first?" he suggests.

"Tony, you order," Sally says. "You know what's good."

'A glass of Soave to start," Ricci says rapidly to the waiter. "Then the cold antipasto, lobster diavolo, linguine, and maybe a salad of arugola and raddichio. With a bottle of that chianti classico I had the other night. The Monte Vertine."

"Very good," the waiter says, nodding approvingly.

"Sound good to you?" Tony asks Sally.

"Sounds yummy. You eat like this every night?"

He gives her his sizzling smile, eyes half-lidded. "This is an occasion. Dinner with the boss."

"Let's forget about that," she says, touching his hand, "and just enjoy."

The food is unexpectedly good. Maybe a little harsh, a little too garlicky, but Sally exclaims with delight over every course, the wine, the crusty bread, the prompt and efficient service.

"You know how to live," she tells Tony.

"Everyone knows how to live," he says. "All you need is money."

"That's so true," Sally says. "It's what makes the world go 'round, isn't it?"

She gets him talking about himself, his family, his boyhood in Salerno, a motor scooter he owned, a job he had making plaster statues of saints. She bends close to listen to his nonstop monologue over the loud talk and shouted laughter of the other diners, all the deafening sounds bouncing off the low tin ceiling. But, by leaning forward, she gets a whiff of his cologne mixed with the garlic, and she sits back.

She has one glass of the red wine and lets him finish the bottle. He drinks and eats enthusiastically with, she is bemused to note, a corner of the paper napkin tucked into his collar and the remainder spread over his chest, hiding a tie of hellish design.

He insists on tortoni and espresso, and then amaretti with ponies of Strega. Sally takes one sip of the liqueur and then pushes the glass toward Tony.

"You finish," she says.

"Sure," he says, and downs it in one gulp.

It's after ten o'clock when they rise to leave. He pays the bill with cash, Sally sees—no plastic for him—and leaves a lordly tip. They come out into a black, close night, the sky clotted with clouds and a warm, soft mist drifting. They stand for a moment in the doorway.

"Hey," he says, "I didn't tell you how great you look. That's the way a woman should dress. Very *elegante*."

"Thank you," she says, smiling.

"I mean, a woman doesn't have to show everything she's got in public. Am I right?"

"Absolutely," Sally says, taking his arm. "Where are you parked, Tony?"

"Well, uh, my car's in the garage right now. Transmission trouble. I cabbed down."

She knows he's lying; the poor shlumpf doesn't own wheels.

"Then we'll take mine," she says brightly. "It's only two blocks away; we won't get wet."

They skip, laughing, through the mizzle until Sally tugs him to a halt alongside her silver Mazda RX-7. "Here we are," she says.

He looks at the car with astonishment. "This is yours?"

"All mine. You like?"

"*Fantastico*," he breathes, and walks around the car admiring the lines.

"C'mon, get in," Sally says. "You can drive."

They slide into the bucket seats. Tony caresses the wheel with his palms, staring at the dash. "Radio, air conditioner, cassette deck," he says. "Even a compass. You got everything."

"All the comforts of home," she says lightly. "I also own a Cadillac, but this baby is more fun to drive."

"I wish—" he starts, then suddenly stops.

They sit in dimness, windows opened a few inches to let in moist night air. The windshield is beaded with mist, and illumination from streetlights is broken into watery patterns, as irregular as pieces from a jigsaw puzzle.

"If you had your druthers, Tony," she says quietly, "what kind of a car would you like?"

"A Jaguar," he says promptly. "The XJ-SC Cabriolet. You know the car?"

"I've seen it. A beauty. You have expensive tastes."

"Yes," he says sadly, "I do. Maybe someday . . ."

"Maybe sooner than you think," she says. "Do you mind if we sit here a few minutes? There's something I want to talk to you about."

"Sure," he says. "The night's young."

In spite of all her rehearsals and imagined scenarios, she finds it difficult to state or even hint at what she wants. But Tony is no great brain, she tells herself, so she figures her best bet is to come on as blunt and obvious as possible. Then she can gauge his reaction and play him from there.

"That cousin of yours," she says. "Mario. What do you think of him?"

Ricci shrugs. "He's okay, I guess. Sometimes he thinks he's my father. He knows what he wants."

"Yeah," Sally says with a short laugh. "He wants me."

Tony turns to peer at her in the gloom. "What do you mean? What are you saying?"

"The guy is driving me crazy. He's after me every day. He won't let up. I don't know what to do about it."

"He is after you? I don't understand. You pay your dues promptly."

"Do I have to spell it out for you, Tony? That cousin of yours is trying to get me into bed. He's told me a hundred times what he wants to do to me."

"No!"

"Oh, yes. You didn't know?"

"I swear I didn't."

"I thought he might have said something about it. I know how men talk."

"Mario is not like that. He is very—how do you say it?—very nearmouthed."

"Closemouthed."

"Yes, closemouthed. He tells me nothing. Just Tony, do this; Tony, do that. He keeps his secrets."

"Well, I'm one of them. No way am I going to spread my legs for that guy. He disgusts me. But I don't know how to make him leave me alone. I'm not going to ask you to talk to him about it."

"Holy Mother, no! I couldn't do that."

"Of course you couldn't. Because then he'd know I had talked to you about it. He'd get jealous because you're young and handsome, and he'd think you and I have something going."

"Yes," he says, "that's true."

"Tony," she says, putting a hand on his thigh, "what am I going to do?"

"You told him you don't want, uh, what he wants?"

"I told him a hundred times, but he won't take no for an answer. He just keeps after me. Calls me almost every day. Sends me letters. Dirty letters—you know?"

Tony nods. "He is acting like a fool. If a woman says no to me, I say goodbye. There is always another."

"You think I haven't told him that? But it hasn't done any good. I've got to get him out of my life, but I don't know how."

No response from Tony.

"Sometimes," Sally says, deciding this is the moment, "sometimes I wish the same thing would happen to him that happened to Vic Angelo."

"What? What are you saying?"

"You heard me. I just want him gone, and I'm at the point now where I don't care how it's done. I hate the guy, and I hate what he's doing to my life."

They sit in silence then, and Sally gives him time to absorb what she's said. If he belts her, she's sunk. If he gets out of the car and stalks away, she's sunk. If he tells Mario of their conversation, she's sunk. That's a lot of sinking, and her only life preserver is Tony's ambition and greed.

"I'd pay," she says in an aching voice, and she doesn't have to fake the desperation. "I'd pay a nice buck to have it done. Cash. I'd even help plan it. Make it look like an accident."

He doesn't answer, and her hand tightens on his thigh. She moves closer.

"And maybe a good job for the guy who does it," she goes on. "An inside job. No more straining your kischkas lifting pails of garbage in all kinds of weather. You saw that extra desk in my office? That was my father's. I've been handling everything since he died. But the business is getting too big. I need another executive. Someone I can trust. Someone who's done me a big favor by putting Corsini down."

She looks closely into his face and sees something new: stoniness. His eyes are hard and shiny as wet coal.

"No," he says flatly, "I cannot do it. Anyone else, but not Mario. He is my cousin. You understand? He is *family*."

Sally slumps. "Then I'm dead," she says dully.

"No, you are not dead," Anthony Ricci says. "There is a way out for you."

"Yeah?" she says in a low voice. "Like what?"

"Marry me."

She looks at him. "Are you nuts?"

"Listen to me," he says, taking her hand, holding it tightly. "You marry me and Mario will never bother you again. I swear by my mother. And you get to keep the business. Sure, you will still pay dues, but no one will hassle you—because you will be my wife."

"And what's in it for you?"

"First, I marry a smart, beautiful, older woman. It will help me stay in this country. Also I get a good inside job, a desk, maybe a secretary."

"And a piece of the business?"

He gives her his megawatt smile. "Maybe a little piece."

"And what about the sex department?"

"What about it? Am I so ugly?"

"No," she says. "Ugly you ain't."

"So? What do you say?"

"Let me think about it," Sally Steiner says, and doesn't object when he kisses her.

Timothy Cone has covered his table with several thicknesses of old newspaper, and they need it; the barbecued ribs, potato chips, and pickles make for a messy meal. Cleo prowls around, waiting for scraps.

"My live-in garbage disposal," Cone says.

"Cut the small talk," Samantha Whatley says, "and get on with your story. I want to know how it comes out."

As they eat, he describes for the fifth and, he hopes, final time how Sally Steiner was trading stocks on inside information gleaned from the printer's trash. He tells Sam about the mob's control of the private carting business and how Sally was giving tips to Mario Corsini.

"For what reason I don't know, exactly," Timothy admits. "But I think he was leaning on her; that's my guess."

Then he recounts how he went up to see Steiner and did a little leaning of his own, trying to turn her so she'll go to the cops and end extortion by the skels.

By the time he's finished his narrative, they've demolished ribs, chips, and pickles. Sam has provided chocolate eclairs for dessert, but they put those in the fridge and settle down with their beers, feet parked up on the littered table.

"My, oh my," Sam says, "you really have been a busybody, haven't you? But you know what burns my ass?"

"A flame this high?" he asks, holding his hand a yard off the floor.

"Shithead," she says. "When you found the insider leak for Pistol and Burns, your job was finished. Keerect? That's what they hired Haldering for, and you delivered. It should have ended right there. But no, you had to push it and get involved with the Mafia shaking down garbage collectors, and trying to get this Sally Steiner to blow the whistle. Why did you do that, Tim?"

He looks at her. "I don't know," he says. "It just seemed the thing to do."

"Bullshit!" Sam says. "You know what I think your problem is? I think you see yourself as nemesis. Death to all evildoers!"

"Nah, not me. I just saw a chance for the good guys to

make a score, so I played out my hand. Listen, the cops helped me plenty. If I can fiddle a good bust for them, then they're happy and willing to keep cooperating. I wasn't acting out of anything but pure selfishness.''

"Uh-huh," Samantha says. "Get me an eclair, you Masked Avenger."

"Up yours," he says.

They sip their beers, nibble their chocolate eclairs, and agree it's a loathsome combination—but tasty. Their conversation becomes desultory, with Cone doing most of the talking, and Sam replying with monosyllables or grunts.

"Hey," he says finally, "what's with you? Got the fantods or something?"

"Just thinking."

"About what?"

"That Sally Steiner. I feel sorry for her."

He snorts.

"What's that supposed to be?" Sam asks. "A laugh?"

"If it is, it's on me. I went up to see that put-together lady to find out if she was ready to talk to the cops."

"And?"

"She told me to get lost. She's marrying Tony Ricci, Corsini's cousin."

"You're kidding."

He holds up a palm. "Scout's honor. She snookered me. I thought I had her in a bind, but she wiggled out of it. By marrying Ricci she gets to keep the business. And she gets Corsini off her back. Maybe she'll have to give her husband a piece of the action, but I'll bet that garbage dump is going to stay in the Steiner family for another generation. She's a real survivor."

"Is she pretty?" Sam asks.

"She's okay."

An hour later, they're lolling naked on the floor mattress. Popped cans of beer have been placed within easy reach, and Cleo, protesting mightily, has been locked in the loo.

Samantha, sitting up, begins unpinning her magnificent hair. Timothy watches with pleasure the play of light and shadow on her raised arms, stalwart shoulders, the small, hard breasts. Suddenly she stops and stares at him.

"Listen," she says, "you made it sound like Sally Steiner is marrying that Tony Ricci just so she can keep the business in the family. Did it ever occur to you that she might love the guy?"

Cone shrugs. "Could be. There are all kinds of love."

"Yeah," Sam says, reaching for him. "Here's mine."

BOOK II

*A Case of
the Shorts*

One

JOHN J. DEMPSTER, Chairman and Chief Executive Officer of
Dempster-Torrey, Inc., comes charging out of his office
bathroom, a dynamo in overdrive. Gray brush-cut hair is wet
from a shower; he scrubs his scalp furiously with a towel.
He's wearing only boxer shorts imprinted with monetary insignia: dollar, pound, deutsche mark, yen.

Mrs. Esther Giesecke, his executive secretary, follows him
to the dressing room, picking up his damp towel. She stands
in the doorway as he dresses swiftly.

"All right," he says, "what have we got?"

"Tommy called from LaGuardia. The Lear is fueled and
ready to go. He wants to know when you'll be leaving."

"The idiot!" Dempster snaps. "We'll be leaving when I
get there. What else?"

"Hiram Haldering called to confirm your appointment on
Monday afternoon at three."

Another woman appears at the secretary's side. She is Eve
Bookerman, Chief Operating Officer of Dempster-Torrey.

"You sure you want to go to Haldering's office, J.J.?" she
asks. "Why not have him come over here?"

"No," he says brusquely. "I want to get a look at his
operation. Twiggs at Pistol and Burns says it's a raggedy-
assed outfit, but apparently they get results. Eve, I'll want
you to come with me. And Ted Brodsky, too. Tell him about
it. Anything else?"

"Your case is packed," his secretary tells him. "The takeover papers are in there, with a photocopy of your letter of
intent. And a preliminary draft of your speech to the Chicago
analysts."

"That's it?"

"That's it," she tells him.

"Eve, you got anything?"

"*Time* magazine wants to do a profile. They'll assign someone to follow you around for a day. Twenty-four hours in the life of a magnate—that kind of thing."

"A cover?" he asks sharply.

"They didn't say, and I didn't ask."

"Tell them no cover, no story. Did you send flowers to Ed Schanke's funeral?"

"I took care of it, J.J."

"Good. That union should be easier to deal with now. He was a sonofabitch. Well, I guess that's it. If I think of anything else, I'll call from the car or plane. You know where to phone me in Chicago and St. Louis. I'll be back in town Sunday night, so you can reach me at home then if anything comes up."

He inspects himself in a full-length mirror. He's wearing a black suit of raw silk, white shirt, regimental striped tie. His black kilties are polished to a high gloss. His only jewelry is a gold wedding band.

"Okay, Esther," he commands, "check me out."

"Wallet?" she says. "Keys? Handkerchief? Sunglasses? Reading glasses? Credit cards? Pen? Cigarettes? Lighter? Pillbox?"

As she enumerates all these items, he taps trouser and jacket pockets. "Got everything," he reports. "Esther, take my case out to Tim. I'll be along in a minute."

They move into his outer office, a baronial chamber paneled with bleached pine. It is dominated by an enormous desk-table: a solid slab of polished teak supported on chrome sawhorses.

Mrs. Giesecke carries his attaché case into the corridor, closing the door behind her. Dempster puts his back against it and beckons. Eve Bookerman comes into his arms: a long, fervid embrace, lips mashed, tongues seeking.

She pulls away, gasping. "You'll call me tonight, Jack?" she asks.

"Don't I always? That ear of yours still giving you trouble?"

"It's better. The drops are helping."

"Good. I better get moving."

"Jack, you be careful."

"I'm always careful," he says. "See you on Monday."

Tim, his bodyguard, is waiting at the executive elevator. The two men ride down forty-two floors to Wall Street.

"Nice day, Mr. Dempster," Tim says cheerily. "Good flying weather."

"Too bloody hot. But we'll be going from one air-conditioned cocoon to another."

A gray Lincoln limousine is at the curb. Bernie is behind the wheel. He hops out to open the back door, and Dempster slides in. Tim walks around to the traffic side to get in next to his boss.

A black Kawasaki motorcycle is idling about twenty feet to the rear of the limo. It starts up, moves forward so slowly that the man in the saddle drags his steel-toed boot on the pavement. Both driver and the man on the pillion are wearing blue nylon jackets, jeans, massive crash helmets with tinted visors that extend to their chins.

The bike pulls up alongside the Lincoln and stops. The rear rider unzips his jacket. He pulls out an Uzi submachine gun, stock folded down. Firing the weapon with one hand, he sprays the three men in the limousine, shooting through the opened door and the closed windows.

The chauffeur and bodyguard die first, their bodies riddled, jerking as the 9mm slugs cut them open. The muzzle is turned to Dempster. He throws up both hands in angry protest, but the bullets slice through. He is slammed back on the seat, then toppled onto the floor.

The assassin coolly empties the thirty-two-round magazine, then slips the gun back into his jacket. The Kawasaki accelerates, roars away, weaving through traffic. In a moment it is gone.

And so is John J. Dempster.

News headline: MASSACRE ON WALL STREET!

Post headline: WALL STREET BLOODBATH!

Times two-column head: Executive and Two Aides Slain by Motorcyclists in Financial District.

Photographs were gory, but facts were few. Knowledgeable witnesses identified the bike as a black Kawasaki Ltd. 650, and the weapon as a 9mm Uzi submachine gun with folding stock. Descriptions of the killers were meager: two young male Caucasians, medium height, medium build, wearing blue jackets, jeans, visored helmets, boots.

Shortly after the murders, three New York newspapers received phone calls from an organization calling itself "Liberty Tomorrow," and claiming responsibility for the killings. More attacks against "corporate America" were promised, and the callers warned that assassinations of business executives would continue until the "people sit in the seats of the mighty."

The New York Police Department, the FBI, CIA, Interpol, and antiterrorist organizations of foreign governments reported they had no information on a revolutionary group called Liberty Tomorrow, but all cautioned that such anarchic cells formed frequently, were usually short-lived, and sometimes consisted of no more than a half-dozen members.

The police investigation concentrated on finding the Kawasaki and checking all the threatening letters that John J. Dempster, like many business executives, received over the years. Detectives also sought to determine who was aware of Dempster's schedule, knew of his projected flight to Chicago, and was able to direct the killers to the right place at the right time, enabling them to commit their crime quickly and escape with ease.

John J. Dempster was buried on Friday, but even before his funeral (attended by a Deputy Under-Secretary of Commerce), the Board of Directors of Dempster-Torrey, Inc., met in emergency session and appointed a subcommittee to search for and recommend a possible successor to Dempster. Meanwhile the responsibility for keeping the conglomerate functioning was assigned to Chief Operating Officer Eve Bookerman.

On the day of the murders, the common stock of Dempster-Torrey, Inc., was listed on the New York Stock Exchange at $155.250 per share. By the following Monday, it was trading at $119.625.

And on Monday afternoon, at precisely three o'clock, Eve Bookerman is ushered into the private office of Hiram Haldering on John Street.

"My dear lady," he says, taking both her hands in his and twisting his meaty face into a suitable expression of grief, "may I express my extreme sorrow at your loss and my horror at this tragedy."

"Yes," she says, looking at their scabrous surroundings with some astonishment, "thank you. May I sit down?"

"Of course, of course," H.H. says hastily. He drops her hands and pulls an armchair closer to the side of his desk. "After what you've been through in the past few days, I would have been happy to postpone this meeting or at least come to your office."

"No," she says decisively. "Mr. Dempster wanted to come here, and I'm carrying out his wishes as best I can. Our Chief of Security, Theodore Brodsky, was supposed to come along, but he's tied up with the New York police and the FBI."

"I understand completely. And tell me, has there been any progress at all?"

"They don't tell me anything," she says fretfully. "Only that the investigation is continuing. Infuriating!"

Haldering nods his fat head benignly. "I can understand that, having worked for the FBI for many years. They're making progress; I'm sure they are. But nothing will be released until all the facts are nailed down, and either the perpetrators have been taken into custody or suspects identified. I hope, dear lady, that you and other Dempster-Torrey executives are taking extra precautions for your personal safety."

"The police insisted on it," she says, not happily. "My bodyguard is sitting in your outer office right now. Ridiculous! I can take care of myself."

"I'm sure Mr. Dempster thought the same thing," he says. And then, fearing that comment didn't show the proper respect for the departed, he clasps his pudgy hands and leans across the desk. "Well!" he says with a treacly smile. "I'm sure you didn't come here to discuss the murder of Mr. Dempster. Now what can I do for you, ma'am?"

"You're familiar with Dempster-Torrey?"

"Of course. Who isn't? One of the largest conglomerates in the country, I believe."

"Eighth largest," she says, lifting her chin. "Two years ago we ranked number twelve. If J.J. had lived, we would have been the largest within five years. Fantastic! Dempster-Torrey owns twenty-seven subsidiaries with a total of eighty-three divisions. We're into everything from peanut butter to sheet metal. We produce golf carts, paper napkins, scuba diving gear, ventilation ducts, potato chips, ponchos for the U.S. Government, pasta, hair dryers, forklift trucks, and more. That chair you're sitting on was made by a Dempster-Torrey subsidiary. One of our industrial divisions made the tile on this floor. You name it and the chances are good that it is produced by Dempster-Torrey.''

H.H. shakes his head in wonderment, although he knows the chair he's sitting on was purchased secondhand, and the floor tile was part of a job lot—and cruddy stuff it is, too.

''For the past six months or so,'' Eve Bookerman goes on, ''our factories, warehouses, and distribution centers all over the country have been hit by a series of attacks. Deliberate! Fires, vandalism, unexpected strikes, and consumer lawsuits. There have been eighteen separate incidents. Mr. Dempster did not think that was coincidence, nor do I. He was convinced there is a plot by some person or some group directed against Dempster-Torrey. He had no idea what the reason for such hostility might be, nor do I, nor does anyone else in our organization. Mystery!''

''Surely Mr. Dempster must have made enemies during his career.''

''Of course he did. How could a man do what he did without making enemies? But I can't believe any of them would take revenge by setting a fire in a little flag and banner factory we own, a fire that killed two innocent workers. Despicable!''

''You said that Mr. Dempster considered the possibility of a plot by some group. Liberty Tomorrow, for instance—the terrorists who called the newspapers after the murders?''

''It was the first time I ever heard the name. That's one of the most frustrating things about the attacks against Dempster-Torrey. There were no telephone calls, no threatening letters. No one claimed responsibility.''

''And I presume each of these incidents was investigated?''

''Of course. By local police and by our own security people. No arrests, not even a theory on who is responsible. Maddening!''

''Tell me, dear lady, have you told all this to the officers investigating Mr. Dempster's death?''

''I told them,'' she says grimly. ''I don't believe they think there is any connection between the attacks on our factories and J.J.'s murder.''

''But you think there is?''

"I don't know what to think. Nightmare!"

Hiram Haldering, nodding, begins swinging slowly back and forth in his swivel chair. He's getting to look more like a dumpling every day. The double chin is going for a triple. The waistcoat is ready to pop its pearl buttons. And what he fancies is an executive stride comes perilously close to a waddle. He is not totally bald, not quite, but his pate glistens, the color of a peeled apple.

He stops swinging to lean on his desk once again, suety palms clasped.

"I should tell you at once, ma'am," he says, "that Haldering and Company cannot investigate the murder of Mr. Dempster. We have neither the resources nor the personnel. We consider ourselves specialists in corporate intelligence. Buyouts, takeovers, mergers—things of that sort. We provide confidential information on individuals and companies, for a fee. But we are not equipped to conduct homicide investigations."

"I didn't think you were," Eve Bookerman says sharply. "J.J. made an appointment with you on the recommendation of Mr. G. Fergus Twiggs of Pistol and Burns, our investment bankers. The express purpose was to get to the bottom of this series of assaults against our property and our people. We've gotten nowhere in trying to solve them or stop them. Mr. Twiggs suggested you might be able to help."

"Very kind of Twiggs," Haldering says, preening. "It is true that in several cases we have had remarkable success where others have failed."

"Then you'll be willing to take on the job? You can write your own ticket."

"With the understanding that our investigation will deal only with the industrial sabotage and not the assassination of Mr. Dempster."

"I'll accept that," she says crisply. "When will you be able to start?"

"Immediately!" he cries, picking up on her monosyllabicity.

"Excellent! In the hope that we might come to an agreement, I've brought along copies of a file that will give you an idea of what we've been up against. Along with a list of personnel involved, addresses and phone numbers—all of which may be of help."

"I admire your foresight," he says with an unctuous smile.

"Oh," she says, snapping her fingers, "one more thing: Mr. Twiggs urgently recommends that we request the problem be handled by one of your investigators—Timothy Cone. Is that his name?"

"Timothy Cone," Hiram Haldering repeats, smile fading. "Yes, we do employ an investigator by that name. But unfortunately, Mr. Cone is busy with several other cases at the moment. However, we have a number of other investigators who are fully qualified to—"

She interrupts him. "No Cone, no deal," she says.

He shifts uncomfortably in his chair. "As you wish," he says. "Perhaps I should warn you that Timothy Cone is—"

"Mr. Twiggs described him," she says impatiently. "I know what to expect. If he can do the job, it doesn't matter." She rises, holds out her hand. "Nice doing business with you, Mr. Haldering. I'm depending on your shop to make sense out of this whole awful affair. Monstrous!"

He starts to thank her for her trust and confidence, but she is out the door, leaving behind a taped accordion file bulging with documents. H.H. picks up his phone and punches the intraoffice extension of Samantha Whatley.

"Sam?" he says. "Come into my office, please. At once. And if Cone isn't sleeping or beering it up, drag his scruffy ass in here."

Cone lumps up Broadway, that humongous accordion file clamped under his right arm. It's heavy enough so that he lists to starboard, and occasionally has to pause and get a fresh grip.

"Don't you dare take that file out of the office," Sam had warned.

"Sure, boss," he replied. "I'm not about to carry that blivet home with me."

"What's a blivet?"

"Eight pounds of shit in a four-pound bag."

"You're disgusting!" she yelled at him.

"Yeah," he said, "I know."

So now he's plodding home to his loft, lugging the blivet and wondering what he and Cleo might have for dinner. He decides hot Italian sausage might be nice, fried up with canned potatoes. Maybe a charlotte russe for dessert. That sounds like a well-balanced meal.

He stops at local shops for the makings, not forgetting a cold six-pack and a jug of pepper-flavored vodka—something he's been wanting to try for a long time. Thus laden, he trudges up the six flights of iron steps to his loft.

The meal turns out to be okay, but that pepper vodka is sparky enough to make Cone's scalp sweat. He's afraid to light a cigarette, figuring a single belch might ignite and, like a flame thrower, incinerate the joint.

He switches to cold beer to soothe his scorched palate and settles at his desk, feet up, to dig through the contents of that Dempster-Torrey file.

The first thing he finds is three pages stapled together that list names, addresses, and phone numbers of people connected with John J. Dempster and his corporation. Included, Cone sees, are the names of his widow, three young sons, his brother, his parents (still living in Boca Raton, Florida), his deceased bodyguard and chauffeur, and the top rank of Dempster-Torrey execs, the Board of Directors, attorneys, and bankers.

Also on the list, Cone notes with some bemusement, are the names of Dempster's tailor, masseur, physician, dentist, physical fitness instructor, servants, golf pro, pilot, and proctologist.

"Some people know how to live," Cone calls to Cleo. But the tom, sleeping off the Italian sausages under the bathtub, pays no heed.

He starts flipping swiftly through the documents on the attacks that have bedeviled Dempster-Torrey, Inc., for the past six months. There are eighteen reports, all signed by Theodore Brodsky, Chief of Security. They include arson, sabotage, vandalism, product tampering, and similar crimes, all apparently designed to erode the profits and tarnish the public image of Dempster-Torrey. Cone can understand why John J. thought there was a plot against him and his conglomerate; the guy wasn't just being paranoid.

He pops another beer and starts reading the reports again, slower this time, wondering if there's a pattern or link everyone else had missed. He's halfway through and hasn't found a damned thing when his wall phone shrills. He carries his beer into the cramped kitchenette.

"Yeah?" he says.

"You putz!" screams Neal K. Davenport. "Just what the fuck do you think you're doing?"

"Hey, wait a minute," Cone says. "What's this—"

"The Dempster kill!" the NYPD detective shouts at him. "Why are you sticking your nose into that?"

"Come on," Cone says, "don't get your balls in an uproar. Who told you Haldering is involved in it?"

"Eve Bookerman, that's who. She's been running the outfit since Dempster got chilled. She told us that she hired Haldering."

"Then she must have told you that all we're doing is investigating industrial sabotage in their plants. Look, Neal, we don't do windows and we don't do homicides. That job is all yours; Hiram Haldering made it plain to Bookerman. You know about the accidents they've been having?"

"Yeah," the city bull says grudgingly, "they told us."

"You think there's a connection with Dempster's murder?"

"We can't see it."

"So where's the conflict? The Department is after the guys on the motorcycle. We're after the people who are trashing Dempster-Torrey's property. Listen, what's your interest in this? Are you handling the file?"

"Shit, no! I caught the original squeal. I got there right after the blues. But it's too big to leave to little old me. They think I'm only good for busting pickpockets and flashers."

"Tough titty," Cone says. "So who's in charge?"

"Some wet-brained lieutenant who's got a rabbi in the Department with a lot of clout. The guy's a real cowboy. He's riding off madly in all directions. Well, I can't really blame him. This is an important one, and he wants to cover his ass. The first case of terrorism in the Wall Street district."

"The hell it was," Cone says. "A few years ago Fraunces Tavern was bombed by revolutionaries, and long before that a guy drove a horse-drawn cart down Wall Street and set off a bunch of bombs in the wagon. They called them anarchists in those days. Anyway, the explosion blew the hell out of the horses. You can still see the scars on some of the buildings if you look for them."

"Jesus," Davenport says, "you're a veritable gold mine of useless information. Well, regardless of past history, this is still a big case, and everyone wants a piece of it. Not only the Department, but the Manhattan DA, the Federal DA, the FBI, New York State, and the CIA. It's as fucked up as a Chinese fire drill."

"The CIA? What's their interest?"

"They're investigating those wackos, the Liberty Tomorrow gang, to see if it's a terrorist organization with pals overseas, like in Germany, France, or the Middle East."

"Lots of luck," Timothy says. "So everyone is walking up everyone else's heels and fighting for interviews on the TV talk shows. Where do you fit into this mishmash?"

"Christ!" the city cop says. "You know what they've got me doing? A couple of witnesses swear the driver of the motorcycle was wearing a steel-toed boot. So I'm supposed to check out every joint in the city that puts steel tips on shoes and boots. That's like looking for a needle in a keg of nails."

"Yeah," Cone says, "I know what you mean."

"If we could handle it as a simple dusting," Davenport goes on, "an ordinary, run-of-the-mill homicide, things would be a lot easier. But all the people involved are real nobs—or think they are. I mean Dempster-Torrey is a powerhouse in local politics. Charitable contributions, campaign donations, and all that shit. So the heat is on. I get pushed every hour on the hour, and when I heard you were joining the pack, I blew my cork. Sorry I yelled at you."

"That's okay," Cone says. "I can understand how you feel. But believe me, Haldering and Company has no interest in getting involved in Dempster's death. All I'm supposed to do is find out who's torching their factories."

"And you don't think it has anything to do with the murder?"

"Hey, I've just started on this thing. I was reading the file when you called. But you said yourself that you can't see a connection."

"That's right. But that's today. Maybe tomorrow you'll trip over something. You'll let me know?"

"Hell, yes. I'm no glory hound; you know that. If I find anything that sets off bells, you'll be the first to know. You can have the headlines."

"I don't know why I trust you," Davenport says. "You're such a flake."

"Yeah, well, I haven't ever bollixed you up, have I?"

"Not lately you haven't," the NYPD man says, considerably mollified. "Okay, go back to your boozing; you sound half in the bag already. Every time I think of a wild card like you rampaging around in something like this, my ulcer starts acting up. Keep in touch, will you?"

"Depend on it," Timothy says.

He goes back to his desk, back to reading the Dempster-Torrey reports, back to pepper vodka—which now seems mild, light, dry, sparkling, and guaranteed to dull the senses and make life seem interesting and even meaningful.

Finished with the documents, he tosses them aside, parks his feet on the desk, dunks a charlotte russe in the vodka, and ruminates.

As far as finding a link between the eighteen crimes—zero, zip, and zilch. But the lack of a pattern might have significance. It's unlikely one guy is racing around the country setting fires, dumping rice in gas tanks, blowing up warehouses, and slipping cyanide into sealed bottles of diet pills made by Dempster-Torrey's drug subsidiary.

Those sophisticated techniques were devised by someone with a lot of criminal know-how. That makes Cone think it's a gang, bossed by a villain who knows exactly what he's doing and what he wants to accomplish. But what does he want to accomplish? Revenge?

That would point the finger at a fired or disgruntled employee. Or maybe the former owner of some small and profitable company that John J. Dempster gobbled up on his march to power. God knows Dempster must have made enough enemies to last him a lifetime—which didn't, after all, last very long at all.

The Wall Street dick pours another small vodka, swearing to himself it will be a nightcap and knowing it won't because his mind is churning, and he'll be able to sleep only with high-proof oblivion.

He's halfway through that snort when his peppered brain spits out an idea that's so elegant he feels like shouting. It's a neat solution: an organization controlled, or hired, by a tough, determined, brainy guy who knows exactly what he wants and how to get it. Cone walks around his brilliant inspiration, and the more he inspects it from all angles, questions it, analyzes it, the stronger it seems.

And the motive? That's the best part!

"I do believe . . ." he says aloud, and Cleo comes slinking out from under the bathtub to yawn and stretch.

Later, lying in his skivvies on the floor mattress, lights out, his last conscious thoughts are of Neal K. Davenport, and how rancorous the detective must feel at being relegated to a minor role in a big case he thinks of as his own.

Cleo pads up to curl into the bend of his knees.

"He wants praise, kiddo," Cone says, reaching down to scratch the cat's torn ears. "Or maybe justification. He wants recognition that he's doing important work in this screwed-up world. Do you want praise, justification, and recognition, Cleo? The hell you do. I don't either. We've got a roof over our heads and all the hot sausage we can eat. What more do we need?"

Cleo growls agreement.

Two

THE SECRETARY is a middle-aged woman, with a glazed ceramic complexion and wiry gray hair up in a tight bun. She
gazes at the world through hard eyes. He figures it would take
a helluva lot to surprise her—and nothing would shock her.

"Timothy Cone from Haldering and Company," he says.
"To see Miss Bookerman. My appointment's for ten-thirty."

She glances down at a watch pinned to her bodice. She
doesn't have to tell him he's late; her look is accusation
enough.

"I'll tell her you're here, Mr. Cone. Please be seated."

But he remains standing, eyeballing the place. Nothing lav-
ish, but everything crisp, airy, and looking as if it was waxed
five minutes ago. The carpet has the Dempster-Torrey corporate insignia woven into it. A nice touch. Reminds Cone of
the linoleum in his loft. That bears *his* insignia: cracked,
worn, with the brown backing showing through in patches.

"Ms. Bookerman will see you now," the secretary says,
replacing her phone. "Through that door and down the hall to
your left."

"Right," he says.

"No," she says, "left."

He looks at her and sees a glint of amusement in her steady
eyes.

"How about tonight?" he whispers. "Same time, same
place. I'll bring the herring."

That cracks her up. "I'll be there," she promises.

He had called that morning from the loft. Eve Bookerman
could see him at 10:30. Precisely. For a half-hour. Precisely.
Cone said that was fine, and he'd also like to talk to Theodore
Brodsky, Chief of Security. Bookerman said she'd arrange it.
Her voice was low, throaty, stirring. Cone liked that voice.

He figured that if he had a 10:30 appointment, there was no

point in going into the office first. So he spent an hour drinking black coffee, smoking Camels, and finishing the last charlotte russe. He was a mite hung over, but nothing serious. Just that his stomach was queasy, and he was afraid of what might happen if he yawned.

So he plodded all the way down to Wall Street. A hot July day, steamy, with a milky skim over a mild blue sky. By the time he arrived at the Dempster-Torrey Building, he was pooped; the air conditioning was plasma.

Now, scuffing down the inside corridor to his left, he passes a succession of doors with chaste brass name plates: JOHN J. DEMPSTER, SIMON TRALE, THEODORE BRODSKY and, finally, EVE BOOKERMAN. He wonders if, having taken over the murdered man's duties, even temporarily, she has moved into the CEO's office. But when he raps on the gleaming pine door, he hears a shouted "Come in!" and enters slowly, leather cap in hand.

She stands and comes forward to greet him. He is startled. From her voice and determined manner on the phone, he had expected a tigress; he sees a tabby. A short woman, almost chubby, with a great mass of frizzy strawberry-blond curls. She's trying to smile, but it doesn't work.

"Glad to meet you," she says. "Mr. Twiggs has told me so much about you."

"Yeah?" he says. "That's nice."

She's wearing a seersucker suit with a frilly blouse, a wide ribbon bow-tied at the neck. She looks clunky, but she moves well and there's strength in her handshake. Her eyes are great, Cone decides: big, dark, luminous. And she's got impressive lungs. Even with the blouse and suit he can see that.

She gets him seated in an armchair, not alongside her desk but facing her. Then she slides into an enormous, high-backed leather swivel chair. It swallows her, makes her look like a cub.

"Do you smoke?" she asks.

"Thanks," he says gratefully, reaching into his jacket pocket for his pack.

"Please don't," she says sharply. "I can't stand cigarette smoke. Atrocious!"

"Okay," he says equably, "I can live with that."

She sits on the edge of her chair, leans forward, elbows on

the desk, hands clasped: a position of prayer. Her fingers, Cone notes, are unexpectedly long and slender.

"Did you read the material I left with Mr. Haldering?" she demands.

"Yep."

"I hope you realize those reports are confidential. I wouldn't care to have them leaked to the media."

"I don't blab," he tells her.

"And do you have any questions?"

"A lot of them," he says. "Here's one for starters: What's the difference between a Chief Executive Officer—that was Dempster—and a Chief Operating Officer—that's you?"

"It varies from company to company," she says. "At Dempster-Torrey, J.J. made the big decisions and I made the small ones. He got the ulcers and I got the headaches."

"He had ulcers?"

"Of course not. It was just a figure of speech. What I'm trying to say is that he set policy and I carried it out. Expedited things. Found the people he needed and liaised with bankers, attorneys, accountants."

Cone stares at her. "Made his dreams come true?" he suggests.

"Yes," she says with that forced smile, "something like that. But the dreams were his."

"You've been with Dempster-Torrey—how long?"

"Almost eight years."

"Started out as Chief Operating Officer?"

"God, no! I was an MBA fresh out of Harvard. I started in the Planning Section, practically a gofer. I didn't get to be Operating Officer until three years ago."

"And then you worked closely with Mr. Dempster?"

"Yes."

"He made a lot of enemies?"

"Not a lot, but some, certainly. Any man in his position would."

"Any hot-blooded enemies? The type that'll say, 'I'll get you, you dirty dog. No matter how long it takes, I'll ruin you'?"

"None like that I know of. You think it's an old enemy who's engineering all our trouble?"

"I don't think much of anything," Cone says. "I'm just

getting started. Trying to collect stuff. Maybe it would help if you could tell me what kind of a man he was.''

"Very strong," she says promptly. "He couldn't stand to be denied anything he wanted for the company. Couldn't endure defeat. A very forceful personality. Goal oriented. An overachiever. He knew what he wanted and went after it."

"For himself? Or for Dempster-Torrey?"

"Mr. Cone, he *was* Dempster-Torrey. You cannot separate the man from the company he built. They were one. It wasn't just an ego trip. He wanted to make us an international conglomerate, bigger than IBM, General Motors, or the Vatican. And if he had lived, he would have done it. Absolutely!"

"Doesn't sound like the easiest guy in the world to work for."

She slumps back in her big swivel chair, begins curling a strand of hair around a slim forefinger. Those dark eyes glimmer, and Cone wonders if she's trying not to cry. For the first time he sees a wad of cotton batting stuck in her right ear.

"Got a bad ear?" he asks, trying to get her mind off Dempster's death.

She shakes her head impatiently. "A mild infection," she says. "I think I picked it up in the pool at the health club I go to. It's getting better. Look, Mr. Cone, I've tried to describe J.J.'s business personality. Yes, in his business dealings he was hard, demanding, occasionally even ruthless. He believed that was the way he had to be to build Dempster-Torrey. But away from the office, when he could temporarily forget about takeovers and mergers, he was the kindest, sweetest man who ever lived. He was tender, sympathetic, understanding. That's the John J. Dempster you never read about in *The Wall Street Journal* or *Fortune*. The press was just interested in the tycoon. But the man himself was more than just a money- and power-grubber; he was a mensch. You know what a mensch is, Mr. Cone?"

"I know."

"Well, J.J. was a mensch. In his personal life, a man of honor and integrity. I'm trying to be as cooperative as I can. I'm sure that as you get deeper into this thing and talk to more people, you'll hear a lot of bad things about Mr. Dempster. I just want to make sure you understand how I felt about him. I thought he was a marvelous man. Marvelous!"

"Uh-huh," Cone says. "I appreciate that. And how are things going since he died?"

"Lousy," she says with a short, bitter laugh. "It's disaster time, folks. You saw what happened to our stock?"

"I saw."

"All the way down. Because Wall Street knew J.J. *was* Dempster-Torrey. And with him gone, what's going to happen? The market hates uncertainty more than anything else, so the heavy investors and big institutions are dumping shares. Can't say I blame them, but it hurts."

"Sure," Cone says, "it would. But you've still got the factories, the farms, the warehouses, the railroad, the airline, the work force, the management organization. The assets are still there."

"But he's dead," she says darkly. "He was our biggest asset. And the Street knows it."

She peers at a man's digital watch strapped to her wrist.

"Your time's up," she announces. "I've got Ted Brodsky standing by. You want me to bring him in here?"

"No," Cone says. "I'll go to his office."

"Whatever you want," she says, shrugging. "I know you're going to be talking to a lot of people. Just don't believe everything you hear."

"I never do," he assures her. "Thanks for your time. I may be back with more questions."

"Of course. Whenever you like. Just call first. I'm up to my eyeballs until the Board elects another CEO. But I want to help you any way I can."

"Sure," the Wall Street dick says.

Theodore Brodsky's office is small, cramped, and jumbled with file folders, reports, and manuals. There's a national map framed on the wall, studded with pushpins. An American flag on a wooden staff is held erect in a cast-iron base. The room reeks of cigar smoke.

The Chief of Security clears off a two-cushion leather couch, and that's where they sit, half-turned to face each other.

"She wouldn't let you smoke, would she?" Brodsky says with a knowing grin.

"Eve Bookerman? Nah, but that's okay; she's entitled."

"Go ahead, light up. That's why I chain-smoke stogies—

to keep her out of here. She can't stand the stink. Says it gets in her hair.''

Cone lights a Camel, watching as the other man puts a kitchen match to what's left of a half-smoked and chomped cigar.

"I gotta tell you right out," Brodsky says, "I wasn't in favor of Dempster bringing in outside people to investigate what's been happening at our plants. It's a reflection on me. Right?"

Cone shrugs. "Sometimes it helps to get a fresh angle."

"I don't need any fresh angle. When Dempster said he was going to Haldering, I raised holy hell—for all the good it did me. That guy got an idea in his head, you couldn't blast it out with nitro. Anyway, I checked you out with Neal Davenport, and he says you're okay, so I guess we can get along."

"Oh? You and Neal are friends?"

"Haven't seen much of him lately, but him and me go back a long way. Did a tour together in the Two-one Precinct. Then I took early retirement and got this job. Listen, I don't figure you're out to cut my balls off. I mean, you've got a job to do; I can understand that."

"Uh-huh," Cone says. "And I'm not out to make the evening news on TV."

"Sure," Brodsky says. "And if you fall into anything, you'll let me know first—am I right?"

"Absolutely," says Timothy, an old hand at skillful lying.

"Then we can work together," Brodsky says, sitting back and chewing on his cigar. "Like they say, one hand washes the other."

"That's what they say. Suits me fine."

"As I get it, you're just assigned to the industrial accidents—am I right? No interest in the homicide?"

"Nope. I'll leave that to the uniforms."

"Yeah, that's the best thing to do."

Mention of Dempster's murder makes him scowl. He leans forward to drop his cigar in a smeared glass ashtray that already contains three dead butts. Then he rises, begins to pace around the room, jacket open, hands in his pants pockets. He's got a gut, and his belt is buckled low, under the bulge.

If you had called Central Casting, Cone thinks, and said you wanted a middle-aged flatfoot, they'd have sent Theodore Brodsky, and he'd have gotten the part. A big-headed guy with heavy shoulders and that pillowy pot. A trundling gait and a truculent way of thrusting out his face. It's a boozer's face, puffy and florid, with a nose like a fat knuckle.

"My name is shit around here as it is," Brodsky says morosely. "After all, I'm supposed to be Chief of Security, and my A-Number-One job was to protect the boss—am I right? Look, I did what he let me do. I'm the one who talked him into hiring a bodyguard. Tim was an ex-Green Beret, and he'd never dog it. Ditto the chauffeur, Bernie. He used to be a deputy sheriff out in Kansas or someplace. Both those guys were carrying and would have drawn their pieces if they had a chance. But what can you do against a couple of nuts with an Uzi?"

"Not much," Cone says. "And you can't stop a guy with a long gun on a roof across the street. It was just bad luck, so don't worry it."

"I gotta worry it," Brodsky says angrily. "It may mean my ass. I know that Bookerman dame would like me out."

"How come Dempster's limousine didn't have bulletproof glass?"

"You think I didn't think of that? I been after him for months to spring for a custom BMW. It goes for about three hundred Gs, and it's got bulletproof glass, armored body steel and gas tank, remote control ignition, bomb detectors—the whole schmear. He finally agreed, and that car's on order. But it'll take a couple of months to get it. Too late. But the new CEO can use it."

"Who's that going to be—Eve Bookerman?"

"Bite your tongue," Brodsky cries. "If she gets the job, I'm long gone. That lady and me just don't see eye-to-eye."

"What's the problem?"

"Chemistry," the other man says, and Cone lets it go at that.

"Look, Brodsky," he says, "when we first started talking, you said you didn't need any fresh angles on the sabotage. Does that mean you've got an idea of who's behind it?"

"That's exactly what it means."

"There was nothing in your reports even hinting at who's been pulling this stuff and what their motive is."

"Because I didn't have any proof," the Chief of Security says grimly. "But I'm getting it, I'm getting it." He pauses to consider a moment. Then: "I guess there's no reason why I shouldn't tell you. It's the labor unions."

Timothy stares at him.

"Yep," Brodsky says, nodding, "that's who it is. The unions that Dempster-Torrey deals with have got together and are causing all the trouble as bargaining chips to get better terms when their contracts come up for renewal."

"I gotta level with you," Cone says. "I think that idea sucks."

Brodsky flares up. "What are you," he demands, "a wisenheimer? What the fuck do you know about it?"

Cone stands, walks over to the framed map on the wall. He jerks a thumb at it. "All those pins show the location of Dempster-Torrey facilities in this country—correct? There's gotta be over a hundred of them."

"Hundred and fifty-nine."

"So how many local and national unions does Dempster-Torrey deal with? Ten? Twenty? Probably more like fifty, at least. And you're trying to tell me all those unions have joined in some grand conspiracy to damage the company they work for so they'll get better terms on their next contract? Bull*shit!* It just doesn't listen. First of all, you'd never get that many unions to agree on *anything*. Second of all, I'd guess that their contracts come up for renewal at different times. Maybe some next month, some in three years. And finally, what the hell's the point in burning down the place where you work? Manufacturing jobs are too hard to come by these days. No union in its right mind is going to trash a factory where its members earn a living. It's not labor that's causing all the trouble."

"Then who the hell is it?" Brodsky yells.

Cone spreads his hands. "Hey, give me a break. This is my first day on the job. I can't pull a rabbit out of a hat."

"I still think it's the unions," Brodsky says stubbornly. "Who else could it be? Some of those labor guys are out-and-out Commies. Maybe they're doing it for political reasons."

"To destroy American capitalism? I don't know what kind of cigars you smoke, but you better change your brand. You're way off in the wild blue yonder."

"Yeah? Well, you go your way, and I'll go mine. I'm still going to work the union angle."

Cone shrugs. Then, figuring he's gone as far as he can, he collects his cap and starts for the door. But he pauses.

"It might help," he says, "if you could tell me what kind of a man this John J. Dempster was."

Brodsky finds a fresh cigar in the mess on his desk. He bites off the tip, spits it into the overflowing ashtray. He moves the cigar around in his mouth to juice it up.

"They say you should only speak good of the dead," he says, "but in his case I'll make an exception. The guy was a dyed-in-the-wool bastard. A real ball-breaker. When Wall Street heard someone had offed him, the list of suspects was narrowed to ten thousand. He didn't let anyone get in his way, and if you tried, he squashed you. He was just a mean bugger. And he didn't have to be; he had all the money in the world—am I right?"

"You ever have any run-ins with him?"

"Plenty. And so did practically everyone else who works here. His Bible was the riot act. Used to read it all the time."

"Yeah," Cone says, "I know what you mean."

He starts out again, but Brodsky calls, "Hey, Cone," and he turns back.

"I bet what I told you about Dempster doesn't jibe with what Eve Bookerman told you."

"You're right; it doesn't."

Brodsky holds up a hand, middle finger tightly crossed over forefinger. "Dempster and Bookerman," he says with a lickerish grin. "That's Dempster on top."

"Thanks," Timothy Cone says.

He figures plodding back to John Street in that heat will totally wipe him out. So he cabs uptown, but before he goes to the office he stops at the local deli and buys a cream cheese and lox on bagel, with a thick slice of Bermuda onion atop the smoked salmon. He also gets a kosher dill and two cans of cold Bud.

Sitting at his desk, scoffing his lunch while still wearing his leather cap, he reflects that there is no way he can separate an investigation of the industrial sabotage at Dempster-Torrey plants from an inquiry into the assassination of John J.

Despite what Hiram Haldering said, and regardless of what he himself told Neal Davenport, Bookerman, and Brodsky, Cone suspects the sabotage and homicide are connected.

Also, there's a practical matter involved. To limit his detecting to the sabotage, he'd have to travel to eighteen different localities and try to pick up cold trails on cases that had been thoroughly investigated when fresh by local cops and Brodsky's security people, with no results.

All Cone's got to work with is the murdered man's family and friends, his acquaintances, employees, and business associates. Cone pulls out that list of personae that Eve Bookerman provided, from his inside jacket pocket. He looks up the address and phone number of the widow, Teresa Dempster, and dials.

It rings seven times at the other end before it's picked up.

"The Dempster residence." A woman's voice. Chirpy.

"Could I speak to Mrs. Teresa Dempster, please."

"Just a moment."

Long wait. Then:

"This is David Dempster. To whom am I speaking?"

"John J. Dempster was your brother?"

"He was."

"Well, this is Timothy Cone. I'm with Haldering and Company. We're investigating a series of industrial accidents at Dempster-Torrey plants, and I was hoping to talk to Mrs. Dempster for a few minutes. And you're on my list, too."

"Eve Bookerman informed us you'd probably be calling. I must tell you in all honesty, Mr. Cone, that neither Teresa nor I know the slightest thing about Dempster-Torrey operations. But naturally we'll be happy to cooperate in any way we can."

He shouldn't have said "in all honesty." Every time Cone hears that, he gets itchy. Also, Dempster has the plummy voice of a priest who's been unfrocked for waving his dork out a vestry window. Cone wonders what the guy does for a living. His business address on the list is David Dempster Associates, Inc., on Cedar Street.

"Can I see Mrs. Dempster?" he asks.

"As long as you're not a reporter or policeman," the other man says. "I rather think she's had her fill of those."

"I could be up there in a half-hour."

"Come ahead then; I'll tell her to expect you. I'm afraid I'll be gone by the time you arrive, but you'll be able to reach me at my office whenever you wish to see me. You have the address and phone number?"

"Yeah, I've got them. I'll probably get to you tomorrow if that's okay with you."

"Of course. And, Mr. Cone, please make your meeting with Teresa as brief as possible. She's been through a great deal in the past week. She's bearing up well, but we don't want her unduly disturbed, do we?"

"I won't disturb her," Cone promises. "Just a few questions. Won't take long."

But before he starts out, he stops at the office of Sidney Apicella, chief of Haldering's CPAs. As usual, Sid is massaging his nose. The poor guy suffers from rosacea of the beezer. It's big, magenta, and swollen, and he can't leave it alone.

He looks up as Cone enters. "Whatever you want," he says, "I can't do it. I'm too busy."

"Come on, Sid; this'll only take one phone call."

"The last time you told me that it took four days' work."

"One phone call, I swear. I'd do it myself, but you've got the contacts. There's this guy named David Dempster. He's the brother of that pooh-bah who got blasted on Wall Street last week. Anyway, this brother has a business, David Dempster Associates, on Cedar Street. All I want to know is what kind of a business it is, assets, liabilities, cash flow, and all that financial shit."

Apicella groans. "And you think I can get that with one phone call? You're demented!"

"Give it the old college try, Sid. I'll make sure you get special mention in my final report."

"Thanks for nothing," the CPA says. "When are you going to buy yourself a new suit?"

"What's wrong with this one? Sleaze is *in* this year— didn't you know?"

Figuring an outfit as big as Dempster-Torrey isn't going to quibble about expenses, he takes a taxi up to the Dempster residence on East 64th between Third and Lex. The place is practically a mansion and, scoping it from across the street, Cone figures it was probably originally two five-story brownstones. But now, with an expensive face-lift, it's red brick with wide plate glass windows.

The old stoops have been removed, and entrance is via a street-level doorway protected with a wrought-iron gate.

There's a uniformed policeman leaning against the gate, eye-balling all the young ginch passing by.

Cone crosses over and gives the cop what he thinks is an innocent smile. It doesn't work. The blue takes a long look at his black leather cap, cruddy corduroy suit, and yellow work shoes, and says, "Beat it, bum."

"Hey," Cone says, hurt, "watch your language. I'm Timothy Cone from Haldering and Company. I've got an appointment with Mrs. Dempster."

"Yeah? Let's see your ID."

Cone digs out his Haldering & Co. card with his picture attached. Samantha Whatley claims that photo should be on a post office wall with the warning: This man wanted for molesting children.

The officer takes the card, steps inside, and calls on the intercom. Then he opens the gate, returns the ID to Cone, and unlocks the heavy oak door.

"Sorry about that," he says.

"No sweat," Cone says. "You guys on twenty-four hours?"

"Yeah," the cop says. "About as exciting as watching paint dry."

There's a young, uniformed maid waiting for him in the foyer, and he follows her up a wide marble staircase to the second floor. Cone tries to keep his eyes on the stairs, with scant success. Down a carpeted hallway to the rear of the townhouse he gets a quick impression of high ceilings, light, airy rooms, plenty of bright graphics, polished wood, and green plants everywhere.

He is ushered into a greenhouse extending from the back of the building. Wide panes of glass are set in a verdigrised copper framework. The whole faces south and east, and sunlight floods in through glass walls and domed roof. A system of bamboo shades has been designed to mute the bright light, but air conditioning keeps the place comfortable.

The greenhouse is crowded with rough wooden tables, bags of potting soil, fertilizer, crushed shell, sand, and gardening tools. On the waist-high tables, in neat rows, is arranged an impressive assortment of bonsai, each dwarf tree in a splendidly proportioned pot of brown, cream, or dark blue glaze.

Other pots are decorated, and a few are set on lacquered wood pedestals.

The woman who comes forward, brass watering can in her hands, is tall, reedy, and wearing a long, flowing dress that billows as she moves. The gown is voluminous, made of some thin, diaphanous stuff the color of vanilla ice cream. But no paler than the woman herself.

"Mrs. Teresa Dempster?" Cone asks.

She nods vaguely, looking around at her plants. "And you're Mr. Timothy?"

"Cone," he says. "Timothy Cone."

"Of course," she says.

"Thank you for seeing me. I hate to intrude in your time of trial."

At last she looks at him directly. "'Time of trial,'" she repeats. "What a nice, old-fashioned expression. Are you an old-fashioned man, Mr. Timothy?"

He gives up on the name. "I guess I am," he says uncomfortably. "About some things. Beautiful plants you have here, Mrs. Dempster."

"Trees," she corrects him. "All my babies. But such old babies. This one, for instance, is said to be forty-five years old. It's a Japanese red maple. Do you like it?"

"Yeah," he says. "Real pretty."

She puts down the watering can, picks up the little red maple and thrusts it at him. "Then take it," she says. "It's yours."

He moves a startled step backward. "Oh, I couldn't do that," he protests. "It's probably valuable."

"No, no," she says. "If you promise to love it, I want you to have it."

Getting a glimmer of what he's up against here, he says earnestly, "Look, Mrs. Dempster, I appreciate your offer. It's very kind of you. But where I live, there's no sunlight at all. And I've got a nasty cat who'd demolish that thing in two seconds flat. It really wouldn't be fair to the tree for me to take it."

She looks so hurt that he's afraid she might start weeping.

"Tell you what," he says. "Why don't I accept the gift in the spirit in which it's given. But you keep it for me and take care of it. But it'll be my tree."

She gives him a smile as simple and charming as a child's.

"I think that's a wonderful idea!" she says. "I'll tell everyone it's Mr. Timothy's tree, and you can visit it whenever you like. Do you want to name it?"

"Name it?"

"Of course. Most of my trees have names. This juniper is Ralph. That Norfolk pine is Matilda. Would you like your Japanese red maple to have a name?"

"How about Irving?" he suggests, willing to play her game—if game it is.

"How lovely," she says with such evident enjoyment that he stares at her, wary and perplexed.

Everything about her is long: face, limbs, hands, feet. She looks like a tree herself, but not a bonsai. More like a full-grown willow, soft and drooping. There is an ineffable languor, she seems to float, her gestures are flutters. The big azure eyes are more innocent than any eyes have a right to be, and the unbound hair streaming down her back is flaxen and wispy.

Something ethereal there, something unworldly, and Cone has a vision of her galloping through the heather and caroling, "Heathcliff! Heathcliff!" He shakes his head to clear his mind of such nonsense and, to see if she is completely bonkers, asks:

"And what are the names of your boys?"

She looks up into the air as if striving to recall. "Edward," she says. "He's the oldest. And then there's Robert, and then Duane."

"They live here with you?"

"Usually they're away at school. But this summer they're all on a bicycle tour through Europe. They're having tons of fun."

"Did they come back for their father's funeral?"

"No," she says, "they didn't. By the time we got in touch with them, it was too late. Besides, there was no point in their returning, was there?"

Cone has his own idea about that, but doesn't voice it. "Your husband's death must have been a tremendous shock to you, Mrs. Dempster."

"Oh, Jack didn't die," she says, almost gaily. "He just passed over. Nobody and nothing ever dies, Mr. Timothy. Just assumes another form. But everything is immortal: you, me, these trees, the world about us."

Oh, God, he thinks despairingly, she's one of *those*. And he resolves to wind up this interview as speedily as possible, figuring it a total loss. But suddenly Teresa Dempster becomes talkative. He thinks at first she's swaying as she speaks, but then realizes she's standing in the blast of an air-conditioning vent set into the interior brick wall, and the draft is moving her insubstantial gown.

"David, my brother-in-law, was such a help," she says. "He just took care of everything. I know people wanted to be kind, but why did they have to cut down all those flowers? Jack was buried near Schroon Lake. We have a summer home up there, you know, and a family plot in the dearest, sweetest cemetery you ever did see. Mom and daddy are there, and now Jack, and there's a place for me."

The idea seems to enchant her, and she pauses to smile fondly.

"Of course," she goes on, "he's not really there; just the envelope he temporarily inhabited. Because he came to me last night. Yes, he did. 'Terry,' he said. He always called me that. 'Terry, I'm very happy here. I've crossed over, and it's beautiful. I'm waiting for you, Terry.' That's what he said to me last night."

The Wall Street dick can't take much more of this.

"Mrs. Dempster," he says sternly, "did your husband ever mention any enemies he had? Anyone who had threatened him or sworn revenge for one reason or another?"

"So many people have asked me that," she says, and seems genuinely puzzled. "Of course Jack didn't have any enemies. How could he—he was such a *good* man. I've been so fortunate, Mr. Timothy. He was certainly the best husband in the whole wide world. He was away so much—traveling, you know—doing whatever it was he did, but I could understand that; men are so busy. But when he returned, he always brought me a gift. Always! Sometimes it was just a funny little thing like a hand puppet. But he never forgot to bring me something. Never!"

"My sympathy on your loss," Cone mumbles. Then, louder: "Thank you for your time, Mrs. Dempster. I appreciate it."

"You're going away now?" she says, sounding disappointed.

"Yeah, I've got to. Another appointment."

"I suppose I should have offered you a drink or something."

"That's okay. You gave me a tree. Irving."

"And you'll come visit him, Mr. Timothy?"

"I certainly will," he says, and then tries one last time. "The name is Cone. Timothy Cone."

"Oh," she says. "Well, it's not important, is it?"

"Not important at all," he assures her.

He's hoping the lissome maid is lurking around to show him out, but there's no one in sight. He makes his way along the hallway, down the staircase, and out into the hot afternoon sunlight. The same uniformed officer is still on duty at the gate. Cone pauses to light a cigarette.

"You ever talk to Mrs. Dempster?" he asks.

"No," the cop says, "I never have."

"You're lucky," Cone tells him.

"Maybe it was her husband's death that made her flip out," Samantha Whatley suggests. "Maybe she was a perfectly normal woman, but then that awful, bloody murder pushed her over the edge."

"I don't think so," Cone says. "I'm guessing she's been that way all her life. She's not a wetbrain, you understand, but her gears have slipped a little; they don't quite mesh. Not bad enough to have her committed, but the lady is balmy, no doubt about it."

They're sprawled on an oval rag rug in Sam's tiny apartment in the East Village. She's prepared a mess of chicken wings cooked in an Italian sauce with onions and small potatoes thrown in. The big cast-iron pot rests on a trivet between them, and they fill their plates with a ladle. There is also a salad of Bibb lettuce and cherry tomatoes.

"Good grub," Cone says, sucking the meat from a wing. "Maybe a little more pepper and garlic next time."

"Now you're a cordon-bleu? If you stopped smoking, you'd be able to taste food the way it's supposed to taste. So you got nothing from the widow?"

"Nah, nothing important. Except that I'm immortal. That makes me feel swell. Maybe I'll do better with David Dempster, the brother. I called him and set up a meet for tomorrow. I'm also seeing Simon Trale, the Chief Financial Officer of Dempster-Torrey."

"What do you expect to get from him?"

"Nothing, really. I'm just fishing."

She looks at him suspiciously. "When you get that dopey look on your puss I know there's something going on in that tiny, tiny brain of yours. What are you up to, buster?"

"Me?" he says innocently. "I'm not up to anything, boss. Except maybe illicit sex. But I better tell you: I don't think you can separate the industrial sabotage from the murder. I think they're connected. Scratching the Chairman and CEO was just the ultimate act of sabotage. To damage Dempster-Torrey."

"Why? What for?"

"Beats the hell out of me. What's for dessert?"

"Tapioca pudding."

"I'll pass," he says. "You eat the fish eyes and I'll take my portion home to Cleo. That cat'll eat anything."

"Thanks for the compliment. Coffee?"

"Sure," he says. "And I brought a bottle of Spanish brandy. How about a noggin of that?"

"I'm game," she says. "And later do you intend to work your evil way with me?"

"It had occurred to me," he admits.

They watch the *n*th return of *The Honeymooners* on TV while still lounging on the floor, sipping their brandies. It's a nice, lazy evening, but when the show is over, Timothy stirs restlessly.

"What's with you?" Sam demands.

"I don't know," he says fretfully. "I think I'm mellowing out. Look at us: curled up on a rug, watching TV and inhaling brandy. It's all so domestic and comfy I can't stand it."

"The trouble with you is—" she starts, then stops.

"Go ahead," he says, "finish it. What's the trouble with me?"

"You can't endure being happy," she tells him. "You don't know how to handle joy. The moment you start feeling good, you pull back and ask, 'What's the catch?' You just can't believe that occasionally—not always, but now and then—it's perfectly normal to be content."

"Yeah, well, you may be right. I know I don't go around grinning. So I admit I get a little antsy when things seem to be okay, but only because I haven't had the experience. Being happy is like a foreign language. I can't understand it, so naturally I get itchy and think someone is setting me up for a fall."

"You think I'm playing you for a patsy?"

"Oh, Christ, no. I'm talking about God."

"Since when have you been religious?"

"I believe in God," he protests. "He looks a lot like my drill instructor at Parris Island. A mean sonofabitch who kept kicking our ass and telling us it was for our own good. Like my pa walloping me with his belt and telling me it hurt him more than it did me. God always has a catch. Maybe not right away, but sooner or later. You pay for your pleasure in this world, kiddo."

"I'm willing," Samantha says. "Fly now, pay later."

Ten minutes later they're in bed together.

Both would be shocked if someone had suggested anything admirable in their allegiance to each other. Not only their sexual fidelity but their constancy for more years than most of their acquaintances have been married. Each is a half-filled glass, needing the other for topping off. Alone, each is half-empty.

But no such dreary soul-searching for them; all they know, or want to know, is sweat and rut: a gorgeous game of shouted oaths and wailing cries. And in slick slide and fevered grasp they are oblivious to all else. Not even aware that the TV screen has gone blank after the closing rendition of "The Star-Spangled Banner."

Three

A MIDSUMMER HEAT WAVE has Manhattan by the throat. The air is humid, so supersaturated that one drinks rather than breathes it. Clothing clings, feet swell, hair uncurls, and even paper money feels greasy, as if all those engraved presidents are sweating.

Cone shuffles slowly down to Cedar Street, carrying his cap and jacket. He tries to keep to the shady side of streets, but there's no escape. It is the kind of day, as Sydney Smith said, that makes you want to take off your skin and walk around in your bones.

David Dempster Associates, Inc., is located in a building of stainless steel and tinted glass. The lobby is blessedly chilled by air conditioning turned down so low that sides of beef might be hung on the walls without fear of spoilage. Cone just stands there for almost five minutes until his blood stops bubbling. Then he consults the lobby directory and takes a high-speed elevator to the twenty-seventh floor, donning his jacket en route.

The anteroom is small: desk, typewriter on a stand, file cabinet, wastebasket, and a plump, hennaed secretary reading a copy of *Elle*. She looks up as Cone enters and gives him a saucy smile. "Hot enough for you?" she asks.

"It's not the heat," he says solemnly, "it's the humidity." And having completed the New York catechism, he gets down to business. "Timothy Cone from Haldering and Company to see Mr. Dempster. I have an appointment."

"Sure," she says blithely. "I'll tell him you're here."

She pops through an inner door and is out again in a moment. "This way, please, Mr. Cone. Would you like to leave your cap out here?"

"Nah," he says. "Someone might steal it."

"I doubt that," she says. "Very much."

David Dempster's office is large, but only in comparison to the reception room. Actually, it's a modest chamber, skimpily furnished: executive-type desk with leatherbound accessories and two telephones, swivel chair and two armchairs, steel file cabinet and small bookcase. And that's about it. The only wall decoration is a large color photograph of a golden retriever, with an award and blue ribbon affixed to the frame.

The man standing smiling behind the desk is tall and stalwart. He's wearing a vested glen plaid tropical worsted, and the suit is snug across shoulders and chest. Cone figures that if he doesn't pump iron, he does something equally disgusting—like exercise regularly. His handshake is a bonecrusher, as if he's ready to arm wrestle right then and there.

But he's affable enough: gets his visitor seated in one of the armchairs, holds a gold Dunhill to light Cone's Camel and his own Benson & Hedges (filtered). He asks, with a boomy laugh, if it's hot enough for Cone, and the Wall Street dick gives the proper reply. They're like lodge brothers exchanging the secret code.

They settle back, sucking greedily on their cigarettes and regarding each other with cautious ease.

"Teresa informed me you were up to see her," Dempster says. "She was quite embarrassed that she continued to address you as Mr. Timothy."

"That's okay. She said it wasn't important, and it's not."

"What did you think of her?" the other man asks suddenly. "Tell me, what was your initial impression?"

Cone shrugs. "She's different."

Dempster smiles; more fangs than teeth. "Teresa is her own woman. Many people, meeting her for the first time, are put off by her manner. But I assure you, she is not as simpleminded as she might appear. When it is necessary, she can be quite practical and quick-witted. She has handled the tragedy of Jack's death remarkably well."

"He didn't die," Cone can't resist saying, "he passed over."

Dempster becomes serious. "Yes, well, that's what she believes—sincerely believes. And it does no harm to anyone, does it?"

"Not a bit. I asked if her husband had any enemies, and she said no. Now I'll ask you the same thing."

"So have all the police and reporters," Dempster says ruefully. "You must realize, Mr. Cone, that my sister-in-law was not totally aware of her husband's business activities. Or even what Jack did for a living. Not that he ever attempted to conceal anything from her, but she simply wasn't all that interested. She had her sons, her homes, her bonsai, and she was content. As for your question to me: Did Jack have any enemies? Of course he did. He was a ruthless and, at times I fear, a brutal CEO. He built an enormous conglomerate from a small machine shop in Quincy, Massachusetts. You don't do that without making enemies along the way. But no one, to my knowledge, hated him enough to murder him. That is what I have told the police, and it is the truth as I know it."

"Mr. Dempster, I'm not involved in the homicide investigation. I'm supposed to be looking into all the industrial accidents Dempster-Torrey has had lately. You know about those?"

"Vaguely. Jack mentioned them one night at dinner."

"Any idea of who might be pulling that stuff?"

"Discharged or disgruntled employees would be my guess."

Then they are silent. Cone lights another cigarette, but this time David Dempster takes a handsome silver-banded brier from his desk drawer and fills it from a silken pouch. He tamps the tobacco down slowly with a blunt forefinger. Then he lights the pipe carefully, using a wax match from a tiny box. He sits back, puffing contentedly.

Lord of the manor, Cone thinks. With a picture of his favorite hound on the wall.

Dempster has a big face, long and craggy. Big nose, big teeth, and biggest of all, a mustache trimmed in a guardsman's style. It spreads squarely from cheek to cheek, brown with reddish glints. And he has a thick head of hair in the same hues, so bountiful that it makes Cone's spiky crew cut look like a cactus. Dempster's only small feature are his eyes; they're dark aggies.

"What kind of a man was your brother?" Cone asks.

"You know, you're the first investigator who's asked me that. Odd, isn't it? You'd think that would be the first thing the police would want to know. Well, Jack was an enormously driven man. With tremendous energy. And enough ambition for ten. Not for money or power, you understand. He had enough of both to last him two lifetimes. But Jack was a builder. He wanted Dempster-Torrey to become the biggest, richest international business entity in the world. He was intensely competitive. I think business was really a game to him. He played squash, golf, poker, and was a devil at three-cushion billiards. And he always played to win. He couldn't endure losing.''

"Did he ever cut any corners to make sure he won?"

Dempster laughs, flashing the fangs again. "Of course he did! But he rarely got caught. And when he did, he would admit it, grin, and people would forgive him. Because he had so much charm. He was the most charming man I've ever known. And I'm not saying that just because he was my brother.''

"And his opponents in business deals—did they forgive him when he cut corners?"

"That I doubt. I told you he made enemies. But of course I can't speak firsthand. I never had any business dealings with Jack. We went our separate ways.''

"What sort of business are you in, Mr. Dempster?"

"You didn't know?" the other man says, surprised. "Corporate public relations. Not a great number of clients because I prefer to keep this a one-man operation. I am not an empire builder the way Jack was. None of my clients are what you might call giants of industry, but they stick with me and pay their bills promptly. That's all I ask.''

"What sort of things do you do?" Cone asks. "Turn out press releases? Plant photos and bios of clients? Sit in on planning sessions for new products?"

"Ah," Dempster says, relighting his pipe, "I see you know the business. Yes, I do all that, but I suppose my most important function is keeping my clients' names *out* of the newspapers after they've pulled some exceptionally stupid stunt or gotten fouled up in their personal lives.''

"Yeah," Cone says, "there's a lot of that going around these days. How well did you and your brother get along?"

Dempster sets his pipe down carefully. "We weren't as close as we might have been, I suppose. We had such a small family. Our parents are dead, and our few aunts, uncles, and cousins are all out in South Dakota. We should have been closer. And now Jack is gone. I'd say our relationship was cordial but cool. We didn't socialize much. An occasional dinner when he could make it; he was an extremely busy man. And I'd spend a weekend up at their summer place now and then.''

"You ever do any public relations for Dempster-Torrey?''

"No, and I never made a pitch for that account. I didn't want anyone accusing Jack of nepotism. And besides, Dempster-Torrey has a very effective in-house PR department. So it was better all around if I stayed away from my brother's business.''

"Uh-huh,'' Cone says. "Well, you promised to cooperate, and you have. Thanks for your time.''

"If there's anything else I can do to help, don't hesitate to give me a call.''

"I'll do that. Nice dog you've got there.''

Dempster turns to stare at the picture on the wall. *"Had,"* he says in a stony voice. "He was hit and killed last year by a drunken driver who came over the curb while I was walking King along Central Park South.''

"Jesus,'' Cone says, "that's tough.''

"I dragged the guy out of his car,'' David Dempster goes on, "and kicked the shit out of the bastard.''

Again that bonecrushing handshake, and Cone gets out of there. He goes down to the icy lobby, takes off his jacket, and steps out into the steam bath. The heat is a slap in the face, and he starts slogging back to John Street wondering if he'll survive in the office where Haldering & Co. air conditioners, all antique window units, wheeze and clank, fighting a losing battle against the simmer.

He has an hour to kill before his appointment with Simon Trale, Chief Financial Officer of Dempster-Torrey, and he knows there are things he should be doing: checking with Davenport on the homicide investigation; goosing Sid Apicella to get skinny on the balance sheet of David Dempster Associates, Inc.; gathering evidence to back up his grand theory on who's responsible for the campaign of sabotage.

He starts by reviewing his recent conversation with David Dempster. Timothy knows very well that he himself is a mess of prejudices. For instance, he'll never believe a man who wears a pinkie ring, never lend money to anyone who claims to have finished reading *Silas Marner,* never letch after a woman who, on a bright day, wears sunglasses pushed up in her hair.

Silly bigotries, he acknowledges, and he's got a lot of them. And the morning meeting with David Dempster has added a few more. The orotund voice and precise diction. The fanged smile with all the warmth of a wolf snarl. The showy way he loaded his pipe, as if he was filling a chalice with sacramental wine. Wearing a vest on the hottest day of the year and then festooning it with a heavy gold chain from which a Phi Beta Kappa key dangled.

All minor affectations, Cone admits, but revealing. The man comes perilously close to being a poof, or acting like one. Whatever he is, Cone suspects, there is not much to him. Beneath that confident, almost magisterial manner is a guy running scared. Prick him and he'll deflate like a punctured bladder of hot air.

Except . . . Except . . . In David Dempster's final words, regarding the drunken driver who killed his dog, he said in tones of uncontrolled savagery, "I kicked the shit out of the bastard." That shocked Cone, not because of the act or the words describing it, but that it was so out of character for someone he had tagged as a wimp, and a pompous wimp at that.

It's a puzzlement, and Timothy decides to put David Dempster on hold, not that the guy is obviously a wrongo, but only because no one else questioned up to now has given off such confusing vibes. Like all detectives, Cone tends to pigeonhole people. And when he can't assign them to neat slots, his anxiety quotient rises.

The interview with Simon Trale is held in the offices of Dempster-Torrey on Wall Street. Trale elects to meet Cone in the boardroom, a cavernous chamber with a conference table long enough to sleep Paul Bunyan. It is surrounded by twenty black leather armchairs, precisely spaced. On the table in front of each chair is a water carafe, glass, pad of yellow legal paper, ballpoint pen, and ashtray—all embossed with the corporate insignia.

"I brought you in here," Trale says in a high-pitched voice, "because it was swept electronically about an hour ago. The debuggers won't get to my office until this afternoon, so I thought it would be safer if we talked in here."

"Yeah," Cone says, "that makes sense."

He wonders if they're going to sit at opposite ends of that

stretched slab of polished walnut and shout at each other. But Trale pulls out two adjoining chairs along one side, and that's where they park themselves.

The CFO is a short guy. In fact, Cone figures that if he was a few inches shorter he'd qualify as a midget. Usually a man so diminutive will buy his clothes in the boys' section of a department store, but Trale's duds are too well tailored for that. He's wearing a dark blue pinstripe with unpadded shoulders and side vents. His shirt is sparkling white, and he sports a paisley bow tie. Small gold cuff links. A wide gold wedding band. A gold Rolex. Black tasseled loafers on his tiny feet.

He's got a full head of snowy white hair neatly trimmed. The white hair is understandable because Timothy guesses that Simon Trale is pushing seventy, if he's not already on the downslope. But his movements are sure, and that reedy voice has no quaver.

"Mind if I smoke?" Cone asks.

"Go right ahead," Trale says. "The doc limits me to one cigar a day, but it tastes all the better for that."

"When do you smoke it—at night after dinner?"

"No," Trale says, smiling. "First thing in the morning. It gets the juices flowing."

"If you don't mind my asking, how old are you?"

"I don't mind. I'll be seventy-three next year."

"I should look as good next year as you do right now," Cone says admiringly. "No aches or pains?"

"The usual," the little man says, shrugging. "But I still got my own teeth, thank God. I use reading glasses, but my hearing is A-Okay."

"How come you're still working?" Cone asks curiously. "Doesn't Dempster-Torrey have a mandatory retirement at sixty-five?"

"Sure we do. But Jack Dempster pushed a waiver through the Board of Directors allowing me to stay on. You know why he did that?"

"Because you're such a hotshot financial officer?"

"No," Trale says, laughing. "There's a hundred younger men who could do my job. But my wife died nine years ago, and all my kids have married and moved away. I don't play golf, and I've got no hobbies. Dempster-Torrey has been my whole life. Jack knew that, knew how lost I'd be without an office to come to and problems to solve. So he kept me on, bless him.''

"Very kind of him," Cone says, looking down at the cigarette in his stained fingers. "But that doesn't sound like the John J. Dempster I've been hearing about."

"Oh, you'll hear a lot of bad things about him," Trale says cheerfully. "And most of them will be true. I'm not going to tell you he was a saint; he wasn't. But do you know anyone who is?"

"I heard he was ruthless and brutal in his business dealings."

The CFO frowns. "Ruthless and brutal? Well . . . maybe. But when you're wheeling and dealing on the scale that Dempster was, you can't afford to play pattycake. He was hard when he had to be hard."

"So he made enemies along the way?"

"Sure he did. The police asked me to make out a list. I told them it wouldn't be a list, it would be a book!"

He smiles at the recollection. He has the complexion of a healthy baby, and his mild blue eyes look out at the world with wonder and amusement. Small pink ears are set flat to his skull, and his lips are so red they might be rouged. It is a doll's head, finely molded porcelain, with every detail from black lashes to dimpled chin painted just so.

"How long have you been with Dempster-Torrey, Mr. Trale?"

"From the beginning. I was the bookkeeper with the Torrey Machine Works up in Quincy, Massachusetts, when John Dempster came to work for us as sales manager. Within a year he had doubled our revenues. And a year after that he married Teresa Torrey and was made vice president."

"Oh-ho," Cone says, lighting another Camel. "He married the boss's daughter, did he?"

"He did. But he'd have been made vice president even if he hadn't. Sanford Torrey knew what a wizard he had in J.J. Also, Sanford and his wife were worried about their daughter. She had plenty of beaux, but they didn't stay around long. Have you met Teresa?"

"Yeah, I met her."

"And what do you think?"

"Off the wall."

"Yes," Trale says sorrowfully, "that's what other young

men thought—but John Dempster saw something in her. She's really a dear, loving woman, Mr. Cone. When my wife was ill, she couldn't do enough for us. I'll be eternally grateful. John saw that side of her—the warm affection, the innocent openness. Yes, he married the boss's daughter, but there was more to it than that. I may be a foolish old romantic, but I've always thought that he loved her and married her for the qualities he knew he himself lacked: sympathy, sweet naiveté, absolute honesty.''

"But it was also a financial leg up for him."

"Of course. A year after the marriage, the company became Dempster-Torrey—notice that his name came first!—and he started his campaign of acquisitions and mergers, diversifying into areas that had nothing to do with our original business. I went along for the ride, and what a ride it turned out to be!"

"How did this Sanford Torrey like what Dempster was doing?"

"He and his wife were killed in a plane crash a few years after John Dempster began putting the conglomerate together. It turned out that Sanford had left everything he owned, including a majority interest in Dempster-Torrey, to Teresa. But I guess he had some reservations about John Dempster, because he tied up his daughter's inheritance in a trust fund that J.J. couldn't touch. But he didn't have to be afraid of Teresa being left destitute. John took the company public, and it tripled the value of the trust. Provision has been made for the three sons, but she is still a very, very wealthy woman."

Cone stirs restlessly. "This is all interesting, Mr. Trale. Good background stuff. But it really doesn't cut any mustard with what I'm supposed to be doing—finding out who's behind the eighteen cases of industrial sabotage to Dempster-Torrey plants and equipment."

Unexpectedly, Trale smiles. "Those accidents," he says, "they infuriated J.J., but I never could see that they were such a big deal. Every large corporation suffers the same outrages occasionally. But John thought there was a plot against us."

"You don't think so?"

"It's possible, but I doubt it. Insurance covered most of

our losses, and they never affected our basic financial structure.''

"Did your common stock drop after each of the incidents?"

"Oh, sure. But it came right back up again."

"And what's happened to the stock since Dempster's murder?"

The little man pulls a face. "Not good," he says. "I estimate the total value of our common stock has dropped about thirty percent since his death."

"Still falling?"

"It seems to have stabilized the last few days. Wall Street is waiting to see who'll be named the new CEO."

Timothy punches out his cigarette and takes a deep breath. "Mr. Trale, I'm going to throw a wild idea at you. It's something I've been kicking around ever since I was handed this file. I gotta tell you, I haven't got any hard evidence. But you have a helluva lot more business savvy than I do, so I'd like to get your reaction."

"All right," the CFO says mildly, "let's hear your idea."

"Suppose, just suppose, some corporate raider wants to make a move on Dempster-Torrey. He's got to—"

"Whoa!" Trale protests, putting up a white palm. "Hold your horses. You're talking about a takeover of almost three billion dollars. That's *billion*, with a capital B."

"I know that," Cone says patiently. "And I could name you a dozen pirates—American, English, Australian—who could raise that kind of loot. What if some takeover bandit gets the bright idea that he can force down the price of Dempster-Torrey stock and cut the cost of the raid? So before he starts buying, he engineers a program of industrial sabotage, figuring that he's saving money every time Dempster-Torrey stock dips even a point."

"Assuming what you say is true, it didn't work. As I told you, Mr. Cone, the price of the stock didn't decline that much following the incidents, and it came right back up again."

The Wall Street dick stares at him.

Simon Trale returns the stare, then begins biting at his thumbnail. "I see what you're getting at," he says, his voice suddenly bleak. "The acts of sabotage didn't have the desired effect, so the corporate raider, if he exists, murdered John J. Dempster.''

"*Had* him murdered. I know a little about violent crime, Mr. Trale, and Dempster's death had all the earmarks of a contract kill. Two wackos on a motorcycle with a submachine gun. They were hired hands. And it worked. You just told me the total value of Dempster-Torrey common stock has dropped about thirty percent. What a bonanza for some bandido who's after your company.''

"Wait a minute," Trale says, visibly upset. "First of all, about two years ago we restructured the corporation to make a takeover extremely difficult and expensive. Since then I've heard absolutely nothing about anyone making a move on us."

"The wife is always the last to know," Cone says, but the other man ignores that.

"Second, if anyone has accumulated even five percent of Dempster-Torrey stock, he'd have to file with the SEC informing them of the purchase and stating his intentions."

Cone pauses to light another cigarette. "Come on, Mr. Trale," he says, "you know better than that. Let's say four rich outlaws are sitting around a ginmill somewhere, having a few snorts, and one of them says, 'Hey, what say we put the XYZ Corporation into play.' So they all agree to have a fling. Each man will pick up four percent of XYZ's stock, so no SEC statement has to be filed—correct? But between them they'll be holding sixteen percent. In addition to that, they'll tip off some friendly arbitrageurs to start buying XYZ. And all this time they're trading as individuals. There's nothing on paper to show they're working in cahoots. That'll come later when they figure they've got the muscle to make their move. Then it's goodbye XYZ."

"A very imaginative scenario, Mr. Cone," the CFO says worriedly.

"But possible—isn't it?"

"Yes, it's possible."

"Damned right. It's been done before and it'll be done again."

"And you think that is what's happening to Dempster-Torrey?"

"I don't know," Cone says. "I told you it's just a theory. But I can't spot any holes in it—can you?"

"I just can't believe that any corporate raider would murder Dempster just to inflate his profits."

"You can't believe it because you're a moral man with no more than a normal share of greed. But believe me, there are guys on the Street who'll run a bulldozer over their grandma to make a buck."

Trale is silent. Suddenly he looks even smaller, shrunken and defeated. "Maybe I should retire," he says in a low voice. "Jack Dempster played rough, and I went along with him. That was *business*. But murder? Never! I get the feeling that the world has passed me by. I don't recognize it anymore. I've become obsolete."

"Nah," Timothy says, reaching out to pat the little man's shoulder. "You're not obsolete, and you're not going to resign. I need your help."

"Yes?" Trale says, looking up. "What can I do?"

"You have contacts on Wall Street?"

"Of course. A lot of them. . . . Oh, I understand. You want me to find out if there are any rumors about an attempted takeover of Dempster-Torrey."

"Right," Cone says approvingly. "I've got a few snitches myself, but nothing like what a man in your position must have."

It buoys Trale, and he straightens up in his chair, squares his shoulders. "Yes," he says, "I can do that. I have a number of chits out on the Street, and I'll call them in."

"Just what I was hoping you'd say. How long do you think it'll take?"

"Not long. Probably by tomorrow."

"Good enough. You'll let me know?"

"Of course. As soon as I have anything definite—for or against."

"Thanks," Cone says. "Now I've got a couple of more short questions and then I'll let you off the hook. You told me that John Dempster loved his wife, and I accept that. As a matter of fact, Teresa told me they had a happy marriage. But I also heard that he was playing around."

"What does that have to do with industrial sabotage?"

"Probably nothing," Cone admits. "But I just like to know as much as I can about the people involved. Was John Dempster a tomcat, Mr. Trale?" And then, knowing when to lie, Timothy adds, "Several people have told me he was."

"What people told you that?"

Cone sighs. "You're stalling, Mr. Trale. If you don't want to answer, tell me and I'll accept it. And go on believing what I've heard."

The CFO hesitates a long moment. "It can do no harm now," he says finally. "And besides, too many people know to try to keep it a secret. It's true, Mr. Cone: Dempster was a womanizer. It was almost a carryover from his business methods. When he saw something he wanted, he went after it, regardless of the cost, the risk, or how long it might take. He was that way in his pursuit of women as well. But he always went back to Teresa. I know that for a fact."

"Uh-huh," Cone says, figuring the Security Chief, Theodore Brodsky, was probably right on the button when he implied Dempster and Eve Bookerman were having an affair. "Thanks for the talk; it's been a help. I'll wait for your call on takeover rumors."

They rise, shake hands, start out. But Timothy pauses at the door. "One final question, Mr. Trale: Do you know David Dempster?"

"I've met him," the other man says.

"Do you happen to know if he's married?"

"Divorced. About five years ago, as I recall."

"Has he remarried?"

"I don't know. Why are you interested in David Dempster?"

"I'm trying to figure out the guy," Cone says, leaving the Chief Financial Officer to wonder what that meant.

He slouches into Samantha Whatley's office, and she looks up.

"I'm busy," she says.

"So am I," he says. "Puddling around in this heat, doing God's work. I need a couple of things."

She tosses her pen onto the desk and sighs. "Make it short and sweet."

"That's not what you said the other night."

She looks around nervously. "Keep your voice down." She still believes their co-workers are unaware of their relationship, but he thinks a few of the other dicks guess what's going on.

"I need a rental car," he says. "This Dempster-Torrey

thing is spreading out, and I've got to get around. Tell H.H.
the client will okay the expense."

"How do you know—did you ask them?"

"No, I didn't ask them. Come on, don't bust my balls, just
get me some wheels."

"I'll try. That's it?"

"No, that isn't it. I want you to pull a telephone scam for
me. I'd do it myself, but it needs a woman's voice."

"I don't know," she says doubtfully. "Is it important?"

"It's not my main lead, it's sort of a fallback position. You
know what that is, don't you?"

"Yeah," she says in a low voice. "I fall back and you
jump my bones. All right, what's the scoop?"

He explains: She is to call the office of David Dempster
Associates, Inc., and speak only to the secretary. If Dempster
answers, hang up. She is to tell the secretary that she's an old
friend of Mrs. Dempster but hasn't seen her for years. Now
she's in town for a few days and would love to chat with her
old school chum. But she understands Mrs. Dempster has
been divorced, and she doesn't have her new address and
phone number or even the last name she's using now. Could
the secretary help her out?"

"What's Mrs. Dempster's first name?" Sam asks.

"Don't know."

"Shithead!" she says wrathfully. "How can I claim to be
the woman's old school chum if I don't know her first
name?"

"You can finagle it. At least it's worth a try."

He gives her the number and she dials.

"Hello, there!" she carols. "Is this the office of David
Dempster? Well, my name is Irma Plotnick, and I'm an old
friend of Mrs. Dempster—school pals, you know. I'm in
town for a few days—South Bend, Indiana, is my home—
and I was hoping to get together with Mrs. Dempster. Well, a
mutual friend tells me she's divorced now. I tried her at the
number I have for her, but she's no longer there. So I guess
she didn't get the apartment as part of the settlement—right,
dear? Well, goodness, I don't even know what name she's
using now, let alone where she's living. Anyway, dear, I was
hoping you'd be able to give me the name she's using, her
address—and the phone number if you have it. I so want to
get together with her and talk about old times. . . . You do?

Oh, that's great! Now just wait half-a-mo until I get a pen. All right, I'm all set now. Uh-huh. Uh-huh. Uh-huh. I've got it. Thank you so much, dear. You've been a love and I'll certainly tell her when I see her. 'Bye now!"

Whatley hangs up and skids the scratch paper she's been scribbling on across the desk. "Name, address, and phone number," she says triumphantly. "How did you like that performance?"

"Not bad," Cone says grudgingly. "But long-winded. When you're pulling a telephone con, keep it as brief as you can. The best lies are short ones."

"I should have known better than to expect thanks from you," Sam says. "Now take off and let me get some work done."

"One final question that's been bothering me," he says. "If a guy who plays around a lot is called a womanizer, what do you call a woman who does the same thing—a manizer?"

Sam points at the door. "Out!" she says.

Four

IT RAINS HARD that night, breaking the back of the heat wave. When Cone slogs down Broadway to work—only a half-hour late this time—the air is breathable and the sky is clear.

The new receptionist at Haldering & Co. hands him a telephone message on a pink slip: *Call Simon Trale at Dempster-Torrey, Inc.* Cone carries the message and his brown-bagged breakfast into his office. He has a chomp of buttered bialy and a gulp of black coffee before he phones Trale.

"Good morning, Mr. Cone."

"'Morning. I hope you have good news."

"Good news for us, but I'm afraid you will be disappointed. I spoke to a half-dozen of my most knowledgeable contacts. None has heard a word about anyone planning a raid on Dempster-Torrey. To be quite frank, they thought the idea implausible. The way we're structured would make any pirate think twice before he made a run at us."

"All right," Cone says, "I'll accept that. Thanks for your help, Mr. Trale. I'll be in touch if I get another brainstorm."

He hangs up, lights his third cigarette of the day, finishes his breakfast. So now he's back to square one. That's okay; he's been there before.

But the big question remains: Who would benefit from the death of John J. Dempster? Could his wife have learned of his infidelities and hired a couple of punks to ace him? Unlikely. If she knew about his dedicated search for the perfect bang, she probably didn't give a damn; she had her bonsai—and all the money in the world.

Ditto the underlings at Dempster-Torrey. They might think their boss was a double-dyed bastard, but they had high-paying jobs and weren't about to scratch the fount from whom all blessings flowed. The one exception might be Eve Bookerman: an energetic and brainy lady who was sleeping with J.J.

Maybe he threatened to dump her for a younger twist, or maybe she coveted his job. Either one would be motive enough for her to take out a contract on the Chairman and CEO.

A discharged or disgruntled employee? Another possibility. But as Brodsky said, that would narrow the list of suspects to ten thousand. Where do you start digging into something like that?

And then there's David Dempster, that prig. But what reason could he have for putting his brother down? Unless he was hurting for cash and needed an inheritance.

At that moment, as if reading his mind, Sid Apicella comes into his office. He's gripping a sheet of scratch paper.

"You and your lousy 'one phone call,'" he says grumpily. "It took me four calls and almost half a day to get any info on David Dempster. How the hell do you get other people to do your job for you?"

"Boyish charm," Cone says.

"You've got about as much charm as my wife's old poodle—and that monster farts, has fleas, and a breath that would knock your socks off. Anyway, David Dempster Associates, Inc., is a legit outfit that's been in business about twelve years. They do corporate publicity and public relations, and seem to be doing just great. Good cash flow and some heavy clients."

"Bull*shit!*" the Wall Street dick says angrily. "I was up at their place, and it's practically a hole-in-the-wall. Dempster's private office is not much bigger than this latrine."

"So? What do you need in the publicity business? A telephone and a lot of good contacts—right?"

"Maybe. But with all the high-powered PR outfits on the Street, I can't see Dempster attracting any blue-chip clients. How much money they got?"

"The corporation? They keep a minimum hundred-thousand balance. When it gets over that, Dempster pays himself a bonus."

"A sweet setup. And what's he worth?"

"Personally?" the CPA says, consulting his notes. "About four mil, give or take. How does that grab you?"

"It doesn't," Cone says. "You just blew another of my half-assed ideas out of the water. The second time that's happened in the last hour. What a great morning this is. But thanks anyway, Sid; that's one I owe you."

"*One?*" Apicella shouts, rubbing his rosy schnoz furiously. "You owe me so much I'll never get even."

He stomps out after tossing his scrawled notes onto the desk. Cone leans forward to read them, then sits back and lights another Camel. So David Dempster has a personal net worth of four million. That doesn't sound like a man who'd have his brother chilled just to inherit a few more bucks—unless the guy is suffering from terminal greed.

But something smells. Cone well knows that public relations outfits deal with images and perceptions. It's a way of life that carries over into the way the flacks do business: impressive offices, flashy secretaries, a hyperactive staff, and autographed photos on the walls of the boss posing with important people. Dempster has a telephone booth office, one pleasant but plain secretary, and a picture on the wall of his dead hound.

And from this mom-and-pop bodega the cash flow has enabled him to amass a fortune? That just doesn't add up.

He chews it over for a while. Then, groaning, he gets to his feet and wanders down the corridor to the office of Fred Burgess, another Haldering & Co. investigator. Fred is on the phone, but when he sees Cone standing there, he motions him in, points to the armchair alongside his littered desk.

"Marcia," he's saying, "I've already apologized twice, but if you want, I'll do it again. You're the one who picked the Japanese restaurant. I'm not blaming you, but it was the combination of the sashimi and sake that did it. How the hell can you know how much you're drinking when they serve it in thimbles? It didn't hit me until we got up to your place. All that raw fish and rice wine. . . . Marcia, I've already explained I couldn't make it to the bathroom. So your aquarium seemed the best bet. I know it killed all your guppies, but I'll buy you more guppies. Marcia? Marcia?"

He replaces the phone. "She hung up," he says gloomily.

"Have a pleasant evening?" Cone asks.

"Go to hell," Burgess says. "It took me weeks to get this date. She's gorgeous, got a great job on the Street, and beautiful digs up around Gramercy Park. I thought sure last night was going to be *the* night. Then I have to vomit into her goddamned fish tank and kill all her goddamned guppies. I guess I'm on her shit list now.''

"Good detecting," Cone says. "Look, I didn't come in here to discuss your love life. You still got that collection of business cards?''

Burgess, a youngish, fattish, liverish guy, stares at him suspiciously. "Yeah, I still got it. And I'm going to keep it.''

"One card," Timothy says. "Just one. On loan.''

"What's in it for me?''

"I'll tell you how to bring Marcia around.''

"Deal. How do I do it?''

"Buy her the most expensive tropical fish you can afford. Something really exotic with big fins. Like a Veiltail Angelfish. Have it delivered to her apartment with a simple, heartfelt note like, 'I'm sorry I puked in your aquarium.'''

"Yeah," Fred says, "that might work. What do you need?''

"The business card of a writer.''

"Writers don't have business cards. But I got one from a magazine editor. Will that do?''

"It'll have to.''

Burgess pulls out a long file of business cards he's collected over the years at cocktail parties, conventions, and press conferences. He thumbs through them, pulls one out, hands it over.

"Waldo Sperling," Cone reads. "Feature Editor, *Zebu Magazine*. What the hell does Zebu mean?''

"If you did crossword puzzles, you'd know. It's an Asian ox. But don't worry about it; the magazine is out of business and it can mean anything you want it to.''

"Okay," Cone says, rising, "I'll give it a try. Do I look like a Waldo to you?''

"To me," says Burgess, "you look like a schmuck.''

Cone goes back to his office and digs out the name, address, and phone number of David Dempster's ex-wife. He dials and waits for nine rings before a woman's voice comes on.

"H'lo?" she says sleepily.

"Am I speaking to Miss Dorothy Blenke, the former Mrs. David Dempster?''

"Yeah," she says, "that's right. What time is it?''

"Almost eleven-thirty, Miss Blenke.''

"Jesus! I got a lunch date at noon. Who the hell are you?"

"My name is Waldo Sperling, and I'm the Feature Editor of *Zebu Magazine*. We're planning an article on the life of the late John J. Dempster, Chairman of the Board of Dempster-Torrey, and I'm trying to talk to as many people as possible who knew him."

"I don't want to talk about it."

"You knew John Dempster, Miss Blenke?"

"Of course I knew him. Better than most."

"All I ask is a few moments of your time. To get your personal reactions to the man. His good points and his bad points."

"He didn't have any," she says.

"Didn't have any what?"

"Good points."

"Just a few moments at your convenience," Cone urges. "If you don't wish your name to appear in print, we'll respect that. But we would prefer to use your name in the article and perhaps publish your photograph since you obviously represent a key source for our story."

"Listen," she says, "you got my address?"

"Yes, I do, Miss Blenke."

"Okay," she says. "I got this stupid lunch date I'm late for already, but if you can be here around two-thirty or so, I'll give you some time."

"Thank you very much," Cone says humbly. "The name is Sperling. Waldo Sperling."

He hangs up, grinning, and sees Samantha Whatley standing in his doorway. "I heard that, Waldo," she says. "Kind of long-winded, wasn't it?"

"Up yours," he says.

She growls at him. "Go pick up your rental car," she says, and he winks at her.

So there he is, tooling around Manhattan in a new Ford Escort GT and feeling like King Shit. As usual, traffic is murder, but Cone doesn't care; he's got time to kill, and he wants to get the feel of the car. Even the frustrations of stop-and-go city driving are better than cramming aboard a bus or trying to flag down a cab.

But there is the problem of parking. Cone finally finds a slot on East 83rd Street, just west of First Avenue. He locks up and walks back to Dorothy Blenke's address on Third Avenue, north of 85th. It's a sliver of a high-rise, faced with alternating vertical bands of precast concrete and green-tinted glass. The doorman is dressed like someone's idea of a Hungarian hussar, with a braided jacket, frogged half-cape, and a purple plume hanging limply from his varnished shako.

"I have an appointment with Dorothy Blenke," Cone tells him.

"Not in," the hussar says. "Try later."

"She said she'd be here at two-thirty. It's past that now."

The doorman looks at Cone's shoddy corduroy suit with some distaste. "I'm telling you," he says, "she's not back yet. Why don't you take a nice walk around the block."

"Splendid idea," Cone says, and does exactly that. He takes his time, looking in store windows and gawking at the construction work going on in the neighborhood. He returns to Blenke's high-rise and looks inquiringly at the doorman.

"Not yet," the hussar says.

So Cone circles another block, smoking a cigarette, and returns to the apartment house.

"Yeah," the doorman says, "she just came in." Then, formally: "Who shall I say is calling?"

"Waldo Sperling from *Zebu Magazine*."

"Zebu?" the hussar says. "What's that?"

"It's an Asian ox," Cone says. "I thought everyone knew."

The doorman calls on the intercom, talks a moment, then turns to Cone. "Okay," he says, "you can go up. Apartment 18-A. To your left as you get off the elevator."

"Thanks," Cone says. "I admire your uniform."

"Yeah?" the hussar says. "Try wearing it in the summer. You sweat bullets."

He unlocks the inner door, and the Wall Street dick enters a narrow lobby lined with ceramic tiles. It has all the joyful ambience of an underground crypt, and a couple of desiccated ficus trees add the proper mortuary touch. The automatic elevator is more cheerful, and music is coming from somewhere. Timothy recognizes the tune: "Puttin' on the Ritz."

The woman who opens the door of Apartment 18-A is a tall, glitzy blonde with too much of everything: hair, eye shadow, lipstick, bosom, hips, and perfume. And there are three olives in the oversized martini she's gripping.

"You a cop?" she demands.

"Oh, no," Cone says. "No, no, no. Waldo Sperling from *Zebu Magazine*." He proffers his business card, but she doesn't even glance at it.

"I hate cops," she says darkly. "Well, come on in. Would you like a drinkie-poo?"

"No, thank you. But you go right ahead."

"I intend to," Dorothy Blenke says. "What a shitty lunch that was. The guy looked like Godzilla, and he's *on salary*, for God's sake. Hey, I like the way you dress. You just don't give a damn—right?"

"Right," Cone says.

"That's the way I am, too," the woman says. "I just don't give a damn. Now you sit in that fantastic tub chair—twelve-hundred from Bloomie's—and I'll curl up here on the couch."

"From Bloomie's?" Cone asks.

"Yep. Three grand." She gives him a vapid smile. "I even got Bloomie's printed on my panties. Wanna see?"

"Not at the moment," Cone says, "but I appreciate the offer. Lovely home you have here, Miss Blenke."

But the living room is like the woman herself—too much of everything: furniture, lamps, rugs, paintings, knick-knacks, vases, silk flowers, even ashtrays. The place over-flows.

"May I smoke?" Cone asks.

"Why not?" she says with that out-of-focus smile. "This is Liberty Hall. Let it all hang out."

He offers her a Camel, but she shakes her head. So he lights up while she works on her drink. Two of the three olives have disappeared along with half of the martini. Cone figures he better make this fast.

"Miss Blenke," he starts, "as I told you on the phone, *Zebu Magazine* is—"

"What the hell is that?" she interrupts. "I've never seen it on the newsstands."

"Controlled circulation," Cone explains. "By subscription only. We go only to top executives in the financial community."

"No kidding?" she says with that bleary smile again. "I don't suppose you want to sell your mailing list."

"I'm afraid not," Cone says, and tries again. "Miss

Blenke, as I told you on the phone, we're planning a defini-
tive article on John J. Dempster, and I'm trying to—"

"I don't want to talk about it," she says.

Cone, who's beginning to feel like that hussar-doorman—
sweating bullets—plunges ahead. "So we'd be very interested in your personal recollections of the late John
Dempster."

"Late," she says gloomily. "The sonofabitch was always
late."

"I don't understand, Miss Blenke."

"There's a lot you don't understand," she says porten-
tously. "Just take my word for it."

They sit silently while she takes small, ladylike sips from
her giant martini. The third olive has disappeared, and she
peers into the tumbler, puzzled.

She's a big, florid woman with shards of great beauty. But
it's all gone to puff now. It could be the sauce, but Cone
reckons that's only a symptom, not the malady. Thwarted
ambitions, soured dreams, chilled loves—all came before the
booze. Now her life is tottering, ready to fall. It's there in her
glazed eyes and sappy grin.

"You were married to David Dempster for—how long?"
he asks, determined to be gentle with this ruin.

"The nerd? That's what I call him: Lord Nerd. Years and
years."

"No children?"

"No, thank God. His kids wouldn't have been much anyway. He just hasn't got the jism. But I'll say this for him: The
alimony checks are never late."

"And what were his relations to John Dempster?"

"The nerd's?" she says, startled. "He was John's
brother."

"I know," Cone says patiently. "I meant their personal
relationship. How did they get along?"

"Not like gin and vermouth," she says. "Hey, my drink is
gone. Must be evaporation. Have you ever noticed that New
York City has a very high rate of evaporation?"

"Yeah," Cone says, "I've noticed."

She heaves herself off the couch, goes into the kitchen. He
hears her banging around in there, humming a song he can't
identify. He sits hunched forward in the velvet-covered tub

chair, hands clasped between his knees, and wonders if there's another line of business he can get into.

She comes back in a few moments, still humming, with a full tumbler. She plops down on the couch again and crosses her knees. Like many heavy women, she's got good legs and slender ankles. "One martini and I can feel it," she says. "Two martinis and anyone can feel it. What were we talking about?"

"David and John Dempster. How they felt about each other."

"Yeah," she says, "that's right. Well, Jack thought Dave was a washout—which he is. Dave was always bitching because Jack wouldn't give him the Dempster-Torrey PR account, but Jack knew better than that."

"Oh? When was this?"

"Years ago. Lord Nerd finally gave up. He gave up on a lot of things. Jack never gave up. He'd never take no for an answer."

"He must have been quite a man to build a business like that."

"Jack? He was Napoleon, Hitler, and Attila the Hun all rolled into one. You never knew what he was going to do next. That was the fun of him."

Cone stares at her. "But he always went back to his wife," he says softly.

"That dingbat? She'd blow away in a breeze. I'll never, till the day I die, understand what he saw in her. I'll bet she puts on her nightgown before she takes off her underwear. But I don't want to talk about it."

"If you don't mind my asking, Miss Blenke, why did you divorce David Dempster?"

"Galloping boredom," she says promptly. "You've met the guy?"

"Yes."

"Then you know. He'd have to drink Drano to get his blood moving. Jack had all the get-up-and-go in that family. He could work twenty-four hours and then party for another twenty-four. Dave has to have his nappy-poo every afternoon or he'll collapse. The funny thing was . . . What's the funny thing?"

"Something about the brothers?"

"Yeah. Jack was three years younger, but usually it's the older brother who's the big success. Am I right?"

"Usually. But not always. Did you socialize much with John and his wife? When you and David were married?"

"Socialize? Jesus, if we saw them twice a year it was a lot. Those two guys couldn't stand each other, I couldn't stand that ding-a-ling Teresa, and I guess she felt the same way about me. It was not what you'd call close family ties."

Timothy wants to ask her the key questions, straight out, but hasn't the courage. Besides, he has a fairish idea of what had happened.

"Thank you very much, Miss Blenke," he says, rising. "You've made an important contribution to our article. I'll make certain the writer calls you to confirm the accuracy of your quotes."

"You're going so soon?" she says. "Leaving me all alone?"

"Yeah," he says. "I gotta. What was that song you were humming?"

"Song? What song?"

"You were humming it while you were in the kitchen."

"Oh, that . . . 'It Had to Be You.'"

"Uh-huh," he says. "Thanks. Nice meeting you, Miss Blenke."

He figures it's too late to go back to the office. And besides, what the hell would he do when he got there? So, sitting in his rented Escort, he pulls out his tattered list of names and addresses. David Dempster's home is in the Murray Hill section, not out of his way. Cone drives south, planning to eyeball the place—just for the fun of it.

It turns out to be a limestone townhouse on East 38th between Park and Madison. A smart building, well maintained, with pots of ivy on windowsills and small ginkgo trees in tubs flanking the elegant entrance. The place looks like bucks, and the Wall Street dick guesses it went co-op years ago.

He double-parks across the street and dashes over, dodging oncoming cars. He scans the names on the bell plate. There it is: David Dempster, third floor. There are only five apartments in the building, all apparently floor-throughs and the top one probably a duplex. Nice. On the drive back to his loft, Cone spends the time stalled in traffic estimating what a floor-through in a Murray Hill townhouse might cost. Whatever, it wouldn't much hurt a guy with a net worth of four mil.

He gets back to his own floor-through to find that Cleo has pawed open the cabinet under the sink, plucked out a plastic bottle of detergent and gnawed a hole in it. Then apparently the demented cat jumped up and down on the punctured bottle. The detergent is spread all over the linoleum. And the cat is sitting gravely in the midst of it, paws together and a "Who—me?" expression on its ugly mug.

"You dirty rat!" Cone yells, and Cleo darts under the bathtub.

It takes twenty minutes to clean up the mess. By this time, Cleo is giving him the seductive ankle-rub treatment along with piteous mews.

"I don't want to talk about it," Cone says.

He's in the kitchenette, opening a beer, when the wall phone jangles.

"Yeah," he says.

"Mr. Timothy Cone?" A woman's voice.

"That's right."

"Miss Bookerman calling. Just a moment, please, sir."

Eve Bookerman comes on the line. "Hello!" she says breathlessly. "Forgive me for calling you at home, but I tried your office and you weren't in. Mr. Haldering gave me your home phone number. I hope you aren't angry."

"Nah," he says, "that's okay."

"I haven't heard from you and wondered if you were making any progress on the industrial sabotage. Simon Trale told me about your suggestion that it might be a corporate raider. That was a brilliant idea. Brilliant!"

"Brilliant," Cone says. "Except it was a dud."

"But it shows you're thinking imaginatively," she says. "I like that. Do you have anything new to report?"

"Nope. More questions than answers. I think you and I better have another meet, Miss Bookerman."

"I'm tied up most of tomorrow, but I'll make time if it's important."

"I think it might be better if we talked outside your office."

Long pause. Then: "Oh? Well, let's see what we can arrange. I'm working late tonight, and then I've got a dinner appointment. I should be home by eleven o'clock. Is that too late for you?''

"I'll still be awake."

She laughs gaily, but it sounds tinny. "You have my home address, don't you? Suppose you come up here at eleven. I'll tell the concierge you're expected. Will it take long?''

"Probably not. Maybe a half-hour."

"Splendid! See you tonight, Mr. Cone."

He hangs up, stares at the dead phone a moment. He figures he'll come down hard on her. She dresses for success; she can take it.

About a week ago he bought a corned beef that weighed almost five pounds. He spent an entire evening boiling it up, spooning off the scum and changing the water to get rid of the salt. While it was cooking, he dumped in more peppercorns, bay leaves, and garlic cloves—just as the butcher had instructed.

When he could dig a fork into it, he figured it was done. By that time the loft was filled with a savory fog, and Cleo was trying to claw up his leg to get at the stove top. Cone chilled the boiled beef for twenty-four hours, then he and the cat began to demolish it. The first night he had it with boiled potatoes, but after that he just had the meat and beer.

He's eaten it every night for almost a week now, except for that one dinner at Sam's, but there's still some left. It's getting a little green and iridescent around the edges, but it tastes okay. It's not too tender, but he's got strong teeth, and so does Cleo.

So that's what the two have that night, finally finishing the beef, with enough crumbs left over to see the cat through the night.

After cleaning up, Cone lies down on his mattress.

"It's called a nappy-poo," he tells Cleo.

He dozes fitfully, wakes about nine-thirty. Then he showers and dons a clean T-shirt that's been laundered so many times it's like gray gauze. He straps on the ankle holster stuffed with the short-barreled S&W .357 Magnum and sallies forth.

Eve Bookerman lives in a high-rise near Sutton Place. Her building makes Dorothy Blenke's look like a pup tent. It seems to soar into the clouds, all glass and stainless steel, and there's a Henry Moore sculpture on a pedestal in front of the splendid entrance.

The concierge is wearing a claw-hammer coat, starched shirt, and white bow tie. He inspects the Wall Street dick and sniffs.

"May I be of service?" he says in a fluty voice.

"Timothy Cone to see Miss Eve Bookerman."

The twit isn't happy about it, but he makes the call, murmuring into the phone.

"You're expected, sir," he reports. "Apartment B as in Benjamin on the thirty-first floor."

"Floor as in Frederick?" Cone says.

"Beg pardon, sir?"

But Timothy is heading toward the elevator bank, wading through a rug so thick and soft he'd like to strip bare-ass and roll around on it.

No music in the elevator this time, but a lingering scent of perfume. The high-speed lift goes so fast that Cone has a scary image of the damned thing bursting through the roof and taking off for the stars.

More plush carpeting in the thirty-first-floor corridor. The door to Apartment B as in Benjamin is open a few inches, and Eve Bookerman is peering out.

"Ah," she says, "Mr. Cone. Do come in."

She swings the door wide, he takes off his cap and follows her into a foyer about as big as his loft, with black and white tiles set in a diagonal checkerboard pattern. She leads him into a living room with floor-to-ceiling windows overlooking the East River.

Some expensive decorator has done a bang-up job. The whole place is right out of *Architectural Digest,* and Cleo would have a ball destroying that collection of Steuben glass. It's all so clean and polished that Cone wonders if he should remain standing.

"Nice place," he offers.

"Thank you," she says lightly. "I've come a long way from Bensonhurst. I'm having a cognac, Mr. Cone. Would you like one?"

"Yeah, that'd be great."

She brings him a snifter and places the bottle on a Lucite table between two rocking chairs. They're in one dim corner of a room that goes on forever. Noguchi lamps are lighted, but it would take a battery of TV floodlights to chase the shadows in that cavern.

She raises her glass. "To your health," she says.

"And yours. How's the ear?"

"My," she says, "you do remember things. It's much better, thank you."

"Any news on who takes over as CEO?"

"No," she says shortly. "The Board appointed a special subcommittee to come up with recommendations, but they haven't reported yet."

He looks at her closely. "Lots of luck," he says.

She giggles like a schoolgirl. "I haven't a prayer."

"Sure you have," he tells her. "You were the person closest to John Dempster, weren't you?"

She stiffens. "What do you mean by that?"

"Listen, Miss Bookerman," he says, "thanks for the brandy, but let's not play games. Okay? I'll ask you questions and you answer. If you don't want to, that's your choice. But it means I'll have to get the answers from someone else. I'm hoping you'll save me time."

"I fail to see what my relationship to John Dempster has to do with your investigation of industrial sabotage."

He sighs. "Look, you have your own way of working—right? And I have mine. You've got to give me wiggle room. All those attacks on Dempster-Torrey property—what do you want me to do: go to eighteen different places around the country and investigate cases that have already been tossed by the local cops and your own security people with no results? I'd just be spinning my wheels. Does that make sense to you?"

She nods dumbly, takes a sip of her cognac.

"So I figure the solution—if there is one—is right here in New York. I also think Dempster's death is tied in with the assaults against your property. His murder was the final act of sabotage."

"But why?" she cries. "For what reason?"

He shrugs. "My first idea about a corporate shark on the prowl got shot down, so now I'm looking for another motive. And all I've got to work with are the people involved—like you. That's why I'm putting it to you straight: Did you have a thing going with Dempster?"

She raises her chin defiantly. "You really go for the jugular, don't you? Incredible!"

"You going to answer my question or not?"

"Yes, I had a *thing* going with John J. Dempster—if that's what you want to call it."

"Okay," he says mildly, "that clears the air a little. You knew he was a womanizer?"

She pokes fingers into her blond curls, then tugs them in a gesture of anger. "You have been busy, haven't you? Of course I knew he played around. I worked closely with the man for years, and we had what you call a *thing* for the past three. He cheated on his wife from the moment he was married. But don't get the wrong idea, Mr. Cone. My balling J.J. had nothing to do with my keeping my job or moving up at Dempster-Torrey. I happen to be damned good at what I do. Besides, that wasn't the way Jack worked. If I had said no, I'd still be Chief Operating Officer because he knew I had earned the title. Also, he could have had any other woman he wanted—younger, prettier, skinnier than I."

"You do all right," he says, and she gives him a faint smile. "Tell me something, Miss Bookerman—and this is just curiosity—how come he was such a hotshot with the ladies? His money? Power?"

She shakes her head. "He could have been a cabdriver or a ditchdigger and he'd still be a winning stud. He had energy and drive and—and a forcefulness I've never seen in anyone before and will probably never see again. Physically he wasn't all that handsome. I mean he was hardly a matinee idol. But when he zeroed in, I don't think there's a woman in the world who could have resisted him. And when he wanted to, he could be kind, considerate, generous, loving."

Suddenly she begins weeping, tears spilling from those big, luminous eyes and down her cheeks. She makes no effort to wipe them away. She reaches out with a trembling hand to pour herself more cognac, but Cone takes the bottle, fills her glass, and helps himself to another belt.

"Sorry about that," she says finally, taking a deep breath. "I thought I was all cried out, but I guess I wasn't."

"That's okay," he says. "You're entitled."

She sits back, takes a gulp of her drink. Tonight she's wearing another suit: glossy black gabardine, with a pale pink man-tailored shirt and a ribboned bow at the neck. She looks weary, and there are lines in her face that Cone didn't spot at their first meeting.

He wonders if she's just a nice girl from Bensonhurst who's suddenly found herself in over her head, her mentor gone, her lover dead, and a lot of business pressures she can't handle. But her next comment disabuses him of that notion; she has spunk to spare.

"What the hell has J.J.'s sexual habits got to do with the sabotage and his murder?" she wants to know.

"Listen, I told you I had more questions than answers. When I work a case, I try to collect as much stuff as I can. Ninety percent of it turns out to be junk, but how do you know what's meaningful when you start? So far you've been very cooperative, and I appreciate that. I hope you'll keep it up. You've got a big stake in this."

"What's that supposed to mean?"

"You're the one who hired Haldering and Company. If I can figure out who pulled the sabotage jobs, and maybe who iced your boss, you'll get brownie points with the Board of Directors, won't you? That should help if they're considering you for the CEO job."

She looks at him in amazement. "You're something, you are," she says. "You think of everything. Fantastic! Well, for your information, Mr. Cone, making CEO comes pretty far down on my anxiety list."

"Uh-huh," he says. "Now can we get back to the Q and A for a few more minutes?"

"Sure. Fire away."

"You've met his brother, David Dempster?"

"I've met him."

"What's your take?"

"A neuter."

"How did John Dempster feel about him?"

"Ignored him. He thought David was a joke."

"Did David try to get the Dempster-Torrey PR account?"

"My God, how have you found out these things? Yes, David made a pitch—but that was years ago. Jack turned him down, of course. We set up an in-house publicity and corporate advertising division, and it's worked out very well."

"So there was hostility between the brothers?"

"Not hostility. Just nothing."

"I've talked to Dorothy Blenke, David's ex-wife."

"Have you? I've never met the lady."

"I got the feeling—though she never said yes or no, either way—that maybe John Dempster had a fling with her while she was married to his brother. You know anything about that?"

Eve Bookerman struggles out of the armchair and stands stiffly erect. "Get out!" she yells at him.

"Okay," Timothy says equably. He rises, reaches for his cap.

"No," the woman says, holding up a palm. "Wait a minute. Sit down and finish your drink. I apologize."

They both sit again, stare at each other warily.

"Maybe," she says. "I don't know for sure. But from little things Jack said, it could have been that way."

"There are a lot of 'coulds' and 'maybes' in this file," Cone says. "All right, let's say John and Dorothy had an affair. That was before his thing with you—right?"

She nods.

"And maybe, just maybe, that affair led to David Dempster's divorce. Do you think that's possible?"

"Anything is possible," she says.

"Thank you," he says, "but I knew that when I was four years old." He finishes his drink, rises, takes up his cap. "I appreciate your seeing me."

"I talked too much," she says dully.

"Nah," Cone says. "You really didn't tell me much I hadn't already guessed. Besides, I'm not wired, so who's to know what you did or didn't say. Get a good night's sleep, Miss Bookerman."

"Fat chance," she says bitterly.

Cone rides down in that same scented elevator, flips a hand at the tailcoated gink behind the desk, and exits into a night that's all moon and grazing breeze. He feels loose and restless, and considers his options. He could go directly home. He could drop in at the nearest bar for a nightcap or two. He could call Samantha and see if she's in the mood to entertain a visitor at that hour.

So fifteen minutes later he finds himself double-parked on East 38th Street, scoping the townhouse where David Dempster lives. The third-floor lights are on, front windows opened but screened. Cone can't see anyone moving behind the gauzy curtains.

He sits there for almost a half-hour, smoking two cigarettes to make up for his abstinence in Bookerman's apartment. Finally the third-floor lights go out. Now for the moment of truth: Did the guy sack out or is he planning an excursion? Cone waits patiently for another twenty minutes, but no one comes out of the townhouse.

"What the hell am I doing?" the Wall Street dick asks aloud, and then wonders if he's losing his marbles because he hasn't even got a cat there to listen to him.

Five

IT'S A SATURDAY, and usually he and Samantha spend the day together—and sometimes the night. But she has shopping to do in the afternoon and then, in the evening, she must attend a bridal shower for one of the secretaries at Haldering & Co.

"Gonna miss me?" she asks.

"Nah," he says. "I got a lot of things to do."

"Oh, sure. Like smoking up a storm, slopping vodka, and kicking the cat."

"I wouldn't kick Cleo. Strangle maybe, but not kick."

"How about tomorrow?"

"Let me take a look at my appointment book."

"Keep talking like that, buster, and you'll be singing soprano. Listen, we haven't had pizza for a long time—maybe a week or so. How's about you pick up a big one—half pepperoni for you, half anchovies for me—and bring it over here tomorrow. I've got some salad stuff."

"Sounds good," he says. "Around noon?"

"Make it later," she says. "I've got to read the Sunday *Times*. Unless you were planning a matinee. Were you?"

"The thought had crossed my mind."

"What mind? How about threeish or fourish?"

"How about twoish?"

"Okay," she says agreeably. "We can read the Real Estate Section in bed together."

"Whoopee!" he cries.

He really does have things to do—not a lot, but some. He changes Cleo's litter and damp-mops the linoleum. He takes in his laundry and decides the corduroy suit will do for another week without drycleaning. He goes shopping for beer, vodka, wine, brandy. And he buys a loaf of Jewish rye (without seeds) and a whole garlic salami. It's about two feet long and looks like an elephant's schlong.

Back in the loft, he and Cleo have salami sandwiches, two for him, one for the cat. Cone's sandwiches have hot English mustard smeared on them. Cleo prefers mayonnaise.

He reads *Barron's* as he eats, marveling at all the reports of chicanery on Wall Street. Most of them involve inside trading, stock manipulation, or fraudulent misrepresentation on a company's balance sheet. The Street has its share of gonnifs, and the fact that they wear three-piece pinstripes and carry alligator attaché cases doesn't mitigate their corruption.

What never ceases to amaze Cone is how few of these moneyed crooks are stand-up guys. Once they've been nabbed by the Securities and Exchange Commission or the Federal DA, they sing like canaries, happy to squeal on their larcenous associates, willing to be wired or have their phones tapped so old school chums can share the blame. Cone knows that when you drive a BMW and summer on the Cape, you'd be eager to cooperate with the fuzz if it means probation rather than a year in the slammer. But Timothy has known cheap boosters, purse-snatchers, and yeggs with more honor than that.

"It's money," he tells a snoozing Cleo. "Everyone quotes 'Money is the root of all evil,' but that's not what the Good Book says. It says, 'The *love* of money is the root of all evil.' Big difference."

Cleo is not impressed.

Cone finishes his reading and then falls asleep at the table, bent forward with his head on folded arms. He wakes early in the evening, feeling stiff from his awkward position, with pins and needles in both hands. He stalks up and down the loft, jangling arms and legs to get jazzed up again.

There's a greasy spoon around the corner, run by a Greek who can do nothing right but double-cheeseburgers and home fries with a lot of onions. So that's what Timothy has, sitting at the counter and wondering if this is the way he's going to die someday, toppling off the stool, OD'd on cholesterol.

He returns to the loft and mooches around for almost an hour, smoking two Camels and buying himself another robust drink. He knows what he's going to do that night, but the prospect is so depressing he puts it off as long as possible.

Finally he can postpone it no longer and calls David Dempster.

"Hello?" Dempster says. Cone recognizes that spoony voice.

"Sam?" the Wall Street dick asks.

"No, you've got the wrong number," Dempster says, and hangs up.

So now Cone knows the guy is home, and he has no excuse for stalling. He makes his preparations swiftly: a jelly jar filled with vodka, the lid screwed on tightly; a plastic bag of ice cubes, closed with a metal tie; a fresh pack of cigarettes; a book of matches; a pencil stub; an empty milk carton in case he has to relieve himself.

He gets up to East 38th Street about 8:30 and double-parks across from the limestone townhouse. There's a streetlight right in front of the building, so Cone backs up the Escort to get out of the glare. He still has a good view, and is happy to see the third floor is lighted. In fact, a couple of times David Dempster comes to the front window, pulls the curtains aside, and peers down into the street.

"Waiting for someone, honey?" Cone says softly. He settles down, knowing it's going to be a long night. He figures he'll stay double-parked as long as he can, and if a prowl car rousts him, he'll drive around the block and take up his station again.

One cigarette later, a beige Jaguar Vanden Plus pulls up in front of Dempster's townhouse. It double-parks, a guy gets out, locks up, goes into the building. In a few minutes, Cone sees the shadows of two men moving behind the thin curtains on the third floor.

He hops out of his car, trots across the street, walks purposefully past the Jaguar, and eyeballs the license plate. Back in his Ford, he jots the number on the inside cover of his matchbook. He's no sooner done that when a dark blue, four-door Bentley pulls up behind the parked Jaguar. Guy gets out, locks up, hurries into the townhouse. Then Cone can spot three shadows moving back and forth on the third floor.

He goes through the same drill: crosses the street, takes a long look at the license plate, returns to the Escort to jot down the number. One more and it'll be a poker game, Cone thinks.

But he has to wait almost fifteen minutes before the fourth visitor appears. He arrives in a chauffeured black Daimler that pulls in ahead of the Jaguar. Man gets out, enters the townhouse. Cone doesn't even glance at the third-floor windows; it's a good bet the Daimler owner is going to join the crowd.

But the Wall Street dick has another problem: The chauffeur steps out of the car, slouches against a fender, lights a cigar, and inspects the night sky. Cone decides to give it a try. He crosses the street, glances at the car, then stops as if entranced.

"Wow," he says to the lounging chauffeur. "What kind of a car is that?"

The guy inspects him coldly. He's a big bruiser with shoulders so wide he'd have to go through a door sideways.

"Daimler," he says.

"Expensive?" Cone asks.

"Nah," the guy says. "Just save your bottle caps."

Cone laughs appreciatively. "Mind if I take a look?" he asks.

"Look but don't touch," the guy says.

So the Wall Street dick walks slowly around the Daimler, eyeballing the license plate.

"Beautiful job," he says. "Who's so rich he can afford something like this?"

The chauffeur stares at him. "I thought everyone had one."

Cone knows he's not going to get anything from this tight-mouth, so he returns to his car and adds the Daimler's license number to his list. There's no movement behind the third-floor curtains, and he wonders if it really is a poker game, or bridge or tiddlywinks, and the whole night is going down the drain.

He opens his jar of vodka, takes a sip to lower the level, and tips in two cubes and some ice water from the plastic bag. As he drinks, he adds more cubes and more water, stirring with a forefinger until he's got the mix just right. Then he slouches down, keeping an eye on the townhouse entrance and hoping for action.

It doesn't take too long. In about twenty minutes, three men come out. They stand a few moments on the sidewalk, talking, laughing, gesturing. Under the streetlight they all look well-fed, well-dressed, well-fixed. Pinkie-ring guys, Cone figures, or maybe the blow-dried type. They all shake hands, real pals, and go to their cars. The Daimler pulls away first, then the Jaguar, then the Bentley. Cone watches them go.

Now what the hell was that? he wonders. Obviously not a poker game. And too short a time for them all to get fixed by a call girl in a back bedroom or watch a porn flick on Dempster's VCR. Is the guy dealing crack? Just what in God's name is going down to bring three apparent richniks to Dempster's apartment on a Saturday night? Clients on business? If that's what it was, why three of them at one time? And why couldn't they have met in Dempster's Cedar Street office or consulted by phone?

It's getting close to 10:30, and Cone sits patiently, still watching those third-floor windows. Suddenly the lights go out and Timothy straightens up. Too early for beddy-bye; the guy *has* to be on his way out. And he is. He leaves his building, walks swiftly toward Park Avenue. He passes under the streetlight and Cone definitely makes him as David Dempster. He starts the Escort and moves slowly after his target.

David Dempster turns south on Park Avenue. Cone pulls up to the corner and stops as if he's waiting to make a turn. He watches, hoping the guy isn't just out for an evening stroll. He isn't. About halfway down the block he pauses under the marquee of a residential hotel. The doorman comes out. The two men talk a moment. Dempster takes out his wallet, plucks a bill, slips it to the doorman. Then he unlocks and gets into a white Cadillac Seville sitting in the No Parking zone in front of the hotel.

The action is obvious to Cone: Dempster is greasing the doorman to "rent" a convenient parking space. When the Seville pulls out, Cone completes his turn and follows. There's enough traffic so that chances are good Dempster won't spot a tail even if he's looking for one.

They go west, they go north, farther west, farther north. For a few moments Cone fears the Seville might be heading for the Lincoln Tunnel. The prospect of a late-night hegira through the wilds of New Jersey doesn't fill the Wall Street dick with glee. But no, Dempster drives north on Eighth Avenue to 45th Street, turns west, slows down in the block between Tenth and Eleventh avenues. Awesome neighborhood for anyone in a white Cadillac at night.

But Dempster knows exactly what he's doing. A tenement has been demolished, the vacant area paved, and it now serves as a narrow parking lot. It's completely dark, with a heavy chain across the entrance. Cone stops well back in the shadows and watches. The Cadillac pulls up. A guy comes out of a little hut. Dempster hands him a bill. The chain is unlocked and dropped, the Seville enters.

By the time Dempster comes walking out, Cone has parked alongside a fire hydrant and doused his lights. He isn't worried about a ticket—the client can take care of that—but the possibility of being towed away is a real downer. But he figures he's got no choice. So he gives David Dempster a good lead, then sets off after him on foot.

The tailee walks quickly down the deserted street to Eleventh Avenue. Just as Cone makes the corner, Dempster disappears into a grungy saloon with a spluttery blue neon sign outside: Paddy's Pig.

Cone saunters up, peers through the flyspecked window. He spots David Dempster seated at the bar talking earnestly to a fat guy who's wearing a seaman's watch cap and a T-shirt that was white a long time ago. Cone can't figure Dempster's choice of a drinking companion. Could the guy be a closet faigeleh? Not likely.

There's no way he can enter the bar; Dempster would make him for sure. So Cone spends the next half-hour meandering up and down the block, stopping at Paddy's Pig occasionally to look through the window and make certain his quarry is still inside. There's a faded menu taped to the inside of the window that Timothy finds interesting. It advertises "Turkey dinner with all the tremens." Of the delirium variety, Cone has no doubt.

He's a half-block away, on the corner of 46th Street, when he sees David Dempster come out of the bar and walk quickly toward 45th, probably to reclaim his car. The Wall Street dick lets him go, waits a few minutes, then returns to Paddy's Pig. Unexpectedly, it has a fine front door of oak, inset with panels of beveled and etched glass.

But the tavern itself is a swamp. The bar is gouged and burned mahogany. The sawdust on the floor dates from Year One, being liberally mixed with peanut shells and cigar butts.

Cone looks around as if he's trying to locate a pal. The scarred bar is on his left. There's a line of booths on the right, and down the middle is a double row of flimsy wood tables and fragile chairs. The tables are crowded with Saturday night boozers who look like seamen, longshoremen, thieves, and over-the-hill ladies of the evening. Noise slams down from the tin ceiling, and there's a stink of scorched grease and phenol.

The booths on the right are occupied by a different breed. Mostly youngish guys dressed for flash. Some are with women, but all look like hardcases. Cone reckons a few have got to be Attica alumni; they've got that lag look about them: talking without moving their lips, eyes constantly on the qv.

He moves up to the bar, one empty stool away from the fat guy in watch cap and T-shirt. He has faded blue tattoos on his flabby arms and a long, pale scar across his chin as if someone went for his throat with a straight razor and he ducked just in time.

On Cone's right, practically rubbing elbows, is a tall dude with the jits. He's either scratching his acne or probing an ear with a matchstick. Both his little fingers have been lopped off at the second joint, and he's got a greasy black ponytail bound with a rubber band.

A mustachioed bartender wanders up and stands in front of Cone.

"Yeah?" he says.

Cone looks around. Everyone seems to be drinking boilermakers, but he includes himself out.

"Vodka," he orders. "On the rocks."

The mustache looks at him. "Bar vodka?" he asks.

"No, no," Cone says hastily. "What have you got?"

"Bar vodka and Smirnoff."

"Give me the Smirnoff," Cone says. "And there's an extra buck in it for you if you open a fresh bottle."

The bartender stares at him. "We don't water our booze in here, mister."

"Didn't say you did. Do you want the buck or don't you?"

The mustache looks over at the watch cap.

"Give the man what he wants, Tommy," fatso says. "The customer is always right."

Grumbling, Tommy fishes out a fresh bottle of Smirnoff from under the bar and uncaps it in front of Cone.

"Okay?" he says truculently.

"Fine."

He's taking his first gulp when the tall dude on his right leans toward him.

"Hey," he says, "I like the way you handled that. You got class."

Cone shrugs, turns away. He sees tubby is giving him the double-O. He seems to approve of what he sees because he pushes his boilermaker closer to Cone and shifts his bulk onto the barstool next to him.

"You from around here?" he asks in a raspy voice.

"Used to be," Cone says. "I been away for a while."

"Yeah," the guy says. "Ain't we all. Need anything? Boom-boom? Wanna be a winner? Check it out?"

"Not tonight."

"Merchandise?"

Cone stares at him. "That fell off the truck?"

"That's right. Cassettes, TV sets, VCRs, microwaves. You name it. All in the original cartons. Sealed."

The Wall Street dick considers that a moment, takes another swallow of his drink. "A motorcycle?" he suggests. "I got a buddy looking for a good buy."

"You're talking to the right man. You name it—make and model—and you got it."

"I'll send him around," Cone says. "You hang here?"

"Every night. I own the joint. Name's Louie."

Cone nods, finishes his drink. He slaps a finif on the bar, turns to go. The tall gink has disappeared. Suddenly there's a great crash behind him and he whirls. A wild, drunken fight has erupted between two men and two women seated at the tables. Screaming curses, they go at each other with fists, feet, elbows, weighty handbags. The melee grows more vicious, with bottles swung, tables upset, chairs splintered.

"Tommy," the fat guy calls, and points under the bar. He's handed an aluminum baseball bat. He slides off the stool and waddles into the donnybrook. He starts bouncing the bat off the skulls of everyone within reach. The hard guys in the booths are spitting with merriment. Timothy decides it's time to leave.

He's heading back to his car, walking along 45th Street, when someone calls, "Hey, mac." He stops and turns slowly. The tall, jittery cat from Paddy's Pig comes up close.

He's got a knife in his hand that looks to be as long as a saber.

"Let's have it," he says in a whispery voice.

Cone backs up a step. "Have what?" he asks.

The guy sighs. "Whaddya think? Money, credit cards, whatever you got."

"Oh, my God!" Cone cries, clutching at his chest. "My heart! My heart!" He doubles over as if in agonizing pain, bending low. When he comes up, he has the S&W .357 in his fist. "Here's what I got," he says.

The man looks at the gun. "Hey," he says, "wait a minute."

"Drop the toothpick," Cone says. "Drop it!"

The knife clatters to the sidewalk. The Wall Street dick steps in and kicks the stupe's shin, just below the knee, as hard as he can. The mugger screams, bends, and Cone cold-cocks him behind the ear with the short-barreled Magnum. The guy goes flat out on the pavement, but Timothy takes him with his heavy work shoes, heeling the kidneys and family jewels.

He finally gets control of himself, tries to breathe slowly and deeply. He picks up the knife and drops it through the first sewer grating he comes to. He drives home to the loft, deciding he shouldn't have given the guy the boot. That was overkill, and it wasn't nice.

"Not nice?" he asks aloud, and wonders if he's ready for the acorn academy.

"What did you do last night?" Samantha Whatley asks.

"Nothing much," Cone says. "Had a few drinks, went to bed early."

"Liar," she says. "I called you around midnight; you weren't in."

"Was that you?" he says. "I was sacked out. I thought I heard the phone ringing, but by the time I got up it had stopped."

"Uh-huh," she says.

It's Sunday afternoon, they're lying together in her fancy bed, and she really is reading the Real Estate Section of the *Times*, the rest of the paper scattered over the sheet. She's sitting up, back against the headboard, heavy, horn-rimmed glasses down on her nose. Cone is just lying there lazily, not caring if school keeps or not.

"Will you listen to these rents?" Sam says. "A studio for twelve hundred a month. A one-bedroom for fifteen hundred. How does that grab you?"

"It's just money," he says.

"*Just* money? Don't try to be so fucking superior. You like it as much as anyone else."

He turns his head to look at her. "Sure I do. But I wouldn't kill for it. Would you?"

"You're the only one I want to kill, and you don't have all that much gelt."

"Bupkes is what I've got. No, seriously, would you kill for money?"

"Of course not."

"Ever talk to a homicide dick about why people kill?"

"I dated a guy from Homicide for a while, but I had to give him the broom. Whenever he got bombed he started crying. But no, I never talked to him about why people kill."

"I'll tell you why," Cone says. "Subtract the weirdos who murder because God told them to. And subtract the ones who kill because they find hubby or wifey in the sack with someone else. Those are impulse murders."

"Crimes of passion," Sam says.

"If you say so. Well, subtract those cases and just consider the murders that are premeditated—sometimes for a long while—and carefully planned. Now you're dealing with two main motives. One is revenge, which isn't too important unless you're a Sicilian."

"And the other is money," she says.

"Bingo," Cone says. "I'd guess that greed tops everything else. It may be for a couple of bucks in a muggee's pocket or for a couple of billion in a corporate treasury."

"Oh-ho," Whatley says, peering at him through her half-glasses. "Now I know why I'm getting this lecture on mayhem on a nice, bright, Sunday afternoon. You're brooding about the Dempster case, and you think greed was the motive for the industrial sabotage."

"And for John Dempster's murder. What else could it be?" he says fretfully. "I'm not saying other motives might not be involved, but it was greed that sparked the whole thing."

"How do you know?" she asks.

"I don't," he says. "And that's what's sending me up the wall. I thought I had it figured, but I struck out."

Then he tells her about his great inspiration: a corporate raider trying to put Dempster-Torrey into play, and conniving to reduce the price of the stock by sabotage and, eventually, assassination.

"Good thinking, Tim," she says.

"Not good," he says mournfully, shaking his head. "Simon Trale, the CFO, checked it out for me, and there's no evidence at all, not even a rumor, that some pirate is making a move. So that's that. Ahh, the hell with it. Let's forget about it."

"Should I heat up the pizza?" Sam asks. "You getting hungry?"

"Yeah," he says, looking at her. "But not for pizza."

"Oh, you sweet-talking sonofabitch," she says. "Can we fornicate on top of the Sunday *Times*? Isn't that sacrilegious?"

"What's the worst that could happen—you get a headline printed backwards on your ass? Leave your glasses on. I've never balled a woman while she's wearing specs."

"You're depraved," Sam says.

"Just a mood. It'll pass."

"Oh, God!" she says. "I hope not."

A few hours later, after a lukewarm shower during which they take turns picking up the soap, they have their pizza, salad, and wine.

Cone gets back to the Dempster case; he just can't get rid of it.

"Of course," he says, "it's garbage to claim anyone kills from one motive alone. Usually it's a tangle of reasons, justifications, and past history."

"Who are you talking about?" she demands.

"Oh . . . just people," he says darkly.

"You're closing up again," she says. "I know that shriveled brain of yours is going 'round and 'round like a Roller Derby, and you're not going to tell me about it."

"Nothing to tell," he mutters, head lowered. "You got any more salad?"

"That's it," she says. "Sorry I ran short."

He raises his head slowly, glares at her.

202 / LAWRENCE SANDERS

"Jesus," she says, "what are you looking at me like that for? I just said there's no more salad; so sue me."

"You remember the Laboris case?" he asks. "The guy who was pulling a Ponzi scam so he could launder money from dope and art smuggling?"

"Yeah," she says, "I remember. So what?"

"Without knowing it, you gave me the lead that broke it. Now you've done it again."

"Done what?" she cries desperately. "Just exactly what are you talking about?"

"Forget it," he says, grinning at her. "Have some more wine."

"Up yours," she says grumpily. "Were you labeled 'Most Likely to Fail' in your high school yearbook?"

"I'm a dropout," he tells her.

"I'm willing to testify to that," she says, and they both crack up.

After the pizza is gone, they stay on the floor, sipping the chilled wine, schmoozing about this and that. These are their most intimate moments, the closest. Sex is brutal warfare, but this is gentle peace, and there's a lot to be said for it—though neither would admit it.

Samantha has a choice collection of old 78s, and she puts a stack on her player, selecting the records she knows he likes best. She starts with Walter Houston's "September Song," Bing Crosby's "Just a Gigolo," and Billie Holiday's "Fine and Mellow."

"I've also got her 'Gloomy Sunday,'" Sam says. "I'd play it, but it ain't."

"That's right," Timothy Cone says happily. "It ain't."

He has many illusions about himself. One of the most mundane is that if, before falling asleep, he tells himself exactly when he wishes to arise, then lo! he will awake at that exact hour.

So on Sunday night, curled on his mattress, he instructs himself, "You will wake up at eight o'clock. You will definitely wake at eight." He sleeps soundly and rouses at precisely ten minutes after nine. Cursing, he lights a cigarette, puts water on to boil, and tosses Cleo a small dog biscuit. It's a cat, but not racist.

Still in his underwear, smoking a cigarette and sipping black coffee, he phones Neal Davenport.

"You're up so early?" the city detective says. "Don't tell me you're at the office."

"On my way," Cone says, unshaven and standing there in his Jockey shorts. "How's the Department doing on the Dempster homicide?"

"That's why you called at this hour? To make me feel more miserable? It's a cold trail, sonny boy, and getting icier every day. This one's a pisser. We're getting flak from everyone, and just between you, me, and the lamppost, we haven't got a thing."

"What about the hotshot lieutenant who was running the show? Is he still around?"

"Nah," Davenport says, "he's long gone. Now we got a deputy inspector, and he's feeling the heat, too. Turning into a lush. This goddamned file is going to ruin a lot of careers—mine included."

"Anything on that terrorist group that called the newspapers? The Liberty Tomorrow gang."

"No trace. The thinking now is that it was all bullshit. A stunt pulled by some wild-assed leftists to grab headlines, or maybe by the finks who actually offed Dempster and just wanted to throw us a curve. This is why you called—just to listen to my kvetching?"

"Not exactly," Cone says. "I want to ask a favor."

"No kidding? I never would have guessed."

"Look," Cone says, "you owe me one—right? The Laboris drug deal—remember?"

"Well . . . yeah, I guess maybe. Waddya got?"

"Three license plates. I need to know who owns the cars."

"What for?"

"Neal," the Wall Street dick says softly, "this could involve the Dempster kill."

Long silence. Then: "You shittin' me, sherlock?"

"I swear to God I'm not. It's not definitely connected, but it might be. Come on, take a chance."

Davenport sighs. "Okay, I'll see what I can do. Give me the numbers."

Cone reads off his scrawls from the inside of the

matchbook cover. "Push this," he urges. "It really could be something."

"And if it's not?"

"Then you've wasted a phone call. Big deal."

"I'll get back to you," the NYPD man says and hangs up.

Cone, anxious to get things moving, fills his coffee cup again, lights another Camel, and calls Simon Trale at Dempster-Torrey. He has to hold for a few minutes before he's put through. And while he's waiting, he has to listen to music. "Climb Every Mountain," no less.

"Sorry to keep you waiting, Mr. Cone."

"That's okay, Mr. Trale. Listen, I warned you I might contact you again if I needed more poop."

"Poop?"

"Information. Someone accused me recently of using other people to do my job for me. But sometimes it's the only way to get the job done, so that's why I'm calling. All right with you?"

"Of course," Trale says.

"When I talked to you about all those industrial accidents, you said most of the losses were covered by insurance. Have I got that right?"

"Correct."

"Does Dempster-Torrey buy insurance from individual companies or do you use a broker?"

"We use a single broker, Mr. Cone. We've found it more efficient and economical that way."

"One broker for all of Dempster-Torrey's property and casualty insurance?"

"Yes."

"Lucky broker. That must add up to a nice wad."

Simon Trale laughs quietly. "It does indeed."

"So I'd guess that Dempster-Torrey, and you in particular, have got heavy clout with the broker."

"A fair assumption. What are you getting at, Mr. Cone?"

"Here's what I need. . . . There's got to be an association of all the property and casualty insurance companies in the country. Some outfit that lobbies in Washington and also collects statistics on property and casualty losses and the insurance business in general."

"Of course there is. The Central Insurance Association, a trade group."

"The CIA?" Cone says. "That must raise a few eyebrows. But I'll bet they've got all the facts and figures on their industry on computer tapes—right?"

"I would imagine so, yes."

"Well, here's what I'd like you to do: Call your broker, ask him to contact the trade association and get a list of the ten companies in the country that suffered the heaviest property and casualty losses in the last year."

There's a long pause. Then: "You think there may be a connection with our losses, Mr. Cone? That there may be some kind of a conspiracy directed against large corporations?"

"Something like that," Cone says. "Look, Mr. Trale, I wouldn't blame you for thinking I'm a bubblehead after I fell on my face on that corporate raider suggestion."

"Don't apologize for that," the old man says. "It was a very ingenious idea that just didn't work out. Happens to me all the time. But now you feel there may be a link between our accidents and those of other companies?"

"Could be."

"All right," Trale says without hesitation. "I'll call our broker and ask him to get the information."

"Lean on him if you have to," Cone says.

Trale laughs. "I don't think that will be necessary; I'm sure he'll be happy to cooperate. Shall I have him contact you directly?"

"Yeah, that'd help. I want to move on this as fast as I can, Mr. Trale, but I'm not promising anything."

"I understand that. I'll call immediately."

Cone hangs up, satisfied he's started things rolling. Now he's got to wait for Davenport and the insurance broker to get back to him. He could do it all himself, but it would take weeks, maybe months, of donkeywork. And he has the feeling that something is going down that better be squelched in a hurry.

Having done a morning's labor for Haldering & Co. with two phone calls, he feels no great obligation to occupy his desk at the office. So he has a whore's bath, shaves, and dresses at a languid pace, pausing to make a small aluminum foil ball for Cleo to chase. He even has time for a morning beer to excite the palate and cleanse the nasal passages.

He ambles downtown, frowning at a summer sun that

beams back at him. It's a brilliant day, and he might glory in it if he was not a man of a naturally morose nature, a grump still studying joy and how to achieve it. The brimful day is an indignity; he still prefers sleet and wet socks.

The snarly Haldering receptionist gives him a glare for his tardiness, and his cramped office is no great solace. There's a chilly memo from Samantha Whatley on his desk: "Your progress reports for the past three weeks are overdue. Ditto expense account vouchers. Please remit ASAP."

He folds the memo into a paper airplane and sails it up. It flutters, falls. Just like his mood. He wonders if he might not improve his lot in life by learning how to slice Nova thin in a high-class deli. He could force that career switch by marching in and slamming Hiram Haldering in the snout. Attractive thought.

He knows why he is suddenly afflicted with a galloping case of the glooms. Having set the wheels in motion on the Dempster file, there's not a damned thing he can do until Neal Davenport and Simon Trale respond to his requests. The inaction chafes, and he hopes to God his second brainstorm isn't going to prove as big a blunder as his first.

He grimly sets to work on those accursed progress reports, trying not to think of the possibility of another balls-up on the Dempster case. But when his phone rings about 11:30, he reaches for it cautiously as if it might bring news of disaster.

"Yeah?" he says warily.

"Davenport. You got pencil and paper? I got names to go with those license plates you gave me."

"Jeez, that's quick work," Cone says. "I didn't expect you to get back to me so soon."

"Well, you said it might have something to do with Dempster. You know how to jerk my chain. I'll give you the names, but I also got addresses if needed. Ready? Samuel Folger is the first. The second is Jerome K. Waltz. That's W-a-l-t-z. Like the dance. The third plate is a company car registered to an outfit named Simon and Butterfield, Incorporated. Got all that? Now never say I don't deliver."

"Yeah," Cone says, "thanks."

"Those names mean anything to you?"

"They're all Wall Street guys. They call themselves investment advisers or financial consultants or whatever. But what they really are is money managers—other people's money."

"They're legit?"

Cone doesn't answer directly. "They're all heavy-weights," he goes on. "Mostly in trust and pension funds. I mean we're talking about billions of dollars."

"So what's the connection with the Dempster homicide?"

"Well, uh, it's iffy right now."

"You bastard!" Davenport shouts. "I knock myself out getting this stuff, and you clam up on me. You got nothing to trade? What kind of horseshit is that?"

"Calm down, Neal," the Wall Street dick says. "I got something to trade. You ever hear of a scabby joint over on the West Side called Paddy's Pig?"

Silence. It goes on for so long that Cone says, "Hey, are you there?"

"I'm here. You said Paddy's Pig?"

"That's right."

"You think it might be tied to the Dempster kill?"

"Yeah."

"You and I better have a meet," the city detective says.

Six

CONE PROVIDES the lunch. He's standing outside the office with a shopping bag when Davenport drives up. He double-parks his unmarked blue Plymouth and props up a "Police Officer on Duty" card inside the windshield. Timothy climbs in with the bag.

"Hey, sherlock," Davenport says, "that smells good. What'd you get?"

"Rare burgers on soft buns with a slice of onion—just like you ordered. Also, French fries, a couple of dills, and a cold six-pack of Bud."

"Sounds good," the NYPD man says, tossing a chewed wad of Juicy Fruit out the window. "You can diddle your expense account?"

"No problem."

"Then let's get at it."

They open up the smaller bags, pop two beers, divide the paper napkins, and start gorging.

"There's mustard and ketchup in those little packs," Cone says.

"I'll skip," the city bull says. "I'm on a diet. Listen, I haven't got much time, so I'll give you the background fast. There's a gang up in Hell's Kitchen—only it's Clinton now—called the Westies. Mostly Irish, and a meaner bunch of villains you never want to meet. I mean they make the outlaws in Murder, Inc., look like Girl Scouts. There's a story that one of the Westies walked into a bar up there carrying the head of a guy he had just popped."

"And the bar was Paddy's Pig?"

"You got it. That's where the Westies hung out. They were mostly into gambling and loan-sharking on the piers. But when the West Side docks dried up, the Westies went into everything else—drugs, prostitution, porn—you name it.

Then, about ten years ago, they got into contract killings, including some for one of the Mafia families. We figure they pulled off at least thirty homicides. Most of the victims were chopped up. One guy had his head put in a steel vise, and it was tightened until his skull cracked open like a ripe melon.''

''Beautiful. Have some more fries before I eat them all.''

They start on their second burgers.

''These onions are hot,'' Davenport says. ''Just the way I like them. But I'll be grepsing all day. Anyway, about three years ago the Department organized a strike force—us and state and federal people. It worked out real good. About a dozen of the Westies were sent up, including some of the bosses, and the rest laid low. Paddy's Pig was closed down for a while, but it reopened with a new owner. And lately our snitches have claimed the gang is back in business again. Now you tell me there's a tie-up between Paddy's Pig and the Dempster homicide. In the first place, what were you doing in that joint?''

Cone wipes his mouth with a paper napkin and opens another beer. ''I tailed David Dempster up there.''

The NYPD man turns to stare at him. ''You shittin' me again?''

''I shit you not,'' Cone says. ''That's where he went, and had a confab with the owner, a fat slob named Louie. Listen, when the Dempster investigation began, did you run everyone involved through Records?''

''Whaddya think? Of course we checked them out. David Dempster's got a sheet—but not much of one. A charge of battery for beating up a drunk driver in Central Park who, Dempster said, killed his dog. And two arrests for assault. Nothing ever came to trial.''

''My, my,'' Cone says. ''So the wimp's got a streak of the crude, has he? That figures.''

Davenport rattles the windows with a reverberant belch, then unwraps a fresh stick of Juicy Fruit. ''It doesn't figure to me,'' he says. ''So David Dempster went slumming and was observed talking to the owner of Paddy's Pig. What does that prove?''

''When I talked to Louie after Dempster left, he tried to push dope. When I wasn't interested, he switched to merchandise that fell off the truck. I told him a buddy of mine was looking to buy a motorcycle. He said sure, send him around.''

The two detectives stare at each other.

"Thin stuff," Davenport says.

"You got anything thicker?"

"No," Davenport admits. "We got a lot of doughnuts that are all hole. Look, could you go back to this Louie and see if he can get you a black Kawasaki, Model 650?"

"Well, ah, that might be a problem. To tell you the truth, I got in a slight disagreement with a guy who may be hanging out there.''

"A *slight* disagreement? With you that's like being slightly pregnant. Okay, I'll do it myself."

"Neal," Cone says gently, "don't do that. They'll make you for a cop the minute you walk in the place."

Davenport looks down at his stained, off-the-rack brown suit, his belly, plump hands. "You really think so?" he asks.

"Definitely. Why don't you get an undercover guy who can act a scuzz. Bring him around and I'll prep him. He can spend time at Paddy's Pig until he's accepted as just another barfly. Then he can move in on Louie and see if he can get a line on the cycle. I'm betting they didn't drop it in the Hudson or send it to a chop shop. It's too valuable."

"Yeah, that makes sense. If it works out, it'll put David Dempster in the crapper. You know that, don't you?"

"Of course I know it."

"Well, what the hell was his motive? Jealousy? Sibling rivalry?"

"Sibling rivalry? That's fancy talk for a gumshoe."

"I read books," Davenport protests. "Come on—what's the motive?"

"I'm working on that."

"Jesus," the detective says disgustedly, "you always hold back, don't you?"

"You handle Paddy's Pig," Cone says, "and let me go after David Dempster. A guy shouldn't chill his own brother. That's not right."

"You got a brother?"

"No."

"Then what the hell are you talking about?"

"I got my standards," Timothy says.

* * *

He carries the two remaining beers up to his office in a brown paper bag. There's a scrawny guy in a seersucker suit waiting in the reception room. He's wearing wire-rimmed cheaters, and there's a straw boater balanced on his knee. He's got the face of a pale hawk, with a droopy nose and a mouth so tight it looks like a lipless slit.

"Man to see you," the antique receptionist snaps at Cone. The visitor stands and tries a smile that doesn't work.

"Mr. Timothy Cone?"

"Yeah. Who you?"

The guy whips out a business card and proffers it. "Bernard Staley from International Insurance—"

"Whoa," Cone interrupts, holding up a hand. "I'm not buying."

"And I'm not selling. It's International Insurance Investigators. The Triple-I. Have you ever heard of us?"

"Nope."

"Good," the guy says, and this time the smile works. "We like it that way. This concerns Dempster-Torrey. Can we talk?"

"Sure," Timothy says, taking the business card. "This way."

Staley follows him down the corridor and into Cone's littered cubbyhole office.

"This looks like my place," the insurance man says, "but it's bigger."

"Bigger? My God, you must work out of a coffin. Listen, I've got a couple of beers here. They're not too cold, but they're wet. You want one?"

He has the guy figured for a stiff, but Staley surprises him. "Sure," he says. "That'd be good."

They open the cans, take a gulp, stare at each other with cautious interest.

"This Triple-I you work for—" Cone says. "What is it?"

"Claims investigations. Most insurance companies have their own claims department. But some of the smaller ones can't handle anything that's complicated or suspicious. And sometimes the big boys get backed up with a lot of claims at once and need temporary outside help. That's where we come in."

"I follow," Cone says. "But what's your interest in Dempster-Torrey?"

Staley drums his fingertips on the top of his sailor. "The way I get it," he says, "you were hired to investigate their industrial sabotage. Correct?"

"That's right."

"So you call Dempster-Torrey. They call their insurance broker. The broker calls the Central Insurance Association. And they call us."

"There's a helluva lot of phoning going on today," Cone says. "Maybe I should buy some Nynex stock. But how does your company come in on this?"

"About three years ago the computers at the CIA—that's a great name, isn't it—picked up a big increase in property and casualty claims by large corporations. It was a jump that couldn't be explained by normal growth, so the Triple-I was hired to take a look-see."

"So you've been looking into property and casualty losses for the past three years."

"Just for a year. The eye who had the file before me retired, and I inherited it. He got nowhere with it, and that's exactly where I've got."

"Did you investigate this stuff personally?"

"You better believe it," Bernard Staley says. "Traveled all over the country. Spent a lot of the CIA's money—and delivered zilch. And I usually got there a day or two after it happened. Sometimes within hours. Not only torching factories, but sabotage, and vandalism, product tampering, bribery of union leaders, consumer lawsuits, and hiring away or corrupting key personnel—in other words, a complete program to ruin the reputation and profits of the targeted company."

"Any homicides?" Cone asks.

Staley gives him a strange look. "Funny you should ask," he says. "The chief researcher for a biomedical outfit got wiped out in a car crash. Clear night. He wasn't drunk or stoned. The official verdict was that he lost control of his car and drove into a concrete abutment. But the guy was some kind of a genius, and there was talk he was working on a cure for baldness. After he died, the stock of the company went way down, and the new product never did hit the market."

"You think the guy's accident wasn't kosher?"

Staley shrugs. "Just a feeling," he says. "No hard evidence at all. But I keep remembering it. He left a pretty wife and three young kids.''

''Yeah,'' Cone says, ''that's hard to forget. And you've gotten nothing from all your digging?''

The other man blinks behind his specs. ''Nothing you can take to the bank. Just a crazy notion that all these jobs— different companies, different places—were pulled by the same guy, or the same mob. A lot of similarities. In several of the arson cases, the MO was practically identical. But don't ask me who's behind it or what the motive might be—I haven't a clue. Anyway, I won't bore you with my tale of woe any longer. You wanted a list of the ten companies that had the biggest property and casualty losses. Here it is, with their total claims.''

He fishes into his inside jacket pocket, comes out with a folded sheet of typing paper, hands it over.

''You'll notice that Dempster-Torrey is at the top as far as dollar losses go.''

Cone scans the list quickly. ''I recognize most of the names,'' he says. ''Not all, but most. What do these dates mean?''

''That's when the accidents happened,'' the Triple-I man says. ''I thought it might possibly help. You'll notice some of the dates go back more than a year. I know you asked for losses in the past year, but this thing has been growing for three years now, so I decided to include the biggest losers.''

Cone looks at him admiringly. ''You know your job,'' he says.

''No, I don't,'' Bernard Staley says. ''If I did, I'd have closed this file a year ago. I hope you have better luck. I've got a lot more on my plate besides this, but it keeps bothering me.''

''Yeah. The pretty wife and three young kids.''

The insurance investigator nods, rises, extends his hand. ''Nice meeting you, Mr. Cone. I hope that list is what you wanted. I swear to God that something is going down, but what the hell it is, I have no idea.''

''Thanks for your help,'' Cone says, shaking his hand.

''And if you come up with anything you'll let me know?''

''Absolutely. We're both working the same side of the street.''

Staley gives him a wan smile. "Some street," he says sadly.

After he's gone, Cone reads over the list again. This sabotage is not piddling stuff; the claims are heavy: millions of dollars of losses. Which means if someone has deliberately planned the damage, he's a professional or, more probably, has hired professionals. Two of the companies on the list suffered arsonous fires on the same day, and they're half a country apart. No one torch could have managed that.

Cone ruminates a moment, searching through the mess in his top desk drawer for the phone number of his contact at the Securities and Exchange Commission. He calls.

"Jeremy Bigelow, please. Timothy Cone calling."

"He's on the phone at the moment, Mr. Cone. Would you care to wait?"

"Yeah, I'll wait."

He waits, and waits, and waits. Finally Bigelow comes on. "Hiya, Tim," he says.

"What were you doing on the phone so long—trying to explain to your wife why you take off your wedding ring the moment you leave the house?"

"My God," the SEC man says with an empty laugh, "you never forget anything, do you. What's happening?"

"The usual bullshit. Jerry, I need a small favor."

"Well, uh, I'm awfully busy right now."

Bigelow is a nice guy but not too swift. Cone has had to strong-arm him more than once.

"Look," he says in a hard voice, "don't get snotty with me. In the first place, you owe me one for that Sally Steiner scam. Don't think I didn't see your name in *The Wall Street Journal*. But that's okay; I told you to grab the glory. In the second place, if you stiff me on this, you'll be passing up something that could be bigger than the Boesky affair. If you and the SEC don't want a piece of the action, just say so and I'll get out of your hair."

"Bigger than the Boesky affair?" Jeremy repeats. "You just said the magic words. What have you got?"

"A list of ten companies. I need to know the amount of short sales in each company's stock on the dates I'll give you."

"My God," Bigelow says, "it'll take a month of Sundays to dig that out."

"Jerry, stop trying to jerk me around. You've got it all on your computers and you know it. *The New York Times* runs a list of big-board short positions every month. It shouldn't take you more than an hour or two to come up with what I need."

"Well, all right," the other man says grudgingly. "Mail me the list and I'll see what I can do."

"Mail *shit!*" Cone says wrathfully. "I haven't got the time, and if you'd like maybe to see your name in *Business Week,* you'll want to get on this as fast as you can. Have you got a bug on your phone wired to a tape recorder?"

"Well . . . yeah," the SEC man says hesitantly. "For when informers call."

"I'm the best informer you'll ever have. Switch it on and I'll dictate the names of the companies and the dates."

He hears fumbling, clicking, and then Bigelow says, "Okay, go ahead."

Cone reads aloud the list from Triple-I. He concludes by saying, "That's all for now, folks. Keep those letters and postcards coming."

Jerry gets back on the phone again. "All right," he says, "I'll get it to Research right away. You're sure this is a biggie?"

"Makes the Teapot Dome Scandal look like the Gypsy Handkerchief Switch," Cone assures him. "I'll expect to hear from you tomorrow. If not, look for me at your office with a cast-iron shillelagh. Have a nice day."

"Yeah," Jeremy Bigelow says faintly. "You, too."

Cone disconnects, convinced the pace of the investigation is picking up. He lights a Camel, lifts his work shoes on top of his battered desk, and considers. Where are the flaws? If not flaws, where are the gaps? He spots one, and reaches for the phone again. He calls Mrs. Teresa Dempster.

She answers the phone herself, and he wonders, sorrowfully, if the nubile maid has been canned.

"Hello, there!" she says cheerily. "This is Teresa Dempster speaking."

"How are you, Mrs. Dempster? This is Timothy Cone."

"Mr. Timothy!" she carols. "How nice to hear from you again."

"I was wondering how my bonsai is doing. The Japanese red maple you gave me—remember?"

"Irving! Of course I remember. Well, Irving is doing just

wonderfully. Growing enormously. I think we'll have to repot him.''

''I was wondering if I might stop by—just for a few minutes—to take a look.''

''Of course you may,'' she says gaily. ''Irving will be so happy to see you.''

''Be there in a half-hour,'' he says.

He grabs his cap and starts out. He meets Samantha Whatley in the corridor.

''Where are you going now?'' she demands.

''Nutsville,'' he tells her.

She's wearing a long denim apron over a white linen jumpsuit, but no costume could conceal her feyness. The big azure eyes are widened in constant wonder, and the webby wheaten hair drifts down her back. She greets him at the door and seems genuinely delighted to see him.

''You're the first visitor I've had today,'' she says breathlessly, taking his hand and drawing him inside. ''It's Jeanette's day off, so I've been all by my lonesome—except for my friends, of course.''

''Of course,'' Cone says, figuring she's talking about her trees and plants. ''No police guard outside?''

''Not anymore. It was really so unnecessary. Goodness, who'd want to hurt me?''

Cone doesn't answer, but follows her up the stairs and down the hallway to the greenhouse. She stops suddenly and turns to him.

''Would you like a blueberry yogurt?'' she asks. ''Really delicious.''

''Thanks, but no, thanks. I had a heavy lunch.''

''I can imagine,'' she says. ''You men with your rare roast beef and Yorkshire pudding—it's not good for you, you know.''

''I know,'' Cone says. ''I try to avoid it.''

''Well, there's Irving!'' she says, pointing. ''Isn't he beautiful?''

''He surely is,'' Cone says, meaning it. ''You have a way with growing things, Mrs. Dempster.''

''Oh, well, I try,'' she says, blushing. ''I have my share of failures, I do assure you, but I keep trying. Now look at this one, Mr. Timothy. A new arrival. It's a Chinese elm, and it's older than you and I put together. But isn't it magnificent?"

"Very impressive. Have you named it yet?"

She stares at the little tree. It's thick and sturdy—and stunted.

"Yes," she says in a low voice. "I call it John J. Dempster. For my late husband, you know."

"I know," Cone says. "I hope you haven't been lonely since your husband di— since your husband passed over."

"Lonely? Oh, no. I know so many wonderful people who call and visit. I'm so fortunate. And my sons are coming home next month. I don't have time to be lonely."

"Good for you," he says. "And I'm sure your brother-in-law comes by occasionally."

"Occasionally?" she says, and laughs: a high-pitched trilling sound. "Why, he's here almost every day."

"Since you lost your husband?"

"Oh, long before that. David and I are such good friends. Heavens, he practically lives here. John was away so much— on business, you know—and David would take me out to dinner and to the theater."

"So David would know when your husband was leaving on a business trip?"

"Of course," she prattles on. "I'd tell him, and we'd plan what we'd do while John was gone. The opera or ballet or just a long walk through Central Park. Once we went to the Cloisters. David is so good to me. And especially since John went on. You know it's difficult for a woman to get around and see things by herself."

"I know," Cone says sympathetically. Then he leans close to her with a viperish smile. "You don't suppose, do you, Mrs. Dempster, that David has a crush on you?"

It's a calculated risk. He knows she is not a total meshuggeneh, and if she resents his question and tells him to get lost, he won't be a bit surprised. But she leans even closer, and her voice is lower than his.

"How odd you should suggest that. You know, it had occurred to me, but I thought I was imagining things. I do that at times."

"No reason why he shouldn't be attracted to you," Timothy says bravely. "You're a fascinating woman."

"Oh, my!" Teresa says, blushing again and putting her long fingers to her cheek. "I thank you, sir. What a nice thing to say."

"The truth," he says. "Well, I'm afraid I must go now, Mrs. Dempster. I hope you won't be alone all evening."

"Oh, no," she says. "I have so much to do, and later David is coming over to take me to dinner and a Mostly Mozart recital at Lincoln Center. Do you like Mozart, Mr. Timothy?"

"Oh, yeah," Cone says. "Can't get enough of him. Thanks for letting me see Irving, Mrs. Dempster."

"He's yours, you know. And you have visitation rights whenever you wish."

He wants to kiss that velvety cheek, but resists. He leaves her home, not proud of what he has done, but telling himself it was necessary. That doesn't help much.

He drives back to the loft, wondering how the possible destruction of David Dempster might affect that sweet, innocent woman. Not a happy thought. But she impresses him as being a survivor, able to endure grief and tragedy. He hopes his appraisal is correct. It's even possible that her wackiness is her salvation. A more rational woman might crack.

When he gets to his building, he finds the front door has been jimmied—again. But it's not yet 6:00 P.M., so the elevator is still working, and he doesn't have to trudge up six flights. Cleo greets him with an ankle rub and a desperate growl that signals starvation.

Cone brings out that length of garlic salami—still plenty left—and whacks off a thick chunk. Cleo takes it under the bathtub to enjoy. Cone opens a cold beer and, on impulse, pours it into an empty jelly jar. Then he sprinkles it with salt.

He can't remember why they did that when he served with the USMC. For the flavor? To raise a head on the brew? But the taste of salted beer brings back old memories, most of which he'd like to forget forevermore.

He slumps at his spavined table, feet up, totally drained by the day's events. All those people, all that pushing and shoving to get what he wants. And then, most recently, duping an ingenuous woman. He's wiped out.

Before he knows it, he's brooding about the victim, John J. Dempster. From what he's heard from everyone, he figures the guy was a hustler—in the boardroom and in the bedroom.

With all the chutzpah in the world. Willing to risk his balls in the coliseum. In fact, going from risk to risk because that's where the fun is.

Cone has known a lot of hustlers, on the street, in combat, in the business world. He admires them all, straight or crooked, for their gall and their energy. They play the cards they were dealt to the best of their ability and never whine that they didn't draw a better hand.

Occasionally, but not often, Cone wishes he could be like that. But he hasn't got the temperament, and he knows it. Instead, he seems destined to plod through life armed with a push broom and dustpan, cleaning up after the hustlers.

These melancholy reflections are interrupted by ferocious pounding at the loft door. He slips the magnum out of his ankle holster. Standing to one side of the door, he shouts, "Who is it?"

"The police!" Neal Davenport shouts back. "Open up! Have you got a naked cat in there?"

Cone replaces his revolver, unchains, unbolts, unlocks the door. The city detective lumbers in, followed by a skinny, stooped guy who's wearing a costume so decrepit that he makes Cone look like a candidate for *GQ*.

Davenport jerks a thumb at his companion. "Meet Officer Sam Shipkin," he says.

"You could have fooled me," Cone says, shaking the man's hand.

He's got a black beard that looks as if mice have been at it, and he's wearing shades that are practically opaque. His ragged jeans weren't stone-washed, they were ground between boulders, and his scuffed motorcycle boots look like Salvation Army castoffs. He's got on a sweat-stained T-shirt bearing the legend: ALL THE NUDES FIT TO PRICK.

"How d'ya like this dump?" Neal asks Shipkin. "As ratty as I told you?"

The undercover cop looks around. "I like it," he pronounces. "Poverty chic."

"Listen," the NYPD bull says, "let's not waste time. I've got to get home to Staten Island—and don't ask me why."

"You don't want a drink?" Cone asks.

"Who says so? What've you got?"

"Vodka, beer, wine, some brandy."

"A beer for me. Sam?"

"A little brandy."

They sit at the rickety table, and the host serves them.

"What in God's name is that?" Davenport cries, pointing.

"A garlic salami. Want a hunk?"

"Jesus, no! You want a slice, Sam?"

"I'll pass," Shipkin says. "My ulcer would be infuriated."

"Sam's going up to Paddy's Pig," Neal says, "and see what he can work. I told him you'd prep him."

"Sure," Cone says, and describes the tavern to the undercover man: the physical layout of the place, the patrons, what they drink.

"The hard guys are in the booths on your right," he says. "Down-and-out boozers at the tables in the center. Louie, the owner, is a fat crud with old tattoos. The night I was there he was wearing a watch cap and T-shirt."

"He's dealing drugs?"

"He's dealing *everything*. He offered me Boom-boom. What the hell is that?"

"Gage," Shipkin says. "From Florida. Heavy stuff."

"Screw the drugs," Davenport says. "It's the motorcycle we want."

"I told this Louie I got a buddy looking to buy a bike," Cone says. "He said just tell me the make and model and he'll come up with it."

Shipkin nods, sips brandy from his jelly jar. "I get the picture," he says. He turns to the other detective. "How about this scenario: If I get a lead on the Kawasaki, I'll make a dope buy from Louie with marked bills. Then we'll have him on a drug rap and can lean on him about the cycle. How does that listen?"

"Sounds good to me. How about you, sherlock?"

"Makes sense," Cone says. "We're not going to get anywhere with this unless someone caves. The more clout we have, the better. The way I figure it, this Louie is the broker between David Dempster and the Westies. He arranges the deals and turns over the cash after taking his cut. And once we've got enough to cuff Dempster, even on some shitty charge, I can finger three or four other guys who'll be happy to make deals to save their ass."

Davenport looks at him curiously. "Still holding out on

me, huh? Okay, play it your way. Right now, all I want is that motorcycle. Anything else Sam should know?''

"Yeah," Cone says, turning to Shipkin. "If you spot a tall guy at the bar with a black ponytail and a bad case of acne, watch your back. You can't miss him; someone chopped off both his little fingers."

"What's queer about him?" Sam asks.

"He's stretched," Cone says. "Carries a long switchblade and thinks he's a hero."

"Okay," the undercover cop says, "I'll keep an eye out. Thanks for the tip." He finishes his brandy and rises. "Well, I better get to work. The more time I spend up there, the easier it'll be."

"The bartender's name is Tommy," Cone adds. "He's got a big mustache. If that's any help."

"You never know," Shipkin says. He looks around the loft. "It's really getting to me," he tells Cone. "If you ever decide to move, let me know first."

"You kidding?" Davenport says. "This *scroccone* is going to die here. They'll find him under the bathtub someday, OD'd on garlic salami."

"There are worse ways to go," Timothy says.

Seven

It TURNS OUT to be a real nothing morning. The summer sky is somber, and there are rumblings of thunder over New Jersey. The stuffed air smells of turps; there's an ugly ocherous glow over everything.

Grousing, Cone shambles down to John Street, convinced that a day starting so dismally can only end in disaster. He stops at the local deli for black coffee and a bagel with a shmear. He takes his breakfast up to the office, exchanging silent glares with the ancient receptionist. It's that kind of day.

He hasn't slept well, but he doesn't blame the junk food he pigged on the previous night. He's eaten salami, anchovies, and chocolate pudding before, and the mixture never depressed him. But this morning engenders thoughts of making out a will and investing in a cemetery plot.

When his phone rings, he stares at it balefully, convinced it's going to bring him news that he's overdrawn at the bank or the IRS has found another flaw in their annual audit of his return. He finally picks it up.

"Yeah?"

"Tim? This is Jeremy Bigelow. Tell me something: Do you always fall in an outhouse and come up with a box lunch?"

"What the hell is that supposed to mean?"

The SEC investigator is bubbling with excitement. "Those ten companies you gave me—Research says that eight of them had very, *very* high short positions on the dates you mentioned. We got a computer sharpie who loves puzzles like that, and he did some back-checking. He claims that in the month before your dates, the total of shares sold short more than tripled in all eight companies. What in God's name is going on?"

Cone sighs. This time he *knows* he is right, but he feels no elation. "It's a ripoff," he tells Bigelow. "A beautiful swindle that might be funny, but people have been dusted—and there's nothing ha-ha about that. Jerry, I think you better bring the Federal DA in on this one."

"The SEC can handle it."

"No, you can't," Cone says. "This isn't just a civil matter. If it pans out, there are going to be criminal indictments. You got a pet in the DA's office?"

"A pet?"

"A contact. Someone you've worked with before. Preferably someone who owes you."

"There's an ADA named Hamish McDonnell. I've had some dealings with him."

"Hamish McDonnell? Italian, of course."

"No," Bigelow says seriously, "I think he's a Scotsman. He's a hardnose, but he gets things done. You think I should call him?"

"It would be the smart thing to do. Cover your ass. Tell him what I gave you and what your computers came up with. Give him my number. If he wants more skinny, he can give me a call."

"Well, all right," the SEC man says hesitantly. "I'll do it, but don't cut me out of this, Tim."

"Don't worry," Cone says. "You'll see your name in print again."

He hangs up and waits, smoking a cigarette, feet up on his desk. Samantha Whatley, coming along the corridor, stops and looks in.

"Working?" she asks.

"Yes, I'm working," he says irritably. "What the hell do you think I'm doing—fluffing my duff?"

"What a lovely mood you're in," she says. "No wonder the whole office calls you Mr. Congeniality."

"The whole office can go hump," he says angrily. "You think I—"

But she walks away, leaving him with his sour thoughts. He hears the grumble of thunder outside—"The angels are bowling," his mother used to say—and he supposes it'll start pouring any minute now. Or maybe it'll hold off until he goes out for lunch. That'll be nice. When his corduroy suit gets wet, it smells like a Percheron's jockstrap.

His phone shrills, and he lets it ring seven times before he picks it up. Sheer perversity.

"Yeah?" he says.

"Timothy Cone?" A man's voice: sharp, brisk, demanding.

"That's right."

"This is Hamish McDonnell, Assistant DA, Federal. Jeremy Bigelow called, said you had something to talk about."

"He told you about the short sales?"

"He told me," McDonnell says, "but I have to know more about it before I set the wheels in motion. I've got a very busy schedule today, but if you can be at my office at three-thirty this afternoon, I'll give you a half-hour."

That's all Cone needs. "Forget it," he says.

"What?"

"Forget it. Unless you want to drag your ass over to my office within an hour, I'll take it to the FBI. I've got a pal there who loves headlines."

"Now wait just a—"

But Cone hangs up. He gives the guy three minutes to get back to him, but the phone rings again in less than a minute.

"Yeah?"

"Hamish McDonnell here. Listen, I think we got off on the wrong foot."

"Not me," Cone says, "I know the drill: hay foot, straw foot, hay foot, straw foot."

"I don't understand."

"Not important. You interested or aren't you?"

"You really think something is going down with those short sales?"

"Oh, yeah. There's frigging in the rigging."

"All right," the ADA says, "I'll get someone to fill in for me over here, and I'll be at your place in an hour. Now are you happy?"

"Creaming," Cone says.

He's there in a little more than an hour, his rubberized raincoat streaming and his red hair plastered to his skull.

"Aw," Cone says, "did you get caught in the rain?"

McDonnell stares at him. "You're a real comedian, aren't you?"

He's a young guy, broad and beefy. He looks as if he might have been a hotshot in college football but didn't have the moves or speed to make pro. But he's still in good shape: flat belly, hard shoulders, a jaw like a knee, and hands just slightly smaller than picnic hams.

"Where can I hang my raincoat?" he asks.

"Throw it on the floor," Cone says. "That's what I do."

But the ADA sits down in the armchair in his wet coat. He pulls out a clean white handkerchief and swabs his dripping hair. "All right," he says, "let's stop playing games. What've you got?"

Cone takes him through the whole thing: How Haldering was hired to investigate sabotage at Dempster-Torrey factories; how he, Cone, decided the motive was to bring down the price of the common stock so short-sellers could profit; how he suspects that David Dempster might be the knave behind the manipulation.

"David Dempster?" McDonnell says sharply. "The brother of the guy who got scragged?"

"That's right."

"You think he had anything to do with John Dempster's death?"

"How the hell would I know?" Cone says. "I'm just a lousy private eye interested in industrial sabotage."

"What have you got on David Dempster?"

"He runs a two-bit PR operation from a small office on Cedar Street, but his net worth is like four mil. That's got to tell you something—right?"

"Unless he inherited it."

"That I doubt. But you can check it out."

McDonnell looks at him a long time, eyes like wet coal. "It stinks," he says finally.

"Sure it does," Cone agrees. "A dirty way of making a buck."

"That's not what I mean," the ADA says. "I mean your story stinks."

The Wall Street dick jerks a thumb toward the door. "Then take a walk," he says. "Sorry to have wasted your time."

"Jesus, what a hard-on you are! Can you blame me for doubting you? What the hell have you given me? A lot of numbers on a computer tape. Those short sales could have been lucky guesses and you know it. All you've said is that you 'suspect' David Dempster might be finagling it. Where's your hard evidence?''

Cone shrugs. ''Take it for what you think it's worth. It's your decision.''

McDonnell leans forward to slam a meaty palm down on the desk. ''Goddamn it!'' he cries. ''You're holding out on me and I know it. You want to be charged with obstruction of justice?''

''Be my guest,'' Cone says. ''I'll be delighted to see you make a fucking idiot out of yourself—if you're not one already.''

They lock eyeballs, both infuriated. It's Hamish McDonnell who blinks first. ''Can't you give me anything to go on?'' he says hotly. ''Anything at all that will make me think you're just not blowing smoke.''

''Yeah,'' Cone says, ''I can give you something. Three names. Two guys and a company. They're all hotshot financial advisers, with pension and trust funds to diddle. They're the weasels who are financing this scam. There may be others, but these three are in it up to their pipiks.''

''How do you know?''

''I don't. You want the names or not?''

The ADA groans. ''Give me the goddamned names,'' he says.

It turns out that Cone's ballpoint pen has run dry and he can't find a clean piece of paper to write on. So his triumph is somewhat diminished by having to borrow McDonnell's pen and a sheet torn from his pocket notebook.

''You're a winner, you are,'' the ADA says. ''How do you get across the street—with a Boy Scout?''

Cone jots down the three names provided by Neal Davenport. ''You won't have any trouble getting addresses,'' he tells McDonnell. ''They're all well-known operators on Wall Street. And listen, do me a favor and do yourself a favor, get moving on this fast. These bums are planning another trick. It's going down right now.''

''Yeah? And how do you know that?''

''You'll have to take my word for it.''

''Seems to me I'm taking your word for a helluva lot.''

''What do you want—a list of personal references?''

''This is going to take a lot of work, and if—''

''Bull*shit*,'' Cone says. ''You pick up these chiselers,

sweat them a little, tell them you've got all the facts and figures on their smelly deals with David Dempster, and I guarantee at least one of them is going to crack. He'll spill his guts to wangle a lesser charge. Wall Street villains are not stand-up guys; you know that.''

"If you're scamming me on all this, Cone, I'm going to come back to this shithouse and personally take you apart. And believe me, I can do it.''

"Maybe,'' Timothy says.

Hamish McDonnell rises and buttons his raincoat. He makes no effort to shake hands, and neither does Cone.

"And don't call me,'' the ADA says. "I'll call you when and if I've got something.''

Cone leans back and lights a cigarette. He figures McDonnell for a tough nut who's not afraid to use the muscle of his office to get the job done. That's okay; the pinstriped types will find themselves confronted by a heavyweight with none of the deference of their golf club pros or private nutritionists.

He pulls on his leather cap and leaves the office. He discovers the rain has stopped. But the sky is still leaden with drizzle. He curses his stupidity for not having driven to work that morning. He tries to find an empty cab and fails. Damning the weepy day, he starts the long hike back to his loft, convinced there's no productive work to be done in the office.

It's true that he persuades other people to do his job for him. Neal Davenport, Jeremy Bigelow, and now Hamish McDonnell—all cooperate, but only because they believe it's to their own profit. Everyone acts out of self-interest—right? Because self-interest is the First Law of Nature. You could even make out a case that a guy who devotes his whole life to unselfish service—like spooning mulligatawny into hopeless derelicts or converting the heathen—is doing it for the virtuous high it gives him.

But even assuming that no one acts without an ego boost, there's a very practical problem Cone has in farming out his investigative chores. Once he's done it, all that's left for him is twiddling his thumbs—or anything else within reach. No use leaning on his helpers; that would just make them sore and earn him static. So there's nothing for him to do but be quietly patient—which is akin to asking a cannibal to become a vegetarian.

These rank musings occupy his mind during his sodden

toddle back to his cave. There he finds that Cleo, apparently surfeited with garlic salami, has upchucked all over the linoleum.

He spends the remainder of that day futzing around the loft, smoking too many cigarettes and drinking too much vodka. He goes over the caper a dozen times in his mind, looking for holes in the solution. No holes. Then he wonders if another meet with Dorothy Blenke or Eve Bookerman would yield anything of value. He decides not.

In the evening, warned by what happened to Cleo, he shuns the salami and opens a can of pork and beans.

"Beans, beans, the musical fruit," he sings to the cat. "The more you eat, the more you toot."

He finishes the can (eaten cold), leaving just a smidgen for the neutered tom, figuring to give the poor creature's stomach a rest. Then he gets caught up on his financial newspapers and magazines, devouring them with the avidity of a baseball maven reading box scores. Wall Street is his world, and he's long since given up trying to analyze his love-hate feelings about it.

On Wednesday morning, he calls Samantha Whatley at the office.

"I won't be in for a couple of days," he tells her. "I'm sick."

"Oh?" she says. "Don't tell me it's the fantods and megrims again. You pulled that one on me once before."

"No," he says, "this time I think I got coryza and phthisis. With maybe a touch of biliary calculus."

"I'll tell you what you've got, son," she says. "More crap than a Christmas goose. Hiram was asking about you. He hasn't seen you around lately and wanted to know if you still worked here."

"Tell fatso to stuff it," Cone says angrily. "I'm working the Dempster-Torrey file and he knows it."

"How you coming on that?"

"Okay."

She sighs. "I should have known better than to ask. Will you be in tomorrow?"

"Probably not."

"Friday?"

"Maybe."

"It's payday, you know."

"Well, if I don't make it, will you pick up my check?"

"No," she says. "If you want it, do us the honor of stopping by."

"Now you're acting like a shithead."

"Asshole!" she says and hangs up.

He goes out to buy cigarettes, food, cat litter, newspapers, and to replenish his liquid assets. The low-pressure area is still hanging over the city, and the denizens are beginning to snarl at each other. That's all right with Cone; at least it's better than everyone giving him a toothy "Have a nice day."

If it wasn't for the Dempster-Torrey case, he would have enjoyed that solitary day in the loft. The phone never rings—not even a wrong number—and Cleo snoozes away the hours under the bathtub. Cone rations his drinks carefully, just keeping a nice, gentle buzz as he reads his newspapers, takes a couple of short naps, showers with his stiff brushing and cornstarch treatment, and changes his underwear and socks.

Several times he's tempted to call Davenport and McDonnell, but resists. He just hopes to God they're doing their jobs. If not, it'll take him weeks, maybe months, to bring down David Dempster and put that gonzo behind bars.

Late that night, stripped to his briefs, he's ready to sack out. He's got a little high-intensity lamp he uses for horizontal activities. He's also got his copy of *Silas Marner,* which he's been reading for four years now. He's already up to page 23, and has discovered it's a better somnifacient than any flurazepam he can buy on the street.

He reads another half-page and has just enough strength left to put the book aside and turn off his lamp.

Thursday starts in the same lethargic pattern. But then, close to noon, Detective Neal K. Davenport calls, and things start jumping.

"Hiya, sherlock," Neal says breezily. "I called your office but they said you were home sick. I figured that was horseshit, and you're just fucking off."

"You got it," Cone says. "What's doing?"

"Everything's coming up roses. Today is D-Day and H-hour is three o'clock. That's when we're going to raid Paddy's Pig. Sam Shipkin's done a great job. He found the motorcycle, and guess where they've been keeping it."

"In the john?"

"Close but no cigar. There's another building behind the tavern. Like a big shed. Sam says it looks like a department store—everything from condoms to cassettes. All hot. The cycle is the same make, model, and color used in the Dempster kill."

"But you don't know if it's the actual bike?"

"Of course not. But it'll do as corroborative evidence. The icing on the cake is that it's owned by the Ryan brothers, a couple of no-goodniks who got their start as smash-and-grabbers when they were in their teens. They've both done time for strongarm stuff and have sheets that don't end. They fit the witnesses' description of the guys on the motorcycle when Dempster was put down. And to top that, Shipkin says that when he met them, they were both wearing steel-toed boots. How does that grab you?"

"Sounds okay," Cone says cautiously, "but I wouldn't call it an airtight case. Any two-bit shyster could get them off in five minutes if all you've got is a similar motorcycle, descriptions by eyewitnesses, and the boots."

"You think I don't know that?" Davenport says indignantly. "That's why Sam Shipkin made a big drug buy from Louie about an hour ago with marked bills. So we got him cold, and we can lean on him. I figure he'll make a deal and sing. Anyway, we're going to give it the old college try. Listen, the raid on Paddy's Pig is going to be what you'd call a media event. We've tipped the newspapers and TV stations, so it should be a circus. I figured you might want to be there."

"Yeah," Cone says. "Sure. Neal, there's a guy named Hamish McDonnell in the Federal DA's office. I think you should call him and invite him to the bust."

"No way!" the NYPD man says. "This is our party, and we're not sharing the headlines with the Feds or anyone else."

"Now look," Timothy says, "right now you got peanuts. If this Louie is afraid of the Westies and decides to clam up and take his lumps, then where the hell are you? The Ryan brothers waltz away and you guys are left looking like idiots. Is that the kind of headlines you want?"

Silence. Then: "Well, yeah, that could happen. But what's this Hamish McDonnell got to do with the price of tea in China?"

"He's coming at David Dempster from a different angle. Dempster was the brain behind all the industrial sabotage I was assigned to investigate. If McDonnell pins him on that— and I think he will—you'll have insurance in case Louie decides to keep his mouth shut. David Dempster will take a fall either way—or both.''

"Goddamn it!" Davenport yells. "Why the fuck couldn't you have told me all this from the start?"

"Because it's outside your jurisdiction," Cone explains patiently. "Granted that the dusting of those three guys on Wall Street is local. And the Department deserves the credit for breaking it. But there's more to it than just those homicides; there's arson, sabotage, bribery, and maybe conspiracy to commit murder. I think David Dempster is up to his ass in all that shit, but they're *federal* raps, Neal. Like crossing state lines to commit a felony. I really think you should invite Hamish McDonnell on the Paddy's Pig raid. You'll make a friend—which might prove a benefit. And you'll have a fall-back if you can't nail the Ryan brothers on a homicide charge.''

"Well . . . maybe," the city bull says reluctantly. "I'll have to get an okay from the brass. What kind of a guy is this McDonnell?"

"He thinks he's hard-boiled," Cone says, "but I think he's half-baked. But that's neither here nor there. Come on, Neal, once you guys get this thing wrapped up and tied with a ribbon, there'll be enough glory to go around. The Department will get their headlines, and the Feds will get theirs, and everyone will live happily ever after. Will you call McDonnell?"

"I don't like it," Davenport says grumpily. "This is our baby, and I don't want people thinking we can't clean up the garbage in our own gutters. But like you say, it could be insurance for getting an indictment. Okay, I'll see what the higher-ups think about it. If they say go ahead, I'll give the Feds a call. And next time, for Christ's sake, will you try to be a little more open so I know what's going on?''

"I certainly will," Cone says warmly. "See you at three."

But Davenport has already hung up. Cone replaces the wall phone slowly, and his hand is still on it when it rings again. He picks up, wondering if the city dick has already changed his mind.

"Yeah?" he says.

"Tim? This is Jeremy Bigelow. You really sick?"

"Slightly indisposed. What's with you?"

"I got some good news. I went to my boss with the story of the short traders, and he got the Commission to issue a formal order of investigation. That means we can get subpoenas and question the guys who were selling short so heavily before the dates you gave me."

Cone takes a deep breath. "Jerry," he says, "why did you do that? I thought you turned the whole deal over to the Federal DA. You contacted Hamish McDonnell—remember?"

"Well . . . yeah," Bigelow says, "but why should they get all the credit? It was the SEC that uncovered it—right?"

Cone doesn't comment on that. "You'll get your share of the credit," he tells the investigator, and then repeats what he said to Neal Davenport: "There'll be enough glory to go around. Take my advice, Jerry, and give McDonnell a call before you go ahead with your subpoenas. Otherwise you're going to find there are two identical investigations going on, with everyone walking up everyone else's heels, and bad blood between you and the Feds."

"You really think so?" Bigelow says worriedly.

"I really think so. Be smart and play it cool. Call McDonnell and tell him the SEC has launched a formal investigation and can issue subpoenas, but you don't want to do it if it'll interfere with what he's doing. Be nice and you'll score brownie points. And meanwhile, call your favorite reporters and leak just enough to get their juices flowing. Tell them it's going to be the biggest Wall Street scandal since Boesky. They'll jump at it."

"Yeah," Bigelow says happily, "I could do that."

"Just make sure they spell your name right," Cone says.

He hangs up, shaking his head in bemusement. He can't understand all these headline-hungry guys. Cone couldn't care less about personal aggrandizement, and he doesn't give a tinker's dam about the reputation of Haldering & Co. In a hundred years, who'll remember all this shit?

But meanwhile it's fun. By three o'clock he's tooled his Ford Escort up to 45th Street. He finds a parking space around the block and walks back to join the small crowd of rubbernecks that's appeared out of nowhere to watch the police raid on Paddy's Pig.

There's not much to see. No excitement. No wild-and-woolly shoot-outs. The tavern is blocked off by a jam of official and unmarked cop cars. There's also an NYPD truck pulled up in front, flanked by a mobile TV van. Cone edges into the mob and watches.

There's a parade of sweating cops going into Paddy's Pig empty-handed and coming out lugging cartons, crates, unpacked television sets and VCRs. Then two come out wheeling a black motorcycle, and that's hoisted into the truck.

Louie is brought out, cuffed, held firmly between two uniformed mastodons. He's thrust into a squad car. A younger guy, similarly cuffed, is treated the same way. He's grinning like a maniac. One of the Ryan brothers, Cone assumes. Finally Detective Davenport and ADA Hamish McDonnell exit from Paddy's Pig and stand on the sidewalk, talking rapidly and gesturing.

The vehicles begin to pull away, the rubbernecks disperse. A non-event, Cone figures, and wonders why he bothered to show up. He's about to leave when Hamish McDonnell spots him, yells, "Hey, Cone!" and beckons. Davenport gives him a wise-ass grin and goes back inside the bar.

"You sonofabitch," McDonnell says furiously, "why the hell didn't you tell me the NYPD was after David Dempster for the homicides?"

"Hey," Cone says, "don't get your balls in an uproar. First of all, you had no need to know. Those killings are a Department squeal—correct? I work with the locals just the way I work with you. Everyone gets a piece of the pie."

McDonnell gives him a close look. "I gotta admit you didn't shaft me. Those names you gave me are panning out. All we had to do with one guy was mention the name David Dempster, and he broke. Started blubbering. You know what worries him most? That we'll take his vintage Daimler away from him. How d'ya like that?"

"Beautiful," Cone says. "You got enough on the short-selling and sabotage?"

"We're getting it," the ADA says. "All these guys are going to do time. Maybe not a lot, but some." Suddenly he becomes Mr. Nice. "Listen, Cone," he says, "I'm sorry if I came on heavy. I apologize."

"That's okay. You're entitled. You didn't know me from Adam and probably figured I was handing you a crock."

"Yeah, something like that. Tell me, how did you get onto David Dempster?"

"It was easy," the Wall Street dick says. "I didn't have anyone else."

McDonnell laughs. "And what are you getting out of it?"

"I'll get my reward in heaven."

"Loser!" McDonnell jeers. Then: "Look, I owe you one. We're taking David Dempster tomorrow at four o'clock at his office. Davenport will be there. You want to be in on the kill?"

"I got nothing better to do," Timothy says.

Neal Davenport is waiting in the overchilled lobby of David Dempster's steel and glass office building on Friday afternoon when Cone shows up. They waste no time in greetings.

"How you doing with Louie?" Timothy wants to know.

"We're not ready to dance the fandango yet," the NYPD man says, "but his lawyer sounds like he wants to make a deal. I think we'll nail the Ryan brothers on the kills."

"What about the sabotage?"

"My guess is that David Dempster was directing the whole operation, and paying for it. He gave the orders to Louie, and that shmegegi sent the Westies into action. It was a sweet setup. Louie was Dempster's cutout; he never met the mugs who were doing his dirty work. So naturally they can't finger him."

"Yeah, that's how I see it. But if Louie doesn't talk, Dempster walks away from the homicide rap?"

"Maybe. But McDonnell will get him on the sabotage and conspiracy-to-defraud charges."

"Big deal," Cone says disgustedly. "He'll squirm out of that with a slap on the wrist."

"Don't worry it," Davenport advises. "Louie is going to spill, take my word for it. He's never done time before, and we've been telling him how wonderful Attica is and what a prize his fat ass will be up there."

"You tell him that in front of his lawyer?"

"Of course not. But right now he's being held without bail, and his cellmate is doing us a favor."

"Good," Cone says. "Let the bastard sweat a little."

Then Hamish McDonnell comes marching into the lobby,

carrying a scuffed attaché case. He's flanked by two U.S. marshals, both as big as he.

"You three guys look like a half-ton of beef on the hoof," Davenport says to the ADA. "Did you get your warrant?"

"Signed and sealed," McDonnell says, patting his case. "Now we deliver."

"You going to cuff him?"

"Oh, hell yes. You'd be surprised at the psychological effect handcuffs have on these Ivy League types. Takes all the starch out of their boxer shorts." He turns to Cone. "You been up to his office?"

"Yeah. It's a small place; I'm not sure we'll all fit in. There's this little reception room. A secretary at a desk. One door that leads to Dempster's private office."

"Sounds good. Let's go."

They all jam into a high-speed elevator. They exit on the twenty-seventh floor, tramp down the hallway to Dempster's office in a phalanx. The plump secretary looks up from her magazine in amazement when they come crowding in.

"What—" she starts.

"Don't bother announcing us," McDonnell says. "It's a surprise party."

He strides to the inner door, jerks it open. The five men go charging in. David Dempster, crisply clad, is seated behind his desk, talking on the phone. He hangs up slowly, rises slowly, looks slowly from face to face. One of the marshals glides to his left, the other to his right, as if they've performed this ballet a hundred times.

"David Dempster?" McDonnell asks.

"Yes. And who, may I ask, are you?"

"Hamish McDonnell, Assistant District Attorney, Federal." The ADA flaps his ID at Dempster. "I believe you've met Mr. Cone. This gentleman is Detective Neal K. Davenport of the New York Police Department. These two men are United States marshals. I have a warrant for your arrest."

"Warrant?" Dempster says, the plummy voice suddenly dry and strained. "Arrest? For what?"

"Mr. Dempster," McDonnell says, "the charges against you would fill a windowshade. Will you waive the reading of your rights?"

"Now wait a minute . . ."

"No, Mr. Dempster, you wait a minute. You can waste our time or you can make it easy on us and yourself and just come along quietly. Cooperate—okay?"

David Dempster manages a smarmy grin. "You don't mind if I fill a pipe first, do you?" he asks and, without waiting for a reply, opens a side desk drawer and reaches in.

Surprisingly, it's Davenport who reacts first. The portly detective moves so fast that Cone can't believe it. He launches himself across the desk, grabs Dempster's wrist in both hands, twists in opposite directions. There's a howl of pain, and Neal plucks a nickeled pistol from Dempster's nerveless fingers.

"Nice pipe," the city cop says. "What're you smoking these days—thirty-twos?"

"Cuff him," McDonnell orders, and the marshals bend Dempster's arms behind his back, not gently, and click the steel links on his wrists. They clamp their big mitts on his upper arms.

"Not smart, Mr. Dempster," the ADA says. "What were you going to do, kill all five of us? Or just wave your popgun and make a run for it? It's tough getting a cab on Fridays."

"I wish to speak to my attorney," Dempster says stiffly.

"You'll get your chance," McDonnell says. "Let's go."

Cone stands aside to let the entourage file by. David Dempster pauses a moment, pulling back against the marshals' grip. He stares at Cone.

"You?" he says. "You did this?"

The Wall Street dick nods.

Dempster takes in the rumpled corduroy suit, grayed T-shirt, yellow work shoes.

"But you're a bum!" he says in outraged tones.

"Yeah," Cone says, "I know."

He lets them all go ahead. He dawdles a moment in the reception room where the hennaed secretary has her back pressed against the wall, a knuckle between her teeth.

"I think you can close up now," Cone tells her gently.

"He's not coming back?" she asks.

"Not for a while."

"Shit!" she says unexpectedly. "Best job I ever had."

By the time Cone gets down to the street, the others have disappeared. He glances at the clock over the entrance and figures that if he hurries, he can get back to Haldering & Co.

in time to pick up his paycheck. But hurrying anywhere in that heat is not a boss idea.

"Ahh, screw it," he says aloud, causing passersby to look at him nervously and detour around him.

Stripped to their skivvies, they're lazing around the loft on a late Saturday afternoon. The front windows are open, and Cone's antique electric fan is doing its whirry best, but it's still bloody hot.

"When the hell are you going to spring for an air conditioner?" Samantha Whatley demands.

"One of these days," Cone says.

"That's a lot of bull," she says. "You're such a skinflint you'd rather suffer."

It's the truth, and he knows it. Tightwadism is his philosophy, if not his religion, and the thought of shelling out hundreds of dollars for a decent window unit is more than he can bear.

"It's not so bad," he says defensively. "And they say it's going to cool down tonight."

"Yeah," she says, "maybe to eighty. What are we eating?"

"I got nothing in the house. I figured I'd run out to the deli. What do you feel like?"

"Anything as long as it's cold."

"How about a canned ham, potato salad, some tomatoes and stuff?"

"I can live with that," she says. "And see if they've got any Heavenly Hash."

"What the hell is that?"

"Ice cream, you asshole. What world do you live in?"

They're drinking jug chablis poured over ice cubes, and working on a can of honey-roasted peanuts. Occasionally they flip a peanut to Cleo, who'd rather cuff it and chase it than eat it.

"So?" Sam says. "How you doing on the Dempster-Torrey file?"

"Oh, that," he says casually. "It's over. All cleared up. Finis."

Her feet hit the floor with a thump. She bends across the table and glares at him. "You crapping me?"

He raises a palm. "Scout's honor. I'll write up the final report next week."

"Next week sucks," she says wrathfully. "I want to know right now. Who did it—the butler?"

"Nah," he says. "David Dempster."

She draws a deep breath. "David Dempster? The brother?"

He nods, pours them more wine. "Listen, you know what it means when you sell short?"

"Vaguely. It means you sell something you don't own."

"That's about it, kiddo. When you sell a stock short, you don't own it. But it's perfectly legit."

"So how do you sell it if you don't own it? And what's the point?"

"Let's say that the stock of XYZ Corporation is selling at a hundred dollars a share. You don't own any XYZ but you think, for whatever reason, that the stock is going to take a nosedive. So you *borrow* a hundred shares of XYZ and sell them. You get ten thousand bucks—right? Disregarding the broker's commission. Follow?"

"Sure. But who do you borrow the stock from?"

"Your brokerage house—or anyone else willing to lend the shares to you. Anyway, say the shares of XYZ Corporation do just what you figured and go down to eighty. Then you *buy*. Those hundred shares cost you eight thousand. You return the borrowed shares, and you've made yourself two grand."

"Beautiful," Sam says. "How long has this been going on?"

"Since Eve shorted the apple to Adam."

"But what if the stock goes up?"

"Then you slit your wrists and do a swan from your penthouse terrace. Nah, I'm kidding. Selling stock short isn't much chancier than buying it long because you expect it to go up."

"And that's what David Dempster was doing—selling short?"

"I doubt it," Cone says. "He doesn't strike me as being much of a plunger. But he figured out a handy-dandy scheme for the heavyweight short-sellers on Wall Street. I think it started about three years ago. He knew what an emotional, irrational world the Street is. It's really a loony bin. The silliest rumor or statement by some high-muck-a-muck can send the Dow up or down. So the way I figure it, David Dempster worked out a way to depress the price of particular stocks. Maybe he began by just starting rumors. God knows he had the contacts in his PR business to do that. Or perhaps the Tylenol scare in Chicago gave him the idea. He probably reckoned he could sink the value of shares in a drug or food company just by phoning the cops and newspapers anonymously and claiming he had poisoned the product. Then there's a lot of publicity, products are pulled off the shelves—just to be on the safe side—and the manufacturer's stock takes a tumble.''

"Jesus," Samantha says, "what a perverted mind to think of that."

"Sure, but it worked. Because Dempster realized that even if the stock slid just a couple of points, you can make a bundle if you're trading thousands of shares. A guy who sold short ten thousand shares of XYZ Corporation at a hundred simoleons a share would receive a million bucks—correct? Then, after a product-tampering scare or some other disaster to the company, the stock falls to ninety dollars a share. He *buys* his ten thousand shares at that price and nets a cool hundred thousand smackers. Nice? Now figure what the profit would have been if he had traded a half-million shares!''

"Disgusting," she says. "You're telling me that David Dempster devised ways to make certain that stocks went *down?*"

"You better believe it. And from anonymous phone calls and product tampering he soon began organizing real sabotage like arson and vandalism—and corrupting key personnel. Anything he could do to damage the company, depress the stock price, and benefit his short-selling clients. The Bela Lugosi of Wall Street.''

"And they paid him for the service?"

"Sure. Either a fee or percentage of the take. How do you think he rolled up a personal net worth of four million? He probably had a small list of very greedy customers. Mostly guys who managed OPM—Other People's Money—in pensions and trusts. They'd get together in his townhouse, decide on a victim, and Dempster would get to work. He didn't do the dirty stuff himself, of course; he paid a gang of hoods called the Westies to do that.''

"My God," Sam says, "the things people will do for the almighty buck. You think David Dempster arranged his brother's murder?"

"Hell, yes," Timothy says. "He engineered it, even to the extent of using Teresa Dempster to find out when her husband was leaving on a trip so he could set up that Wall Street ambush. And just like he figured, after his brother died the price of Dempster-Torrey stock took a bath, and all his short-selling clients made a bundle."

They sit silently then, sipping their chilled wine and watching Cleo stalk a peanut across the linoleum. Maybe it really is cooling off, a little, but they have no desire for an aerobics session—at least not the vertical variety.

"Tim," Samantha says in a low voice, "he really had his brother put down? His *brother*, Tim?"

"Oh, yes, he did it."

"But *why?* Just for the money?"

"That was part of it, sure. But I told you that none of us acts from a single motive. People aren't that simple. Yeah, David killed his brother for money. But also he did it because John put the horns on him by enjoying fun and games with Dorothy, David's wife. And you've got to figure there was a lot of sibling rivalry as Neal Davenport, of all people, suggested. Listen, just because two guys are brothers doesn't mean they think alike or have the same personalities and temperaments. Ask any horse trainer. Or even people who breed dogs or cats. They'll tell you that every animal in a litter is different, with its own traits and characteristics. John J. Dempster may have played hardball in his business and personal life, but he was genuine. David Dempster is a small, mean, hypocritical bastard."

Sam holds up her palms in protest. "Enough already!" she pleads. "I'll read all about it in your report. Right now I don't want to hear any more about money, greed, and fratricide. It's all too depressing. I just want to think nice thoughts. Give me a couple of more ice cubes and pour me some wine."

The loft is dimming, and a blessed breeze comes sneaking in the front windows. Cone turns off the fan, and that helps. The traffic noises seem muted and far away.

"How you coming with your nice thoughts?" Cone asks.

"Getting there," Samantha says.

"You be nice to me, I'll be nice to you."

"Best offer I've had all day. Did you change the sheets?"

"Of course. It's the last Saturday of the month, isn't it?"

"My hero," she says. She stands, ambles over to the mattress. She peels off bra and panties. Still standing, a pale wraith in the darkling, she begins unpinning her long, auburn hair.

"Maybe I should go get the ham first," Timothy says.

"Screw the ham!" she says, then pauses, arms still raised, tresses half unbound. She looks at him thoughtfully. "You know who I feel sorry for in that whole Dempster mess?"

"Who?"

"Teresa. She sounds like such a nice, nutty lady. But she was married to a rakehell. And then he gets killed, and it turns out her brother-in-law, who's been a real pal, was involved in the murder. My God, what that woman's been through."

"Yeah, well, she's coping. I went up to see her this morning. She's thinking of going to Japan for a while."

"What for?"

"To study Zen. Says she wants to be closer to the cosmos—whatever that means. She told me she thinks everything happens for the best."

Hair swinging free, Sam comes over to stand close in front of him. He bows his head to kiss her pipik.

"But not you," she says, stroking his bristly hair. "You think everything happens for the worst."

"Not everything," Cone says.

BOOK III

One from Column A

One

It NEVER occurs to Cone that Samantha Whatley doesn't want to be seen with him in public because he dresses like a refugee from Lower Slobbovia. She says it's because she doesn't want to run the risk of being spotted by an employee of Haldering & Co., and then their rare liaison will be trivialized by office gossip.

So their trysts are limited to her gentrified apartment in the East Village or his scuzzy loft in a cast-iron commercial building on lower Broadway. That's okay with Timothy; he's a hermitlike creature by nature, and perfectly willing to play the game according to her rules.

So there they are in her flossy apartment on Sunday night, August 8th, gnawing on barbecued ribs and nattering of this and that.

"When are you going to take your two weeks?" she asks him.

"What two weeks?"

"Your vacation, you yuck. When do you want to take it?"

He shrugs. "Makes no nevermind to me. Anytime."

"Well, I'm taking off on Friday. I'm going home."

He ponders a moment. Then: "You're flying on Friday the thirteenth?"

"Best time. The plane will be practically empty. I don't want you tomcatting around while I'm gone."

"Not me."

"And try to cut down on the booze."

"Yes, mother. Who's going to fill in for you at work while you're gone?"

"Hiram himself."

"Oh, Jesus!" he says, dropping his rib bone. "Don't tell me that while I'm eating."

On Monday morning after Sam leaves, Cone wanders to

work an hour late, as usual. He finds two file folders on his desk: assignments to new investigations. He flips through them listlessly; they look like dullsville to him. One concerns a client who's invested a nice chunk of cash in a scheme to breed miniature horses. Now, with his money gone and the phones of the boiler shop operation disconnected, he wants Haldering & Co. to locate the con men and get his investment back. Lots of luck, Charlie.

The second case concerns a proposed merger between two companies that make plastic cocoons for scores of consumer products—the kind of packaging that breaks your fingernails and drives you to stabbing with a sharp paring knife to open the damned stuff. One of the principals wants a complete credit check on the other. Instant ennui.

Cone tosses the folders aside and finishes his breakfast: black coffee and a buttered bialy. He's on his second cigarette when his phone rings. He picks it up expecting a calamity. That's always safe because then a mere misfortune arrives as good news.

"Yeah?" he says.

"Cone? Hiram Haldering. Come here at once, please."

He was right the first time. It's usually a calamity when H.H. says, "Please."

He slouches down the corridor to the boss's office, the only one with two windows. The bright summer sunlight is bouncing off fatso's balding pate, and he's beaming and nodding like one of those bobbing dolls in the back windows of cars driven by morons. But at least his two air conditioners are wheezing away, so the room is comfortably cool.

Which is providential because the visitor, who rises when Cone enters, is wearing a black three-piece suit that looks heavy enough to be woven of yak hair. He's a tall, cadaverous gink with a smile so pained it surely seems his drawers must be binding. The hand he gives to Cone when they're introduced is a clump of very soft, very shriveled bananas.

"This is Timothy Cone," intones Hiram Haldering. "He is one—and I repeat *one*—of our experienced investigators. Cone, this gentleman is Mr. Omar Jeffreys."

"Of Blains, Kibes and Thrush," Jeffreys adds. "Attorneys-at-law."

Everyone gets seated, and H.H. turns to the lawyer.

"Mr. Jeffreys," he says, "will you explain to Cone what it is you want."

"It is not what *we* want," the other man says. "Oh, dear me, no. Our desires are of no import. We merely wish to present, to the best of our abilities, the wishes of our client."

"Yeah, well," Cone says, "who's the client?"

"For a number of years Blains, Kibes and Thrush, P.A., has provided legal counsel to an Oriental gentleman, Mr. Chin Tung Lee. He is the Chairman and Chief Executive Officer of a corporation that processes and markets a variety of Chinese foods under the White Lotus label. You are, perhaps, familiar with the products?"

"Oh, hell yes," Cone says. "Lousy grub."

"Cone!" Haldering shouts indignantly.

"Well, it is," he insists. "Take their chicken chow mein, for instance. My God, you can hardly find the meat in it. They must be using the same chicken for ten years. So what I do is buy a small can of boned chicken and add it to the chow mein. That makes it okay. Even my cat loves it."

He ends triumphantly, and the other two men stare at him glassily.

"Very interesting, I'm sure," the attorney finally says. "But I do not believe the ingredients in White Lotus chicken chow mein are germane to this discussion. Mr. Chin Tung Lee is presently faced with a financial problem outside the expertise of Blains, Kibes and Thrush. He wishes to employ the services of Haldering and Company, and I am authorized to conclude an oral agreement, prior to the execution of a written contract that will finalize the terms of the aforementioned employment."

"Why didn't he just pick up the phone and call us?" Cone wants to know. "Or come over here himself?"

"Mr. Lee is an elderly gentleman who, unfortunately, has been confined to a wheelchair for several years and is not as physically active as he would like to be. He specifically asked for your services, Mr. Cone."

"Yeah? How come? I never met the guy."

"He is a close personal friend of Mr. Simon Trale of Dempster-Torrey, and I believe it was Mr. Trale's recommendation that led to Mr. Lee's decision to employ Haldering and Company, and you in particular."

"And I'm sure he'll be happy with our services," Haldering booms. "We guarantee results—right, Cone?"

"Nah," the Wall Street dick says. "No one can do that. Mr. Jeffreys, you said that Lee has a financial problem. What is it?"

"I'm afraid I am not at liberty to reveal that at this particular time. Our client wishes to discuss the matter with you personally."

"Okay," Cone says equably. "If he wants to play it cozy, that's fine with me. How do I get hold of him?"

The attorney proffers a business card. "This is the address on Exchange Place. It is the corporate headquarters of White Lotus. On the back of the card you will find a handwritten telephone number. That is Mr. Chin Tung Lee's private line. Calls to that number will not go through the company's switchboard."

Cone takes the card and stands. "All right," he says, "I'll give him a call and find out what his problem is. I also want to tell him to put more chicken in his chow mein."

He shambles back to his office, digs through the mess in his desk (what's a stale package of Twinkies doing in there?), and finally roots out an old copy of Standard and Poor's Stock Guide. He looks up White Lotus.

The corporation, listed on the OTC exchange, sells packaged Chinese foods to consumers, restaurants, and institutions. It is capitalized for slightly over two million shares of common stock, no preferred. It has no long-term debt. It has paid a cash dividend every year since 1949. What is of particular interest to Cone is that the price range of the stock for the past fifteen years has varied from 31 to 34, never below, never above.

Similarly, there has been little change in the annual dividend rate. White Lotus stock is currently yielding slightly over 5 percent. Its financial position appears exemplary: high assets, low liabilities, and a hefty bundle of surplus cash and cash equivalents.

All in all, it seems to be a solid, conservative outfit, but maybe a bit stodgy. It sounds like the kind of stock Chinese widows and orphans would love to own: a nice 5-percent return come wars, inflation, or financial foofarows. No one's going to get rich trading White Lotus, but no one's going down the drain either. So what could their financial problem be?

"Ah so," Cone says aloud in a frightful Charlie Chan accent. "It is written that when icicles drip on the mulch bed, the wise man hides his peanut butter."

He then dials the direct line to the Chairman and Chief Executive Officer of White Lotus. But when Mr. Chin Tung Lee comes on the phone, he sounds nothing like Charlie Chan. And nothing like an invalid confined to a wheelchair. His voice is strong, vibrant, with good resonance.

He says he will be happy to see Mr. Timothy Cone in an hour, and thanks him for his courtesy. A very polite gent.

Cone plods down Broadway to Exchange Place. It's a spiffy day with lots of sunshine, washed sky, and a smacking breeze. Streets of the financial district are crowded; everyone scurries, the pursuit of the Great Simoleon continuing with vigor and determination.

But as he well knows, Wall Street is usually a zero-sum game: If someone wins, someone loses. That's okay; if you can't stand the heat, get out of the kitchen. And thinking that makes him smile because once, not too long ago, Samantha was bitching about how difficult it was for women to rise to positions of power on the Street. To which Cone replied, "If you can't stand the heat, go back in the kitchen." She kicked his shin.

The corporate offices of White Lotus are in a lumpish building that looks in need of steam cleaning. The frowsy lobby is vaguely Art Deco, but the old elevators still have operators—which has become as rare as finding a shoeshine boy or paperboy on the streets of Manhattan.

Timothy, a fast man with a stereotype, figures the offices of any outfit that sells canned chop suey are going to look like a joss house: carved teak furniture, brass statues, and paneled silk screens. But the offices of White Lotus are done in Swedish modern with bright graphics on the walls and, on the floor, a zigzag patterned carpet that bedazzles the eye.

The receptionist—female, Caucasian, young—phones and says Mr. Lee will see Cone in a few minutes. The Wall Street dick spends the time inspecting a lighted showcase in the reception room. It contains packages of all the White Lotus products: noodles, fried rice, chop suey, chow mein, pea pods, water chestnuts, soy sauce, fortune cookies, bean sprouts, bamboo shoots. Cleo would approve.

It really is no more than two minutes before he is ushered into the inner sanctum. Lee's personal office is a jazzy joint with not a hint of any Oriental influence or even the slightest whiff of incense. It's all high-tech with splashes of abstract paintings and clumpy bronze sculptures that look like hippopotamus do-do. There's a mobile hanging from the high ceiling: a school of pregnant pollack in flight.

"You like my office, Mr. Cone?" Chin Tung Lee asks in his boomy voice.

"It's different."

Lee laughs. "My wife decorated it," he says. "I admit it took some time getting used to, but now I like it. My son says it looks like a garage sale."

He presses buttons on the arms of his electric wheelchair and buzzes out from behind the driftwood desk to offer a tiny hand.

"So pleased to make your acquaintance, sir," he says. "Mr. Trale has told me a great deal about you and what a fine job you did for Dempster-Torrey."

"That was nice of him," Cone says, shaking the little paw gently. "You and Trale old friends?"

"Please sit down there. I insisted I have at least one comfortable chair for visitors. As you can see, my chair is mobile, but I must sit on a Manhattan telephone directory to bring me up to desk level."

He laughs again, and Cone decides this guy is the most scrutable Oriental he's ever met. Timothy flops down in the leather tub chair, and Lee whizzes around behind his desk again.

"Oh, yes," he continues, "Simon and I have been friends for many, many years. We play chess together every Friday night."

"And who wins?"

"I do," the old man says, grinning. "Always. But Simon keeps trying. That is why I admire him so much. Mr. Cone, I received a phone call from Mr. Jeffreys of Blains, Kibes and Thrush. He informed me that he has negotiated a satisfactory service contract with Haldering and Company, and that you have been assigned to our case. I was delighted to hear it."

"Thanks," Cone says. "So what's your problem?"

"Before I get into that, I'd like to give you a little background on our company."

"I got all the time in the world," Cone says. "You're paying for it."

"So we are. Well, I'll try to keep it mercifully brief. I emigrated from Taiwan—called Formosa in those days—in 1938, just before the beginning of the war. I had been waiting several years to get on the quota. At that time it was extremely difficult for Asians to enter the United States legally."

"I can imagine."

"However, eventually I did arrive. I came to New York and, with the aid of relatives already here, started a small business on Mott Street. It was really a pushcart operation; I couldn't afford a store. I sold Chinese fruits and vegetables. Well, one thing led to another, and now I own White Lotus. A typical American success story."

"You make it sound easy," Cone says, "but I'll bet you worked your ass off."

"Eighteen hours a day," Lee says, nodding. "In all kinds of weather. Which is probably why I'm now chained to this electric contraption. But the family members I eventually employed worked just as hard. The pushcart became a store, offering poultry and meats as well as vegetables. That one store became four, and we began selling prepared foods. And not only to local residents but to tourists and uptown visitors who came to Chinatown. They wanted mostly chop suey and chow mein in cardboard containers, so that's what we sold. It was merely a small step from that to the canning process. We went public in 1948."

"And the rest is history."

Chin Tung Lee smiles with a faraway look, remembering.

"Do you know, Mr. Cone," he says, "I miss those early days. The hours we worked were horrendous, but we were young, strong, and willing. And you know, I don't think any of us doubted that we'd make it. This country offered so much. If you devoted your life to your business, you would succeed. It seemed that simple."

"Things have changed," Cone offers.

"Yes," Lee says, looking down at the spotted backs of his hands. "I try not to be a boring ancient who talks constantly of the 'good old days,' but I must admit that things have changed—and not always for the better.''

He pauses, and Cone has a chance to take a close look. The man has got to be Simon Trale's age or more—well over seventy. And he's even smaller than Trale, though it's hard to judge with him sitting in the wheelchair, propped on a telephone book, short legs dangling.

He's got a polished ivory complexion and sports a faded and wispy Vandyke that makes his face appear truncated and incomplete. His eyes are dark and sparkling—nothing enfeebled about those eyes—but he's wearing what is obviously a toupee, and a hellish one at that: a mustardy mixture of white, gray, black, with reddish strands. The guy who made that rug, Cone decides, should be shot.

"All those relatives," Chin Tung Lee goes on, "who worked so hard with me—brothers, sisters, aunts, uncles, cousins—I'm afraid I've outlived them all. Their portions of the business have passed to the second and, in some cases, to the third generation. But I still think of White Lotus as a family business, Mr. Cone. Not as large as La Choy, certainly, but with a personality and distinctiveness all its own. I am sorry to bore you with all this; you must forgive the maunderings of an old man.''

"No, no," Cone says. "I'm getting the picture. But how come you haven't retired?"

"To what?" Lee says, flaring up. "To chess every Friday night with Simon Trale? No, thank you. White Lotus has been my life and will continue to be while life lasts.''

"You mentioned the second and third generations—you've brought them into the business?"

"Only my son, Edward Tung Lee. He is my child by my first wife, who died several years ago. The others—nephews, nieces—none showed any interest in White Lotus, other than cashing their dividend checks. Perhaps they all thought devoting their lives to the production of quality canned chop suey was beneath them. However, I must admit that most of them have done very well—doctors, lawyers, musicians. One nephew is doing computer research at M.I.T. I'm very proud of him.''

"And the son who works for the company—what is his position?"

"Edward? I suppose you might call him our Chief Operating Officer. He oversees production, labor relations, marketing, financial planning, advertising, and so on. I want him to be experienced in every department.''

''That means you expect him to take over someday.''

''Perhaps,'' Chin Tung Lee says, looking at Cone queerly. ''Perhaps not. But enough of these personal details. They really have nothing to do with why you are here.''

''Your financial problem?''

''More of a puzzle than a problem. Mr. Cone, have you any idea what price White Lotus common stock closed at on Friday?''

The Wall Street dick shrugs. ''I don't know exactly, but I'd guess it was somewhere between thirty-one and thirty-four dollars a share.''

Lee stares at him a second, then breaks into a jovial laugh again, tugging at his silky beard. ''Ah,'' he says, ''I see you have been doing your homework. I like that. Well, if you had given me that answer six months ago, you would have been exactly right. But as a matter of fact, on last Friday White Lotus stock closed at forty-two and a half.''

''Oh-ho,'' Cone says, ''so that's it. How long has this been going on—for six months?''

''Approximately.''

''Has the volume of trading increased?''

''Appreciably. And the price of the stock continues to rise.''

''Are you planning anything? Like a buyout? A merger? A big expansion? New products?''

''No to all your questions. We are a very well-structured corporation, Mr. Cone. Profitable certainly, but not wildly so. We keep a low profile. We don't dabble in anything in which we have no expertise. As far as I'm concerned, our product line is complete. No increase in the dividend has been declared or even discussed. You may think we are ultraconservative, perhaps dull, but that has been my business philosophy all my life: Learn what you can do, do it as well as you possibly can, and don't take risks trying to conquer new worlds. So I really can't account for the run-up in our stock. As I say, it puzzles me—and it disturbs me. I'm at an age where I don't enjoy surprises—especially unpleasant surprises. I want to know what's going on.''

''Yeah,'' Cone says, ''can't blame you for that. Okay, I'll

254 / LAWRENCE SANDERS

look into it and see if I can come up with something. I'd like to talk to your son if that's all right.''

"Of course. Today he's at our factory in Metuchen, New Jersey, but he should be back later this afternoon. I'll tell him to expect a call from you and to cooperate fully.''

"Thanks. That should help. All of your stuff is produced in New Jersey?''

"Only the consumer products. The restaurant and institutional sizes are made up at a new facility in the industrial park at what used to be the Brooklyn Navy Yard. We also have several small buying offices around the country to ensure a steady and dependable supply of fresh ingredients.''

"That's another thing,'' Cone says. "Why don't you put more chicken in your chicken chow mein? There's no meat in there.''

Chin Tung Lee looks at him with an ironic smile. "Eat more noodles, Mr. Cone,'' he advises.

"Yeah,'' Cone says, "I guess that's one solution. Well, thanks for the information. I'll ask around and see what else I can pick up. And I'll get back to you if there's anything more I need.''

"Whenever you wish; I am at your disposal. You may think it odd that I should be concerned at this sudden and unexplained increase in our stock price and trading volume. Other companies would welcome such activity, I know. But it's so unusual for White Lotus that I can't help wondering what is going on. And I must admit to a fear that if you discover what it is, it will not be pleasing. I hope you will expedite your investigation, Mr. Cone.''

"I'll see what I can do,'' Cone says. "If I come up with something, you'll be the first to know.''

He rises, reaches across the desk to pump the little hand again. He's still in that position when he hears the office door open behind him. He straightens, turns slowly.

A woman has come bursting into the room. She is young (about twenty-five), tall (almost six feet), blond (very), with a velvety hide (tawny), and summer-sky eyes. She is wearing a cheongsam of thin, pistachio-colored silk that clings.

Those jugs have got to be silicone, the Wall Street dick decides, because if they were God-made there'd be a slight sag just so He could remind the public of human imperfection.

"Oh, darling," she carols, "please excuse me. I didn't know you had a visitor. Sorry to interrupt."

"Come in, Claire," Chin Tung Lee says gently. "You're not interrupting at all. Mr. Cone, I'd like you to meet my wife."

Cone nods from where he stands across the room. Which is just as well, he figures, because if he went close to shake her hand he might flop to his knees in humble obeisance.

He meanders back to John Street, inspecting the women he passes and comparing them to Mrs. Claire Lee. She's got them all beat by a country mile.

So stricken was he by her sudden appearance that his impressions are still confused, and he tries to sort them out. He debates if she is the model type, the dancer type, the actress type.

"The goddess type," he says aloud.

He buys a meatball hero and a couple of cold cans of Bud, and goes up to his office. He reflects mournfully that it's a fitting lunch; that's exactly what he is—a meatball hero. Besides, she's the client's wife, and he doesn't dast fantasize depraved dreams about her. A waste of time. Still, a few modest dreams couldn't hurt anyone. Not even Samantha.

He resolutely vanquishes the scintillant image of Claire Lee, and unwraps his oozing sandwich. While he's scoffing, he calls Jeremy Bigelow at the Securities and Exchange Commission.

"Hey, old buddy," Jerry says happily, "that short-trading scam is really panning out. The bad guys are falling all over themselves to squeal and cop a plea."

"Yeah, I read about it," Cone says. "So you owe me one—right?"

"Oh-oh," Bigelow says, instantly worried. "Now what?"

"Very easy. Your secretary could look it up. There's this outfit on the OTC exchange. White Lotus. They sell canned chop suey. I just want to know if anyone has filed a 13-D public disclosure form on them."

"Why would anyone want to buy five percent of canned chop suey?"

"Beats the hell out of me. Look it up, will you?"

"Okay," the SEC man says. "I'll get on it and let you know."

"How soon?"

"As soon as my secretary gets back from lunch."

Cone finishes his hero and starts on the second beer. He leans back in his squeaky swivel chair, puts his feet up on the desk, and broods about what he knows and what he doesn't know.

He knows that a sudden run-up in stock price and an increase in trading volume is frequently—not always, but frequently—a tipoff that someone is going to make a tender offer for the company concerned. Usually the first step is to accumulate sufficient shares to prove you're serious and then make a bid to purchase enough stock from other shareholders—customarily at a premium over the current market price—to give the offeror control.

It can be a friendly takeover in which the company's management cooperates, or unfriendly, during which the company's executives and directors fight tooth and nail to defeat the bidder—and keep their jobs. The benefaction of shareholders is not always the highest good on Wall Street. "Corporate democracy" has all the modern relevance of "Fifty-four forty or fight," and sometimes the poor shareholders have to take their lumps.

One kicker here is that when any entity—individual or corporate—accumulates 5 percent or more of another company's stock, the entity must file a 13-D public disclosure form with the SEC, stating the purpose of the purchase: tender offer or simply an investment.

Jeremy Bigelow's secretary calls in about an hour and tells Cone there is no record of a 13-D form having been filed for White Lotus. He thanks her, hangs up, and goes back to his pondering, demonstrating his enormous physical strength by crumpling an empty aluminum beer can.

The absence of a 13-D form doesn't faze him; it's still possible a tender offer for White Lotus is in the making. There are several ways of getting around the 13-D law, all of them devious. If you like things in black and white, security regulations are not for you. Wall Street prefers grays.

Cone is certain of one thing: If a tender for White Lotus is in the works, it's going to be treated as an unfriendly offer by Mr. Chin Tung Lee. Cone will not soon forget the little man's passion when he spoke of a "family company" and how White Lotus was his entire life. Any hopeful raider is in for a knock-down-and-drag-out fight before Lee surrenders White Lotus—if he ever does.

What Cone can't answer is the question Jeremy Bigelow asked: Why would anyone *want* White Lotus? Admittedly it has a clean balance sheet; the bottom line looks good. But it has no subsidiaries that could be spun off for instant profit. Its product line offers nothing new or different. It would take an enormous infusion of advertising dollars to increase its market share at the expense of La Choy.

Figure White Lotus stock is selling at forty bucks a share. That means, with two million shares outstanding, anyone taking over the company would have to come up with eighty million dollars. That may not sound like much, Cone acknowledges, in this era of megadeals, but it's still a nice piece of change.

And Cone doesn't think White Lotus is worth it. There's little opportunity for growth there, and even with a more dynamic leadership than Chin Tung Lee offers, the company seems fated to amble along at a tortoise pace, paying a nice dividend but with no potential of becoming a real cash cow. Cone can name a dozen companies at the same price, or lower, that would provide a better chance to make a killing.

All this cerebral activity makes him drowsy. His chin sinks onto his chest, and he dozes at his desk for almost an hour. He doesn't even dream of Claire Lee, but he twitches awake when the phone rings. He picks it up.

"Mr. Timothy Cone?"

"Yeah. Who's this?"

"Edward Tung Lee. Mr. Cone, I'm still in New Jersey, but I just spoke to my father and he said you'd like to talk to me."

"That's right. Whenever you have the time."

"Well, I'm about to drive back to Manhattan. I have a business appointment at a restaurant on Pell Street at five o'clock. It shouldn't take long—ten or fifteen minutes. If you could meet me there, perhaps we can have a drink together."

"Sounds good to me," Cone says. "What's the name of the place?"

"Ah Sing's Bar and Grill. They're in the book."

"I'll find it. I better describe myself so you can spot me."

"Don't bother," Edward Lee says, laughing. "You'll be the only honkie in the joint."

He disconnects, and Cone hangs up thoughtfully. The guy sounded high. Maybe he's snorting monosodium glutamate or mainlining soy sauce. Cone shakes his head to rid his still sleep-befuddled brain of such nonsense, and starts flipping through his tattered telephone directory to find the address of Ah Sing's Bar & Grill on Pell Street.

It turns out to be exactly like a hundred other cheap Chinese restaurants Timothy has frequented from Boston to Saigon: all Formica and wind chimes, fluorescent lights and plastic poppies. The walls are white tile, reasonably clean, decorated with paintings of dragons on black velvet and a calendar showing Miss Hong Kong in a bikini.

A small bar is on the right just inside the entrance. Drinkers have a fine view of the frenetic activity on Pell Street through a big plate glass window, though right now the bar is empty. But the remainder of the long, narrow restaurant has plenty of early diners, all men, all Asian, seated at tables and in booths.

Cone has no sooner swung aboard a barstool when there's a slender guy at his elbow. He's dressed like an Oriental yuppie.

"Mr. Cone?" he says in that bouncy voice. "I'm Edward Tung Lee." They shake hands. "Look, why don't you have a drink. I'll be finished in a few minutes and join you here."

"Take your time," Cone says. "No rush."

"Henry," Lee calls to the bartender, "put this on my tab, please."

Cone watches him stride back to a booth. He's tall, about Cone's height, but with better posture. He moves with quick grace: a young executive on the fast track. His jetty hair is blow-dried, and during the few seconds they talked, Timothy noted the gold Rolex, gold chain bracelet, diamond cuff links. Edward Lee doesn't need a fortune cookie to predict a glorious future; he picked the right father.

"Sir?" the bartender asks.

"As long as he's paying for it," Cone says, "I'll have a double Absolut vodka on the rocks. Splash of water. No fruit."

"Very wise," Henry says.

He gets to work, playing a conjuror. Tosses ice cubes into the air. Catches them in the glass. Begins to pour from the vodka bottle. Raises the bottle high without spilling a drop. Sets the glass smartly in front of Cone and adds a dollop of ice water with a flourish.

"Nicely done," Cone says. "If I tried that, I'd need a mop."

"Too much water?" the bartender asks anxiously.

Cone takes a sip. "Just right," he says.

Henry moves away, and Cone works on his drink slowly, looking out the big window at the mob scene on Pell: pedestrians rushing, street vendors dawdling, traffic crawling, a guy carrying a clump of live chickens (heads down, feet trussed), and a young woman strolling in a sandwich board covered with Chinese characters.

He turns to look back into the restaurant. Lee was right; Cone is the only Caucasian in the place. That makes him think the food must be something special. But then he decides that conclusion is probably as stupid as the belief that truckers know where to eat. Follow that dictum and you're in for a humongous bellyache. Those guys are interested only in quantity and low price. Cone figures the patrons of Ah Sing's Bar & Grill have the same needs.

He spots Edward Tung Lee sitting in a booth against the far wall. Lee is leaning over the table, talking rapidly and earnestly to a roly-poly Asian with three chins and a gut that doesn't end. The two have their heads together, which looks funny because Edward has thick, glossy hair and the fat guy is bald as a honeydew melon.

While Cone watches, Lee slides out of the booth, shakes hands with the other man. He comes quickly to the bar, threading his way through the tables, and takes the stool next to Cone. Henry is in front of him instantly.

"The usual, Mr. Lee?" he asks.

"Why not."

They both watch as Henry goes into his act, mixing a scotch sour with all the showy skill of a professional juggler.

"Best bartender I've ever seen," Cone says.

"Henry belongs uptown," Lee says. "I could get him a job like that"—he snaps his fingers—"but Chen would kill me. That's the tubby gentleman I was talking to: Chen Chang Wang. He owns this joint and a dozen others like it around the city. He has enough labor problems without me luring away his favorite bartender."

"Chen Chang Wang is the owner?" Cone says. "What happened to Ah Sing?"

"Long gone," Lee says with his burbling laugh. "But the name lingers on. Ah Sing's is a lot easier to remember than Chen Chang Wang's Bar and Grill."

"A good customer?" Cone guesses.

"A *very* good customer. You'd be amazed at the quantity of White Lotus products he moves. Not exactly gourmet food, but he gives good portions and his prices are reasonable."

"You call on customers yourself? I should think your salesmen would do that."

"Oh, they do, they do. But I like to visit all our wholesale customers myself now and then. Listen to their complaints, make sure they're getting deliveries on time, ask for suggestions on how we can improve our service. Orientals place a lot of importance on close personal relationships, Mr. Cone."

"It makes sense. Listen, I don't want to take up too much of your time. I talked to your father this morning and got most of the information I need. I also met your stepmother," he adds.

Edward Lee makes a face. "There's no fool like an old fool," he says.

Timothy doesn't like that. If Chin Tung Lee wants to marry a dish one-third his age, it's nobody's business but his own. Edward has no call to bad-mouth his father—unless the luscious Claire cut him out of an inheritance he expected.

"I thought she was a nice lady," Cone says, "but that's neither here nor there. I guess your father told you why he hired Haldering and Company."

"The run-up in our stock price? Nothing to it. Much ado about nothing."

"Yeah?" Cone says. "How do you account for it?"

"Easy," Lee says. "With this bull market, a lot of people are getting nervous. There's going to be a huge correction. I don't mean there's going to be a calamitous crash, but what goes up has got to come down. As they say on Wall Street, trees don't grow to the sky. So a lot of investors are getting out of the high-fliers. Lately there's been a stampede to quality. And White Lotus has always been an undervalued stock. My God, where else can you get a safe five-percent return year in and year out from a solid, well-managed company?"

While he expounds all this, Cone has been inspecting him in the mirror behind the bar. In that blued reflection Lee looks older than Cone first thought. His wrinkle-free skin seems more the result of facials and bronzing gel than the placidity of a man at peace with himself and the world.

He's a handsome guy with gently curved lips, cleft chin, and a high unblemished brow. The slant of the eyes is slight but exotic, and the black, horn-rimmed glasses with tinted lens give him the appearance of an off-camera movie star. He's not wearing a wedding band, but Cone wonders if he's married, and makes a mental note to find out.

His glib explanation of why White Lotus stock is on a rampage disturbs the Wall Street dick. Too much frowning sincerity. The guy seems to be pushing when there's no need to push.

"Well, you may be right," Cone says. "I've just started on this, so I've got no ideas, one way or another."

Edward signals the bartender and points to Cone's empty glass and his own. Henry gets to work.

"Take my advice, Mr. Cone," Lee says, "and don't waste your time. Believe me, it's just a demonstration of normal market forces at work. In another six months or so, I expect the price of White Lotus stock will be back in its usual range."

"Have you told your father this?"

That's when the man's ire becomes apparent. "Tell him? Who the hell can tell him anything? He's always been stubborn, but he's getting worse. Ever since he married that— Well, ever since my mother died and he remarried. Sometimes I wonder if he's getting senile. Let me give you a for-instance. A year ago I went to him with what I thought was a great idea—and everyone in the business I talked to said it would fly. I wanted White Lotus to get into frozen dinners. Packaged gourmet Chinese food. Slide them in the oven or microwave and you'd have a delicious meal as good as anything prepared fresh by the best Chinese chefs. I'm talking about steamed sea bass, salt-baked chicken, mu shu pork, five-fragrant beef, smoke tea duck, and things like that."

"Yeah, well, I don't know much about highfalutin food, but it sounds like a commercial idea."

"Commercial?" Lee cries. "A blockbuster! I spent six months researching it. The numbers looked good. I'm not only talking about frozen Chinese dinners sold to consumers in supermarkets, but the restaurant trade, too. So a joint like this could expand its menu. The cost would be doable. No chefs to hire. No fresh produce going bad on you. Someone orders, say, twice-fried shredded beef, you just pop the package in the microwave, and that's it. Sensational!''

"And what did your father say?"

"He said no. He wants to stick to the same old crap we've been turning out for forty years. Damn it!'' Then, as if ashamed of his vehemence, Edward Tung Lee tries a smile. "Ah, well,'' he says lightly, "you lose one, you win one—right?"

The owner, Chen Chang Wang, comes waddling by. He gives them a Buddha smile, waves a flabby hand, goes out the door to Pell Street.

"Well,'' Cone says, "I think I—"

Then the world comes to an end. They hear sharp explosions—more booms than cracks. The plate glass window shatters, comes crashing down. A hole and star appear in the mirror behind the bar. Someone starts shrieking and can't stop. There are more shots.

Cone falls off his barstool and drags Edward Lee to the floor along with him. He goes for the magnum in his ankle holster.

"Stay down!'' he orders the other man. "Don't even raise your head.''

He looks cautiously to the rear of the restaurant. Tables and booths are empty; the patrons are flat on the floor.

"Keep down,'' he cautions Lee again.

He rises slowly to a crouch. No more explosions, the shrieking has finally ended. Now there are shouts, and someone is blowing a whistle: short, loud, repeated blasts.

Cone slips the .357 into his jacket pocket. Gripping it, he goes out the front door onto Pell Street. People are coming from doorways, from behind parked cars and pushcarts. A uniformed cop is already there, and another comes pounding up. A circle of gawkers forms.

And in the center, spread-eagled on the sidewalk and leaking blood, lies the body of Mr. Chen Chang Wang, looking like a beached and punctured whale.

Cone goes back inside. Edward Lee is standing, brushing

off his black silk suit. Henry rises slowly from behind the bar.

"Sorry I knocked you over," Cone says.

"Glad you did. What the hell happened?"

"I'm afraid," says Timothy, "you just lost a good customer."

Lee stares at him, face twisted. "Chen?"

Cone nods.

"Dead?"

"Very."

Lee's face scrunches up even more. He begins pounding on the bar with a clenched fist. "Bastards!" he spits out. "Oh, the rotten bastards!" Then, calming: "Henry, pour me a brandy, and one for Mr. Cone, and you better have one yourself."

No tricks this time, no wizardry; the bartender fills three snifters with a trembling hand. He drains his glass in one gulp. Cone and Lee right the toppled barstools, sit down, turn to watch the confusion on Pell Street. A squad car, siren growling, has nosed through the mob and parked. They hear more sirens coming closer.

"Ah, Jesus," Lee says, taking a swallow of his brandy, "he was a sweet man."

"Someone didn't think so," Cone says. "Who are the bastards?"

"What?"

"When I told you he was dead, you said, 'The bastards, the rotten bastards.' Who did you have in mind?"

"Oh," Lee says, "that. I meant the man who shot him."

"Uh-huh," Cone says. "Probably more than one. Wang is pretty well perforated. Sounded like forty-fives to me."

Two uniformed officers come into Ah Sing's Bar & Grill. One is Chinese, the other black. They have notebooks and pens ready. The Chinese goes to the back of the restaurant where the patrons, now seated at tables and booths, are again digging into their rice bowls. The black officer stops at the bar.

"Were you gentlemen seated here when the incident occurred?" he asks them.

"Yeah," Cone says. "Having a drink. Then all hell broke

loose. We heard shots, and the plate glass window came down.''

"Did you see anything that happened outside?"

"Not me," Cone says.

"You?" he asks Edward.

"I saw nothing," Lee says. "We were talking together, facing each other."

"Okay," the cop says. "This is just preliminary. Could I have your names, addresses, and phone numbers, please. And I'd like to see any identification you have."

He copies everything down in his notebook.

"Thank you for your cooperation," he says politely. "Anything else you can tell me?"

"Yeah," Cone says, pointing at the holed and starred mirror. "A wild slug went in there. You'll be able to dig it out if you need it."

The officer looks. "Thanks again," he says gratefully. "I might have missed that."

"Can we leave now?" Lee asks him.

"Sure," the cop says. "Everything's under control." He moves down the bar to question Henry.

"He didn't even search us," Lee says.

"Why should he? They've probably got witnesses who saw the shooters make their getaway. I doubt if killers would pop Mr. Wang and then come into his bar and order drinks."

"If he had searched us," Lee persists, "he'd have found your gun. I saw you take it from a holster on your leg."

"So?"

"You always carry it?"

"Yep. My security blanket. I've got a permit for it."

"You're a valuable man to know," Edward Tung Lee says in a low voice.

What he means by that, Cone has no idea.

Two

HE WAKES in a grumpy mood, hauls himself off the mattress, lights his first cigarette of the new day. He goes growling around the loft, washing and shaving, drinking black coffee and then adding a smidgen of brandy just to get his eyelids up.

"So I tell him a good customer has been scragged," he says to Cleo, who is working on a breakfast of leftover chicken chow mein. "And he says, 'The bastards, the rotten bastards.' So I ask him who the bastards are, and he says he meant the guy who popped Chen Chang Wang. Now I ask you, does that make sense? Of course it doesn't. So he was lying. But why? No skin off my ass. I couldn't care less who ventilated Mr. Wang. Cleo, you dirty rat, are you listening?"

It's a peppy August day, which does nothing for his crusty mood. So the sun is shining. Big deal. That's what it's getting paid for, isn't it? And that mild azure sky with fat little puffs of clouds—it all looks like a sappy postcard. "Having fine time, wish you were here." And when the hell was Samantha coming home?

There's a guy waiting for him in the Haldering reception room. He looks short and squat sitting down, but when he stands up, he's lean and mean, only an inch or two shorter than Cone. He's Chinese, with black hair cut *en brosse,* and he's got a mouthful of too many white teeth.

"Mr. Timothy Cone?"

"That's right. Who you?"

The gink hands him a business card, and the Wall Street dick reads it aloud: "Johnnie Wong. Federal Bureau of Investigation." Cone inspects the card, feeling it between thumb and forefinger. "Very nice. Good engraving. You mind showing me your potsy?"

"Not at all." Wong whips out his ID wallet and displays it.

"Uh-huh," Cone says. "Looks legit. What's with the Johnnie? Why not just plain John?"

"Take it up with my mom and pop," the FBI man says. "I've been suffering from that all my life. The Wong I can live with, but please don't tell me 'Fifty million Chinese can't be Wong.'"

"I wasn't going to," Timothy says—but he was. "You want to palaver, I suppose. This way."

Johnnie Wong follows Cone back to his weeny office and looks around. "I like it," he says. "It's got that certain nothing."

"Yeah," Cone says, and holds up the brown paper bag he's carrying. "My breakfast: coffee and bagel. You want something? I'll call down for you."

"No, thanks," Wong says, "I've had mine. You go ahead."

Cone lights a Camel, starts on the container of black coffee, the bagel with a shmear. "So?" he says to the other man. "How come the FBI is parked on my doorstep?"

"You were in Ah Sing's Bar and Grill on Pell Street when the owner, Chen Chang Wang, was killed."

"Oh-ho," Cone says, "so that's it. Yeah, I was there. But how come you guys are interested? I should think it was something for the locals to handle."

"We're working with the NYPD on this," Wong says. "That's how I got your name. Would you mind telling me what you were doing there?"

"Yeah, I'd mind. There's such a thing as client confidentiality."

"Sure," the FBI man says. "And there's such a thing as obstruction of justice."

The two men stare at each other a moment. Johnnie Wong is a jaunty guy with eyebrows like mustaches. He's a little chubby in the face, but there's no fat on his frame; he looks hard and taut. He grins a lot, flashing all those Chiclets, but it's tough to tell if it's genuine merriment or a grimace of pain.

"Tell you what," Cone says, "you tell me why the FBI is interested in Wang's murder, and I'll tell you what I was doing there."

Wong considers that a moment. "Fair enough," he says finally. "But I trade last."

It's Cone's turn to ponder. "Okay," he says, "I'll deal. I was with Edward Tung Lee, the chief operating officer of White Lotus. You've heard of them?"

Wong nods.

"Haldering and Company was hired by White Lotus to find out why the price of their stock has shot up in the last six months. That's what Edward Lee and I were talking about."

"Interesting," the FBI man says, "but not very."

"Now it's your turn."

"It's a long story."

"I got nothing better to do than listen," Cone says.

"All right then, listen to this: Since 1970 the number of Chinese immigrants in this country has almost doubled. I'm talking about people from Taiwan, mainland China, and Hong Kong. Add to those the immigrants from Macao, South Korea, Singapore, Vietnam, Cambodia, and Thailand, and you'll see there's a helluva lot of Asians here. Ninety-nine percent of the come-ins are law-abiding schnooks who just want to be left alone so they can hustle a buck. The other one percent are dyed-in-the-wool gonnifs."

"And that's where you come in," Cone says.

"You got it. I'm a slant-eye, so the Bureau assigned me and a lot of other Oriental agents to keep tabs on the Yellow Peril. What's happened is this: In the past few years the Italian Mafia has taken its lumps. The older guys, the dons and godfathers, are mostly dead or in the clink. The new recruits from Sicily are zips, and the guys running the Families today just don't have the clout and know-how. There's been a vacuum in organized crime. Or was until the Asian gangs moved in. The biggest is United Bamboo. They're mostly from Taiwan but have links with the Yakusa, the Japanese thugs. Their main competitor, not as big but growing fast, is the Giant Panda mob, mostly from mainland China and Hong Kong."

"United Bamboo and Giant Panda," Cone repeats. "Nicer names than La Cosa Nostra. What are these bad boys into?"

"You name it," Wong says. "United Bamboo is in the heroin trade because they've got good contacts in the Golden Triangle. Now they're making deals with the Colombians and pushing cocaine. They also own a string of prostitution rings around the country, mostly staffed by Taiwanese women. Giant Panda does some dope dealing—a lot of marijuana—but most of their money comes from shakedowns: a classic protection racket aimed at Chinese restaurants, laundries, and groceries. Lately they've been trying to take over legitimate businesses.''

"Any homicides?" Cone asks.

"Hell, yes! Practically all United Bamboo or Giant Panda soldiers. But a lot of innocents, too. People who refused to pay baksheesh or just had the bad luck to be in the wrong place at the wrong time. Anyway, the reason I'm telling you all this is because Chen Chang Wang, the guy who got chilled yesterday, was an officer in Giant Panda. Not the top general of the New York organization, but a colonel."

"So that's it. You've had your eye on him?"

"Not a tail—we don't have the manpower for that. Just loose surveillance."

"And you think it was United Bamboo who knocked him off?"

"It had all the earmarks of a United Bamboo kill. They use very young punks—guys in their teens—and give them stolen U.S. Army forty-five automatic pistols. They just squat, close their eyes, and blast away. They've got to hit *something*. Then they take off, sometimes on foot, sometimes in a car or on a motorcycle. Get this: Last month there was a murder in Seattle's Chinatown, and the killers made their getaway on bicycles! How does that grab you?"

"Beautiful," Cone says. "So there's no love lost between the two gangs?"

"None whatsoever," Johnnie Wong says with his glittery grin. "They're competing for the same turf. Each wants to take over when the Mafia goes down. Listen, they've got more than a million Asian immigrants to diddle. That can mean a lot of loot."

"No difference between the two?"

"I wouldn't say that," Wong says cautiously. "First of all, United Bamboo speaks mostly the Cantonese dialect while Giant Panda is mostly Mandarin."

"Which do you speak?" Cone asks him.

"Both," the FBI man says, and the Wall Street dick decides his grin is the real thing. Here's a guy who gets a laugh out of the world's madness.

"Also," Wong goes on, "United Bamboo are the heavies. I mean they're really vicious scuts. Burn a guy with a propane torch before they chop off his head. Or take out a victim's family in front of his eyes before they off him. The old Mafia would never touch a target's family—I'll say that for them. But United Bamboo will."

"Like Colombian coke dealers?" Cone suggests.

"Yeah, those guys are savages, too. But the Giant Panda mob is softer. Not saints, you understand. They kill, but it's all business with them. They're putting a lot of their young guys in banks and brokerage houses on Wall Street. Listen, all this bullshit is getting me nowhere. Isn't there anything else you can tell me about your meeting with your client in Ah Sing's?"

"Not a thing," Cone says. "He was talking with Chen Chang Wang when I got there. Then he left Wang in a booth, came over and joined me at the bar. In a little while, Wang walked by, smiled and waved at us, went out—and that's when the fireworks started."

"And that's all you can tell me?"

"That's all."

Johnnie Wong looks at him closely. "You wouldn't be holding out on me, would you?"

"Why would I do that?" Cone says. "I know from nothing about United Bamboo and Giant Panda and who blasted the late Mr. Wang."

"Uh-huh," the FBI man says. "Well, I'll take your word for it—for now. I checked you out before I came over. You add up: the tours in Vietnam, the medals, and all that. Where are the medals now?"

"I hocked them," Timothy says.

Wong flashes his choppers again. "Keep in touch, old buddy," he says. "We haven't got all that many warm bodies assigned to Asian gangs in the New York area, and I have an antsy feeling that something is going down I should know about and don't. So consider yourself a deputy. If you pick up anything, give me a call. You have my card."

"Sure," Cone says, "I'll be in touch. And you've got my number here."

"I do," Johnnie Wong says, rising. "And I've also got your unlisted home phone number."

"You would," Timothy says admiringly. "You don't let

any grass grow under your feet, do you? We can work to-gether.''

"Can we?" Wong says, staring at him. "You ever hear the ancient Chinese proverb: *A freint darf men zich koifen; sonem krigt men umzist.* A friend you have to buy; enemies you get for nothing.''

"Yeah," Cone says.

After the FBI man leaves, Cone flips through the morning's *Wall Street Journal.* Then he lights another cigarette, leans back, clasps his hands behind his head. He knows he should be thinking—but about what? All he's got is odds and ends, and at the moment everything adds up to zilch. No use trying to create a scenario; he just doesn't have enough poop to make a plot.

So he calls Mr. Chin Tung Lee on that direct number at White Lotus. The Chairman and CEO picks up after one ring.

"Yes?" he says.

"Mr. Lee, this is Timothy Cone at Haldering."

"Ah, my young friend. And how is your health today?"

"Fine, thanks," Cone says, willing to go through the cere-mony with this nice old man. "And yours, sir?"

"I am surviving, thank you. Each day is a blessing."

"Uh-huh. Mr. Lee, the reason I'm calling is that I'd like to get hold of a list of your shareholders and also a copy of your most recent annual report. Is that all right with you?"

"Of course. I'll have a package prepared for you."

"If you could leave it at the receptionist's desk, I could pick it up without bothering you."

"Oh, no," Chin Tung Lee says. "I will be delighted to see you. And there is something I wish to ask you."

"Okay," Cone says. "I'll be there in an hour or so."

He wanders down the corridor to the office of Louis Kier-nan, a paralegal in the attorneys' section of Haldering & Co. Cone prefers bracing Kiernan because the full-fledged lawyers give him such a load of gobbledygook that he leaves them with his eyes glazed over.

"Lou," he says, lounging in the doorway of the cubby, "I need some hotshot legal skinny so gimme a minute, will you?"

Kiernan looks up from his typewriter and peers at Cone

over his wire-rimmed reading glasses. "A minute?" he says.
"You sure?"

"Maybe two. There's this rich old geezer whose first wife
has died. Now he's married to a beautiful young knish. He's
also got a son by his first wife who's older than his second
wife—dig? Now my question: If the codger croaks, who inherits?"

"The wife," Lou says promptly. "At least half, even if the
deceased leaves no will. The son would probably be entitled
to a third. But listen, Tim, when you get into inheritance law
you're opening a can of worms. Anyone, with good cause,
can sue to break a will."

"But all things being equal, you figure the second wife for
at least fifty percent of the estate and the son for, say, thirty
percent?"

"Don't quote me," Kiernan says cautiously.

"You guys kill me," Cone says. "When a lawyer's wife
asks, 'Was it as good for you as it was for me?' he says, 'I'd
like to get a second opinion on that.' Thanks, Lou. See you
around."

He rambles down to Exchange Place, sucking on another
cigarette and wondering how long it'll take nonsmokers to
have the streets declared off-limits. Then nicotine addicts will
have to get their fixes in illicit dens, or maybe by paddling
out into the Atlantic Ocean in a rubber dinghy.

Twenty minutes later he's closeted with Chin Tung Lee.
The old man looks chipper, and since he's puffing a scented
cigarette in a long ivory holder, Cone figures it's okay to light
up another coffin nail.

"I know it's too early to ask if you have made any progress, Mr. Cone."

"Yeah, it is. I'm just collecting stuff at this stage. That's
why I wanted your shareholder list and annual report."

"Right here," Lee says, tapping a fat package on his desk.
"I hope you will guard this well. I would not care to have the
list fall into the hands of an enemy."

"I'll take good care of it," Cone promises. "I notice
White Lotus stock is up another half-point."

"It continues," the little man says, nodding. "My son believes it is of no significance, but I do not agree."

"By the way," Cone says, as casually as he can manage, "is your son married?"

Chin Tung Lee sets his holder and cigarette down carefully in a brass ashtray made from the base of a five-inch shell. "No, he is not," he says with a frazzled laugh. "It is a sadness for me. Men my age should have grandchildren. Perhaps great-grandchildren."

"He's still a young man," Cone says. "He may surprise you one of these days."

"A very pleasant surprise. Family is important to me. Are you married, Mr. Cone?"

"No," the Wall Street dick says, stirring uncomfortably in the leather club chair. "You said you had something to ask me."

"Ah, yes," Lee says, and now his laugh is vigorous again. "Happy news, I am glad to say. Today is my dear wife's birthday. To celebrate, we are having a cocktail party and buffet dinner in our apartment this evening, and I hope you will be able to join us."

"Hey," Cone says, "that sounds great. What time?"

"From five o'clock until the wee hours," the gaffer says gleefully. "I must admit I am looking forward to it. I enjoy celebrations."

"Fireworks?" Timothy says, grinning.

"Regretfully, no. The popping of champagne corks will have to do."

"Your son will be there?"

"Naturally," Chin says, astonished at the question. "He lives in the apartment. With his own private entrance, I might add. In any event, we are expecting almost a hundred guests, and I trust you will be one of them."

"Sure will," Cone says. "You in the book?"

"We are indeed. But to save you from searching through four pages of Lees in the Manhattan directory, I have written out our address and home telephone number. You will find it in the package. Then we may expect you?"

"Wouldn't miss it," Cone promises. "Should I bring a birthday present?"

The old man waves a hand in protest. "Of course not. Your presence will be gift enough."

A lesson to Cone in grace and civility.

He's down in the lobby carrying the fat package when he

realizes what was missing from that conversation. Chin Tung Lee never asked if Cone had spoken to his son. And he had said nothing of the murder of Chen Chang Wang, a good customer of White Lotus products.

Which meant—what? That he considered it of no importance, or that his son had not told him that he and Cone were in Ah Sing's when Wang was sent to join his ancestors.

The Wall Street dick begins to appreciate what is meant by a "Chinese puzzle."

He can go back to the office—but that's not a cheery prospect. Haldering might come nosing around, demanding to know what progress Cone has made on the White Lotus case as well as those other two files, real yawners, he's supposed to be investigating.

So he decides to hike all the way back to his loft, breathing deeply to get the cigarette smoke out of his alveoli. That lasts for six blocks; then he lights up, cursing himself for his weakness as he inhales deeply and wonders which will rot first: lungs, liver, or kidneys.

He doesn't bother picking up lunch, figuring he can last till that buffet dinner. Then he'll gorge and maybe slip something special in his pockets for Cleo. Meanwhile the cat can subsist on refrigerator grub: cheddar and bologna.

In the loft, he strips to T-shirt and baggy Jockey briefs and mixes himself a jelly jar of vodka and water, with plenty of the former, little of the latter, and lots of ice.

"Here's looking at you, kid," he toasts Cleo, who has come out from under the bathtub and is now lying in a patch of diffused sunshine coming through the dirt-encrusted skylight.

The first thing Cone does is phone Eve Bookerman at Dempster-Torrey, something he should have done a week ago.

"I'm so glad you called, Mr. Cone," she says in her ballsy voice. "I wanted to thank you personally for the job you did on our sabotage problem. Marvelous!"

"Yeah," he says, "it turned out okay, and for once the nice guys didn't finish last. Listen, the reason I'm calling is this: When I was working your case, we rented a car for a month. It's a Ford Escort and was charged to Dempster-Torrey. By rights the car should have been turned in when the file was closed. But there's still about two weeks left on the rental, and I wanted to ask if it's all right with you if I keep the car until the month runs out.''

She laughs. "Mr. Cone, you keep the car as long as you need it, and don't worry about the billing. It's the least we can do.''

"Thanks," he says. "It'll be a big help. Anything new on who's going to be the CEO at Dempster-Torrey?''

"I didn't make it," she says.

"Tough," Cone says. "But tomorrow's another day.''

"Thank God for that," she says. "Nice talking to you, Mr. Cone. Let's have a drink sometime.''

"You name it," he answers, knowing she never will.

He sits at the kitchen table with his drink and opens the White Lotus package. The first thing he goes through is the annual report, knowing full well that like most corporation reports, it should be submitted for the Pulitzer Prize in fiction.

White Lotus is a four-color, slick-paper job. It doesn't tell him much more than he's already learned except that the number of registered stockholders is slightly over 2,000—which seems high for a company as modest as this chop suey producer. On the opening page are photographs of Chin Tung Lee and Edward Tung Lee, facing the camera with frozen smiles.

The Board of Directors is interesting. Of the ten, three are outsiders, all with Caucasian names. Of the remaining seven, five are named Lee and the other two have Chinese monikers. All seven are officers of White Lotus. Sounds to Cone as if the Chairman and CEO is keeping a very tight rein indeed on his company.

The computer printout of shareholders' names, addresses, and the number of shares held provides more provocative stuff. Cone flips through the list quickly, getting an instant impression that at least 90 percent of White Lotus shareholders are Chinese, or at least have Oriental names. Then he zeros in on the largest holdings, those of Chin Tung Lee, Claire Lee, and Edward Tung Lee.

He does some rough estimates because the battery of his handy-dandy pocket calculator went kaput a long time ago and he hasn't gotten around to replacing it. He figures Chin Tung Lee owns about 26 percent of White Lotus, wife Claire 11 percent, and son Edward 16 percent.

Those numbers add up to some ripe conclusions. The three of them combined hold a majority interest in White Lotus. Chin and Claire can easily outvote Edward. Chin and Edward can easily outvote Claire.

And Claire and Edward can outvote Chin.

The other 47 percent of White Lotus is held by the 2,000 shareholders, mostly in odd lots. There are few investors with as many as 1,000 shares. And they, Cone notes, are all Chinese.

"I don't know what it all means," he says to Cleo. "Do you?"

The cat gives him the "I am famished" signal, which consists of ankle rubs and piteous mewls.

So Cone tosses the beast a slice of bologna and mixes himself a fresh drink. He opens a bag of Cheez Doodles and goes back to his arithmetic.

He thinks of it as getting "spiffed up," but no one else would. The thready tweed jacket with greasy leather patches on the elbows isn't quite the thing for a cocktail party in August. The gray flannel slacks, recently laundered, still bear the stains of long-forgotten sausage submarines. The button-down shirt is clean, even if one button is missing. He wears the collar open, of course, and the T-shirt shyly revealed is almost white.

Donning this finery puts him in an antic mood, and on the drive uptown in his red Escort he bangs his palm on the steering wheel and sings as much of the Marine Corps hymn as he can remember—which is not much. Finished with his caroling, he wonders if his frolicsome mood is due to the prospect of free booze and a generous buffet or the hope of seeing Claire Lee again, a woman he wouldn't sully with his dreams.

The Lees live in a Fifth Avenue apartment house just north of 68th Street. It is an old building with heavy pediments and carved window casements. It is planted solidly on the Avenue, turning a stern and forthright stare at the frivolity of Central Park. The building is a dowager surrounded by teeny-boppers.

The Lees' apartment is something else again. It occupies the entire ninth floor with two entrances and enough space to accommodate a convention of sex therapists. The crowd that has already assembled when Cone arrives is wandering through room after room, seemingly lost in this high-ceilinged, air-conditioned warren. There's enough furniture to equip a small, slightly shoddy hotel.

Three bars have been set up, and two long buffet tables. Repressing his appetites, Cone first seeks out Chin, Edward, and Claire Lee to pay his respects. Duty done, he shuffles off to the nearest bar for a vodka (Finlandia), gulps that, orders a refill, and carries it to an adjoining buffet. There he piles a platter with rare roast beef, sliced turkey breast, cherry tomatoes, cukes, and radishes. He also ladles out a bowl of something that looks Chinese. It turns out to be shrimp in lobster sauce, Szechwan style. It makes his scalp sweat.

He does his scarfing in a corner where he can eyeball the parading guests. They're mostly Orientals, but there's a good representation of whiteys and blackies. All are thin, elegantly dressed and, Cone figures, perform no more arduous chores than clipping coupons from their tax-exempt bonds. But that's okay. Life is unfair; everyone knows that.

He finishes his food but is not ready for seconds—yet. He hands the plate to a passing waiter and joins the wanderers, reflecting that occasionally his job does have its perks. He finds a large room, furniture pushed back against the wall, rug rolled up, where a three-piece combo is playing Gershwin, Cole Porter, and Irving Berlin. It's the kind of toe-tapping music Cone enjoys—he hates any song he can't whistle—and he dawdles there awhile watching a few couples dancing on the waxed parquet floor.

Then he repairs to the closest bar and, since no one is going to hand him a tab, asks for a cognac. He's smacking his chops over that when Edward Tung Lee, wearing a dinner jacket, comes swaying up. It doesn't take a sherlock to deduce that the guy is half in the bag.

"So glad you could make it," he says with a crazed smile.

"I'm glad, too," Cone says. "I wish your stepmother would have birthdays more often."

"Did you see what she's wearing?" Edward demands. "Disgusting!"

The Wall Street dick doesn't think so. Claire is tightly enwrapped in a strapless wine-colored velvet gown with bountiful décolletage. There's a star-shaped mouche stuck to her right clavicle, so adroitly placed that the most jaded observer must become a stargazer, an eager student of heavenly bodies. It happened to Cone.

"It's her birthday," he advises Edward. "Let her enjoy."

But the son's anger will not be mollified. "Let her enjoy," he repeats darkly. "The day will come . . ."

With this dire prediction, he weaves away, and Cone is happy to see him go. His hostility toward his stepmother is understandable—but that doesn't make it right. Timothy just doesn't want to get involved.

He has one final sandwich of smoked sturgeon on Jewish rye (seedless), and a portion of ice cream he can't identify. But it's got cut-up cherries and chunks of dark chocolate mixed in. Cleo would love it.

One more brandy, he decides, and when the black bartender asks, "Sir?" Cone grins foolishly and says, "Double cognac, please."

Working on his drink, he goes back to the buffet table and filches some slices of roast beef, baked ham, and sturgeon, which he wraps in a pink linen napkin and slips into his jacket pocket. And he's not the only guest copping tidbits; a lot of the elegant ladies are loading up their handbags.

He's about to search out Chin Tung Lee and make a polite farewell when he feels a soft hand on his arm. He turns to see that velvety star, the beauty patch adhering to skin as creamy as the ice cream he just scoffed.

"Mr. Cone," Claire Lee says with a smile that buckles his knees, "I'm so glad you could make it."

"Happy Birthday," is all he can manage.

"You already wished me a Happy Birthday," she says, laughing. "When you arrived—remember?"

"So?" he says. "Two Happy Birthdays. A dozen."

"Thank you," she says, suddenly grave. "I know that my husband was delighted that you could come. He likes you, Mr. Cone."

"And I like him. A fine gentleman. I was just about to find him and say goodnight."

"No," she says sharply, "not yet. Have you seen our terrace?"

He shakes his head.

"Let me show you," she says, taking his arm.

It turns out not to be a world-class terrace. First of all, it faces eastward with a dead view of the bricked backs of buildings on Madison Avenue. Also, it is narrow—hardly enough room to swing a cat—and the lawn chairs and tables look like castoffs from a summer place in the Hamptons. There are a few hapless geraniums in clay pots.

Still, it is outdoors, and a number of people have found their way there, carrying drinks and plates of food. They seem to enjoy dining alfresco, and the guy in the white dinner jacket snoring gently in one of the rusted chairs is feeling no pain.

Claire leads Cone down to one end, away from the other guests. They stand at the railing, looking down into a paved and poky courtyard. They'd have been wiser to look up at a cloudless sky made luminous by moonlight. It's a soothing night with a blessed breeze and the warm promise of a glorious day to come.

"Did you see Edward?" she asks in a low voice. "The man is drunk."

"Nah," Cone says. "Just a little plotched. He's navigating okay."

"You don't think he'll make a scene, do you?"

"I doubt it."

"My husband worked so hard to make this party a success. I'd hate to have it spoiled."

"It is a success," he assures her, "and nothing's going to spoil it."

She is silent, still gripping his arm. He is conscious of her softness, her warmth. And her scent. It is something tangy, and he has a terrible desire to sneeze.

She is a lofty woman; in her high heels she is as tall as he. She stands erectly, and he wonders if that's her natural posture or if she's just trying to keep her strapless bodice secure. The moonlight paints a pale, silvery sheen on her bare shoulders, and her long, slender arms are as smooth and rounded as if they had been squeezed from tubes. The wheaten hair is braided and up in a coil.

"He hates me," she says quietly. "Edward. I know he does."

Cone doesn't like this. He's a shamus and doesn't do windows or give advice to the lovelorn.

"He's an awful, awful man," Claire Lee goes on, "but I can understand the way he feels. I'm so much younger than Chin. I'm even younger than Edward. Naturally he thinks I'm a gold digger. But I happen to love my husband, Mr. Cone; I swear I do.''

"Yeah," he says, acutely uncomfortable.

She takes her arm from under his and turns suddenly to face him. He is proud that he can return her stare and not let his eyeballs drift downward into the valley of the damned.

"You're a detective, aren't you?" she asks, her voice still low but steady and determined.

"Well, my boss calls us investigators. Most of our work is financial stuff. Wall Street shenanigans. I mean, we don't handle burglaries or homicides or crimes like that—"

"But you know *about* them, don't you?"

"Some," he says, totally confused now and waiting to hear what she's getting at.

"Listen," she says, "I need your advice."

"Not me," he says hastily. "If it's something personal, I'm just not qualified. Sorry."

She turns away to peer down into the concrete courtyard again.

"I've got no one else I can talk to," she says.

"No one? What about your husband?"

"No."

"A girlfriend? Family?"

"No one," she repeats.

The wine-colored velvet gown has no back. He can see gently fleshed shoulders, the soft channel of her spine. His weakness makes him angry.

"Just what the hell are you talking about?" he says roughly, then finishes his drink and puts the empty snifter in his pocket.

"I need help," she says, turning her head toward him, the big baby-blues widened and softened with appeal.

He realizes it's a practiced come-on, but he can no more resist it than he could resist that final double cognac.

"What's the problem?" he says in a croaky voice.

"I can't talk about it now," she says, speaking more rapidly. "Not here. You know Restaurant Row?"

"Forty-sixth Street between Eighth and Ninth? Yeah, I know it. Some good take-out joints."

"There's an Italian place called Carpacchio's on the north side of the street, middle of the block. They've got a small bar in the back. It can't be seen from the street. Can you meet me there at three o'clock tomorrow afternoon? The lunch crowd will have cleared out by then.''

So she had it all planned, he reflects mournfully, and knew I'd jump. Sucker!

"Sure," he says, "I could do that. Carpacchio's at three tomorrow. I'll be there."

"Oh, thank you," she says breathlessly. "Thank you so much." She leans forward to kiss his cheek fleetingly. "You stay here a minute; I'll go in alone."

"Yeah," he says, "you do that."

He waits a few moments after she's gone, then leaves the Lees' apartment without saying goodnight to the host.

On the drive back home, he tries to con himself by reasoning that all he's doing is helping a damsel in distress. But that won't wash. He wonders if he would have agreed to the meet if Claire was ugly as a toad and caused warts. He knows the answer to that one.

Then he figures that it's possible that whatever her problem is, it just might have something to do with what he's supposed to be investigating: the run-up in the price of White Lotus stock. There's no way he can deny that possibility and no way he can confirm it except by appearing at Carpacchio's at three o'clock tomorrow.

Feeling better about his decision, telling himself it's all business, just business, he climbs the six floors to his loft to find Cleo in an agony of hunger. When he pulls the napkin-wrapped package from his pocket and opens it, the demented animal, sniffing the odors, begins leaping wildly at him, pawing his legs.

Cone tears off bite-sized pieces of beef, ham, and sturgeon and puts them in the cat's dish, a chipped ashtray. Cleo starts gobbling, then stops a moment in the ingestion of these rare delicacies to look up at him in astonishment, as if to say, "How long has *this* been going on?"

He pulls the empty snifter from his other pocket and pours himself a jolt of harsh Italian brandy for a nightcap. He sucks on it slowly, sitting at his table, feet up, trying to imagine what the lady could want. He thinks about possible motives for a long time, and then realizes his primal urge has cooled.

There's something more, or less, to Claire Lee than a goddess. She was rehearsed and knowing. Very sure of her physical weapons and how to use them. Nothing wrong with that except his vision of her is shattered. But it's not the first time his hot dreams have been chilled. He can endure it.

But what, in God's name, could Claire Lee *want?* Considering that, he looks down to see Cleo crouched at the table. The cat's dish is empty, and the ravenous beast, mouth slightly open, is staring at him with a feral grin that seems to be saying, "More, more, more!"

Three

HE SPENDS the morning at the office, groaning over the composition of the weekly progress report that each of the five Haldering & Co. investigators is required to submit. With Samantha on vacation, the reports will go to Hiram Haldering himself, known to his employees as the Abominable Abdomen.

Cone composes what he considers a masterpiece of obfuscation. It hints, it implies, it suggests, and is such an incomprehensible mishmash that he figures it'll send Hiram right up the wall. The report ends: "Will the White Lotus investigation be brought to a successful conclusion? Only time will tell."

Satisfied with his literary creation, he tosses it onto the receptionist's desk and flees the office. He stops at a nearby umbrella stand for a Coney Island red-hot with mustard, onions, and piccalilli, washed down with cherry cola. Eructing slightly, he pokes back to his loft. But instead of going up, he finds his Ford Escort, unticketed and with hubcaps intact, and drives uptown.

Parking anywhere near the Times Square area is murder, and he has to go over to 44th Street and Tenth Avenue before he discovers an empty slot. He walks back to Restaurant Row, pausing en route to buy a lemon ice from a sidewalk vendor and watch the action at a three-card monte game. The dealer is really slick, and Cone, making mental bets, loses fifty imaginary dollars.

He gets to Carpacchio's on West 46th Street about twenty minutes early, figuring it'll give him a chance to have a drink and scope the place. But when he enters and walks to the back, Claire Lee is already there, sitting alone at the little bar and working on something green in a stemmed glass.

The only other people in the dim restaurant are six waiters

having their late lunch at a big table up front. Cone takes off his cap and slides onto the barstool next to Claire. She gives him a thousand-watt smile.

"I was afraid you wouldn't show up," she says.

"I told you I would," he says gruffly. "What do I have to do to get a drink in this joint?"

She swings around to face the table of waiters. "Carlos," she calls. "Please. Just for a minute."

One of the guys rises, throws down his napkin, comes back to the bar. He isn't happy at having his lunch interrupted.

"Yeah?" he says.

"Could I have another of these, please. And my guest will have—what?"

"Vodka rocks," Cone says. "And you better give me a double so you don't have to stop eating again."

Carlos shoots him a surly look but serves them, then returns to the noisy table up front.

"A real charmer," Cone says.

"Carlos isn't angry at waiting on us during his lunch. He just doesn't like seeing me with another man."

"Oh-ho," Cone says. "It's like that, is it?"

She takes a cigarette from a platinum case. He holds a match for that and his own Camel, noticing that her fingers are trembling slightly.

She looks smashing in a printed silk shirtwaist with a rope belt. Her hat is enormous: a horizontal white linen spinnaker. It would look ridiculous on a smaller woman, but she wears it with all the aplomb of a nun in a starched wimple.

"Lovely day, isn't it?" she says.

"Oh, my, yes," Cone says. "And here it is Wednesday, and don't the weeks just fly by."

She stares at him, outraged, then tries a weak grin. "I guess I deserved that. But it's hard to explain why I asked you to meet me."

"Just say it. Get it over with."

"Yes, well, I'm afraid it's a confession. I hope I can trust you, Mr. Cone. If not, I'm dead."

"I don't blab."

"First of all, I want to hire you, Mr. Cone."

"I told you," he says patiently, "I've got a job. Financial investigations. If what you want comes under that heading, then you'll have to make a deal with my boss."

"Then I want your advice," she says, looking at him directly. "Will you give me that?"

"Sure. Advice is free."

"Before I married my husband, I was living in California. I was very young and hadn't been around much. I went to Los Angeles hoping to get in the movies or television."

"You and a zillion others."

"I found that out. Everyone told me I had the looks. I don't want to sound conceited, but I thought I did, too. Prettier than a lot of girls who made it. And a better figure."

"I'll buy that," he says.

"What I didn't have," she goes on, "and don't have, is talent. I did one test and it was a disaster. My aunt, my closest relative, sent me the money for acting school. I tried, I really did, but it didn't help. I just couldn't act or sing or dance. Have you ever been to southern California, Mr. Cone?"

"Yeah, I spent some time there."

"Then you know what it's like. Life in the fast lane. Sunshine. Beaches. Partying. Twenty-four-hour fun."

"If you've got the loot."

She drains her first green drink and takes a little sip of the second. "Exactly," she says. "If you've got the loot. I ran out. And I couldn't ask my aunt for more."

"Why didn't you go home?"

"To Toledo? No, thanks. No surfing in Toledo. And it would have been admitting defeat, wouldn't it?"

"I've done that," he tells her. "It's not so bad."

"Well, I couldn't. So, to make a long story short, I ended up in a house in San Francisco. Not a home—a house. You understand?"

"I get the picture," he says.

"Don't tell me there were a lot of other things I could have done: sell lingerie in a department store, marry a nebbish, go on welfare. I know all that, and knew it then. But I wanted big bucks."

He doesn't reply.

She is silent a moment, and he stares at her, wondering how much of her story is for real and how much is bullshit. Her face reflects the innocence of Little Orphan Annie, but he suspects that inside she's got a good dollop of Madame Defarge.

Her nose is small and pert. A short upper lip reveals a flash of white teeth. The complexion is satiny, and if she's wearing makeup it's scantily applied. He finds something curiously dated in her beauty; she could be a flapper: She's got that vibrant look as if at any moment she might climb atop the bar and launch into a wild Charleston that would shiver his timbers.

"So?" he says, wanting to hear all of it. "Now you're in a house in San Francisco. A cathouse."

"That's right," she says, lifting her chin. "In Chinatown. It was called the Pleasure Dome. Very expensive. It catered mostly to Oriental gentlemen. It was run very strictly. No drugs, believe it or not, and no drunks tolerated. We accepted credit cards."

"Beautiful. Were you the only white in the place?"

"There were two of us. The other girls were mostly Chinese, some very young, from Taiwan."

"And you made the big bucks?"

"I surely did. I had my own apartment, a gorgeous wardrobe, and for the first time in my life I had money in the bank. I even filed a tax return. In the place where you have to put in your occupation, I wrote Physical Therapist."

"I'll drink to that," Cone says, and does. "How long were you there?"

"Almost two years. Then the place was raided and closed down."

"Oh? Local cops?"

"No, FBI. According to the newspaper stories, the Pleasure Dome was part of a chain of fancy houses owned and operated by some Chinese gang."

"Uh-huh. Were you charged?"

"I wasn't caught. I lucked out. On the weekend the place was busted, I was up in Seattle with a Chinese gentleman who was on a business trip. They let us do that occasionally—take short trips with some of the wealthier clients. The tips were great. Anyway, I got back to Frisco on Monday and discovered I was out of a job. More important, the other girls who had been picked up during the raid were still in jail. It turned out that most of them were here illegally and would be deported. I decided the smart thing would be to put distance between me and the Pleasure Dome. In one day I closed out my bank account, packed my favorite clothes, and got a plane to New York.''

He looks up at her admiringly. "No flies on you," he says.

"I've learned," she says. "The hard way. But I did all right. I had some names to look up in New York."

"Chinese gentlemen?"

She looks at him sharply but can see no irony in his face or hear sarcasm in his voice. "That's right," she says. "Old friends. Then, about three years ago, I was introduced to Chin Tung Lee. He was and is the sweetest, dearest, most sympathetic and understanding man I've ever met. His wife had died, and he didn't want to live out his life with just that miserable son of his for company. Chin is almost three times my age, but when he asked me to marry him, I said yes."

"You were tired of the game?" Cone guesses.

"Yes, I was tired."

"And Chin was wealthy."

She shows anger for the first time. "What the hell did that have to do with it? All my friends were wealthy, but I had enough money in the bank to tell any one of them to get lost—and I did it, too, on a couple of occasions. I don't care what you may think; I didn't marry Chin for his money."

"Okay, okay," Cone says, "I'll take your word for it. Did you tell him any of your past history before you married him?"

"No."

"Did he ever ask?"

"Once. I made up some stuff about teaching school in Ohio."

"Sounds like a happy ending to me," the Wall Street dick says. "So what am I doing here listening to your soap opera? What's your problem?"

She sighs and opens an alligator handbag that probably cost more than Cone makes in a week. She pulls out an envelope and hands it over.

"I got this in the mail last Friday," she says. "Take a look."

He inspects the long white envelope. Addressed to Mrs. Claire Lee at their Fifth Avenue apartment. No return address. Postmarked New York. Cone looks at her. "You sure you want me to read this?"

"That's why I'm here," she says determinedly.

It's a single sheet of white paper folded in thirds. Two lines of typewriting: "Remember the Pleasure Dome? We have the photographs."

Cone reads it again and looks up at her.

"Blackmail?" she asks.

"Sounds like. What photographs do they mean?"

"No porn, if that's what you're thinking. But on the Chinese New Year we always had a big party at the Pleasure Dome. Free food and booze for our best clients. All of us girls would be there. Fully clothed, of course. Maybe our gowns would be low-cut or very short, but all our bits and pieces were covered. It was just a big, noisy party, and pictures would be taken as souvenirs for the clients. Those were the only photographs taken in the Pleasure Dome as far as I can recall."

Timothy stares at her. "You may have learned the hard way, as you say, but I wonder if you learned enough. When you had a scene with a customer at the Pleasure Dome, where did you take him?"

"Upstairs. To one of the bedrooms. They were beautifully decorated and furnished."

"I'll bet. Mirrors on the walls?"

"Of course."

He gives her a cold smile. She returns his stare, her face becoming as white and stiff as her hat. "Jesus!" she gasps. "You don't think they took photos through the mirrors, do you?"

Cone shrugs. "It's been done before. It's a smart move for any guy who runs a kip. First of all, it helps keep his girls in line. Second, he can always sell the photographs or videotapes to jerks who get their jollies from that kind of stuff. And third, the possibility of blackmail is always there. So he shoots the action through a two-way mirror and builds up a nice file that his girls and clients don't know about. He can lean on them anytime he wants."

"Oh, my God," Claire Lee says despairingly, "what am I going to do?"

"Right now? Nothing. This is just the opening move. A blackmailer wants the victim to sweat a little first, lose sleep, think of nothing but what it's going to cost to keep the secret hidden. Have you been sleeping since you got the letter?"

"With pills."

"There you are. You're getting nervous already, anxious enough to tell me about it, and you don't even know what the blackmailer's got and what he wants for it. You'll get another letter, Mrs. Lee, with maybe a sample photograph attached. Then you'll get more letters, spelling out exactly what you'll have to pay. You have any idea who might be pulling this?"

"No. Not the slightest. Isn't there anything you can do to stop it?"

"Nope. This first letter is completely innocent. Take it to the cops and they'll laugh. You haven't been threatened—yet. This is only the opening move in a dirty game. You'll just have to play it out. Mrs. Lee, why don't you let me keep this letter."

"Why do you want it if you can't do anything?"

"So you don't keep reading it and driving yourself nuts. How many times have you looked at it already? A dozen? A hundred? A thousand times?"

"At least," she says with a wan smile. "All right, you take it."

"Let me know when the second letter arrives," Cone says. "Because you're going to get another; I guarantee it."

She finishes her drink. "You know, Mr. Cone," she says, "I feel better just telling you about it. I guess confession really is good for the soul."

"Is it?" he says. "I wouldn't know."

He drains his vodka and stands up. "Keep in touch," he says, trying to keep it light. "And thanks for the drink."

He walks slowly toward the outside door and pauses to pull on his cap. He glances back. Carlos, the waiter, is already at her side. The two are talking earnestly, their heads so close together that the guy is practically standing under her broad-brimmed hat.

He's back in the loft before five o'clock, nods at Cleo, and immediately gets on the horn to Johnnie Wong at the Federal Bureau of Investigation.

"Can I buy you a drink?" he asks.

"Hey, old buddy," Wong says, "that's the best bribe I've had all day. Where?"

"How about my place?"

"Sounds good. How do I find it?"

Cone laughs. "If you've got my unlisted phone number,

you've got to have my address. If you can get here before six, the downstairs door will be open and the elevator will be working. I'm on the top floor, a loft.''

"I'll find you."

Cone gives Cleo fresh water, half a can of human-type tuna, and sits back to review that wacky conversation with Claire Lee.

He can't for the life of him think of any reason why she would make up a history like that. And after all, it wasn't so unusual that it couldn't be true. But what was her motive for telling Cone, practically a stranger, all the squalid details of her past when, according to her, she hadn't even told her husband?

Cone decides he'll buy her story. The lady is terrified—or at least badly spooked. She can't ask help from Chin or Edward Lee, and apparently has no close friends she can consult. So she picks the only guy in the law enforcement business she knows. Looking at it from that angle, her confession makes a crazy kind of sense.

He pulls the letter from his pocket and reads it again. "Remember the Pleasure Dome? We have the photographs." That tells him exactly nothing, unless Claire's horror was feigned when he told her about a camera clicking away through a two-way mirror. Maybe she had willingly posed for centerfolds with men, women, donkeys, and dalmatians. That would account for her fear of a letter that apparently said zip.

He is still trying to puzzle out what's going on in that beautiful head, and wondering about the extent of her chicanery or absence thereof, when there's a sharp rapping on the door. He moves to one side of the jamb.

"Yeah?" he calls. "Who is it?"

"Johnnie Wong."

Cone unchains, unbolts, unlocks the door. The FBI man comes in, flashing his toothy grin. He takes a look around the place.

"Holy Christ!" he says. "You live here? If I were you, I'd sleep in the office. What's that thing under the bathtub?"

"Cleo, my cat," Cone says. "Listen, this joint's not so bad. It was neat and clean when I moved in, but I grunged it up a little to make it livable."

"You call this livable? It's the biggest Roach Motel I've ever seen. Where's that drink you promised me?"

They sit on opposite sides of the table. Wong has a beer. "No, thanks," he says when Cone offers a jelly jar. "I'll drink it right out of the can. That way the worst thing that can happen to me is a cut lip." He takes a gulp, then looks at the Wall Street dick thoughtfully. "Okay, you didn't ask me up to admire the interior decoration. What do you want?"

"I told you Haldering was hired to investigate the run-up in the price of White Lotus stock. I've got a list of the shareholders here. There're more than two thousand names, so I don't expect you to study the whole printout. But would you take a quick look and see if you recognize any of the names."

"Oh, God," Johnnie Wong says, sighing. "This I've got to do for a free beer? All right, let me see the damned thing."

He flips through the pages swiftly, then goes back to the first and starts again, slower this time. Cone sits silently until Wong tosses the list aside.

"Interesting," the FBI man says. "The second time I went through it, I looked for people with big holdings, a thousand shares or more."

"You recognize any of the names?"

"About a half-dozen. They're all members of the Giant Panda gang."

The two men stare at each other a moment.

"What does that mean?" Cone asks.

"Beats the hell out of me," Johnnie says. "I guess it means that Giant Panda is assembling a heavy position in White Lotus stock. But for what reason, the deponent knoweth not. Got any ideas?"

"Not a one," Cone says fretfully. "They're a long way from having control of the corporation. And the stock pays five percent. That's a nice return for legitimate equity investors, but it's bupkes for a criminal gang."

"Well," Wong says, "it's your problem. Now do you figure I've paid for my brew, or have you got something for me?"

Cone admires the guy. He's a no-horseshit operator, cards on the table, everything up front. Timothy figures he better give him something if he wants the agent on his side.

"I've got a weirdie for you," he says. "It may be a bone or there may be some meat to it. Ever hear of a cathouse in San Francisco called the Pleasure Dome?"

Wong is about to take a swallow of his beer, but he stops and puts the can back on the table.

"The Pleasure Dome," he repeats. "How in God's name did you come up with that one? Have I ever heard of it? You bet your sweet patootie I have. I was stationed in Frisco when we busted the joint. What a palace that was! White girls, blacks, Chinese, Koreans, Hispanics, Japanese. It was a House of All Nations. Very exclusive. Very expensive. No sailors allowed. How do you know about the Pleasure Dome?"

"It just came up in conversation," Cone says. "Who owned the joint?"

The FBI man shoves his beer away and stands up. "Okay," he says, "you wanna play hard to get, so be it. Don't call me again."

"Wait a minute," Cone says. "Let me think."

"Yeah," Wong says, sitting down again, "you do that."

He is quiet then, sipping his suds slowly, his eyes on Cone.

The Wall Street dick knows that he needs this guy. He's got a pipeline into the Asian underworld that Cone could never match. Secretiveness is Cone's nature, but here's a case where it could work against him, make his job twice as hard, if not impossible. He ponders a long time, trying to decide where his loyalties belong. How much does he owe the client? And the client's wife?

"Who owned the Pleasure Dome?" he asks again, trying one last time.

Wong gives him a mocking grin. "Trade last," he says. "Who told you about the place?"

Cone gives up, figuring he's got no choice. "A woman named Claire," he says. "Ring any bells?"

"Good God, this is like pulling teeth. What's Claire's last name?"

Cone hesitates a beat or two, then realizes he's in for a penny, he might as well be in for a pound. "Lee," he tells Wong. "Claire Lee. She claims she worked in the Pleasure Dome."

"So? She might have; a lot of women worked there. What's your interest?"

"She happens to be the wife of Chin Tung Lee, the CEO and largest shareholder of White Lotus."

"Oh, boy," the FBI man says with a grin. "The shit is beginning to hit the fan, old buddy."

"How so?"

"Because the Pleasure Dome was owned by the United Bamboo mob. It was one of the string of whorehouses they operated up and down the West Coast. So now let's recap . . . Giant Panda is buying into White Lotus. And the wife of the bossman at White Lotus once worked in a crib owned by United Bamboo. What do you make of that?"

"Nothing," Cone says. "I can't figure it."

Johnnie Wong leans across the table, thrusting his face close to Cone's. "You wouldn't be holding out on me, would you?"

"Not me. I'm just as flummoxed as you are."

The FBI man sits back, then slaps the tabletop with a smack of his palm that brings Cleo growling out from under the tub.

"Damn!" Wong says angrily. "I told you I felt in my stones that something is going down. I pick up rumors and get tips from my snitches. The big guns of United Bamboo and Giant Panda are in town. A lot of meetings. A lot of comings and goings. That murder of Chen Chang Wang. And now this business with White Lotus. Something's cooking. Maybe a full-scale gang war. Maybe just a fight for the New York territory. Who the hell knows? Listen, if you get anything, give me a shout. Even if you think it's not important. I'll do the same with you. I'd like to stop these assholes before they start shooting up Manhattan. Keep in touch, and thanks for the beer."

"Anytime," Cone says.

After Wong leaves, Cone goes into the kitchenette and starts heating up a can of corned beef hash. He wonders if he spilled too much in revealing the identity of Claire Lee. He decides not. After all, he didn't say a word about the blackmail letter.

Because the FBI agent has no need to know. Not yet.

Cone spends Thursday morning in the office making a series of desultory phone calls on those two tedious files he was assigned. It's donkeywork, and while he's talking to people and scribbling notes, he's thinking about the White Lotus affair and remembering how great Claire Lee looked in her spinnaker hat. The life she's led hasn't raddled her beauty; she looks untouched by human hands.

Maybe, Cone imagines, she sold her soul to the Devil in exchange for eternal youth. He'd be willing to sign a contract like that, but the Devil has never asked him.

He finally gets all he needs to close out the two cases. The shlumpf who fell for the miniature horse scam ain't going to get his money back. And the two plastic manufacturers can merge with confidence and live happily ever after. *Sic transit . . .*

He's smoking his fourth cigarette of the day, scanning the stock tables in *The New York Times,* when his phone rings. He stares at it a moment, then puts his newspaper aside and picks it up, thinking it might be the Devil calling, ready to make a deal.

"Yeah?" he says.

"Mr. Cone, this is Edward Tung Lee. How are you this morning?"

"Surviving."

"I'm going to be in your neighborhood shortly and wondered if I could stop by your office for a few minutes. There's something I'd like to discuss with you."

"Sure," Cone says, "come ahead. I'll be here."

Lee arrives in less than ten minutes, which makes Cone think the guy called from around the corner; there's no way he could have made it from Exchange Place that quickly.

He's dressed as dapperly as he was at Ah Sing's Bar & Grill, this time in a gray silk suit that glints like a newly minted silver dollar. But the breezy self-confidence is dented; he's got the jits. That high, broad brow is sheened with sweat, and he can't stop twisting his gold bracelet around and around.

He slumps into the chair facing Cone's desk with no digs about the claustrophobic office.

"First of all," he starts off, "I want to thank you for not telling my father that you and I were at Ah Sing's when Chen Chang Wang was killed."

"Yeah, well, since you hadn't told him, I figured you must have a good reason."

"I didn't want to upset the old man," Lee says earnestly. "He and Chen were friends from way back."

"Uh-huh," Cone says. "But he must have read about it; all the papers carried it. And I suppose it was on local TV."

"Oh, he knows about it, but I didn't want to be the one to tell him."

"Sure," Cone says.

"About your investigation," Lee goes on. He plucks a white handkerchief from his breast pocket and dabs at his forehead. "Hot day."

"Yeah," Cone says. "Usually is in summer."

Lee ignores that. "About your investigation," he continues. "Have you been getting anywhere?"

"Not really," Cone says. "I had a couple of other files I had to work on."

"Well, I'm sure you'll find it's just the way I explained at Ah Sing's: normal market activity, a flight to quality."

"Could be," Cone says. "I see where White Lotus was up another seven-eighths yesterday. Heavy volume for a stock with your capitalization."

"Just a blip," Edward says. "Nothing to it."

The Wall Street dick makes no reply, waiting for this Nervous Nellie to speak his piece.

"Actually," Lee says, swabbing his brow again, "what I wanted to talk to you about has nothing to do with White Lotus. It's more of, ah, a personal matter."

"Oh?" Cone says, wondering when he was ordained and became a father confessor. "What's that?"

"It's silly, really," the man says with a shaky smile. "Probably nothing to it."

Cone waits silently, giving him no help at all. If this guy, he thinks, tells me he once worked at the Pleasure Dome, I'm going to toss his ass out of here.

"As you probably know," Lee plunges ahead, "I live in my father's apartment. But I have my own suite with a private entrance. I also have my own phone, an unlisted number. Last Friday night, at about eleven o'clock, I was reading when the phone rang. A man's voice asked, 'Edward Tung Lee?' I said yes, and he said, 'We know about the Bedlington.' And then he hung up. Well, naturally I thought it was just a crank call. But it did worry me that he had my unlisted number and called me by my full name."

"Recognize the voice?" Cone asks.

"No," Lee says. "A BBC English accent, but beneath that

I thought I heard something else. Perhaps a Chinese educated in England. A singsong quality you learn to recognize."

"I get it," Cone says. "Instead of emphasizing a syllable, you change the pitch of your voice."

Lee looks at him in astonishment. "How on earth did you know that?"

"I remember a lot of useless stuff," Cone says. "So the guy said, 'We know about the Bedlington.' Then he hung up. Right?"

"Yes, that's correct. Then, last night, he called again. Same voice. He said, as nearly as I can recall, 'About the Bedlington, you'll be hearing from us.'"

"You're sure he said 'us' and not 'you'll be hearing from 'me'?"

"No, he said 'us.' And on the first call, he said, '*We* know about the Bedlington.'"

"Uh-huh," Cone says.

"Does the name Bedlington mean anything to you?" Edward asks.

"Sure," Cone says, all wide-eyed innocence. "It's a dog, a terrier."

Lee gives a short honk of laughter. "True," he says. "It also happens to be a hotel on Madison Avenue. About three blocks from my apartment. From my father's apartment."

"So?"

"Well, ah, as you probably know, I am not married. But, hah!—that doesn't mean I must live like a monk—right? So, on occasion, I have taken a woman to the Hotel Bedlington. You've shacked up with women in a hotel or motel, haven't you?"

"Not recently," Cone says.

"Well, I do. I have an understanding with the desk clerk at the Bedlington. Everything is handled very discreetly. I mean, I have no wild parties or anything like that. I've had absolutely no problems until I got those stupid phone calls."

"How long you been using the Bedlington for fun and games?"

"Oh, about two years now."

"You trust the desk clerk?"

"Completely. He'd never try to blackmail me."

"What makes you think it's blackmail? You're over twenty-one. So you're having a toss in the hay with a consenting adult. Big deal. Your playmates *were* adults, weren't they?''

"Of course," Edward says, offended.

"Well, then? How can anyone blackmail you? What are you worried about?"

Lee shifts uncomfortably in the creaky armchair. "It's my father, d'ya see," he says. "He's from the old school. Very straitlaced. I know that if he found out, there'd be hell to pay."

Cone shrugs. "Sounds thin to me," he tells Lee. "You've got a right to live your own life. If those phone calls are driving you bananas, why don't you go to your father, confess all, ask for his forgiveness, and promise to be a good little boy in the future. He impresses me as being a very shrewd, intelligent man. He's lived a long life, and I'd guess he's seen everything and probably done more than you realize. I just can't see him making a federal case out of your occasional bangs at the Bedlington."

"You just don't know him," Lee says in a low voice. "He can be a very vindictive man when he's angered."

"Well," Cone says, "I don't see that there's a helluva lot you can do about it. You could have your private number changed, but they'd just call you at the office."

"And there's nothing *you* can do about it?"

"Like what?"

"Find out who's behind it."

Cone shakes his head. "Not on the basis of what you've told me. I could get someone to put a tap on your phone and record the calls—but what good would that do? If the guy only talks for a minute or two, the chances of tracing the call are zero. The only thing I can suggest is this: If it *is* blackmail, sooner or later your mystery caller is going to tell you how much he wants and how it's to be delivered. If it's a person-to-person payoff, I can handle it for you and maybe collar the guy or at least get a line on him. If the payoff is to be made by drop or by mail, it'll still give a possible lead. Right now we've got nothing."

"Then if I do get another call and I let you know, can I depend on your help?"

"Sure."

"Thank you!" Edward Tung Lee cries fervently. He rises

and leans across the desk to pump Cone's hand. "I can't tell you what a load you've taken off my mind. Thank you!"

After he's gone, Cone lights another Camel, leans back, parks his feet on the desk. That had to be, he reflects, one of the sleaziest stories he's ever heard in his life. It's got more holes than a wheel of Emmentaler. The only reason he's giving it a second thought is that the guy who called Edward Lee said, "*We* know about the Bedlington." And the guy who sent the letter to Claire Lee wrote: "*We* have the photographs."

That's interesting.

Four

On Thursday evening Timothy Cone ambles up Broadway at a leisurely pace, stopping in bars twice en route to have a beer and smoke a cigarette. He can't get Edward Lee's fish story out of his mind. It may have elements of truth in it, but it also has gaps big enough to drive a Mack truck through.

For instance, if Edward wants to make nice-nice with a tootsie, why doesn't he invite her up to his apartment? He's got a private entrance, hasn't he?

And that business of dreading his father's wrath is so much kaka. Chin Tung Lee may be old and straitlaced, but Cone can't believe he'd go into an Oriental snit upon discovering that his Number One son likes to get his ashes hauled occasionally.

No, Edward isn't Telling All. His report of the phone calls may be legit, but Cone would bet the family farm that those calls are making Edward sweat for a more significant reason than fear of shocking dear old dad.

It's a creamy night, pillow soft, with a clear sky and a teasing breeze. Stars are beginning to pop out, and a waning moon is still strong enough to silver the city. Cone hates to go up to the loft, but figures he'll eat, feed the cat, and later do a little more pub crawling if the mood is on him.

His phone is ringing when he enters, and he kicks Cleo out of the way to get to it.

"Yeah?" he says.

"Hello, asshole," Samantha Whatley says. "I figured I better call you early before you started pub crawling."

"Nah," he says. "Farthest from my thoughts. How are you?"

"Eating up a storm. Mom is stuffing me. I've gained three pounds so far, all in the wrong places. How are things at the office?"

"Okay."

"Hiram giving you any problems?"

"Not me. I'm keeping out of his way."

"I spoke to him this afternoon. He says you're working on some Chinese thing."

"Yeah, I'm up to my tail in chop suey."

"Anything exciting?"

"Not very," Cone says.

"Jesus, you're a chatty sonofabitch," Sam says. "Cutting down on your smoking?"

"Trying to," he says, fumbling the pack out of his jacket pocket and shaking a cigarette free.

"And how's that miserable cat?"

"Hungry. When are you coming back?"

"A week from tomorrow. But I'll be in late. See you on Saturday?"

"Sure," he says, "sounds good."

"Take care," she says lightly.

"Yeah," he says. "You, too."

"That was Sam," he tells Cleo after he hangs up. "She says to give you her best."

He inspects the contents of the refrigerator. It's famine time. There's a half-can of tuna, a couple of odds and ends of this and that, but nothing to *eat*. He gives Cleo the tuna and fresh water, then heads out again.

"Be back soon," he promises the cat, "but don't wait up."

There's a Greek joint around the corner that's usually open till nine o'clock. Cone calls it the Ptomaine Palace. "The food is poisonous," he once told Samantha, "but the portions are big."

He sits on a stool at the Formica counter and orders a bowl of lamb stew with rye bread and a bottle of Heineken. He finds a few shreds of lamb floating in the viscid gravy, but there are chunks of potatoes, carrots, celery, and onions. He uses a lot of salt and pepper and fills up, which is all he asks of any meal.

He finishes by sopping puddles of gravy with pieces of bread. Before he leaves, he orders another lamb stew to go, figuring it'll keep Cleo happy for at least a couple of days. It's poured into a Styrofoam container and put into a brown paper bag.

Carrying that, he heads back for the loft. He's on Broadway, close to home, when two short guys step out of a doorway and crowd him. They're both wearing black trousers and gray alpaca jackets. He makes them as young Chinese.

"You are Mr. Timothy Cone?" one of them asks.

"Not me, friend," Cone says. "I'm Simon Legree from Tennessee."

There's a rapid jabber of Chinese, then the other man stoops swiftly and runs his hands down Cone's shins. He plucks the .357 magnum from the ankle holster and hands it to his partner.

"So you are Timothy Cone," the speaker states. "Come this way, please."

Since he's now waving the S&W, Timothy goes along, still carrying the lamb stew. They lead him to an old, black, bulge-bodied Buick, a real doctor's car. There's a third Chinese sitting behind the wheel. They get Cone in the wide back seat, between the two men who took him.

"I must blindfold you now," the leader says. "So sorry."

The blindfold is white, padded, and is put on so slickly that Cone figures it's got to be fastened with Velcro. The car starts up.

"Nice night for a drive," he offers, but no one answers, and after that he doesn't try any chitchat.

He lets his body go slack, feeling gravity and momentum, swaying slightly when the car takes a corner. He tries to imagine the route. A right-hand turn, a straightaway with the Buick accelerating, then slowing to make another right. Now we're around the block and heading uptown, he guesses.

He can't get a glimmer through that thick bandage over his eyes, but he can hear traffic noises change as they pass cross-streets. He counts the number of blocks, and when the Buick veers slightly to the left, he estimates they're about at 14th Street. They pause awhile, probably for a traffic light, then make a left turn. Heavier traffic noise now, and Cone thinks it's got to be a wide east-west street, either 14th or 23rd.

The car slows after traveling for about four minutes, and Cone sways as it turns to the right. They go down an incline, and the Buick's engine takes on a reverberant sound, almost like an echo. An underground garage, Cone decides. The car comes to a stop, a back door is opened. He's helped out, gently, no rough stuff, and still carrying his lamb stew, is led about twenty feet, hands gripping both his arms. He scuffs his work shoes on concrete and smells gas and oil fumes. Now he's convinced it's an underground parking garage.

The men holding him press closer, and the three of them slow, stop, wait a minute. Sound of elevator door opening. Forward, with a smoother floor under his feet: tile or linoleum. Metallic sound of elevator door closing. Then they go up, and Cone silently counts off seconds: A hundred and one, a hundred and two, a hundred and three . . . He's figuring two seconds per floor; the elevator stops at 118. The doors swish open, he's ushered out.

Now he's walking on a rug, springy beneath his feet. A long walk and Cone, counting his paces, estimates forty feet at least. His captors are no longer pressing him, so it's got to be a wide corridor. A hotel maybe? No, they wouldn't run the risk of bumping into guests while hustling a blindfolded man.

They halt. Three sharp raps on wood. Small squeak of a door opening. Cone's pulled forward, stumbling a bit on thicker pile carpeting, maybe a deep shag. Around a corner. He's thrust forward, hands on his back. Stop. A fast spatter of Chinese. Then . . .

A precise voice: "Mr. Cone, what is that you are carrying?"

"Lamb stew," he says. "You can have some if you like."

There's a snap of fingers. The brown paper bag is taken, and Cone hears the crinkle of paper, the pop of the lid coming off the Styrofoam container.

"You are right," the voice says, "it is lamb stew. It looks and smells dreadful."

"It's not so bad," Cone protests. "It's filling."

"Mr. Cone, I must apologize for this unconventional method of making your acquaintance. I trust you were not physically harmed."

"Nah," Cone says, "your guys did a nice job. Can you take the blindfold off now?"

"I fear that would be most unwise. And please do not try to remove it yourself. There are two very quick men standing behind you, both of them armed."

"Okay," Cone says, "I'll be good."

"Excellent. This will only take a few moments, and then you will be returned to your home. Mr. Cone, I understand you are investigating the increase in the price of White Lotus stock.''

"Where did you hear that?" Cone says. Then: "Listen, if we're going to have a confab, could I sit down?"

"I prefer you remain standing," the voice says sharply. "I am not going to ask you to terminate your investigation, Mr. Cone. I know you are an employee of Haldering and Company, and have been assigned to the case. All I am asking is that you delay your inquiries for perhaps another week. Two weeks at the most. Surely you could do that without insurmountable objections from your employer."

"Maybe I could," Cone says. "But why should I?"

"Because I request it," the voice says with a silky undertone. "In return, naturally, you may expect to profit."

"Yeah?" Cone says. "How much?"

"Five thousand dollars. In small, unmarked bills."

"Forget it. I work for a salary. It's not king-sized, but it's enough."

"Come, Mr. Cone," the voice says softly, "it is never enough. We all want more, do we not?"

"I got enough," Cone insists stubbornly.

"And there is nothing in this world you want?"

"Yeah, I've always wanted to screw a contortionist. It's something I've dreamed about for a long time."

The voice gives a chuff of laughter, then rips off some Chinese, and the two men standing behind Cone also laugh.

"That could be arranged, Mr. Cone," the voice says dryly.

"Just kidding," Cone says. "Listen, I don't like standing here with this shmatteh over my eyes, so let's get down to the nitty-gritty. If I refuse to stall on this White Lotus thing, what happens then?"

"Please do not ask me to say it."

"Go ahead; say it."

"Then I am afraid we shall have to kill you, Mr. Cone."

"Okay," the Wall Street dick says cheerfully. "As long as I know where I stand. Give me a chance to think about your cash offer—all right?"

"How long?"

"A week."

"Three days," the voice says sternly. "Then we must come looking for you. You can run, but you cannot hide."

"Good line," Cone says, "but it's not yours. Joe Louis. Can I go home now?"

"We shall contact you on Monday, and expect your answer at that time. Yes, you may go now."

"Can I take my stew?"

"Please do."

"And how about my piece?"

"Your piece?"

"My gun. Revolver. Your guys lifted it."

"Your weapon will be returned to you, Mr. Cone. Thank you for your kind cooperation."

There's a long chatter of Chinese. The brown paper bag is thrust into his hands, he is gripped, and the film starts running in reverse: Around the corner, across the shag rug, through the door, along the corridor, down in the elevator to the garage, into the car, and then the drive back. Cone, counting to himself, figures it takes about fifteen minutes.

The car stops, he's helped out, still carrying his lamb stew. The blindfold is whisked away. He stands there, blinking.

There's another rat-a-tat of Chinese between the two alpaca jackets. One turns and starts walking south on Broadway toward the corner. The speaker is now armed with a sleek 9mm Luger which he waves at Cone.

"Your revolver will be left on the sidewalk," he explains. "Please do not attempt to reclaim it until we have left, or we will be forced to return."

Through bleary eyes Cone watches the other guy place his magnum on the pavement near a fire alarm box. Then he returns, and the two young Chinese climb into the car.

"Good night, Mr. Cone," the leader calls, and the Buick accelerates, turns the corner with a chirp of tires, and is gone.

Cone goes down to the corner and reclaims his iron. He inspects it quickly under a streetlight. It looks okay. Still loaded. He slips it into his jacket pocket. Then he walks slowly back to his building. But before going upstairs, he stands a moment on the deserted street.

It has been a scarifying experience, being blind. He doesn't want to go through that again. Now he can see the haloed glimmer of the streetlight, see the gleaming gutters of his city and, looking upward, see the glittering stars whirling their ascending courses. A blessing. More than that: a physical delight. Almost a thrill.

Up in the loft, he pours some of the gelatinous stew into Cleo's dish. The happy cat goes to work on it immediately. Cone goes to work on a stiff shot of brandy while he undresses, staring with new eyes at Cleo, the loft, furniture, everything.

He strips to his skivvies, turns out the lights, and rolls onto his floor mattress.

"Now for a lot of Z's," he calls to the cat, but all he gets in reply is the noisy slurping of lamb stew.

He's still in his skivvies when he phones Johnnie Wong on Friday morning.

"Don't tell me you're in the office already," the FBI man says.

"On my way," Cone says. "Listen, you told me to contact you if anything happened, even if I didn't think it was important. Okay, something happened; I got taken for a ride."

"Well, you're talking to me so it couldn't have been a one-way trip."

Timothy describes the events of the previous evening. Wong listens without interrupting. Then, when Cone is finished, he says, "Could you ID the two foot soldiers who picked you up?"

"I doubt it."

"I know," Johnnie says. "We all look alike to you blue-eyes."

"Not me; my eyes are shit-brown."

"What about the boss?"

"I'd make him for a Chinese. He speaks English like a professor or like it's his second language. I mean he never uses contractions. Never 'I'm' or 'You're' but always 'I am' or 'You are.'"

"I know what contractions are. Anything else about him?"

"An iron fist in a velvet glove kind of guy. Very polite. He'd apologize before he had your head blown off. He talked about me stalling for two weeks, so you're right; something's going down soon."

"And that's all you can give me on him?"

"I told you I was blindfolded the whole time."

"Any idea where you were?"

"I figure I was in an apartment house on West Fourteenth Street, somewhere around Tenth Avenue. It's on the north side of the street. At least nine stories high. It's got an underground garage and automatic elevators. The corridors are wide and carpeted. The apartment I was in had a wood door and a thick shag rug."

"I thought you said you were blindfolded."

"I was, but I could hear and smell, and feel things under my feet. Also, I counted seconds and minutes."

"You're something, you are," Johnnie Wong says. "Well, you've given me enough to make an educated guess. You were in a twelve-story apartment house owned by the Giant Panda mob. It's on West Fourteenth Street like you said, but it's between Eighth and Ninth. It's all rentals, but the entire tenth floor is the East Coast headquarters of the Pandas. The bossman you talked to was probably Henry Wu Yeh. He's the warlord of the New York branch. From Hong Kong. Educated at UCLA. A very flinty customer. And a real tycoon type. He's the guy who's trying to muscle Giant Panda into legitimate businesses. You will turn General Motors over to us—or else! That kind of guy."

"Yeah, that sounds like him," Cone says. "One minute he's Mr. Nice and the next he's the Voice of Doom."

"By the way," Wong says, "you'll find Henry Wu Yeh on that list of White Lotus shareholders you showed me."

"No kidding?"

"No kidding. I forget how many shares he owns, but it's more than a thousand. Listen, do you want protection?"

"What for?"

"Well, Yeh said they're going to come looking for you on Monday, didn't he?"

"So? That's Monday. I got three days before they yank my chain."

Johnnie Wong laughs. "As we Chinese say, 'Rots of ruck, old buddy.'"

After he hangs up, Cone stands a moment, staring at the wall. It comes as no surprise to him to learn he was rustled by the Giant Panda gang. His reasoning goes like this:

He meets Edward Tung Lee at Ah Sing's Bar & Grill on Pell Street.

He sees Lee and Chen Chang Wang in deep conversation.

Wang gets blown away and is later revealed to be an officer in the Giant Panda organization.

During the excitement, Edward Lee notices that Timothy Cone carries a shooter in an ankle holster.

When the Giant Panda soldiers pick Cone up, the first thing they do is dust him down for an ankle holster. It was no normal frisk; the alpaca jackets went directly to his shins.

Ergo: Edward Tung Lee is a member of, or working closely with, the Giant Panda mob and tipped them off that Cone was carrying on his leg bone.

So, if Edward Lee is buddy-buddy with the Giant Pandas, those phone calls he received must have come from someone else. The United Bamboo gang maybe? And are they also responsible for the letter to Claire Lee? United Bamboo owned the San Francisco kip where she worked, and could easily have taken the photographs.

Musing on all these permutations and combinations, Cone lights his first cigarette of the morning, coughs, and wanders over to his desk to consult the White Lotus shareholder list. He's curious about how many shares are owned by Henry Wu Yeh, the pooh-bah of the Giant Pandas.

No list. He can't find it. He searches, even in such unlikely places as the cabinet under the kitchen sink. No list. He gets down on hands and knees and peers beneath the claw-footed bathtub, thinking Cleo might have dragged it there. No list. The White Lotus annual report is still on his desk, but that confidential record of shareowners has disappeared.

He inspects the locks on the loft door. No signs of a break-in. But that doesn't mean shit. A good picklock could open almost any door and never leave a trace. And no use wondering when it was done. Last night or yesterday afternoon while Cone was at work. Whenever, the White Lotus shareholder list has been snaffled.

Cone glares accusingly at Cleo.

"What a lousy attack cat you turned out to be," he says to the beast. "What'd the gonnif do—toss you a fish head? You fink!"

He's in his office in a sour mood and telling himself he's got a lot to be sour about.

That missing list bothers him, mostly because he promised Chin Tung Lee he'd take good care of it. It would be easy to assume it had been glommed by the Giant Pandas while they had him in custody, but that just won't wash. If Edward Lee is snuggling up to the Pandas—and Cone believes he is—he could easily provide a shareholder list anytime it was wanted.

That probably means the guy who burgled the loft was a paid-up member in good standing with the United Bamboo mob. But what would that gang of cutthroats want with a list of White Lotus investors? Unless they were going to put the company into play.

Three days, he reflects: that's how long he's got before he faces the long knives. The prospect of his immediate demise doesn't dismay him as much as fears for Cleo's future without him. He wonders if he should leave Samantha Whatley a letter, willing the cat to her. Unless, of course, when he is knocked off, Cleo is also sent to the great litter box in the sky.

Engrossed with these morose musings, he suddenly becomes aware that his phone is ringing. He picks up, wondering if it's Mr. Yeh, calling to remind him that the clock is ticking.

"Yeah?" he says.

"Mr. Cone? This is Claire Lee. I'm calling from home. My husband is with me and would like to see you as soon as possible."

She sounds breathless. Maybe distraught.

"At your Fifth Avenue apartment?" he asks.

"Yes. Please. As quickly as you can, Mr. Cone."

"Okay," he says, "I'll be there."

He has no idea what it's all about, but figures that maybe it would be smart if he had wheels. So he grabs a cab back to his neighborhood, reclaims the red Ford Escort from a parking lot on Wooster Street, and heads for the Lees' Fifth Avenue apartment.

Finding a parking space in that area is like the search for the Holy Grail. Finally Cone gives up, double-parks on East 68th Street, and locks up. If the Escort is towed, so be it; the client will pay the ransom to get it out of hock.

Claire meets him at the door of the apartment. She looks yummy in a white linen jumpsuit with an alligator belt. But her face is drawn, and when she clasps Cone's hand in both of hers, her skin feels moist and clammy.

She draws him into the apartment, closes and bolts the

door, then turns to face him. He wonders if she's been weeping; her eyes are lost in puffy bags. She leans close, and he catches a whiff of 80-proof something.

"My husband is ill," she says in a low voice. "Maybe not ill, but very upset. Troubled."

"Sorry to hear that," Cone says. "What's he troubled about?"

"You better hear it from him."

She leads the way through a maze of hallways, corridors, empty rooms, up two steps, down two steps, until they finally reach what is apparently the master bedroom.

It is a huge, high-ceilinged chamber dominated by an enormous oak four-poster that could sleep the Celtics, spoon-fashion. And there are armoires, dressers, escritoires, cabinets, chests, cupboards, étagères—all in dark, distressed woods, looking as if an entire Scottish castle had been denuded to furnish this one melancholy room.

In the center of the immense bed is Mr. Chin Tung Lee, shrunken under a sheet and light blanket drawn up to his scrawny neck. His complexion is tallowy and his eyes are dimmed. Even his little beard seems limp. He withdraws a hand from beneath the covers and offers it to Timothy. The skin is parchment, the bones as thin and frail as a chicken's wing.

"Thank you so much for coming," he says in a wispy voice. "Please, pull up a chair."

Cone wrestles one as heavy as a throne to the bedside and sits, leaning forward.

"Sorry you're feeling under the weather, Mr. Lee. Is there anything I can do?"

Claire Lee is standing on the other side of the bed, opposite Cone. Her husband turns his head slowly in her direction.

"The first letter, dear," he says, and there's no vigor in his voice. "Please show it to Mr. Cone."

She plucks a single sheet of paper from a bedside table and brings it around to him. It's heavy stationery, thrice folded. The letterhead is embossed. Cone scans it, then looks up at Chin Tung Lee.

"Yangtze International, Limited," he says. "On Pine Street. Never heard of them. Have you?"

"Oh, yes, I've heard of them. My countrymen." Then, bitterly: "I understand criminal elements are involved."

"Uh-huh," Cone says, and reads the letter. It's in polite legalese, but the meaning is clear. Yangtze International has accumulated 16 percent of all White Lotus stock, with the pledge of proxies by "many other shareholders" and requests a personal meeting with Mr. Chin Tung Lee with a view toward "proper representation" on the Board of Directors.

Cone reads it twice, then folds it and taps the letter on his knee.

"I checked with the SEC early this week," he says. "No one has filed a 13-D notifying an investment in White Lotus of five percent or more and declaring intent. But that doesn't necessarily mean anything; there's a ten-day delay allowed."

"But what does it *mean*, Mr. Cone?" Lee asks.

"You know what it means," Cone says harshly. "They're making a run on your company. Now we know why the stock has been going up, up, up."

"I'll never sell out," the old man wails. "Never!"

"You won't have to," Cone says, "if you play your cards right. You've got options. You can pay them greenmail— more than the market value of the stock—and buy *them* out. You can start a poison pill defense to make it so expensive to take over White Lotus that they'll just go away. You can look for a friendly buyer. You can consider a leveraged buyout: You buy everyone's shares and go private. You'll have to take on debt to do that. But then, in a couple of years or so, depending on what the Dow is doing, you can go public again. It could make you a zillionaire. But I'm not the one to be giving you advice on this. Have you got an investment banker?"

"No. I've never had the need for one."

"Well, you've got the need for one now. Mr. Lee, you're in a war, and you better have the best strategist money can buy. Ask around, then pick one. If you want a tip from me, try Pistol and Burns on Wall Street. It's an old outfit. Very conservative. Talk to G. Fergus Twiggs. He's a full partner and a smart apple."

Lee looks imploringly at his wife. "Claire, will you remember that?"

"Yes, daddy," she says. "Pistol and Burns. G. Fergus Twiggs."

"Thank you, dear. Now show Mr. Cone the second letter."

She goes back to the bedside table, returns with a sheet of white foolscap. She hands it to Cone with fingers that are trembling even more than they did at Carpaccio's bar.

Timothy unfolds the paper and reads. No letterhead on this one. Just two typed lines: *We have Edward. Do not go to the police if you wish to see your son alive again.*

He looks up in astonishment. "What the hell is this?" he demands. "Has someone grabbed him?"

"I checked," Claire says, gnawing at a knuckle. "He didn't sleep in his bed last night. No one's seen him or heard from him since yesterday afternoon."

"Oh, Jesus," Cone says. "No wonder you're in bed, Mr. Lee."

The oldster sighs. "As the Good Book says, 'Man that is born of a woman is of few days and full of trouble.'"

"I'll buy that," Cone says. "This is the only letter you've received?"

"The only one," Claire says. "It came this morning."

"Phone calls?"

"About Edward? No, none."

"Well, if he's been snatched, you'll be hearing from the people holding him. They'll either phone or send you another letter. I think you should bring the cops in on this, Mr. Lee."

"No," the gaffer says in an unexpectedly firm voice. "Absolutely not. I'll pay anything to get him back, but I won't endanger his life."

"You've got no guarantee," Cone argues. "You could pay off and they still might croak—they still might do away with him because he can identify them. But listen, this is a rough decision and you have to make it yourself. Don't listen to me."

"I want to do the right thing," the septuagenarian says, his voice faint again.

"Sure you do."

"You won't tell the police, will you?"

"If you don't want me to, I won't."

"But is there anything you can do to help?"

"Very iffy," Cone says. "Right now they're just letting you sweat a little. You'll be hearing from them again. Then we'll know where you stand."

He looks at Claire to see if she picks up on that: practically the identical language he used at Carpacchio's. But she won't look at him.

"Tell me something," Cone says. "How did this letter arrive? In your regular mail delivery?"

"No," Claire says, "it wasn't mailed. A messenger left it with our concierge this morning. The other letter—the one from Yangtze International—that was hand-delivered, too."

"Uh-huh," Cone says. "Both letters came at the same time by the same messenger?"

"No," she says. "I asked. They both came this morning but at different times. About an hour apart. The letter from Yangtze came first, delivered by a commercial service. Then, an hour later, the letter about Edward was brought by a young Chinese boy. The concierge says he dropped the letter on his desk and ran out."

"I get the picture," Cone says. "Look, I'm going to leave you folks now. I've got some calls to make to people who may be able to help." Then, when Chin Tung Lee glares at him, he adds hastily, "Not the cops. Just some guys who might have heard some talk. It's worth a try. Listen, do you mind if I take this letter about Edward along with me? I got a pal in the typewriter business. He'll be able to identify the machine used. That might help; you never know."

"Take it," Lee says wearily.

"And call me if you hear anything more. Either by letter or phone. And don't forget to contact an investment banker. I know that your son's disappearance is enough troubles, but you've got to start moving to protect your business, too."

The old man nods and holds out his hand. Cone shakes it gently, afraid the wrist bone might snap.

"I'll be in touch, Mr. Lee," he says as lightly as he can. "I'm not going to tell you not to worry because I know you will. But you've lived a long life and had a lot of problems, and you solved them all, didn't you?"

"Yes," Chin Tung Lee says, straightening up a little and raising his head from the pillow. "That is true."

"So? I'm betting you'll grab the brass ring on this one, too."

Claire Lee leads the way to the front door. Cone appreciates that or he'd be lost in the warren.

"First that letter I got," she says in a low voice, "and now this. I think I'm going nuts."

"Nah," Cone says. "You're a survivor. And your husband needs you. Got any ideas who might have snatched Edward?"

"Anyone out to make a lot of fast bucks," she says bitterly. "But no, I have no idea who it might be."

"How about your problem? Did you get another letter or phone call?"

"No."

"Okay," Cone says at the door, "hang in there and take care of your husband. He looks shvach."

"Just the way I feel," she says. She puts a hand on his arm. "Please, Mr. Cone, help us."

"I'll see what I can do," he says gruffly.

Mercifully, the Ford Escort is still peaceably double-parked, which Cone considers a good omen—but of what he cannot say. He drives back to the loft, his brain whirling like one of those spheres of ivory intricately carved by Chinese artists. Within the outer ball, the size of a softball, is a smaller one, turning freely; within that a golf ball; within that something smaller, the balls dwindling down to a carved pea, and all these nesting globes are perforated with ornate designs and revolve dizzily like Timothy's brain.

The first thing he does in the loft—even before he pours a vodka—is to compare the letter from Edward Lee's kidnappers with the letter from Claire Lee's blackmailers. Even to his inexpert eye it's obvious the two letters are of different sizes and grades of paper and were typed on different machines.

"Shit!" he says aloud.

Then he mixes a vodka and water.

He works on that, smokes a butt in short, angry puffs, and ponders his next move. First things first, he finally decides, and calls Johnnie Wong at FBI headquarters on Federal Plaza. A real grouch of a guy tells him Wong is not available, but he can leave a message if he wants to. Cone wants to, and does.

It's one hour, two drinks, and three cigarettes later before Johnnie gets back to him.

"The office told me you called," he says breezily. "Second time today we've talked. When are we going to start living together?''

"God forbid," Cone says. "Where are you—can you tell me?"

"Sure," Wong says, laughing. "I'm calling from my car. I was over in Jersey on a job, and just came through the Lincoln Tunnel. Traffic is murder! Right now I'm heading south on Ninth Avenue. What's up?"

"Listen, I think we better meet as soon as possible. The pasta fazool just hit the fan.''

"Yeah? Well, don't say any more about it. Too many big ears on these mobile circuits.''

"So I've heard," Cone says. "How's about you stopping by my place? Don't come up; I'll wait for you downstairs. Double-park and we can talk in your car. How does that sound?''

"Okay by me," Johnnie Wong says. "Give me fifteen minutes or so. I'm driving a black Chrysler two-door."

Cone's waiting on the sidewalk when the Chrysler pulls up about twenty minutes later. He slides into a leather bucket seat.

"Nice yacht," he says to Wong. "So this is where the taxpayers' money goes.''

"This is where," the FBI man agrees. "What've you got?''

"The first thing I got is a question. Then I'll trade. Ever hear of Yangtze International, Limited?''

Johnnie turns sideways to stare at him. He's not smiling. "You really come up with some doozies," he says. "Yeah, I've heard of that outfit. It's the business arm of the Giant Panda mob. Handles all their purchases, leases, rentals, and investments. How did you hear about it? And don't tell me it was in idle conversation.''

"Chin Tung Lee, the boss of White Lotus, got a letter from Yangtze this morning. They claim they now own sixteen percent of White Lotus stock and want to put their people on the Board of Directors. Sounds like the start of a takeover to me.''

"I'll be damned," Wong says thoughtfully. "But then I shouldn't be surprised. I see the fine Italian hand of your old pal Henry Wu Yeh behind that deal. Did I tell you the guy's an MBA? It fits the pattern of the Pandas trying to muscle into legitimate businesses. What's Lee going to do?''

"Fight it, of course. I gave him the name of a good investment banker. The old man really loves that company; it's his whole life, and he's not going to fold because of one letter from Yangtze. But all that is just an appetizer. Here's one from Column A: It's a letter that was delivered to Lee's apartment house this morning.''

He hands over the two-sentence note from the kidnappers. Wong scans it, then looks up in shock.

"Jesus," he says, "they grabbed his son? The guy you were with at Ah Sing's?"

"That's what it says. Listen, Johnnie, you've got to cover my ass on this. I promised the father I wouldn't go to the police.''

"So? We're not the police—exactly.''

"I know, but if you guys go charging up there, install phone taps and tape recorders, put on around-the-clock guards and all that crap, Chin Tung Lee will know for sure I tipped you, and my name will be mud. He'll probably send a hatchetman after me, and I got enough problems with Henry Wu Yeh.''

"Maybe you should read *How to Win Friends and Influence People*. You figure Giant Panda pulled the snatch? It makes sense. They put more pressure on Lee to make him turn over White Lotus to them. And if he pays a hefty ransom, they use the money to buy more White Lotus stock. It's neat.''

"Too fucking neat," Cone says angrily. "And it doesn't listen. Because Edward Lee is palsy-walsy with the Pandas.''

Then he tells Wong the story of how, when he was frisked by Giant Panda foot soldiers, they went directly to his ankle holster. Only Edward could have told them about that. Also, Lee and Chen Chang Wang were thick as thieves at Ah Sing's Bar & Grill before Wang got popped.

"Yeah," the FBI man says, "I see what you mean. It sure sounds like Edward is sleeping in the Pandas' bed. Maybe he's in so deep that he gaffed his own kidnapping. It wouldn't be the first time the so-called victim was working hand in glove with the so-called kidnappers.''

"That's possible, too. But look, you told me the United

Bamboo and Giant Panda gangs hate each other's guts—right?''

"You better believe it. Like Cain and Abel, the Yanks and Red Sox, Texaco and Pennzoil."

"You think they both got spies in the other's camp?"

"You believe there's honor amongst thieves? Of course they do. About a month ago we found two Giant Panda thugs sliced to linguine in a Jersey pig farm. Only it turned out they weren't really Pandas; they were actually United Bamboo undercover guys. Their cover was blown, and they ended up feeding the pigs—personally."

"So you've got to figure both mobs have a pretty good idea what the other one is up to. How's this for a scenario: Giant Panda starts buying White Lotus stock through Yangtze International, planning a takeover. United Bamboo hears about it, takes a look at White Lotus, and decides they want a piece of the action. But Giant Panda has already accumulated sixteen percent of the stock, so United Bamboo has got to move fast. That they do. They kidnap the son of the CEO and biggest shareholder in White Lotus. You want to see Edward alive again? Okay, the ransom will be all your stock in White Lotus. And that amounts to about twenty-six percent of all outstanding shares. So by snatching Edward, United Bamboo ends up with a bigger hunk of the company than Giant Panda assembled by buying shares on the open market."

Johnnie Wong, frowning, considers it for a moment. Then: "I'll buy that. Mostly because it's the way United Bamboo operates: they're tough, direct, violent. They prefer physical action to reading SEC regulations before they move."

"Have you guys got snitches in United Bamboo?"

The FBI man gives him a blazing grin. "You don't expect me to answer that, do you? I will neither confirm nor deny."

"Okay, then I reckon you do," Cone says. "How about contacting your plants and find out if United Bamboo is holding Edward Tung Lee."

"I'll try," Wong says cautiously.

"You've got to do better than that," Cone urges. "This thing has to be wrapped up by Monday, or I may end up in a pig farm."

"All right, I'll move on it as soon as I get back to the office."

"When will I hear from you?"

"Depends. You'll be home tonight?"

"Oh, yeah," Cone says. "With the door locked, bolted, and chained."

"Why don't you teach Cleo karate?" Johnnie Wong suggests.

After the black Chrysler pulls away, Cone goes around the corner to a deli and buys a whole barbecued chicken, a container of potato salad, and two dills. He carries the fragrant bag back to the loft, rips it open, and starts on his dinner, after twisting the tail off the chicken and tossing it to Cleo.

He eats slowly and methodically because he's got a lot to brood about. He figures he's done all he can on Edward's kidnapping; now it's up to Johnnie Wong. But that's not what's bothering him; it's the threatening letter Claire Lee received and those phone calls to Edward Lee.

Cone's first idea had been that the United Bamboo mob was behind both letter and calls. But that no longer makes sense. You don't act like a blackmailer on the phone and then kidnap your intended victim. And it couldn't have been the Giant Pandas for the reason he had given Wong: Edward Lee is playing kneesy with that gang.

Which means, if Cone's reasoning is half-assed correct, there's a wild card in the deck: some free-lancer out to make a nice score by leaning on Claire and Edward. Timothy can't totally buy that notion, but it's the best he can come up with.

He gives the wingtips to Cleo and starts on the second leg, pausing occasionally to gulp potato salad or chomp on a pickle. He's drinking a beer with his meal and making it last because he only wants a single before getting back to vodka.

Vodka, he sincerely believes, is a great aid to mental labor because it frees the mind of discipline and diminishes linear thinking. You can fly on vodka, and if ever a case demanded an unfettered, soaring brain, the White Lotus caper is it.

He bundles up the de-winged, de-legged, de-tushed carcass of the bird and puts it in the fridge along with the remains of the potato salad and the second pickle. He reckons it'll make a nice Saturday morning brunch. Cleo can have the neck and back.

Then he goes back to his cigarettes and vodka. He runs out of ice cubes, but that doesn't annoy him. What nags is a feeling that he's missing something in this whole cockamamy jumble. He's missing something or someone is jerking him around. Either way, he doesn't like it.

Johnnie Wong hasn't called by 11:00 P.M., or midnight, or 1:00 A.M. Finally Cone gives up and undresses. He checks the door, turns off the lights, rolls onto his mattress. The magnum in its holster is close at hand. Cleo comes padding up to curl into the bend of his knees. The two of them sleep, both snoring gently.

When the phone rings, Cone comes groggily awake. It's still dark. He stumbles over to the wall phone, cursing when he stubs his toe on the refrigerator.

"Yeah?" he says, his voice thick with sleep.

"Aw," Johnnie Wong says, "I didn't wake you up, did I?"

"What time is it?" Cone asks.

"After five. But don't complain; I've been up all night."

"Any results?"

"Oh, yeah. I think we got a world-class flap on our hands. Listen, can you meet me down on the street in front of your place in about twenty minutes?"

"Sure. What's going on?"

"I want to drive you somewhere, and I'll tell you about it on the way."

Cone dresses quickly, straps on his shin holster, makes sure he's got cigarettes and matches, waggles his fingers at a drowsing Cleo, relocks the door, and clatters downstairs to an early morning that's just beginning to break over Brooklyn.

Timothy hasn't been out at that hour in a long time, and it's nice. The air is fresh—it hasn't yet been breathed by a million other people—and the sky is a patchwork of grays and violets. Stars are fading, and an unexpectedly cool August breeze is coming from the northwest. Sprinkler trucks have wet down Broadway; the pavement gleams in the pearly light.

Johnnie Wong is late, but Cone waits patiently, walking up and down slowly, smoking his first Camel of the new day. When the Chrysler arrives, Cone slides into the passenger seat.

"Hey, old buddy!" the FBI man cries, clapping him on the shoulder. "Sorry to interrupt your beauty sleep."

Cone looks at him closely. "Christ, you're wired," he says. "Haven't been popping bennies, have you?"

"Nah, I'm just hyper. A lot going on, and it could make me a hero or leave me looking like a putz."

He starts up, turns eastward, accelerates down a deserted street.

"Great morning," he says. "Best time of the day. No traffic. No pollution. Everything fresh and clean."

"That's what you wanted to tell me?" Cone says. "How wonderful the world is at six o'clock in the morning?"

Wong laughs: "Not exactly. Listen, you were right; the United Bamboo pirates are holding Edward Lee. They grabbed him late Thursday afternoon. It took me all night to authenticate that, and I had to call in a lot of chits."

"Where have they got him?"

"Where we're heading: Doyers Street in Chinatown. The Yubies' headquarters. That's what I call them—the Yubies. From the 'U' and 'B' in United Bamboo."

"You don't have to draw me a diagram," Cone says.

"God, you're grouchy early in the morning."

"I'm always grouchy."

"Well, the Yubies have three or four hangouts that we know about. Mostly in Manhattan, but one in Queens. Anyway, their headquarters is on Doyers Street in a five-story tenement. They've got the whole building except for a ground-floor restaurant, which happens to be the best dim sum joint in Chinatown. Edward Lee is being held in a third-floor office. He's been roughed up a little, but he's alive and okay. At least he was a couple of hours ago."

"You guys going in for him?"

"Ah, there's the rub. That's why I'm taking you to see the place. It's a fucking fortress."

Even at that early hour Chinatown is bustling. Merchants are taking down their shutters, street vendors are setting up their stalls, the narrow streets are crowded with men and women carrying live ducks, dead mackerel, and net bags filled with fruits and vegetables. Tea houses are already open for business, and the whole area has a raucous vitality.

Wong finds a parking space on Chatham Square. As they walk back to Doyers, he describes the setup.

"The entrance to the Yubies' headquarters is alongside the dim sum restaurant. There's an iron grille door on the street, kept locked, a small vestibule, and then a steel door painted to look like wood. Also kept locked. And if that wasn't enough, there are always two United Bamboo soldiers on the sidewalk outside the entrance. Twenty-four hours a day. I figure they're carrying. They don't let anyone inside the iron grille or the steel door unless they're recognized or expected. There's an intercom to the upper floors and also an alarm bell the guards can sound in case they get jumped."

"Beautiful," Cone says. "Back entrance?"

"Nope. Just a small blind courtyard. Fenced and topped with razor wire. There it is; take a look."

They saunter along on the other side of Doyers Street, pausing while Cone lights a cigarette, giving him a chance to eyeball the place. Three red-brick tenements in a row. The center building has the ground-floor restaurant. He spots the guards lounging near an iron gate. They look like kids to him: short and wiry.

Cone and Wong continue their slow stroll, turn onto Pell and then Mott Street.

"There's a place up near Canal where we can get coffee and a nosh," Johnnie says. "It's probably open by now."

"Yeah," Cone says, "that sounds good. My treat."

They sit at a table against a white-tiled wall. Wong tucks into a down-home breakfast of buttermilk pancakes and pork sausages with a side order of hush puppies. Cone has a bagel with cream cheese, lox, and a slice of onion. Both swill black coffee.

"You were right," Timothy says. "A fucking fortress. You guys thinking of hitting it?"

"Our legal eagles say we don't need a warrant; we've got probable cause: a kidnap victim being held against his will on the third floor. But how do we do it? We rush the place like gangbusters and already we're in deep trouble. Those two jerko guards will probably draw and start blasting away; you know that. And if they don't, they'll push the alarm button. That's what scares me most, because if the alarm goes off before we get upstairs, the guys in the third-floor office are liable to pop Edward Tung Lee just so he can't testify against them. I told you they were savages, didn't I? Real primitive types."

Cone continues munching his bagel sandwich and gulping black coffee. "So what do you want from my young life?"

"We can't let Edward Lee rot in there, can we? We've got to make a try at getting him out as long as it doesn't endanger his life."

"You could surround the front of the building and make a big show of force. Then bring in your hostage negotiation team."

"You think that would work?" Wong says, pouring more syrup on his pancakes.

"No," Cone says. "Because if they cave and hand you Lee, they'll know you've got them on a kidnap rap."

"Right. Well, you were an infantryman. Vietnam and your medals and all that shit. So what do you suggest?"

Cone pushes back from the table, lights another cigarette. He finishes his coffee and signals for a refill.

"You got some cowboys in your office?" he asks.

"You mean like a SWAT team? Sure, we got guys like that. An assault squad. Specially trained. Real hotshots. They just don't give a damn."

"Uh-huh," Cone says. "Listen, you know anything about the tong wars back in the twenties and thirties?"

"A little. I know the area bounded by Mott, Pell, and Doyer streets was called the Bloody Triangle."

"That's right. Well, during one of those wars the boss of a tong was threatened by an opposing gang. They swore they were going to top him. So he surrounded himself with bodyguards. On the street outside his headquarters. In the room where he worked. Even in his bedroom. But he got slammed just the same. You know how?"

"How?"

"The enemy went up on the roof of the building next to the tong headquarters. Same height. They crossed over and let a shooter down in a bosun's chair. He popped the bossman through a front window."

Johnnie Wong stares at him. "Son of a bitch," he says softly.

"Probably the world's first demonstration of vertical envelopment," Cone goes on. "When you're in a firefight, or going into one, you tend to think horizontally. You figure the enemy will be on the same level. You never expect to get a load of crap dumped on your head. In World War Two it took a while for our guys in the South Pacific to learn the Nip snipers were up in the trees."

Wong leans forward, interested. "You think it would work here?"

"You've got buildings on both sides of the United Bamboo headquarters. All the buildings are tight together and the same height. Crossing to the middle roof should be a cinch. You couldn't lower just one guy; you need more firepower than that. The Yubies' headquarters are three windows wide. You make sure your lines are secure, and then three guys rappel down the face of the building, one guy to each stack of windows. They're armed with Uzis or maybe Ingrams or whatever lightweight choppers you guys are using these days. They rappel down to the third floor and start blasting the bejesus out of everything in sight, keeping their shots high because you don't want Edward Lee cut in two. If you think all that shooting is too risky, then have your hotshots kick the windows out with their boots and toss in stun grenades."

"Or tear gas," Wong says. He's getting excited now.

Cone shakes his head. "Gas would take too long to knock out Lee's guards. And besides, while this is going on, you're going to have a squad charging up the stairs to the third floor. And unless they're wearing masks, the gas will take them out, too."

"And how does this squad get past the guards, inside the two locked doors, and go galloping up to the rescue?"

"When the guys come down from the roof and the party begins, those two guards are going to run out into the middle of the street and look up, to see what's going on. That'll be your chance to grab them—while they're still peeing their pants. As for those locked doors, they shouldn't take more than a minute or two to pry open if you've got the right tools. My advice would be to blow them. Look, I haven't been in the war business for years, so I don't know what new goodies you guys have in your armory. But I'll bet you've got gizmos to get you through locked doors in seconds. Then you go hotfooting up to the third floor where the bad guys are still spooked."

"You really think that meshugass would work?"

Cone shrugs. "Fifty-fifty," he says.

"Come on," Johnnie Wong says angrily, "give it to me straight. If you had to make the top decision, would you say go or no-go?"

"Go," Cone says.

Wong sighs. "All right," he says. "I'll give it the old college try. We'll have to buck this one all the way up the line, probably to D.C. It's the time factor that worries me. I want to get Edward Lee out of there before the media gets wind of it or we'll have a three-ring circus on our hands. By rights, we should have conferences on this, liaise with the NYPD, and maybe even run a rehearsal down at Quantico. But we just don't have the time. Listen, are you going to be home this weekend?"

"I'll be in and out."

"I'll try to keep you up to speed on what's going on. I owe you that; it's your idea."

"Look," Cone says, "if you can't get enough guys to jump off the roof, I could do that. I know how to rappel."

Wong looks at him with amusement. "Smell action?" he asks. "Can't get it out of your system, can you? Thanks for the offer, but we've got weapons you haven't even heard about."

"Guns are guns," Cone says. "You point and pull the trigger."

"Forget it," the FBI man advises. "My God, you're just a lousy civilian."

Johnnie says he wants to get back to his office as soon as possible, so Timothy decides to walk home—a nice hike that'll get his juices flowing. The sun has popped up, but the air is still cool enough. It promises to be a hot, beamy day, not a rain cloud in sight. There's a skywriting plane at work over Manhattan, and Cone wonders what would happen if a berserk pilot spelled out FUCK YOU for all the city to see and ponder.

He buys a morning *Times* and a *Barron's* from a sidewalk kiosk. Then, nearing home, he begins stocking up on groceries and potables, figuring he'll spend the weekend in the loft; he doesn't want to be out if Johnnie Wong calls.

The elevator works until noon on Saturdays so Cone doesn't have to lug all his bundles up six flights of steep stairs. He gets everything stowed away, gives Cleo fresh water, fresh litter, and a Twinkie. Then he undresses and sacks out on the floor mattress to complete his night's sleep.

He awakes a little after noon, feeling grungy and tasting that onion from the bagel sandwich. So he brushes his teeth, showers, shaves, and pulls on fresh skivvies. Then he pops a beer, lights a cigarette, and eats two Mallomars.

He figures the action he suggested to the FBI man has a reasonable chance of success. It's got surprise going for it, and if the guys on the roof and the guys on the street can coordinate, it should go like silk. If their timing is off, it could be the biggest foozle of all time.

What it requires, of course, is luck. Cone has seen perfectly plotted combat operations go awry because of accidents, breakdowns of equipment, or acts of God. Other rumbles, planned by wetbrains who didn't know shit from Shinola about fighting a war, went off without a hitch because they had luck going for them.

He hopes Johnnie Wong has luck, or a lot of good men could get their butts shot off. Still, he reflects, that's what they're getting paid for, and if they don't like the odds, they should get into another line of business—something a front-line grunt in Nam would have found a wee bit difficult.

He resolutely puts memories of that time and that place into the farthest, dimmest corners of his mind, and tries to concentrate on today's trials and tribulations. He wishes Samantha wasn't a thousand miles away. Not that he would ever ask her advice or cry on her shoulder, but her physical presence is spice in a world he finds flat and tasteless without her.

He wonders how he ever got diddled by the fickle finger of fate and ended up an investigator, prying into other people's lives and sticking his nose into financial brannigans. Because, he ruefully admits, his own life is so dull. He's living vicariously, and if it wasn't for Cleo, he could go nights without speaking to a living soul—assuming cats have souls. And why not?

It's that kind of a moony weekend, with a lot of reading, drinking, smoking, and pigging out on food that comes in plastic wrappers. Not a phone call, from Wong or anyone else, and his cabin fever is just about to drive him to a seizure of pub-crawling when his phone rings late Sunday night, and he kisses it for luck before he says, "Yeah?"

"It's on," Johnnie Wong says. "And if I sound whacked-out it's because I haven't slept for forty-eight hours. I can't talk about it on the phone. You remember where I parked my car on Saturday?"

"Sure."

"Can you meet me there at two-thirty?"

"I'll be there. Anything I can do to help?"

"Pray," Wong says, and hangs up.

Cone's got about three hours to kill and figures it's too risky to take a snooze; he might not wake up in time to witness the fireworks. So he spends a half-hour cleaning his S&W .357 magnum and oiling the ankle holster.

Since it's going to be a night operation, he debates the wisdom of wearing a black turtleneck sweater and dark gray slacks. But then he realizes he's just conning himself; he's going to be a spectator, not a combatant, and his costume is of no importance. So he wears a navy blue T-shirt under the usual corduroy jacket, and stuffs his cap in the pocket.

He spends the last hour reviewing the plan again, trying to spot flaws. He can't find any; the plot still looks good to him. If everyone does his job, and Lady Luck is smiling, Edward Tung Lee should be sleeping in his Fifth Avenue apartment by dawn.

He exits his building to find a low-hanging cloud bank over the city. If there are moon and stars up there, they can't be seen—which Cone takes as a promising portent for night action. Also, there's no wind to speak of, nothing strong enough to bother those cowboys rappeling down from the roof.

He drives the red Escort over to Chatham Square, finds a place to park on the Bowery, and walks back. Johnnie Wong is waiting for him. The FBI man is wearing camouflaged combat fatigues and looks unexpectedly bulky. Cone digs a finger into his ribs and feels the armor beneath the cloth.

"Bulletproof vest?" he asks.

"I hope so," Wong says, grinning.

"Don't tell me you're flying off the roof?"

"Hell, no; I'm no bird. I'm leading the squad up the stairs after we blow the outside doors."

"Then it's going down like we said?"

"Pretty much," Wong says. "With a few minor refinements. The guys going off the roof will be carrying Ingram Mark Tens. Plus stun grenades."

"What are you carrying?"

"Old Faithful: a Thompson forty-five with drum magazine."

"How do you blow the doors?"

"Our boffins have come up with a cutie. It's a high-energy explosive made to look like a credit card, and just as thin. You slide it between the door and jamb, pull the friction snapper, and run like hell because it's got a five-second fuse—if you're lucky. Listen, I haven't got much time so let me give you the scoop. We had to liaise with the NYPD, and in about fifteen minutes they're going to close off Doyers Street at both ends with barricades and unlighted, unmarked police cars. They'll position flatbeds at each end loaded with floodlights and searchlights. And portable generators, of course.

"Our combat control is on the roof of the building across the street from the Yubies' headquarters. You get up there by going through a courtyard and climbing six flights of stairs. We've got men posted on every floor to keep tenants inside their apartments. Everyone's connected by walkie-talkies— and let's hope they work."

"What about the guys on the roof of the United Bamboo building—did they get there okay?"

"No sweat. They've been up for about a half-hour now, moving around on felt boots so they don't spook the bandidos downstairs. They report they've got their lines securely anchored—one around a chimney and the other two with grappling hooks. Time's getting short; let's go."

Johnnie leads the way to Doyers, and they begin passing men in dark suits, some of them talking quietly into their radios.

"How many guys you call in on this caper?" Cone asks.

"Almost a hundred. The controller flew up from Quantico. He's run operations like this a dozen times before. He's got a good score, but he's a bastard to deal with. It took me a while to persuade him to let you watch the action. After all, it was your idea."

"I know," Cone says. "But I'm just a lousy civilian."

They go across a bleak courtyard, through the back door of a tenement, and climb the stairs to the top floor, where there's an iron ladder leading through an opened skylight to a tarred roof. There are two brick chimneys and a number of vent pipes protruding from the roof. Cone spots a waist-high wall with a coping of slates facing Doyers Street.

There are five men up there. One has what appears to be a

4X5 Speed Graphic, another has a shoulder-mounted video camera.

"We're recording all this for posterity," Wong says dryly. "I'm not going to introduce you to anyone; they're too tense for politeness."

"Yeah," Cone says, "I know the feeling."

Two of the other FBI men are using their walkie-talkies. The fifth man, apparently the controller, is standing well back from the wall, hands jammed into his pockets. He's staring up at the dark sky, his mouth half-open. Johnnie goes up to him, speaks a few words, and jerks a thumb in Cone's direction. The controller turns to look, nods, then says something. Wong comes back to Cone's side.

"Keep back from the roof edge until the action starts," he says. "And no lighting matches, no smoking. Okay?"

"Sure," Cone says. "Listen, I don't want to put the whammy on this, but have you made plans for casualties?"

"Two ambulances and medical evac teams standing by on Mott Street. And paddy wagons. Only they're buses. Well, I've got to leave now and get on station."

"Look," Timothy says, "do me a favor, will you? Remember that White Lotus shareholder list I showed you at my place? Someone copped it from my loft, and I think it was a United Bamboo picklock. When you get up to their offices, and this whole thing is winding down, will you take a look around and see if you can find it? I promised Chin Tung Lee I'd take good care of it. It's confidential information."

"Sure," Johnnie says, "I can do that. See you soon, old buddy."

"You bet," Cone says.

Wong leaves, and the Wall Street dick reaches into his pocket for a cigarette, then pulls his hand guiltily away. He notices the five FBI men on the roof are inching closer to the wall overlooking Doyers Street. Cone inches right along with them.

The controller is holding what appears to be a stopwatch, big as an onion. He consults it and says quietly to his talkers, "Coming up to one minute."

They murmur into their radios.

"One minute . . . mark," the controller says in dullish tones.

The talkers repeat.

They all wait in silence.

"Forty-five seconds," the controller says. His voice is sluggish. "Thirty seconds . . . twenty . . . ten . . . five, four, three, two, one. Go."

The talkers begin shouting into their walkie-talkies. Everyone moves to the edge of the roof. They grip the wall coping, stare across the street.

Three men drop on lines from the top of United Bamboo headquarters. They rappel swiftly downward. They use leg kicks to keep themselves bouncing off the brick front of the building.

They come to a stop facing the third-floor windows. They smash the glass with their boots. They toss in grenades. The three explosions are almost simultaneous: one titanic *boom!*

"Lights," the controller says in his listless voice.

Searchlights and floods make day of night. The street is frozen in a harsh, greenish glare.

"Go with Unit Two," the controller says.

Cone figures no one is going to send him to Leavenworth for smoking a Camel now. He lights up, leans over the wall, peers down.

One of the Yubie guards has run out into the street, is staring upward. The other has his back against the iron grille door. He's fumbling at his belt.

Wong's squad comes spilling out of tenement doorways. They rush the guards. Grab them. Johnnie works at the iron grille. Motions everyone back, then ducks away. Sheet of flame brighter than the floodlights. Sparks. The grille hangs crazily from one hinge.

Same thing with the inner door. It's blown completely inward. The attackers cram into the entranceway, Wong leading.

Now the three rappelers have disappeared. They're inside, through the shattered windows. Gunfire. Single shots. Then short bursts from automatic weapons.

"Unit Three," the controller says stolidly.

Cone wonders if a reserve has been put on standby. It has. A dozen men come charging down Doyers. These are New York City cops, wearing helmets and flak jackets. Following them is a platoon of uniformed police who set up a cordon around the United Bamboo building.

More gunfire. A lot of it.

"Medics," the controller mentions. Then: "Let's go."

He leaves first, climbing carefully down the iron ladder. Followed by his two assistants. Then the photographers who have been working steadily since the action started.

Cone lights another cigarette and follows them. By the time he hits the street, the small-arms fire is dwindling; just single shots or brief chatters of submachine guns.

An ambulance comes slowly up the street, siren growling. Cone stands in the doorway, watches the stretchers and body bags unloaded. Then an armored bus pulls up.

By this time every building on Doyers Street is lighted. People are leaning out windows; some have gone to their roofs for a better view.

The shooting stops. Cone lights another cigarette and realizes he's got two going at once. He finishes the butt with quick drags and starts on the other.

Two FBI men come out of the United Bamboo building. They're gripping Edward Tung Lee by the arms. His knees are buckling, but he can walk. They help him into the ambulance. Then more cops come out, FBI and NYPD. They're herding a long file of prisoners, some dressed, some in pajamas and robes, some wearing shorts. All have hands clasped atop their heads. They're stuffed into the bus. It pulls away; another takes its place.

Johnnie Wong comes out, helping to carry a stretcher. The supine body is covered to the chin with a blanket. A medic walks alongside, holding a plastic bag high, the connecting tube disappearing under the blanket.

The ambulance pulls away. A second comes purring up. Wong stands dazedly, looking around. The Thompson dangles from one hand.

Cone crosses the street, goes up to him.

"Johnnie," he says gently.

The FBI man turns slowly to stare, not recognizing him at first. Cone knows the symptoms: shock, flood of adrenaline, postaction shakes.

"You okay?" he asks Wong.

"What? Oh, yeah, I'm all right. One of my guys caught it."

"Ah, Jesus," Cone says. "Bad?"

"I think so. It looked bad. Chiang Ho. He's been with the

Bureau almost ten years. A sweet man. Oh, God, what am I going to tell his wife?''

"Maybe he'll make it."

"No," Wong said, "he won't." Then, savagely: "But I got the fucker who chilled him. We grabbed Edward Lee out of there—did you see?"

"I saw. It was a beautiful job, Johnnie."

"I guess. Yeah, it was. It went real good. We're taking everyone in. You know, after Chiang went down, I wanted to dissipate all those guys. I never felt like that before in my life. Not a nice feeling."

"I know. But what the hell, you'll get an 'I love you' letter from the Director for all this."

"Maybe," Wong says. "Hey, I found your fucking list. It was right on top of the desk in the office."

He reaches into his fatigue jacket, pulls out the White Lotus computer printout.

"Thanks," Cone says. "I owe you a big one, payable on demand."

"I'll remember that, old buddy," the FBI man says. "Keep in touch."

By all rights, he should zonk out the moment he hits the loft and sleep until late Monday morning. But he is too wired. Granted he has been a sideliner, not an active player in that raid on United Bamboo headquarters. But the tension and suspense have clutched him. He can still hear the controller's phlegmatic "Go" and then the eruption of gunfire.

It takes a stiff vodka to soothe the jits, and by that time he's concentrating on the remainder of the puzzle—the reason he was dumped into this mishmash in the first place.

Why the run-up in the price of White Lotus stock? Obviously because the Giant Panda mob has been buying up shares through Yangtze International with the aim of taking over the company. That's a perfectly legitimate ploy. So why did Henry Wu Yeh have Cone kidnapped and tell him to stall his investigation or be prepared to knock on the Pearly Gates? That doesn't make sense.

And where do the blackmailing letter to Claire Lee and phone calls to Edward Lee fit into the jumble?

Groaning, he starts flipping through the White Lotus share

holder list. He pays particular attention to investors owning more than a thousand shares—the people Johnnie Wong said were associated with Giant Panda.

Revelation comes slowly, not in a sudden inspiration. No light bulb flicks on over his head as in a cartoon strip. The answer comes from dry numbers which, the Wall Street dick well knows, can relate a tale as gory as bloodstains, a wet knife, or brain-splattered hammer.

The first step is adding up the holdings of all those thousand-share investors and realizing that no way, *no* way can they represent 16 percent of the outstanding shares of White Lotus. Yet that is what the letter from Yangtze International claimed—that they owned 16 percent of the stock, with the pledge of proxies by "many other shareholders."

So how did they come up with that magic number of 16 percent? Timothy knows how. Edward Tung Lee personally owns 16 percent of White Lotus. What a beautiful coincidence. And if you believe that, try the Tooth Fairy on for size.

What it means, Cone realizes, is that Edward Lee is conniving with Giant Panda to make a run on his father's company. But for what reason? Cone thinks he has the answer to that one, too.

He turns to the first page of the glossy White Lotus annual report. There is the photograph of Edward Tung Lee, Chief Operating Officer. Even with his frozen smile he's a handsome devil: curved lips, cleft chin, high brow, blow-dried hair.

He could be a matinee idol. And Cone decides that's exactly what he is.

"Cleo," he calls, and the slumbering cat lifts its head.

"I've been snookered," Cone says.

He wakes late on Monday morning, sits up on his mattress, yawns, roughs his scalp with his knuckles. He thinks of that punky saying: "Today is the first day of the rest of your life." If he doesn't get to work, he reflects sourly, it may be the last day—courtesy of Henry Wu Yeh.

It's almost ten o'clock before he gets his act together; two Camels, two cups of black coffee, and a tot of brandy bring the roses to his cheeks.

He gives Cleo fresh water and a pickled pig's foot to chew

on. He checks the revolver in his shin holster, makes sure his wallet is stuffed with lettuce. Then he tears the photograph of Edward Lee from the annual report and sticks it in his jacket pocket. He sallies forth, feeling full of piss and vinegar, and not a little vindictive.

He drives directly to the Upper East Side and spends ten minutes wedging the Escort into a parking space that would be jammed with a moped. He walks back to the Hotel Bedlington on Madison Avenue, a few blocks away from the Lees' apartment on Fifth.

He knows this joint; it's figured in other cases he's handled. It's a staid, almost mousy establishment, with a lot of over-the-hill permanent residents, a cocktail bar that is proud of its Grasshoppers, and a lobby that smells faintly of must and has a magnificent framed lithograph of Grant's Tomb over the desk.

Cone wanders around a few moments before he spots a bellhop. The guy is short, squat, and has a heavy blue jaw. He looks one year younger than God. Cone figures he belongs in an OTB with a cigar butt stuck in his kisser. He's got that New York wisenheimer look, and Timothy knows it's going to cost him.

"Can I talk to you a minute?" he asks.

The bellhop gives him the up-and-down, taking in the black leather cap, ratty corduroy suit, scuffed work shoes.

"Talk is cheap," he says.

"I hope so," Cone says. "Anyplace where we can have a little privacy?"

"What's in it for me?" the guy says. He looks like a tall midget, and his gut is busting the brass buttons on his waistcoat.

"A couple of bucks?" Cone says hopefully.

"G'wan. I don't even say hello for a deuce."

"A fin," Cone says.

The bellhop jerks a thumb toward the door of the men's room. "In there," he says. "And make it snappy. I got a job to do, you know."

They lean on urinals in the empty loo. Cone hands over a fiver.

"You ain't no cop," the guy says. "That I guarantee. A private eye? Bill collector? Maybe a reporter for a scandal sheet?"

"Something like that," Cone says. "What's your name?"

"Max."

"Listen, Max, I'm going to show you a photograph. I want to know if you've ever seen the guy before. Just a simple yes or no. That's easy enough—right?"

"Let's see it."

Cone pulls out the photograph of Edward Tung Lee and holds it up. The bellhop stares at it.

"Never saw him before in my life," he says, but meanwhile he's rubbing a thick thumb against a bent forefinger.

The Wall Street dick sighs, pulls out his wallet. "You already got a Lincoln," he says.

"It'll cost you a Hamilton," Max says. "Look, you're making a nice couple of Washingtons on your job, aintcha? What am I—chopped liver?"

Cone fishes in his wallet, hands over a ten-dollar bill.

"Yeah, I make the guy," Max says. "He checks in two, three times a week. Always in the afternoon. Stays maybe a couple of hours."

"Since when has this been a hot-pillow joint?" Cone asks.

"Since day one," the bellhop says. "Whaddya think, every hotel in the city don't do it? It's easy money—and fast turnover."

"And how long has this guy been checking in for a few hours of fun and games?"

"Oh, maybe a couple of years now. That's it; you got your money's worth."

"Not yet," the Wall Street dick says. "Different women— or always the same woman?"

Max makes the same gesture, rubbing his thumb on a crooked forefinger.

"You're going to wear out your thumb," Timothy says. "How much?"

"I figure it's worth a Jackson."

"A double-sawbuck?" Cone says, outraged. "Are you sure your name's not Jesse, as in Jesse James?"

"Listen, I know and you want to know. It's supply and demand—get what I mean?"

Groaning, Cone gives him a twenty-dollar bill.

"Always the same woman," Max says. "The guy calls the desk before he shows up so he's got the room number—you cappish? The Hitler on the desk is on the take. So the guy shows up, no luggage, and goes directly to his room. Then fifteen, twenty minutes later, the dame shows up. She's got the room number from him, sails through the lobby, and goes straight upstairs. Nice people. Good tippers. They spread it around like they should.''

"Uh-huh," Cone says. "And I guess she's a short, dumpy broad with dark hair—right?"

The bellhop looks at him with disgust. "Whaddya think," he says, "I was born yesterday?"

"All right," Cone says, sighing. "How much?"

"A Grant. But I won't testify in court if this is a divorce thing like I figure it is."

"This better be good," Cone says, handing over a fifty-dollar bill.

Max slips the folded bill into a waistcoat pocket. "She's a beauty, a real sparkler. Tall as you. Young. Blond. Great jugs. Wears expensive clothes. Once I heard the guy call her Claire. Is that what you wanted?"

"It'll do," Cone says, nodding. "Now can you tell me where the public phone is—or are you going to hold me up for that, too?"

"Nah, that's a freebie. It's on the mezzanine."

Cone finds the phone in an old-fashioned booth with a folding door. It's even got a little wooden seat. He calls the corporate offices of White Lotus on Exchange Place.

"Is Mr. Chin Tung Lee in this morning?" he asks the operator.

"Yes, he is, sir. May I ask who's calling?"

"I have a personal delivery to make to Mr. Lee and just wanted to make sure he's there. Thank you."

He hangs up, leaves the Hotel Bedlington, heads for the Lees' apartment on Fifth Avenue.

There's a monster standing in front of the Lees' door with his arms folded. He looks like a young Genghis Khan, with slit eyes and mustachios bushy enough to sweep out a parrot's cage. Cone decides to play it safe, not knowing if this muscle is FBI, NYPD, or a hired janissary.

"Timothy Cone to see Mrs. Claire Lee," he says. "She's expecting me."

The mastodon unfolds his arms, and the Wall Street dick

wonders if he's going to get a karate chop that will decapitate him.

"You wait," the guy says in an unexpectedly high-pitched voice.

He disappears and Cone waits in the corridor. In a few moments the door is opened again by the juggernaut.

"You come," he says.

Timothy follows him through that maze of rooms and hallways. He's finally ushered through a double set of doors, into a small living room, and then into an adjoining bedroom. The woolly mammoth withdraws.

Edward Tung Lee is seated in a leather club chair. He's wearing cerise silk pajamas under a brocaded dressing gown. There's a white handkerchief neatly peaked in the breast pocket of the robe. His feet are bare. Claire Lee is standing next to him. She looks like a pom-pom girl in a middy, short pleated skirt, bobby socks and white Reeboks.

"Mr. Cone!" she carols. "What a pleasant surprise!"

"I was in the neighborhood," he says, "and thought I'd drop by to see how your husband is doing."

"Much better, thank you," she says. "So well, in fact, that he insisted on going into the office this morning."

"Silly thing to do," Edward says. "He just won't slow down."

They all look pleasantly at each other.

"Now listen," Claire says, "I really don't think it's too early in the morning for a drink. Do you, Mr. Cone?"

"It's never too early," he tells her.

"And I know what you like," she says archly. "Vodka on the rocks with a splash of water. Right? Edward, I think you should have something. Perhaps a brandy. The doctor said it would do you good."

"A small one," he says.

"And perhaps a small something for me," she says gaily. "Be back in a jiff."

She sashays out the door and Edward says, "Pull up a chair, Mr. Cone."

But he sits on the edge of the unmade bed. Now he's facing Lee and the other armchair. He wants them both in his sights when the woman returns.

"You look a little puffy around the gills," he says, "but none the worse for wear. They give you a hard time?"

Edward is startled. "You know what happened to me?"

Cone nods.

"How did you find out? It hasn't been in the papers."

"The grapevine," Cone says. "The FBI did a helluva job grabbing you out of there."

"They saved my life. And one of them was critically wounded in the shoot-out—did you know that?"

"I heard."

"I'll never forget that," Edward says somberly. "Never in my life."

"Yeah," Cone says.

Claire comes bustling in, carrying a silver tray of drinks. She hands them around: vodka rocks to Cone, small snifter of brandy for Edward, and something green in a stemmed glass for herself.

"Cone knows what happened to me," Edward tells her.

"Oh, Mr. Cone knows *everything*," she says lightly. "Don't you, Mr. Cone?"

"Just about," he says.

She takes the armchair, and now he can look at both of them without turning his head from side to side. They lift their glasses in a silent toast, then sip their drinks delicately. Very civilized.

"You two are a nice couple of bums," Timothy says.

Their faces congeal. Edward's hand begins trembling. He sets the snifter down on the floor next to his chair.

"What?" Claire Lee says, voice strangled. "What did you say?"

"Bums," Cone repeats. "Cruds. Both of you. How long did you think you'd be able to have those matinees at the Bedlington? Forever and ever?"

"I don't know what you're talking about," she says hotly. "And I think you better leave right now."

"Oh, stuff it," he says angrily. "I couldn't care less if you rub the bacon every day of the year. What I don't like is that you both played me for a fool, each telling me how much you hated the other. I fell for it because it was a classic setup: younger stepmother, older son, both competing for an old man's inheritance. Only you've been rumpling the sheets together for two years."

"You're a dirty, filthy man," Claire says, glaring at him.

"You better believe it," he tells her, taking a gulp of his

drink. "Look," he says, addressing Edward, "if you want to put horns on your pop, that's your business. *My* business is finding out why the price of White Lotus stock has been going up, up, up. Do you want to hear my scenario? It's a cutie."

Neither replies.

"It goes like this," Cone continues. "And don't interrupt to tell me I'm wrong—because I don't think I am.

"One: Claire and Edward are shacking up and making jokes in the sack about what a senile old fart Chin is. Two: Edward is still steaming because his father wouldn't finance his great idea of having White Lotus market a line of frozen gourmet Chinese dinners. Oh, yeah, I saw how riled you got at Ah Sing's when you told me about it. Three: During those tosses in the hay, Claire eggs you on, and you decide to cut loose from White Lotus, go off on your own, start a new business and make a zillion."

"Now see here—" Edward starts.

"Shut up, you," Cone says savagely. "Nothing wrong with your plan, but it's the way you went about it that sticks in my craw. Your sixteen percent of White Lotus stock at the old price of thirty bucks a share would be worth a nice piece of change if you sold your stock on the open market. But it would take that to open a pizza parlor these days. You needed a lot more loot to start a frozen food operation."

"Claire," Edward says stiffly, "maybe you better phone the police."

"Go ahead and call them," Cone says. "And tell them to bring along reporters and photographers—you jerk! So your problem was how to increase your capital. The answer? Greenmail! You make a deal with Giant Panda. Those thugs play along because they're anxious to get into a legitimate business and put all that money to work they've made from dope and shakedowns. The scam is this: Fronts for Giant Panda start buying White Lotus stock. The price goes up. When it's high enough, as it was last week, Giant Panda makes a play for White Lotus, working through Yangtze International.

"Look, both of you know how much Chin Tung Lee loves his company. It's his whole life. You figured he'd pay a premium to keep control. So Yangtze pretends they want to take over when what they really want is for Chin to pay greenmail—buy their shares at more than the market price. That would yield enough dough for you to start your frozen dinner business."

"You're insane," Edward Lee says in a low voice.

"Sure I am," Cone admits cheerily. "But I'm also right. Almost everything fits: Your father's need to hang onto the company he created. Your need to get your new business started and prove you're as smart an operator as your old man. And Giant Panda's need to get into a legitimate money-maker. What was the deal? Were they going to give you a controlling interest? Like shit they were! Those guys are gangsters, even if they work through a financial front on Pine Street. You'd be lucky to end up with thirty percent. Am I right or am I right?"

Edward Lee, stunned, makes no reply, but Claire does. "You said 'almost everything fits.' What doesn't fit?"

"You don't," he tells her. "You and Edward could have taken over White Lotus anytime you wanted. Between the two of you, there's enough stock to elect your own Board of Directors and put the old man out to pasture. But you didn't go that route. Why not? Mrs. Lee, I make you for a street-wise lady who's always had an eye on the main chance. You're a nice-looking woman, no doubt about it, but when it comes to spine, you got short-changed.

"I figure your thinking went something like this: Yeah, I could go in with Edward on his greenmail scheme, but would it really be smart? What if Chin conks out tomorrow from a stroke or cardiac arrest and I inherit? It's more than possible at his age. So maybe I should play my cards cautiously. If Edward's plot comes off, and his business is a big success, then I'll think about dumping the father and going with the son. But meanwhile I'll play it cozy, let Edward carry the ball and see how far he gets. I'm young; I can afford to wait. If Edward's a winner, I'll go with him. If he takes a pratfall, it's ta-ta, Eddie darling."

"You're disgusting," she says, spitting it out.

"Oh, yeah," Cone says, draining his drink. "Almost as disgusting as you two upright citizens." He rises, places his empty glass on a bedside table. "Thanks for the belt. I've got to run along now. So much to do, doncha know."

"Mr. Cone," Edward Lee says nervously, "you're not

going to tell my father about the Bedlington matter, are you?''

"Like the lawyers say," Cone tells him, "I'll take it under advisement. Meanwhile, sweat a little. Now will someone show me how to get out of this damned place?"

Claire Lee leads the way in silence. But at the outside door she pauses and turns to face him.

"You had eyes for me, didn't you?" she says.

"Yeah," Cone says. "At first. Until I remembered I've got a lady who makes you look like a Barbie Doll. And she's got spine to spare."

"I'm not so bad," Claire says defensively.

"Compared to whom?" Cone asks.

He gets to Exchange Place by one o'clock, after stopping at a Lexington Avenue saloon for a cheeseburger and a bottle of dark Heineken. And another cheeseburger and another bottle of dark Heineken. He's famished because he's coming off a high after that confrontation with Claire and Edward. Feeding his face brings him down, and he can plan what he's going to say to Chin Tung Lee.

But he has to wait in the White Lotus reception room. "Mr. Lee is busy at the moment, sir, but he'll be with you shortly." That's okay; it's still Monday, Cone's still breathing, and if Henry Wu Yeh's hatchetmen are on his tail, Timothy hasn't spotted them.

When he's conducted into Lee's garish office, the old man appears chipper enough. He's got his long ivory holder with a scented cigarette clamped between his plates at a jaunty FDR angle. The mustardy toupee is slightly askew, giving him a raffish look. Even the wispy Vandyke is alive and springy.

"So happy to see you, Mr. Cone," he says in his boomy voice, offering his tiny hand across the desk. "I meant to call you, but this is the first day I've been out of bed. Please, sit down and tell me what you've been doing."

The Wall Street dick slumps into the leather tub chair. He shakes a Camel from his pack and lights it. "Glad you're up and about," he says. "I went to see your son this morning."

"I know," Lee says. "He called right after you left. He said you knew about his rescue."

"That's right."

"What a happy ending to an unfortunate affair. You had nothing to do with it, did you?"

"Not me."

"In any event, all's well that ends well, as your Shakespeare said."

"He's not my Shakespeare," Cone says, "and a lot of other guys said it first."

Then they sit in silence a moment. Lee seems to sober under Cone's hard stare; the sprightliness leaks away, the smile fades. He sets holder and cigarette down carefully in the brass ashtray.

"Is something troubling you, Mr. Cone?"

"Yeah," Timothy says, "something is. You suckered me good, didn't you?"

"What? What are you saying?"

"I thought you were a cocker spaniel, and you turn out to be a pit bull. How long have you known about your wife and son?"

Chin Tung Lee doesn't answer, but he seems to shrivel and slide down in his wheelchair.

"Any other man would have kicked their butts out the window," Cone goes on. "But that's not your style. You're a chess player with a habit of winning. You prefer to think five plays ahead—at least. You like to move people around the way you maneuver chess pieces. So you got a friend or employee to type up a scary letter to your wife and make threatening phone calls to your son. For a man in your position that would be duck soup. You figure to spook them into ending those matinees at the Hotel Bedlington. Then you'd forgive and forget."

"What my son did to me," Chin says stonily, "I can never forgive or forget."

"Come on," Cone says. "If it wasn't Edward, it would be someone else—and you know it. Would you prefer a stranger? Would that make it better?"

"You are a very cynical man, Mr. Cone."

"Nah. Just realistic. How old are you—late seventies?"

"Eighty next year."

"So you're more than three times her age. What did you expect? You probably knew her history when you married her; you must have figured something like this would happen."

"Yes, I anticipated it. But not my son!"

Cone shrugs. "The family that plays together stays together."

That, at least, earns a wan smile. "Tell me, how did you find out I was responsible for the threats?"

"No great job of detecting. Just elimination. It couldn't have been the United Bamboo mob, because they kidnapped your son, and you don't kidnap a potential blackmail victim. And it couldn't have been the Giant Panda gang, because Edward is practically in bed with them."

Then the old man straightens up on the telephone directory he's sitting on. He glares wrathfully at Cone.

"Are you certain of what you're saying?"

"As sure as God made little green apples. Look, this thing between Claire and Edward is a sideshow. It's none of my business. My job was to find out why the price of White Lotus stock has been galloping. All right, here's the answer: Your son and Giant Panda, working through Yangtze International, have been shafting you by driving up the price. Edward has probably pledged his shares to the Pandas to give them more clout."

"My own son? He wants to force me out?"

Cone sits back, lights another cigarette slowly. He sees Chin's hands are trembling, and he gives the geezer a few moments to settle down.

"You got it wrong," Cone tells him. "Your son couldn't care less about taking over White Lotus. He thinks it's got no pizzazz. He wants to start his own company, to market frozen gourmet Chinese dinners—the idea you turned down. The only way he can get enough capital to swing that is to force you to buy him out at an inflated price. And give Giant Panda a nice profit at the same time, of course. It's greenmail, Mr. Lee. They know you'll pay a premium over the market price of the stock to keep control of White Lotus."

The old man tugs gently at his wispy beard. "So other people play business chess, too," he says.

"On Wall Street? You better believe it."

"Mr. Cone," Lee says, "in that ugly commode across the room you will find a bottle of sake. A Japanese drink, but tasty. Rice. Also some crystal sake shot glasses from the

Hoya Gallery. Very handsome. I suggest this might be the right time for a drink.''

"I'm game," Cone says.

He brings bottle and glasses back to the driftwood desk. He pours the miniature tumblers half-full. Chin drains his in one gulp and holds it out for a refill. Cone pours again, filling both. He's glad to see Lee's hand is now steady.

They settle back, smiling at each other.

"Do you play chess, Mr. Cone?"

"Nope. I don't play anything."

"Ah. Too bad. I think you may have the gift. Tell me, how do you suggest I react to this extortion?"

"Have you contacted an investment banker?"

"Yes, I have an appointment tomorrow with Mr. Twiggs of Pistol and Burns.''

"Good. He's a smart man. Well, if this was a purely business decision, there are a lot of things you could do to fight off the greenmailers. Restructure your company. Take on heavy debt to buy up your stock on the open market. Look for a white knight to take over with your approval. Use the poison pill defense and put in golden parachutes to defend your personal position and your closest buddies.''

"I have the feeling you don't support these methods wholeheartedly.''

"I would if it was purely a business decision. But it's not. It's Edward, your only son. We're talking about family here, Mr. Lee, and I know how much that means to you.''

"Yes. So what do you suggest?"

"How about this: You call in your son and make him an offer. You'll pay him whatever he wants, within reason, for his sixteen percent of all White Lotus shares. In addition, you'll help finance his new business up to X dollars. The exact amount you're willing to gamble on him is up to you. The important thing is that your offer will get him off the hook with Giant Panda. If he goes in business with them, he'll be lucky to keep the fillings in his teeth. But if you promise him majority control of his new company, he'll jump at it—unless he's an idiot, which I don't think he is. You follow?"

"I follow."

"Now in addition to getting your son out from under Giant Panda, this plan will also give you such a heavy block of

White Lotus stock that no takeover pirate will even think of making a run at your company."

"You believe Giant Panda will accept defeat gracefully?"

"Of course not," Cone says. "They'll squeal like stuck pigs. You can tell them to go screw, but I think it would be wiser to make a deal with them. You know Henry Wu Yeh?"

"I've met the gentleman."

"Is that what he is? Well, I hear he's got the smarts. First, sew up your deal with Edward. Then go to Yeh and offer him the same share price you gave your son. He'll go for it. What other choice has he got? Fronts for Giant Panda have been buying up White Lotus stock in lots of a thousand shares or more. They should be happy to unload at a premium over the market price. That's why they got into this scam in the first place. The only thing they'll be losing will be majority control of Edward's new company—an iffy proposition."

"This is going to cost me a lot of money, Mr. Cone."

"You bet your sweet ass it will," Timothy says cheerfully. "I don't know what your personal net worth is, but I'd guess you may have to take on some heavy debt to finance the greenmail and investment in Edward's venture. But what's your alternative? Complete estrangement from your son. You don't want that, do you?"

"No. In spite of what he's done, he is still my flesh and blood. More sake, please."

Cone fills their crystal glasses again. The vodka at the Lees' apartment, beers at the Lexington Avenue saloon, and now two shots of rice wine. . . . He figures if he keeps this up, his liver will look like a cellulose sponge.

"So tell me, Mr. Lee—what do you think of my scenario?"

"It has much to recommend it. I will give it very careful consideration."

"Yeah, well, I've got to level with you; I have a personal interest in your going for it. Mr. Henry Wu Yeh isn't happy about my sticking my schnoz in his affairs, and he's suggested his world would be a brighter place without me—permanently. So if you could speed up your decision and, if you decide to go for it, give Yeh a call today, I'd appreciate it. I don't want to lean on you—the choice is yours—but I don't want you to hear from someone else that I suggested this plan just to save my own cojones. I happen to think it would be best for you, your son, and just incidentally for me.''

"Thank you for your honesty, Mr. Cone. Now I hope you will be equally honest about another matter. Was my wife a party to this greenmail scheme?"

"I don't know. All I can do is guess. And my guess is that she may have encouraged Edward to break with you. But that could have been just pillow talk—you should excuse the expression. I don't think she made any commitment or actually pledged her stock. I think she decided to wait and see how the cards would fall—and then go with the winner.''

"Yes," Chin Tung Lee says sadly, "she is capable of that. My wife has a certain peasant shrewdness."

"That she has. Here's a thought: If you decide to cut a deal with your son and help finance his new business, why don't you stipulate that he relocates in California and starts the company out there.''

"Ah, you think that will effectively end their affair?"

Timothy shrugs. "There's always the chance that she'll follow Edward to the West Coast. But I'm betting she sticks in New York. You've got more money than your son."

"Yes," Lee says, "and I'm an old man with not too much time to go. Is that what you're thinking? You *are* realistic."

Then, emboldened by the second sake, Cone says, "Look, Mr. Lee, why don't you say to your wife, 'Hey, baby, straighten up and fly right. Stop playing around or you're out on your ass.' Have you got the gumption to talk to her like that?''

"I may speak to her," the old man says cautiously, "but perhaps not in those exact words."

"Whatever," Timothy says. "You're the chess whiz." He rises, takes up cigarettes, matches, leather cap, and prepares to leave.

"Another sake?" the oldster suggests.

"No, thanks. I know a guy who drank a lot of that stuff and then threw up in his girlfriend's aquarium."

"You know some odd people, Mr. Cone."

"Everyone's odd—including me. You still love your wife, don't you?"

"Yes," says Chin Tung Lee.

* * *

They're humping away as if the Bomb is en route and they've only got minutes to wring the last twinge of joy from sentient life.

"Oh," Samantha Whatley says. "Oh oh oh."

Maybe it's because she's been away so long or because he's missed her so much. But they're playing the brangle buttock game with brutal intensity, perhaps meaning to punish each other for their separation. They couple with the desperation of survivors.

In her bouncy bed, with the pink mattress flounce all around, French dolls tossed to the floor to stare at the ceiling with ceramic eyes, they joust with grunts and fervor, reclaiming their intimacy with groans and curses. No delicacy or gentle caring here, but naked warfare and the fury of combat.

"Ah," Timothy Cone says. "Ah ah ah."

These two demons never have figured out if they're lovers or antagonists—and have no interest in finding out. All they seek is the resolution of their wants. And if the end doesn't justify the means, what the hell does?

So they slide slickly over each other, prying ferociously, grappling, twisting, biting, and losing themselves in a quest they cannot define. There is anguish in their lovemaking as if they mean to perish when all is complete. But meanwhile they practice the age-old tricks and skills that came out of the cave, or might have been perfected by hairy primates swinging from trees.

Neither will surrender, but both must. They end with a duet of moans and yelps, singing a song of longing and need deferred. Then, slackening, they stare at each other wide-eyed, fearful of their release, wondering if the world still turns.

Cone lurches off the sheets, stands a moment until his knees solidify. Then he pads over to Samantha's refrigerator and returns with the chilled California chablis he brought to celebrate her homecoming. He fills their glasses, then sets the jug down on the floor alongside the bed.

They sit up with their backs against the headboard, sipping their wine and content to laze away the late Saturday afternoon.

"Did you miss me?" Sam asks.

"Sure."

"Don't tell me you didn't cut your eyes at another woman while I was gone."

"I might have looked," Cone admits, "but I didn't touch."

"Fair enough," Sam says. "And what have you been up to at the office?"

"Nothing much. The usual bullshit."

She turns her head to glare at him. "Come on, asshole, give me a break," she says. "I'll read your reports on Monday anyway."

"Yeah, well, mostly I was working the White Lotus file."

"Tell me about it."

He gives her a condensed account of his adventures with Chin, Claire, and Edward Lee, with Johnnie Wong and Henry Wu Yeh, with the United Bamboo and Giant Panda gangs. By the time he finishes, they've polished off the wine. Cone refills their glasses. The light is muted now, the apartment mellow with dusk.

"Jesus," Sam says, "you really get the crapolas, don't you. Did the Giant Panda baddies ever come after you?"

"Nah. I got a call on Wednesday from Chin Tung Lee. He made a deal with Yeh—bought back Giant Panda's shares of White Lotus stock at a premium. And Edward is moving to the coast to start his new business."

"Was Chin happy at how it all turned out?"

"I guess so. He sent me a great big carton of White Lotus products. I've got enough Chinese food in the loft to give Cleo slanted eyes."

"Tim," she says thoughtfully, "that Claire Lee—was she the one you had the hots for?"

"She's something. I thought at first she was gold, but she turned out to be tin."

"But her husband loves her."

"Everyone's got problems," Cone says.

"Yeah? What's your problem, sonny boy?"

"I'm horny again."

"Thank God!" Samantha cries.

3